The Butterfly Touch

Hector L. Bones

Library of Congress Control Number: TX0009534650
Book Cover by Hector L. Bones
Illustrations by Hector L. Bones
1st edition 2024

CONTENTS

INTRODUCTION

Welcome to The Butterfly Touch. I'm thrilled to introduce you to Nyomi Boones, a character whose journey has come to mean so much to me. Nyomi's story, at its heart, is one about finding balance: balance between the power she possesses and the person she wants to become, between the pull of expectation and the desire for freedom, between fear and self-acceptance.

When I began writing this book, I wanted to explore what it means to feel different—to carry something within us that we can't always explain, something that perhaps sets us apart. For Nyomi, that "something" is her magic: a mysterious power that brings her art to life but also presents her with profound challenges. Through her eyes, we experience the weight of being unique, and the quiet, often difficult journey of understanding what it means to live with a gift that the world may never fully understand.

At first glance, The Butterfly Touch may seem like a story about magic, but I hope you'll find that it's also a story about self-discovery, friendship, and resilience. Nyomi's journey is filled with the kinds of twists and turns we all encounter in our lives. She faces moments of self-doubt and fear, times when she questions her place in the world. Yet through each challenge, she grows, realizing that her strength lies not only in her powers but in her ability to trust herself and those around her.

As Nyomi navigates this path, two people play pivotal roles in her life: Thomas, a quiet guide with a mysterious past, and Callie, her vibrant, steadfast friend. Thomas represents the mentors and wisdom-bearers we encounter, those who remind us of our potential when we can't see it ourselves. Callie, on the other hand, embodies the grounding presence of friendship, the relationships that keep us connected to reality, to joy, and to who we are at our core.

While Nyomi's world might contain elements of the fantastical, her experiences are deeply rooted in the real emotions we all face. Her struggles with self-acceptance, the process of learning to embrace what makes her different, and the courage it takes to confront her own fears are things I think many of us can relate to. My hope is that readers will see a bit of themselves in Nyomi—her flaws, her hopes, her courage—and find comfort in knowing that growth often comes from the parts of ourselves that challenge us the most.

As you embark on this journey with Nyomi, I invite you to think about your own unique gifts and the ways they've shaped you. We each carry our own "magic," whether it's a talent, a passion, or a perspective that makes us see the world differently. And while those gifts may sometimes feel like burdens, I hope this story reminds you, as it has reminded me, that they can also be sources of beauty and strength.

Thank you for stepping into Nyomi's world. I hope you find her story as inspiring and thought-provoking as it was for me to write. May The Butterfly Touch serve as a reminder that our differences are not just challenges but also possibilities, that our journeys of self-discovery are lifelong, and that, in the end, we all have the potential to create something beautiful from the gifts we hold within.

Enjoy the journey,
Hector L. Bones

SYNOPSIS

The Butterfly Touch tells the story of Nyomi Boones, a high school student with a quiet passion for art—and a mysterious power she can barely control. In a moment of deep frustration, Nyomi sketches a butterfly, and to her shock, it lifts off the page, fluttering into the air as though alive. This miracle is the beginning of an unexpected journey, revealing her power to bring her art to life. But as her creations grow in complexity, so do the challenges of managing her gift.

With each drawing, Nyomi's powers become harder to control, stirring fear and self-doubt. She begins to question who she is beyond her abilities, feeling isolated and misunderstood as she hides her secret from her friends and family. When Thomas Hale—a quiet, enigmatic classmate—discovers her abilities, he offers her guidance, sharing his knowledge of magic's deeper meanings and its potential dangers. With Thomas's mentorship, Nyomi learns to develop "rules" for herself, gaining control over her powers by grounding them in discipline and self-trust.

Amid the chaos of high school life, Nyomi's friendship with her free-spirited best friend, Callie, remains her one constant. Callie, unaware of Nyomi's powers, anchors her to the real world, offering laughter, loyalty, and a connection to life beyond magic. Through Callie's friendship, Nyomi learns that she doesn't have to face her journey alone.

As graduation nears, Nyomi faces her biggest test yet: the decision to embrace her powers as part of her identity rather than a burden. Through Thomas's quiet wisdom and Callie's unwavering support, she realizes that her powers are not something to fear but to celebrate. She envisions a future where her art—and her magic—can bring subtle beauty and wonder to the world.

The Butterfly Touch is a story of self-discovery, friendship, and acceptance. It explores the courage it takes to embrace our unique gifts, even when they make us feel different, and the beauty of finding our own place in a world that doesn't always understand us.

PROLOGUE: THE FIRST FLUTTER

The night was still, the kind of quiet that makes you think the world has paused just for a moment. For Nyomi Boones, that silence felt more like a cage. She sat hunched over her desk in her small bedroom, bathed in the soft glow of a single desk lamp, the tip of her pencil gliding across the paper with the same purpose as the breath she held.

She had been sketching for hours. It was how she escaped the chaos of life—her parents' relentless push for academic excellence, the pressure of looming schoolwork, and the gnawing feeling of not quite fitting in anywhere. Art was her refuge, the one place she could lose herself and not worry about who she was supposed to be. Here, in the fine lines of her drawings, she could breathe.

Tonight, her hands moved mechanically as her mind wandered to the past week—an argument with her mother over homework, another awkward conversation at school where she couldn't bring herself to join in. Her heart ached for something she couldn't quite name, and her pencil traced those feelings into delicate arcs and curves.

On the page before her, a butterfly was emerging—its wings were intricate, adorned with patterns that felt both familiar and strange. Nyomi had always loved butterflies. To her, they were symbols of transformation, fleeting but beautiful, capable of extraordinary change with just the right conditions.

But the butterfly she drew tonight felt different. It was more than just a random creation; it was something personal. As she shaded its wings, she poured into it all the uncertainty she felt—her fear of the future, her frustration with being misunderstood, and the quiet, persistent hope that there was more to her life than just fitting into a box someone else had crafted for her.

As she leaned back to study her work, she sighed. The butterfly stared back at her from the paper, still and lifeless, its beauty trapped in two dimensions. Nyomi's eyes lingered on the drawing as her thoughts drifted. If only she could be like a butterfly—free, unbound by expectations, able to change effortlessly. If only life worked like that.

She blinked, trying to shake the wistful feeling, but something caught her attention. The edges of the butterfly's wings seemed to shimmer under the soft lamplight. She squinted, leaning forward, certain that her tired eyes were playing tricks on her. But no—there it was again, a faint glow, like the wings were catching light in a way that paper shouldn't.

Her heart skipped a beat as she watched, frozen, while the lines of the butterfly's wings seemed to quiver, almost as if the drawing itself were breathing. Nyomi pulled her hand back, her pulse quickening. This couldn't be real. She had spent too many late nights sketching, clearly, and her tired mind was conjuring illusions.

But then, the paper trembled.

Nyomi gasped, her chair scraping the wooden floor as she pushed back. Before her disbelieving eyes, the butterfly's wings slowly began to lift from the page, detaching themselves from the paper as though they were peeling away from the confines of the sketch. The wings beat once, then twice— tentatively, like they were testing the air.

Nyomi clutched the edge of her desk; her breath caught in her throat. The butterfly, impossibly real, fluttered off the page and hovered before her. Its iridescent wings glowed softly in the dim light, casting faint, dancing shadows on her bedroom wall.

She couldn't move. Couldn't speak. Couldn't even begin to understand what was happening. The butterfly floated in front of her face, wings whispering through the air as it circled her head once, twice, and then came to rest delicately on her hand.

Nyomi stared at it, her skin prickling with an odd warmth where its tiny legs touched her. Her mind raced, trying to make sense of this impossible thing. Butterflies didn't just spring to life from drawings. Magic didn't exist. Not in the real world.

And yet, here it was, a small, fragile creature of ink and imagination brought to life by... what? Her will? Her emotions? She didn't know.

The butterfly's wings fluttered gently, and then it lifted off her hand, gliding toward the window. Nyomi watched as it tapped lightly against the glass, as if searching for a way out. She moved without thinking, her legs shaky as she crossed the room to the window. With trembling fingers, she unlocked it and slid it open.

The butterfly hovered for a moment, as if acknowledging her, and then it fluttered out into the night, disappearing into the darkness. Nyomi stood there, the cool night air brushing against her skin, her mind a whirlwind of disbelief and awe.

For a long moment, she didn't move, didn't breathe. It had to be a dream, she told herself. Or a hallucination, maybe. She was stressed. Exhausted. That was all. But when she looked back at her desk, the empty space where her drawing had been confirmed what she already knew.

The butterfly was gone. And it had been real.

She stumbled back to her chair, her body still tingling with the strange warmth that had accompanied the butterfly's touch. Her mind raced through a thousand questions, none of which had answers. What had just happened? How? Why?

Her eyes drifted to her sketchbook, to the blank page that remained where the butterfly had once been. And as she sat there, her thoughts swirling, a quiet certainty began to settle in her chest, along with something else she hadn't felt in a long time.

Wonder.

For the first time in as long as she could remember, Nyomi didn't feel trapped. She didn't feel like she was merely surviving in a world that didn't understand her. Instead, she felt a flicker of something new, something fragile but bright.

Possibility.

She had brought something to life. She didn't know how or why, but it had happened. And if she could do that, what else was she capable of? What else lay within her, waiting to be discovered?

The questions buzzed around her mind like fireflies, each one sparking with excitement and fear. She wasn't ready to confront the enormity of it all just yet, but she knew one thing for certain: her life had just changed.

She spent the next few days in a daze, trying to focus on school, on homework, on the endless demands of daily life. But her mind was elsewhere, constantly returning to that moment when the butterfly had lifted off the page and come to life. Every time she closed her eyes, she could see its wings, shimmering with that strange, ethereal glow.

And every time she thought about it, the same question bubbled up inside her: was it a one-time thing, or could she do it again?

She wasn't sure if she wanted to find out. The idea of having that kind of power both thrilled and terrified her. What if she couldn't control it? What if she brought something else to life, something dangerous? The thought gnawed at her, leaving her restless and distracted.

But as the days passed, the pull of curiosity grew stronger. She couldn't ignore it. Not forever. And so, late one night, after everyone in the house had gone to bed, Nyomi sat down at her desk once again, her sketchbook open before her.

Her hands shook as she picked up her pencil, the weight of her decision pressing down on her. She didn't know what would happen, but she had to try. She had to know.

Slowly, carefully, she began to draw.

This time, it was a small, delicate bird creature with soft feathers and bright, curious eyes. She sketched it with the same care and attention to detail that she always put into her art, but this time, her heart was pounding with anticipation.

When she was finished, she sat back and stared at the drawing, waiting. Her hands were clammy, her breath shallow. Would it happen again? Or had it all been a fluke?

For a long moment, nothing happened. The bird remained motionless on the page, just a collection of lines and shading. Nyomi felt a wave of disappointment wash over her. Maybe it had been a dream after all. Maybe she had imagined the whole thing.

But just as she was about to close the sketchbook, she saw the faint shimmer of light around the edges of the bird's wings. Her heart leapt into her throat as she watched, wide-eyed, as the bird began to move.

Its wings fluttered softly, then lifted off the page, just as the butterfly had done. Nyomi could only stare as the bird hovered before her, its tiny body glowing with that same otherworldly light.

It chirped once, a soft, melodic sound, and then it flitted around the room, its wings beating rapidly as it explored its new surroundings. Nyomi watched it in awe, her body frozen with a mixture of fear and wonder.

This was real. This was happening. She wasn't dreaming.

The bird flew toward the window, just as the butterfly had done, and Nyomi found herself moving automatically, opening the window to let it out. It disappeared into the night, leaving Nyomi standing there, breathless and trembling.

She closed the window and leaned against it, her mind spinning. Twice now. It happened twice. There was no denying it anymore.

She had a gift. A power. And with that power came questions— questions she wasn't sure she was ready to answer.

What did this mean? Why did she have this ability? And most importantly, what was she supposed to do with it?

As the night deepened, Nyomi stood there in the quiet of her room, her heart racing with a mixture of excitement and fear. She didn't have the answers yet, but one thing was clear: her life was no longer ordinary.

The world had shifted, and she was standing on the edge of something incredible. Something terrifying.

Something magical.

And it all began with the first flutter of a butterfly's wings.

DEDICATION

I dedicate this book to my beautiful wife Debbie N. Bones, who has been a great support and source of inspiration. She is the most brilliant person I know to which I can count to bounce off ideas and help me through but also helps me keep on track and complete our projects in life.

Without you Debbie my love I would never have got the courage to get this book out.

I also dedicate this book to my children who inspired me to put my ideas on paper and bring them to life. Thanks Nyomi, Alisher Krystal and Aiden Kalel, for being great kids and an infinite source of inspiration.

CHAPTER 1: THE BUTTERFLY TOUCH

Nyomi Boones sat at her desk, the cool air from the slightly open window brushing against her skin as she stared down at her sketchbook. The pencil in her hand felt light, yet familiar—an extension of her fingers, her most trusted tool. She should have been working on her chemistry homework or finishing the assigned reading for English, but her mind was elsewhere. It had been like this for days now— weeks, even—where her thoughts drifted to the world, she wanted to create rather than the one she was trapped in.

Art was the only thing that made sense to her. In a world filled with tests, expectations, and the relentless drive to succeed in ways she didn't care about, art was her escape. She could lose herself in the lines, the shapes, the quiet details. Her pencil had a way of translating her emotions onto paper, even the ones she didn't fully understand. Here, she could breathe. Here, she could be herself.

But lately, even art had been feeling... heavy. Like there was a weight pressing down on her, something she couldn't quite shake off. The pressure from her parents, the endless push to excel in school, to follow the path they had set out for her, it was suffocating. They never said it outright, but the message was clear: "You're smart, Nyomi. You should aim higher. Art is nice, but it won't get you anywhere." And with every word, every subtle nudge toward science, math, and practical careers, a piece of her dream seemed to crumble away.

She glanced at her closed laptop sitting beside her. The unfinished chemistry assignment stared back at her in her mind, reminding her of everything she was supposed to be doing, everything that was expected of her. But Nyomi couldn't bring herself to care. Not right now. She wasn't like her parents, who saw life as a ladder to climb, step by step, rung by rung, until you reached success. Her mother, a lawyer, and her father, an engineer, were logical, driven, and focused on tangible results. And they wanted the same for her.

But Nyomi wasn't logical. Not in the way they wanted her to be. She saw the world in colors and shapes, in fleeting moments and emotions that couldn't be captured in numbers or equations. She wanted to create, to express something real and raw, something that existed beyond the confines of a classroom or a career plan.

She wanted to be an artist.

Her parents supported her, in their way. They bought her supplies, encouraged her to join art clubs, and praised her drawings when they had time. But there was always a catch, a condition: "As long as your grades are good, Nyomi. School first."

And that was the problem. School always came first, no matter how much Nyomi's heart longed to dive into her art without constraints. The weight of expectations, of being the "good daughter," the "smart one," kept her tethered to a life that didn't feel like her own.

She sighed, looking back at her sketchbook. Tonight, the world felt particularly heavy. Her hand moved absently over the page, sketching without much thought, letting her subconscious guide her. The lines flowed easily, naturally, as they always did when she needed to escape her own mind. She had no plan, no image in mind when she started, but soon, a form began to take shape beneath her pencil—delicate, intricate wings unfolding across the page.

A butterfly.

Nyomi smiled faintly, her pencil continuing its graceful dance over the paper. She had always loved butterflies, their fragility, their beauty, and most of all, their symbolism. Transformation. Freedom. Butterflies represented change, metamorphosis, the idea that something small and insignificant could become something extraordinary with time and patience.

Sometimes she wished she could be like them—able to shed the weight of the world, to break free from the expectations that kept her pinned down, and emerge as something new, something beautiful.

Her hand moved faster now, shading the wings with care, adding detail to each delicate vein, each curve and flicker of light. She lost herself in the process, the act of creating calming her in a way nothing else could. The world outside her bedroom—school, family, responsibilities—faded into the background, replaced by the soft, comforting strokes of her pencil and the butterfly that was slowly coming to life on the page.

For a brief moment, everything felt right.

But the moment didn't last. Nyomi's pencil stilled, hovering above the paper as doubt crept back in. What was she doing? What was the point? A part of her loved these quiet moments, but another part—bigger now than it used to be—couldn't help but question everything. Couldn't help but hear her parents' voices in her head, telling her she was wasting time. Art was beautiful, yes, but it was a hobby, not a future. Not something she could rely on.

And maybe they were right. Maybe she was foolish to think that she could ever make a real life out of this. The world didn't care about butterflies drawn in the margins of notebooks or landscapes sketched in the back of classrooms. The world wanted results. The world wanted practicality. The world wanted her to fit into a mold she didn't belong in.

She dropped the pencil onto the desk with a soft clatter and leaned back in her chair, staring up at the ceiling. The weight of it all pressed down on her, making it hard to breathe. Her chest ached with the familiar, frustrating feeling of being stuck. Trapped between who she was and who she was supposed to be.

Her gaze drifted back down to the butterfly on the page. It was beautiful, with its wings spread wide, as if it were about to take flight. But it was just a drawing. Just a collection of lines and shadows, trapped in two dimensions like she was trapped in her life.

Nyomi sighed again, closing her eyes. She wished she could be like that butterfly—free to fly, free to change, free to escape.

But life wasn't like that. Life wasn't magic. Or so she thought.

It happened so quietly, so subtly at first, that Nyomi didn't even notice.

Her eyes were still closed, her mind still drifting between frustration and longing when a faint shimmer of light caught her attention. She blinked, her eyes snapping open, and for a moment, she thought she had imagined it.

But no—it was real.

Her heart skipped a beat as she leaned forward, staring down at the butterfly on her page. The edges of its wings shimmered in the dim light of her desk lamp, a faint, almost imperceptible glow that made the lines of her drawing seem to pulse, to quiver. Nyomi's breath caught in her throat. Her mind raced, scrambling to find a logical explanation, but none came.

The butterfly's wings moved.

Her hand flew to her mouth as she stifled a gasp. It was impossible. It couldn't be real. And yet, there it was, fluttering its delicate wings, wings that moments ago had been nothing more than pencil strokes on paper.

Nyomi's body froze; her wide eyes locked onto the butterfly as it slowly lifted itself off the page. The sound of its wings was barely audible, like the softest whisper, but it echoed in her mind, drowning out everything else. The butterfly hovered in the air for a moment, its wings beating gently, casting faint, flickering shadows on her desk.

She couldn't move. Couldn't breathe. It was as though time itself had stopped, leaving her suspended in a moment that defied all reason, all logic. The butterfly was alive.

Her mind struggled to comprehend what she was seeing, what she was experiencing. This wasn't possible. Butterflies didn't just spring to life from drawings. This was the stuff of fairy tales, of magic. And magic didn't exist.

Not in her world. Not in the world where everything had to make sense, where everything had to fit neatly into categories and definitions.

But here it was, a living, breathing creature, born from her hands, her art.

The butterfly hovered for a moment longer, its iridescent wings shimmering as it fluttered around her head once, twice, as if trying to understand its own existence. Nyomi's heart pounded in her chest, her breath shallow, her mind racing with a thousand questions she didn't know how to ask.

Before she could move, before she could even think to react, the butterfly drifted toward the window. Its wings beat softly, gracefully, as it tapped lightly against the glass, searching for a way out.

Nyomi stood, her legs shaky, and crossed the room in a daze. Her fingers trembled as she unlocked the window and slid it open, the cool night air brushing against her skin. The butterfly paused for a moment on the sill, its wings glowing faintly in the moonlight, and then it lifted off into the air, disappearing into the night.

For a long moment, Nyomi stood there, staring out into the darkness, her mind numb, her heart still racing. It was gone. The butterfly was gone. And it had been real. It hadn't been a dream, hadn't been a hallucination brought on by stress or exhaustion. She had drawn a butterfly, and it had come to life.

Her fingers brushed against the paper, where the empty outline of her drawing remained, faint and fading, as though the butterfly's essence had been drained from the page.

Nyomi's mind whirled, a storm of emotions swirling in her chest. Fear. Confusion. Awe. And something else, something bright and exhilarating, something that buzzed in her veins like electricity.

Wonder.

She had done that. Somehow, she had brought that butterfly to life. And if she could do that—if she had that kind of power—what else could she do?

Her body trembled, but it wasn't just fear anymore. It was exciting. The weight that had pressed down on her, the suffocating expectations, the doubt—it was still there, but something new had joined it. Something that lifted her, just a little, something that made her heart beat faster in anticipation.

Possibility.

The world had shifted. The rules had changed. And Nyomi Boones was standing on the edge of something extraordinary.

Her hand reached for her pencil again, her fingers brushing the familiar weight of it. She stared down at the empty page before her, her mind still reeling from what had just happened. But now, there was no doubt. There was no fear.

She picked up the pencil. And she began to draw.

Nyomi didn't sleep that night. Every time she closed her eyes, she saw the butterfly again—its delicate wings fluttering in the moonlight, impossibly real, impossibly alive. The faint echo of its existence hummed in her mind, refusing to let her drift off. She couldn't shake the feeling that something within her had shifted, that a door had opened, and now she stood on the threshold of a new, strange world.

The next morning, she stumbled downstairs, bleary-eyed and distracted, as her mother called for breakfast.

"Nyomi, you'll be late for school if you don't hurry."

Her mother's voice was its usual mixture of gentle encouragement and veiled expectation. Nyomi nodded automatically, though she hadn't fully processed the words. She sat at the kitchen table, pushing cereal around in her bowl, her thoughts far away.

Could she do it again?

The question gnawed at her, louder than the clinking of silverware or the quiet hum of the kitchen appliances. She hadn't dared to try again last night. She hadn't been able to bring herself to pick up the pencil again. The weight of what had happened—what might happen—was too overwhelming. But now, in the daylight, the allure of her power felt stronger, more insistent.

Her mother looked at her over the rim of her coffee mug. "You're awfully quiet this morning."

Nyomi blinked, realizing she hadn't said a word since she sat down. "Yeah, I just... didn't sleep well."

Her mother gave her a sympathetic look. "Well, make sure you focus today. You've got that chemistry test coming up."

Chemistry. The very thought made her stomach twist. The test was tomorrow, and she hadn't even cracked open her textbook. How could she? How could anyone focus on something as mundane as formulas and elements when the laws of reality had just bent in her hands?

"Right," Nyomi mumbled, pushing her chair back from the table. "I'll head out early today."

Her mother raised her eyebrow. "Early? That's a first."

Nyomi forced a smile, trying to appear casual. "Just thought I'd get some studying done in the library."

"Good idea," her mother said approvingly. "Keep that focus."

Nyomi nodded, though her focus was nowhere near school. She grabbed her bag and hurried out the door, her heart pounding with a mixture of anticipation and anxiety.

Back in the Safety of Her Room Nyomi arrived home early, avoiding conversation with her classmates and brushing off Callie's questions with vague responses. Her mind was racing, entirely consumed with what she was planning to do.

She dropped her bag on the floor of her bedroom and quickly closed the door. The room felt safe, like the only place where she could explore the impossible without anyone questioning her sanity. She had been distracted all day—her thoughts drifting constantly to the butterfly, to the faint shimmer of life that had risen from her page.

She sat down at her desk, her sketchbook still open to the blank page where the butterfly had once been. For a long moment, she just stared at it, her fingers hovering over the pencil, hesitant.

What if it was a fluke? What if it didn't happen again? Or worse, what if it did, and she couldn't control it?

The questions gnawed at her, but the curiosity was stronger, more powerful than the doubt. She couldn't ignore it. She had to know. She had to try again.

Taking a deep breath, Nyomi picked up her pencil.

This time, she moved more deliberately, her hand steady as it traced soft lines across the page. She wasn't sure what she was drawing at first, just letting her hand guide her, letting her mind focus on the act of creating. The lines slowly formed into a shape, something familiar, something simple.

A leaf.

Nyomi stared at it for a moment, the delicate veins stretching across the surface of the leaf, the soft curves and angles carefully sketched out on the paper. It was nothing extraordinary—just a leaf, like one you'd find on a tree outside. But the simplicity of it felt right, less daunting than the butterfly had been.

She closed her eyes, focusing on the image in her mind. She pictured the leaf as though it were real—sitting in the palm of her hand, soft and fragile, with a slight breeze rustling through its edges.

For a long moment, nothing happened. Nyomi felt a wave of disappointment wash over her. Maybe the butterfly had been one-time thing. Maybe this power, whatever it was, wasn't something she could control.

But then, she heard it—the softest rustle of paper.

Her eyes snapped open, her heart leaping into her throat. The leaf was moving.

It was slow at first, just a faint tremor, like a breeze had passed over it. But then the edges of the drawing began to shimmer, just like the butterfly had, and the lines lifted off the page. Nyomi watched, wide-eyed, as the leaf slowly peeled itself away from the paper, floating gently into the air.

It hovered in front of her, spinning softly as though caught in a gentle wind. Her breath caught in her throat as she reached out, her fingers brushing against the leaf's surface.

It felt real.

Her mind struggled to comprehend what she was seeing, what she was feeling. The leaf was solid, tangible, its veins delicate beneath her fingertips. She held it in her hand, the cool weight of it sending a shiver down her spine.

The leaf fluttered again, slipping from her fingers and floating back toward the window. Nyomi watched as it landed softly on the sill, as if settling itself in the real world.

She stared at it for a long moment, her heart still racing. The butterfly had been real. The leaf was real. This wasn't some strange hallucination or dream. This was something... more.

Her hands trembled as she reached for her pencil again. This time, there was no hesitation. She had to know. She had to push further.

Experimenting with Creation Nyomi spent the next few hours drawing—simple things at first. A small flower. A bird. A pebble. Each time, the result was the same. The object would shimmer, lift off the page, and come to life in her room, as real and solid as anything else.

Her room was slowly filled with these creations—small, delicate things that felt too real to be mere drawings. They were part of the world now, existing alongside everything else, as though they had always belonged there.

Nyomi sat back in her chair, staring at the objects around her. A soft breeze blew through the open window, rustling the leaves and petals scattered across her desk.

She had done this. Somehow, she had brought these things into existence.

Her mind raced with possibilities. What did this mean? How was she doing it? Was it something inside her—some kind of power she didn't know she had? And if she could bring things to life... what else could she do?

Her fingers itched to pick up the pencil again, to keep drawing, to see how far she could push this. But a strange exhaustion had settled over her, a dull ache in the back of her mind. She hadn't realized how tired she was until she stopped, until the rush of creation faded and left her feeling drained.

She rubbed her temples, trying to shake off the heaviness that pressed down on her. Maybe she needed to take a break, to step back and clear her head.

As she stood, her legs wobbled beneath her, a sudden wave of dizziness washing over her. She stumbled, catching herself on the edge of her desk, her heart pounding in her chest.

Something was wrong.

The room felt like it was spinning, the edges of her vision blurring as her pulse quickened. She squeezed her eyes shut, trying to steady herself, but the dizziness only grew worse.

Her breath came into shallow gasps as she clutched the desk, her knuckles white. The objects around her—the leaf, the flower, the bird—seemed to shimmer, their edges flickering in and out of focus.

Panic gripped her, her mind reeling as she tried to make sense of what was happening. Was this a side effect of her powers? Was she pushing herself too far?

She forced herself to take slow, deep breaths, trying to calm the rising tide of fear. After a few moments, the dizziness began to fade, the room slowly settled back into focus.

Nyomi slumped into her chair, her body trembling with exhaustion. She hadn't realized how much energy it took to bring her creations to life, how much it drained from her.

She glanced at the objects around her—the things she had brought into existence—and for the first time, a thought crossed her mind that made her stomach twist.

What if she couldn't control it?

What if she brought something to life that she couldn't handle, something that was dangerous or unpredictable?

The thought lingered, heavy and unsettling, as she stared at her creations. They were beautiful, delicate things, but they were also... alive. And that meant they had the potential to be more than just harmless drawings.

Nyomi's heart pounded in her chest as the weight of what she had done began to sink in. This wasn't just a game; it wasn't just a fun trick. This was real. And it was dangerous.

She had unlocked something inside her—something powerful, something she didn't fully understand. And if she wasn't careful, it could spiral out of control.

The exhaustion pressed down on her, pulling her toward sleep, but her mind was racing too fast to let her rest. She needed answers. She needed to understand what was happening to her, what this power was, and how to control it.

But as she stared at the objects around her, at the things she had brought to life, she couldn't shake the feeling that she had only scratched the surface of what she could do.

There was more. So much more. And she had to find out.

A Moment of Thoughts Nyomi sat in the kitchen, tracing patterns

on the edge of the table as her mother served dinner. Her father was setting his usual stack of files down at the head of the table, his attention half on the conversation, half on the documents he had yet to review. It was a familiar scene, one that often felt like a ritual of routine

—a set of motions that each family member followed without deviation.

But tonight, the atmosphere felt heavier. The memory of the butterfly emerging from her drawing still clung to her mind, making everything around her feel muted, distant. The butterfly had been so vivid, so alive, and it left her struggling to focus on anything else. Her hands tingled with the faint recollection of that impossible warmth, and for the hundredth time, she wondered if it had been real.

"Nyomi?" Her mother's voice cut through her thoughts.

Nyomi blinked, realizing her mother had been speaking. "Sorry, what did you say?"

Her mother gave a soft, patient sigh, a sound that often preceded a reminder about responsibilities. "I asked how your chemistry test went."

"Oh, yeah... it was fine," Nyomi replied, pushing her food around on her plate.

"Just fine?" her mother asked, glancing over with a hint of concern. "You know, your grades have been slipping a little lately. We've talked about this, haven't we?"

Nyomi felt a familiar tension knot in her stomach. "I know, I just... I've had a lot on my mind."

Her father looked up from his files, his gaze sharp but not unkind. "Nyomi, we're just trying to help you stay on track. You're so smart, and you have so much potential. You know we support your art, but..."

"But school comes first," Nyomi finished for him, the words tasting bitter on her tongue.

Her mother nodded, offering a small smile. "Exactly. Art is wonderful, but it's a hobby. You need to be thinking about your future, about building a foundation for something that will last."

Nyomi's chest tightened. "Art can be more than a hobby, though. There are people who make a career out of it."

Her father exchanged a look with her mother, the kind that held unspoken understanding. "Of course, but those are rare cases," he said gently. "Besides, it's important to have something stable to fall back on. Science and math, those are areas where you'll always have options."

Nyomi's fingers curled tightly around her fork. She wanted to argue, to tell them that art was her passion, that it was more than just lines on paper or a passing interest. But every time she tried, the words seemed to stick in her throat, weighed down by the reality of their expectations.

Her mother reached over, placing a comforting hand on her arm. "Sweetheart, we're only saying this because we love you. We want you to have a bright future, one where you're secure and successful. You have so much talent in so many areas. We're just asking you not to put all your focus on one thing."

Nyomi forced a nod, though her thoughts churned with frustration. It was always the same: art was a side note, a temporary escape she was allowed to indulge in only if it didn't interfere with her "real" priorities.

After dinner, she slipped away to her room, the weight of her parents' words pressing down on her. She sat at her desk, the soft glow of her desk lamp casting a small circle of light over her scattered sketchbooks and pencils. For a moment, she stared at the blank page in front of her, the memory of the butterfly still vivid in her mind.

She hadn't imagined it. The butterfly had been real, had lifted off the page, had fluttered around her room. And yet, the moment she tried to wrap her mind around the impossibility of it, reality slipped away, leaving her only with questions.

She picked up her pencil, her fingers moving instinctively as she began to sketch. This time, she didn't have a particular image in mind. Her hand moved almost on its own, tracing lines and curves, her focus turning inward as she let herself sink into the act of creation.

Why couldn't her parents understand?

They loved her, she knew that. They wanted what was best for her. But they didn't see her world the way she did. For her, art was more than an escape, it was the only thing that made sense. In her drawings, she could be anyone, go anywhere. She could transform the ordinary into something magical, something that breathed and had depth.

But even as she let her mind wander, the weight of her parents' expectations lingered. Every line she drew felt like an act of rebellion, a quiet declaration that this part of her—the part that saw beauty in lines and shapes, the part that longed to create—was real and couldn't be dismissed.

Her pencil paused as the lines on the page began to take form. She was drawing another butterfly, delicate and intricate, its wings spreading across the paper with graceful arcs and swirls. She hadn't intended to draw another one, but her hand had moved instinctively, as if it knew what she needed before she did.

She stared at it, her heart tightening. The butterfly was a reminder, a flicker of possibility that she couldn't ignore. Maybe her parents didn't understand her need for art, her need to bring beauty into the world. But at that moment, she realized it didn't matter.

For the first time, she allowed herself to wonder: What if this power— whatever it was—was a gift, something that only she could understand?

The thought filled her with equal parts wonder and fear. Her parents might see her as someone full of potential for things they could understand

—chemistry, math, the sciences. But maybe there was a part of her that was meant to follow a different path, one that didn't fit into the neat, orderly world they had envisioned for her.

With a deep breath, she set down her pencil and stared at the drawing, her fingers tracing the edges of the butterfly's wings. The memory of that first flutter, the way it had come to life, was still vivid in her mind. She could almost feel the magic humming beneath her fingertips, a faint, tingling sensation that sent a shiver up her spine.

She didn't know what this power meant or where it came from, but one thing was clear: this was hers. Her parents' dreams for her future might not align with her own, but in this quiet moment, surrounded by the faint glow of her desk lamp, Nyomi felt a flicker of defiance rise within her.

Maybe she couldn't explain this magic, maybe she couldn't even control it yet. But whatever it was, it was a part of her, just as real as her love for art, just as undeniable as the passion that flowed through her veins every time, she picked up a pencil.

Her fingers hovered over the butterfly drawing; a quiet determination settled in her chest. She might not have answered yet, but she knew one thing: she wasn't going to give this up. She wasn't going to let her magic be another thing she had to hide or sacrifice to fit into a mold she didn't belong in.

As she closed her sketchbook, a calm resolve washed over her. She would keep drawing, keep exploring this strange gift, even if it meant defying the expectations that had been placed upon her. Because in that quiet, private space between her and her art, she had finally found something that felt truly hers.

Nyomi's mind whirled as she stared at the empty space on her desk where the butterfly had been. Her hand trembled slightly as she traced the faint outline on the paper, the ghostly remains of her sketch, as if her drawing had left a trace of its magic on the page.

It was real, she thought, barely daring to believe it. It really happened.

But the doubt crept in almost immediately. Maybe she was just overtired, caught in a dream she couldn't shake off. That had to be it, she reasoned, trying to convince herself. The whole thing felt like something from a fairy tale, a fantastical story she'd read under the covers as a kid. Magic wasn't real—it couldn't be. And yet...

She couldn't ignore the memory of the butterfly's delicate wings brushing her hand, its soft warmth lingering like a whispered promise. Closing her eyes, she tried to recall every detail: the way it shimmered in the moonlight, the way it seemed to look at her as if it understood.

Her heart beat faster as a strange, electrifying thought took root in her mind. What if it wasn't a hallucination? What if I can do it again?

Her eyes snapped open, flickering around her room as she searched for something to test her theory. Nyomi's gaze fell upon the small flower pressed between the pages of one of her art books, its petals faded but still holding the faintest blush of pink. She picked it last spring and kept it as a memento. It was a delicate thing, brittle and dried, yet beautiful in its own quiet way.

Her fingers shook slightly as she lifted it out of the book, laying it gently on a fresh page in her sketchbook. She took a deep, steady breath and picked up her pencil, feeling the weight of her decision to settle over her. This time, she wasn't going to let herself be distracted. She was going to focus, pouring every ounce of attention into her drawing, just to see if she could make something happen.

As her pencil moved across the page, she felt a subtle tension building within her, like a coiled spring tightening with each stroke. She shaded the petals delicately, capturing the faint veins and the soft, curling edges, adding shadows that brought it to life on the page. She became so absorbed in her work that she almost didn't notice the faint shimmer until it was there, glimmering softly around the edges of the drawn petals.

Her breath caught, her fingers freezing mid-stroke as she watched the delicate lines tremble, quivering like they were alive. She half-expected it to stop, for the shimmer to fade as if she were waking from a dream. But the glow deepened, like a pulse growing stronger, gaining life and movement.

The petals began to curl, lifting from the paper as if a breeze were coaxing them upward. Nyomi felt her heart thundering in her chest, a mix of exhilaration and fear threading through her veins as the flower took on a three-dimensional form, its fragile leaves unfurling slowly, reverently, before her eyes. It was like watching a miracle unfold, as if she were seeing something she was never meant to witness—a piece of art made flesh.

With a tentative hand, Nyomi reached out to touch it, her fingertips brushing the edges of the petal. It felt real, soft and cool, and she felt a chill run down her spine. She pulled her hand back sharply, her mind buzzing with a thousand questions.

"What... how...?" she whispered to the empty room, her voice barely audible. The flower hovered in the air for a moment, as if acknowledging her presence, before it gently settled back down onto the page, returning to the stillness of a drawing.

She sat back in her chair, breathless, breathless, her mind a storm of emotions— wonder, disbelief, and a touch of fear. What does this mean? How did I do that? She didn't know, and the not-knowing was as thrilling as it was terrifying. In one night, her entire world had shifted, and she wasn't sure she would ever be the same.

Magic isn't real, she reminded herself. But she couldn't deny what she had seen, what she had felt. The truth settled over her like a whisper, both a promise and a warning.

If I can do this... what else am I capable of?

As the butterfly's delicate wings fluttered out of sight, disappearing into the vastness of the night, Nyomi remained motionless, her hand still hovering by the open window. The cool breeze tickled her fingers, grounding her as she slowly closed the window, almost afraid the moment would vanish as quickly as it had arrived.

A surreal realization settled over her: this power was real, and somehow, inexplicably, it was hers. She could still feel the faint warmth of the butterfly's touch lingering on her skin, its tiny legs pressing against her as if it were somehow part of her. Nyomi's heart raced with exhilaration, but fear prickled at the edges of her mind. Could she control this strange ability? Or was it something that would take control of her?

The light from her desk lamp dimmed, casting the room in softer shadows as she stepped back to her desk. Her gaze fell on her sketchbook, open to a page that only moments ago held the butterfly—her butterfly. Her hands trembled slightly as she picked up her pencil, the familiar weight calming her just a little. What other creations could she bring to life? What secrets lay hidden in the simple graphite lines, waiting for her to release them?

For a fleeting moment, the possibilities felt endless. She could bring to life anything she could imagine—a bird to perch on her shoulder, a flower that would never wither, perhaps even something bigger, something powerful and alive. The thought filled her with both thrill and apprehension. What was the source of this power? Was there a limit, a rule, or was it all bound only by her imagination?

But before she could finish her thought, the faint sound of her mother's voice echoed up the stairs, snapping her back to the present. "Nyomi, dinner's ready!"

Nyomi blinked, as if awakening from a dream. She closed the sketchbook, fingers lingering on the cover. She took one last look at the now-empty page, her heart a conflicted mix of excitement and worry.

"Coming!" she called back, quickly tucking the sketchbook away in her desk drawer, hiding it from view as if it held a secret too precious to reveal.

As she left her room and headed downstairs, her mind swirled with questions, each one more urgent than the last. She forced herself to take a deep breath, to let go of the image of the butterfly, but the mystery lingered, weaving itself into her thoughts.

Stepping into the warm glow of the dining room, she caught sight of her parents already seated, chatting about their day. Their familiar faces and voices, so rooted in the practical world, seemed almost foreign now— almost distant. She wondered what they would think if they knew. What would they say if she told them about the butterfly, about this strange, impossible power hidden within her?

But as she slid into her seat and picked up her fork, Nyomi knew there would be no telling. Not yet. This magic was hers alone—a secret she wasn't ready to share.

Her parents' voices became a gentle hum in the background, comforting yet oddly detached from the new reality she found herself in. As she pushed her food around her plate, one thought repeated in her mind, growing stronger with each passing moment.

What else could I bring to life?

With that thought nestled deep inside her, she made herself a silent promise: later, when everyone else was asleep, she would return to her sketchbook. She would draw again. She would try to control this power, understand it—whatever it took.

For the first time in her life, Nyomi felt like she was on the edge of something extraordinary, and she had only just taken the first step.

Nyomi stared out her window, the cool night air filling her room as the butterfly vanished into the darkness. She'd watched it until it became a faint shimmer, then a memory, and finally just a question floating in her mind. Even as it disappeared from sight, the sensation of its delicate legs brushing her fingers lingered, grounding her in the strange reality of what had just happened.

Slowly, she closed the window, her hands trembling as she reached for the latch. The night seemed darker now, the quiet around her thick and pressing, as though the world itself was holding its breath. Nyomi took a deep breath and returned to her desk, her gaze drifting to the now-empty page in her sketchbook. The intricate pencil lines that had once been the butterfly's wings were gone, leaving only faint smudges where it had been.

This power was real.

A thrill of wonder mixed with a ripple of fear as she placed her fingers lightly on the sketchbook's cover. She could still feel the energy humming beneath her skin, the faint, lingering buzz of something she'd always dreamed about but never believed possible. Her heart raced as she considered the possibilities, each one more thrilling—and terrifying—than the last.

What else could she bring to life?

As she left her room, Nyomi glanced back at the closed sketchbook, a quiet thrill stirring in her chest. Her mind spun with questions, each one feeding a growing sense of wonder and urgency. The world outside her room suddenly felt small, pressing in on the possibilities within her. Tonight, after her family was asleep, she'd returned to the sketchbook. She needed to know if this magic was real, and if it was truly hers to command.

The thought wrapped around her like a promise, one that she would keep only to herself. She slipped down the stairs to join her family at dinner, but every noise and word felt distant, muffled by the rush of anticipation building within her. Her parents chatted about the day's events, their voices familiar yet strangely disconnected from the world she'd just discovered. She forced herself to smile and nod, to join in, but her thoughts drifted back to her room, back to the sketchbook.

Between bites of food, she traced patterns in her mind, each one a hint of what she might try next. A bird with feathers that shimmered in the moonlight, a flower that would bloom with a single touch, or perhaps something larger, something that would let her feel the true extent of this power.

As the evening wore on, her excitement grew, until it was almost too much to contain. Finally, after a polite "goodnight" and a quick retreat to her room, she closed the door and leaned against it, her pulse racing. The house settled into stillness, and she could hear her parents' footsteps fade down the hall as they prepared for bed.

Now, at last, the world was quiet, and it was only her and the waiting sketchbook.

Nyomi crossed the room, her hands steady now, no longer trembling as she reached for the pencil. The page lay before her, blank and open, inviting her to dive deeper, to explore the magic that had begun to stir in her soul. She smiled, a quiet, determined smile. The questions no longer frightened her, they thrilled her, pulled her forward into a world that was hers alone.

Tonight, she will draw again. She would test the boundaries of this gift, this impossible, wonderful thing that had found its way to her. And she wouldn't stop until she understood it, until she made it hers.

CHAPTER 2: THE BUTTERFLY EFFECT

Nyomi sat in the back of her chemistry class, staring blankly at the half– finished worksheet in front of her. The formulas blurred into incomprehensible shapes, their meaning slipping away as her mind wandered back to the butterfly, the leaf, the flower—the things she had brought to life. She could still feel the strange tingle in her fingers from the night before, as if the dormant energy inside her had stirred and couldn't quite settle back down.

She shook her head, forcing herself to focus on the lesson. Her teacher, Mr. Haskell, was explaining something about molecular bonds, but his voice was a distant hum in her ears. No matter how hard she tried, she couldn't stop thinking about what had happened. She couldn't stop replaying the moment the butterfly lifted from the page, the way it fluttered out into the night. The way the leaf had felt so real in her hand.

What was this power? And why did it feel like it was getting stronger? Every time she closed her eyes, she saw those creations again—living, breathing things that shouldn't have existed, yet they had. They had been real. And that terrified her as much as it fascinated her.

Her pencil hovered over the worksheet, but she couldn't bring herself to write anything. The words felt meaningless, the equations irrelevant compared to the questions swirling in her mind. How could she care about chemistry when something inside her had fundamentally changed, something that didn't follow any of the laws of science she had ever learned?

She rubbed her temples, trying to quell the anxiety bubbling inside her. What if she lost control again? What if, the next time, she brought something to life that wasn't so harmless? Something that wasn't just a butterfly or a leaf?

"Nyomi?"

She blinked, realizing Mr. Haskell was standing in front of her desk, frowning down at her. His voice cut through the fog of her thoughts.

"Are you following this?" he asked, his eyes narrowing slightly. "You've been pretty quiet today."

"Uh, yeah. Sorry." Nyomi mumbled, forcing herself to meet his gaze. "I'm just... distracted."

Mr. Haskell sighed, his expression softening. "I know the chemistry test is coming up soon, but you'll do fine if you focus. I'd suggest a bit of extra study time after class."

She nodded automatically, though she wasn't listening. She could feel the eyes of her classmates on her—some curious, others disinterested—but they made her skin prickle with discomfort. Mr. Haskell turned back to the board, and Nyomi slumped lower in her chair, willing herself to disappear.

Focus, Nyomi, she told herself. Just get through the day. Pretend everything normal.

But nothing felt normal anymore.

When the bell rang, she packed her books as quickly as possible and rushed out of the classroom before anyone could stop her. Her legs felt like they were carrying her on autopilot, leading her through the crowded hallways of Riverside High without any real direction.

It was lunchtime, but Nyomi couldn't bring herself to sit in the cafeteria surrounded by noise and chatter. Her head buzzed with too many thoughts, too many questions, none of which had answers. She needed space. She needed quiet.

Her usual hiding place was the library refuge she had discovered in her freshman year when the pressures of high school had first started weighing on her. It was quiet, tucked away at the far end of the school, and no one ever bothered her there. She could sit by the large windows and lose herself in her thoughts—or, at least, she used to be able to.

Today, even the library's comforting silence couldn't calm her. She found her usual spot by the window, setting her lunch tray down in front of her, but her appetite was nonexistent. She stared out at the campus lawn, watching the wind stir the leaves of the trees, the way the sunlight filtered through the branches.

What is happening to me?

The question had been gnawing at her since the butterfly first came to life, but now it felt like it was swallowing her whole. Every moment she wasn't thinking about her power, she was thinking about how to not think about it. It was like a loop she couldn't escape.

"Nyomi!"

The voice startled her out of her thoughts. She turned to see Callie, her best friend since middle school, bouncing toward her with her usual bright energy. Callie was everything Nyomi wasn't—outgoing, talkative, optimistic. Her presence often felt like a warm light that chased away Nyomi's gloom, but today, that light was a little too blinding.

"Hey! Why didn't you meet me for lunch?" Callie plopped down in the seat across from Nyomi, her tray clattering onto the table. "I've been looking for you everywhere."

Nyomi forced a smile. "Sorry, I just... needed some quiet."

Callie took a huge bite of her sandwich and shrugged. "You're always needing quiet. You should try sitting with the group sometime! Everyone was talking about the science fair coming up, and I swear, it's going to be awesome. I'm still deciding what to do for my project, but I'm thinking about robotics. Or maybe holograms. What about you?"

Nyomi shifted uncomfortably. The science fair. It was the last thing she wanted to think about right now.

"I haven't really decided yet," she said, picking at the corner of her sandwich but not eating.

Callie frowned, studying her. "You've been off today. Are you okay? You seem... I don't know, distracted?"

Nyomi's heart raced. She couldn't tell Callie the truth, couldn't even begin to explain what had been happening to her. She barely understood it herself. How was she supposed to tell her best friend that she could bring her drawings to life? Callie would think she was insane.

"I'm fine," Nyomi said quickly. "Just... a lot on my mind."

Callie's face softened, her eyes filled with concern. "Is it your parents again? Are they still on your case about grades?"

Nyomi let out a small, relieved breath. This was familiar territory. Callie knew how much pressure Nyomi's parents put on her, and it was an easy excuse to fall back on.

"Yeah," Nyomi muttered. "They've been... pushing me harder lately.

Chemistry, especially."

Callie rolled her eyes. "Ugh, parents and their obsession with grades. My mom keeps telling me to 'focus on the big picture,' like I'm going to magically know what I want to do with my life right now."

Nyomi laughed softly, grateful for the change in subject. "Yeah, same.

They don't really get it."

Callie grinned, her usual spark returning. "Well, don't worry about it too much. You're smart. You'll figure it out. And hey, when you do, you can ditch the chemistry books and start selling your art! You'll be famous."

Nyomi's smile faltered. Art. It used to be the one thing that brought her peace, the one thing that felt like hers, but now... now it felt different. Ever since the butterfly, drawing wasn't just an escape. It was dangerous. It had power.

"I don't know," Nyomi said quietly, looking down at her hands. "Maybe art isn't enough."

Callie's smile faded, confusion flickering in her eyes. "What? What do you mean?"

Nyomi hesitated, her chest tightening with the weight of everything she couldn't say. How could she explain the fear gnawing at her, the sense that something inside her was spiraling out of control? How could she tell Callie that her art —her one refuge—had turned into something she didn't understand, something that scared her?

"I just... I'm not sure it's what I thought it was," Nyomi said vaguely, picking at her sandwich again.

Callie leaned forward, her brow furrowed. "Hey, don't say that. You love art. You've always loved it. You're amazing at it. Just because your parents don't get it doesn't mean it's not enough."

Nyomi nodded, but the words felt hollow. Callie meant well, but she didn't understand. She couldn't.

Callie nudged her arm playfully. "Come on, cheer up. You've been acting like someone sucked the soul out of you all day. Let's go get a coffee after school. We'll figure out your science fair project, and I bet we can come up with something that'll blow Mr. Haskell's mind."

Nyomi forced a smile. "Maybe."

But her heart wasn't in it. She knew Callie was trying to help, but the more she tried to act like everything was normal, the more overwhelming it all became. The more Callie pushed her to focus on the science fair, on their usual routine, the more Nyomi felt the walls closing in.

As they continued talking, Nyomi's eyes drifted out the window again, her mind only half-listening. She saw a group of students milling around the courtyard, their voices distant through the glass. Most of them she recognized, but one figure caught her attention.

Thomas Hale.

He stood alone, leaning against a tree with a book in his hands. His dark hair fell over his forehead, partially obscuring his face, but there was

something about him that always seemed... different. Quiet. Thomas wasn't like the other students, he kept to himself, always observing, always on the edge of things. Nyomi had seen him around school for years, but they had never spoken.

Today, though, something was different. She couldn't shake the feeling that he was watching her.

As if sensing her gaze, Thomas glanced up from his book. For a split second, their eyes met through the window. Nyomi's heart skipped a beat, and she quickly looked away, heat rising to her cheeks.

What was that about?

Callie was still talking, oblivious to the sudden shift in Nyomi's attention, but Nyomi couldn't focus. She stole another glance out of the window, but Thomas had already looked back down at his book, his expression unreadable.

She shook her head, trying to brush it off. Thomas wasn't important. He was just a quiet kid who happened to be standing outside. It didn't mean anything.

But still, something about the way he had looked at her... it made her uneasy. Like he knew something. Like he had seen more than he was letting on.

"Nyomi? Are you even listening?"

Callie's voice snapped her back to the present. Nyomi blinked, forcing her focus back to her friend.

"Sorry, what?"

"I was saying we should totally do a beach day this weekend," Callie said, grinning. "I need a break from all this school stuff. You in?"

Nyomi hesitated; her thoughts still tangled in the memory of Thomas's glance. "Yeah... maybe. I'll let you know."

Callie frowned. "Come on, Nyomi. You've been acting so weird lately.

You need to relax. We both do."

"I know," Nyomi muttered, but her heart wasn't in it. How was she supposed to relax when everything felt like it was unraveling?

The bell rang, signaling the end of lunch, and Nyomi stood up, grabbing her tray. Callie followed her, chatting away as they walked toward their next class, but Nyomi's mind was elsewhere.

She couldn't stop thinking about Thomas. She couldn't stop wondering if he knew something. And she couldn't stop the feeling of dread that settled in her chest, heavy and cold.

Something was changing. Something inside her. And no matter how hard she tried to pretend everything was normal, she knew the truth.

It wasn't.

The rest of the day passed in a blur, each class dragging on with excruciating slowness. Nyomi went through the motions, nodding when she was supposed to, scribbling half-hearted notes, but her thoughts kept drifting back to her powers. She couldn't concentrate. She couldn't focus on anything but the gnawing fear that had taken root in her chest.

By the time the final bell rang, signaling the end of the school day, Nyomi felt like she was barely holding herself together. She needed space. She needed to breathe.

Callie caught up with her as they walked toward the exit, her usual boundless energy undeterred by Nyomi's quiet mood. "You want to grab that coffee now?"

Nyomi shook her head, forcing a smile. "I think I'm going to head home. I've got... a lot of homework."

Callie pouted but nodded. "Okay, but promise me you'll let me know if you need to talk, okay? You're not yourself lately."

"I promise," Nyomi lied. She wasn't ready to talk. Not about this. Not yet.

With a wave, she turned and hurried out of the building, her feet carrying her toward the safety of home.

That night, Nyomi sat at her desk, staring at her sketchbook. The blank pages seemed to mock her, daring her to try again, to push further, to see what else she could bring to life.

Her hands trembled as she picked up her pencil. The familiar weight of it should have been comforting, but now it felt dangerous. Her mind was filled with fear, but beneath that fear was something else, something stronger.

Curiosity.

What if she could control it? What if she could understand it? Her pencil hovered over the page, her breath shallow.

And then, without thinking, she began to draw.

The next morning, Nyomi shuffled into the kitchen, still bleary-eyed and shaken from the events of the previous night. She didn't sleep well. Every time she closed her eyes, she saw the butterfly again—its wings beating with an impossible life, the glow of its colors blending into the shadows of her room. The memory clung to her like a haunting melody, making it difficult to focus on anything else.

Her mother was already bustling around the kitchen, setting out coffee mugs and pouring milk into a small bowl of cereal. Nyomi's father sat at the table, scanning the newspaper with his usual focused expression.

"Good morning, sweetheart," her mother said, glancing over her shoulder. "Sleep well?"

Nyomi forced a smile. "Yeah, I guess," she replied, though her mind was still lost in the memory of the butterfly. She took a seat at the table and reached for her glass of water, hoping the cool liquid would shake her awake.

But the moment her fingers touched the glass; she felt an odd tingling in her hand. She pulled back instinctively, watching as the water inside the glass began to tremble, tiny ripples forming on the surface.

"Nyomi?" Her mother's voice broke through her thoughts, and Nyomi quickly wrapped her fingers around the glass, holding it steady.

"Sorry, I just... zoned out for a second." She hoped her mother hadn't noticed anything strange. The last thing she needed was for anyone to ask questions she couldn't answer.

But as she lifted the glass to her lips, she could still feel that strange tingling sensation. It was faint, like a whisper just beneath her skin, but it was there—persistent, steady, like a pulse. She took a small sip, her mind racing as she tried to shake off the feeling.

She could still see the glass vibrating slightly, the water shimmering as if touched by an invisible force. She quickly set it down and looked away, trying to ignore the growing unease in her chest.

At school, the strange sensations continued.

In chemistry class, she sat at her usual seat in the back, trying to focus on the lecture. Mr. Haskell droned on about chemical reactions and equilibrium, his voice a low, monotonous hum in her ears. Normally, Nyomi would have been able to tune in and take notes, but today, her mind was elsewhere.

She could still feel that faint tingling, a sensation that seemed to linger at her fingertips, as if something just beneath the surface of her skin was waiting to be released. It was a strange, almost electric feeling, like a soft vibration she couldn't shake.

At one point, her pen slipped from her fingers, and she reached down to retrieve it. But as her fingers brushed the pen, she felt a small spark—a tiny shock that sent a jolt up her arm. She gasped quietly, pulling her hand back as the pen rolled away on its own, moving slightly too fast across the floor.

"Nyomi? Everything alright?" Mr. Haskell's voice brought her back to reality, and she realized he had paused the lecture, his gaze directed toward her.

"Uh, yes. Sorry," she murmured, ducking her head to hide her flushed cheeks.

She picked up her pen, but her fingers still tingled from the shock, and as she gripped the pen, it felt warm—almost as if it were buzzing faintly in her hand. Nyomi took a deep breath, willing the sensation to go away, trying to focus on the lecture. But as the class dragged on, her thoughts kept drifting back to the butterfly, to the glass, to the strange, inexplicable feeling humming beneath her skin.

It felt like something was calling her, urging her to pay attention.

By lunchtime, Nyomi felt like she was teetering on the edge of a dream. She moved through the crowded cafeteria, the noise around her a distant hum, her thoughts swirling in an endless loop of confusion and curiosity.

As she sat down at her usual table with her friends, she noticed a strange flicker in the corner of her vision. She blinked, thinking it was just a trick of the light, but when she glanced down at her backpack, she saw the faintest shimmer of light along the zipper.

Nyomi stared, holding her breath, her eyes glued to the small, flickering glow. It was subtle, almost imperceptible, but it was there—a soft, golden light, like the glimmer of sunlight filtering through leaves. She reached out, her fingers brushing against the zipper, and the shimmer faded, leaving her with nothing but the ordinary fabric of her backpack.

Her heart raced as she pulled her hand back, glancing around to make sure no one had noticed. Callie was busy chatting with another friend, oblivious to Nyomi's distraction, but Nyomi's mind was a whirlwind of thoughts.

The butterfly, the vibrating glass, the sparking pen, and now this. Something was happening to her, something she didn't understand, something that defied everything she knew about the world.

By the end of the school day, Nyomi could barely contain the swirling emotions inside her. The tingling sensation, the shimmering lights, the inexplicable vibrations all pointed to one undeniable truth: the butterfly hadn't been a dream. The magic, whatever it was, was real. And it was still with her.

She hurried home, her mind racing as she replayed the events of the day, each moment adding fuel to the fire of her curiosity. She couldn't ignore it any longer. She had to know more, had to understand what was happening to her.

The moment she was alone in her room, she shut the door and sat at her desk, pulling out her sketchbook with trembling hands. She opened it to a blank page, her heart pounding as she stared down at the clean sheet of paper.

Taking a deep breath, she picked up her pencil, feeling that familiar hum of energy stirs in her fingers. It was faint, a subtle pulse beneath her skin, but it was there—steady and real, like the quiet beat of a drum.

What am I doing? she thought, but she pushed the doubt aside. She couldn't let fear hold her back. Not now.

She began to draw, her hand moving slowly at first, tracing soft lines and gentle curves. She didn't have a clear image in mind; she was simply letting her instincts guide her, allowing her hand to move freely across the page. As the lines took shape, she found herself sketching a small delicate flower bloom with slender petals and a soft, curling stem.

The act of drawing felt almost meditative, a way to channel the energy that hummed beneath her skin. With each stroke of her pencil, the tingling in her fingers grew stronger, more insistent, as if the magic was responding to her touch, feeding off her intent.

She finished the drawing and leaned back, her gaze fixed on the small flower on the page. For a moment, everything was still, her room quiet safe for the faint ticking of the clock on her wall.

And then, just as it had with the butterfly, the edges of the flower began to shimmer.

Nyomi held her breath, her heart racing as she watched the lines quiver, the petals flickering with a soft, ethereal light. The magic was alive, responding to her touch, her intent. She felt a thrill of wonder, mingled with a touch of fear, as the flower seemed to lift slightly off the page, its form becoming more solid, more real.

The petals stretched, unfurling as if in response to sunlight, and Nyomi reached out, her fingers brushing against the flower's delicate surface. It felt cool and soft, its texture impossibly real.

A small, incredulous smile spread across her face as she held the flower in her hand, marveling at the miracle of its existence. The doubts and fears that had plagued her earlier faded away, replaced by a quiet certainty.

This magic—whatever it was—was hers. And if she could bring a butterfly and a flower to life, then maybe, just maybe, there was more she could do.

Setting the flower gently back on the desk, she closed her sketchbook, a new determination taking root within her. She didn't understand this power yet, didn't know where it came from or how far it extended. But she was going to find out.

In that moment, Nyomi made a silent promise to herself: she would explore this gift, this strange, beautiful magic, and learn to control it. She would experiment cautiously, carefully, testing the boundaries of what she could do.

Because for the first time in her life, she felt like she was on the brink of something extraordinary.

Nyomi closed her bedroom door behind her and leaned against it, exhaling slowly as she tried to steady her heartbeat.

The day had felt endless, each moment dragging her further into a web of questions she couldn't shake. She tossed her bag onto her desk and glanced at her sketchbook, half-expecting something to shimmer to life on its own. But it lay there quietly, the pages still and lifeless, as if mocking her.

Moving slowly, she sank into her desk chair and opened her sketchbook, flipping through the pages filled with her art. Each sketch brought a comforting sense of familiarity—the sharp lines of her charcoal, the delicate shading of her pencils, the bright, vivid splashes of color that captured moments of inspiration. But none of them felt quite as real anymore. None of them held the magic she'd experienced with the butterfly and the flower.

Her hand drifted to the empty page, where only a faint outline remained, a fragile remnant of the butterfly that had taken flight. The memory of it flitted through her mind, vivid and undeniable. Yet, a part of her still resisted, searching for an explanation that made sense, that didn't defy everything she knew about the world.

There has to be an explanation, she thought, feeling a hint of reassurance in the idea. Maybe this wasn't magic, maybe there was some logical reason for what she'd seen.

She reached for a pen, tapping it absentmindedly against the blank page as her mind sifted through possibilities. Maybe it's stress, she reasoned, thinking back to her conversations with her parents, the pressure of school, and the gnawing feeling of not fitting in anywhere. Stress could do strange things to the mind—she'd read about people hallucinating under extreme pressure, their brains conjuring images as a way to cope.

Or maybe it's sleep deprivation, she thought, recalling the restless nights she'd spent huddling over her sketchbook. I haven't been getting enough sleep. Maybe my mind is just... slipping.

She repeated these thoughts to herself, almost as if saying them enough times would make them true. Stress, exhaustion, imagination. They were logical, scientific explanations, ideas that fit into the world she understood.

But even as she tried to convince herself, a small, insistent voice in the back of her mind whispered doubts. The butterfly had felt too real, its wings too solid, its touch too warm. And then there was the flower—the way its delicate petals had brushed against her fingers, leaving her with a sense of wonder that lingered long after it had settled back onto the page.

Her hand tightened around the pen as she tried to suppress the feeling rising in her chest—a feeling that maybe, just maybe, this wasn't something science could explain.

"People don't just bring things to life," she murmured, as if saying it out loud would make it more believable. "It doesn't happen. It can't."

But as she stared at the blank page, an unsettling truth began to settle over her. Despite all her attempts to rationalize it, she couldn't shake the memory of the butterfly, of the gentle beat of its wings, of the moment it had lifted off the page and hovered in front of her. It was real. No amount of logical reasoning could change that.

Her thoughts drifted to her science teacher, Mr. Haskell, and his recent lecture on molecular bonds and energy. She remembered his words about how energy flows in patterns, creating forces that hold the world together. She didn't know how her powers fit into any of that, but the idea of energy as a force, invisible but present, made her wonder if there was something to this ability she hadn't considered. Could energy explain it? Could art somehow act as a bridge between imagination and reality?

The thought sent a shiver through her. It was ridiculous—like something out of a fantasy novel. But what if?

Nyomi shook her head, trying to push the notion aside. She didn't want to believe in magic, or powers, or anything that would make her even more of an outsider. If I ignore it, she told herself, maybe it will just go away.

But a small part of her knew that wasn't true. Once opened, some doors could never fully close.

She closed her sketchbook and leaned back, staring at the ceiling as a quiet sense of unease settled over her. She couldn't shake the feeling that something inside her had changed, something fundamental and irreversible. She wasn't sure what it meant, or where it would lead her, but she knew one thing for certain: Her life would never be the same again.

With a sigh, Nyomi turned off her desk lamp and climbed into bed, pulling the blankets up to her chin. She lay in the darkness, her thoughts swirling like leaves in a storm. Her mind kept circling back to the same question, a question that lingered in the quiet corners of her mind long after she drifted off to sleep.

What am I capable of?

As Nyomi sat down to draw again, the familiar weight of the pencil grounding her, a flicker of movement caught her eye by the window. She stilled, pencil hovering just above the page, and glanced up.

In the quiet shadows of the yard, a figure stood beneath the branches of an old oak tree, partially obscured by darkness. Thomas Hale. His face was faintly illuminated by the streetlight, casting strange shadows across his features. His eyes were fixed on her window, his expression unreadable.

Nyomi's heart quickened, her pulse a steady thrum in her ears. Why was he there? She watched him, half-expecting him to turn and leave, but for a long, unsettling moment, he remained still, his gaze locked in her room as if he could see her through the thin curtains.

A chill crept over her, raising the hairs on her arms. Thomas was known for keeping to himself, blending into the background of school life, but something about his presence here felt... intentional. She shivered, feeling exposed, as though he could somehow sense the secret she carried, the strange power that simmered just beneath her skin.

Just as suddenly as he had appeared, Thomas turned and walked away, disappearing into the shadows, leaving only the faint rustle of leaves in his wake. Nyomi let out a breath she hadn't realized she was holding, her eyes lingering on the spot where he had stood. What did he want? The question echoed in her mind, unsettling and unanswered.

She shook her head, forcing herself to focus as she settled into her seat again. She tightened her grip on the pencil, determined to reclaim the sense of control she'd felt slipping through her fingers since her powers had emerged. But Thomas's presence lingered in her thoughts, an uninvited shadow clouding her mind. Her curiosity about her power, once a thrilling and private wonder, was now mingled with an unshakable sense of dread.

With a shiver, Nyomi leaned over her sketchbook, pencil poised above the page. She hesitated, the image of Thomas's expression—a mixture of knowing and something she couldn't quite place—filling her mind. Why had he looked at her that way, like he understood something about her, something she hadn't even begun to understand about herself?

Focus, Nyomi. She took a deep breath, her eyes fixed on the blank page and tried to push everything else aside. The pencil felt steady in her hand, and as she let her mind settle, the whisper of the familiar hum began to stir beneath her fingertips. But Thomas's presence lingered, his face flashing through her thoughts like a silent warning.

Her fingers traced a line across the paper, each stroke a way to channel the tension knotting in her chest. The delicate shape of a leaf began to take form beneath her pencil, and the familiar sense of calm slowly returned. She could feel the warmth of her power beneath the surface, that strange energy thrumming to life, but now it held an edge of uncertainty. Could Thomas have felt it too, somehow sensed it from the darkness outside her window?

The thought made her pulse quicken again, her fingers faltering as the outline of the leaf blurred. She forced herself to continue, but her heart raced with a new, unsettling question. What if she wasn't the only one who could feel it? What if this power wasn't as hidden as she thought?

In the quiet of her room, the shadows felt deeper, more alive. Nyomi could feel the weight of her discovery, as thrilling as it was terrifying, closing in on her.

She set down her pencil, her hand trembling. Her gaze drifted back to the window, to the spot where Thomas had stood. She didn't know why he'd been watching, didn't understand what he might know. But her certainty wavered. Her magic, once a secret wonder, felt suddenly fragile, vulnerable.

Somewhere in the depths of her mind, a quiet resolve settled within her: I have to find out more. About her power, about Thomas... and about what might happen if her secret wasn't so secret after all.

As Nyomi closed her sketchbook and rose from her desk, a sense of determination took root within her, calming her racing heart. She would learn to control her gift, no matter what it took. And if Thomas knew she didn't, she would find that out too.

For now, though, she couldn't shake the image of his eyes watching her from the shadows, and the sense that her life was changing in ways she didn't yet understand.

Nyomi's pencil hovered above the page, her focus slipping as her eyes drifted back to the window. The shadows outside her house remained still silent, yet her heart continued to pound with the feeling that something was watching her. Thomas Hale had stood out there only moments before, his dark silhouette partially hidden beneath the branches, his face half-lit by the streetlight's faint glow. His eyes, intense and unreadable, had been fixed on her window.

Why was he there?

She closed her eyes, trying to brush off the unsettling moment, but the image of Thomas remained, his gaze etched into her mind. Her skin prickled at the memory, her thoughts churning with questions she couldn't quite form. Thomas was quiet, the kind of person who lingered in the background, unnoticed. But tonight, something about his presence felt deliberate, purposeful, as though he'd been there for a reason —and as though he knew something about her, something she barely understood herself.

What did he know? And why did his presence make her feel so exposed?

Nyomi shook off the strange feeling and turned back to her drawing, though Thomas's intense gaze remained in her mind, lingering like a shadow. The sketchbook lay open in front of her, the blank page inviting her to explore again. Her fingers tingled with that familiar pull, the warmth of her power simmering just beneath the surface. But this time, the thrill she felt was tinged with urgency, an unshakable sense that she was on the edge of something vast and unknown. She needed answers—and maybe she wasn't the only one.

With a steady breath, she let her pencil touch the paper, the tip tracing gentle curves as her mind began to settle into the familiar rhythm. But her thoughts wouldn't stay quiet, not tonight. The questions Thomas's presence had stirred within her mingled with her own confusion over this strange power.

She pressed her fingers harder against the pencil, the lines on the page deepening, as if by force of will she could draw out the truth.

What if Thomas did know something? What if he understood the power she was only beginning to grasp? The idea sent a thrill through her, but it also filled her with an almost painful vulnerability. She didn't know him, not really. And yet, a quiet part of her mind whispered that maybe—just maybe—he could help her find answers.

The thoughts lingered, shaping her resolve. She had kept this secret to herself, but now, for the first time, she wondered if she had to. If Thomas had some connection to this magic, then perhaps he held a key she couldn't ignore.

As her pencil moved, lines becoming shapes, she thought of the possibilities that lay before her. She had tasted a hint of something extraordinary, something beautiful and dangerous, but she was reaching a limit she couldn't cross alone. Thomas's face flashed in her mind, and though the thought of sharing her secret with him felt like stepping off a cliff, she knew she couldn't turn back.

Tonight, she would push further. She would try to draw something that revealed the depth of this power. Her fingers tightened around the pencil as she focused, pouring every ounce of her curiosity and fear and hope into the lines forming beneath her hand. The world outside faded, leaving only the soft scratching of pencil on paper and the quiet thrum of magic, steady and insistent.

And tomorrow... maybe tomorrow, she would find a way to talk to Thomas Hale. She would find out what he knew, what he had seen, and whether he held the answers she sought.

Because this time, she couldn't shake the feeling that she was no longer alone.

CHAPTER 3: A SCIENCE FAIR TO REMEMBER

The gymnasium buzzed with an electric energy that rivaled the hum of the machines and projects lining the walls. Every inch of the space was covered in colorful display boards, blinking lights, and the excited chatter of students. The annual science fair was one of the most anticipated events at Riverside High, and this year, the air was thick with competition.

Nyomi stood just inside the entrance, clutching the edge of her project's display board. She felt the vibration of footsteps on the wooden floor as students hurried past, carrying last-minute materials or tinkering with their experiments. Teachers moved between the rows of projects, offering quiet words of encouragement, while the judges—professionals from local universities and tech companies—hovered around the edges, their sharp eyes scanning each display with interest.

Normally, this was the kind of event Nyomi could lose herself in. She'd always enjoyed the creativity that the science fair encouraged, even if her interests lay more in the artistic realm. She'd participated every year, and while she'd never won, it had never really mattered. It was the process of creation, the satisfaction of building something from the ground up, that she loved.

But today, everything felt different.

Her project, a biodegradable packaging material designed to reduce plastic waste, sat in front of her, neatly arranged and ready for demonstration. It was a solid idea, one that could impress the judges—if Nyomi could focus long enough to explain it. But her mind wasn't on the science fair. It wasn't on the judges or the competition or even the project itself.

It was on the butterfly. The leaf. The bird. The strange, impossible creations she had brought to life over the past week.

She hadn't been able to stop thinking about them, no matter how hard she tried. The weight of what had happened clung to her, like an invisible hand pressing down on her chest. She had tried to push it aside, to tell herself that she could handle this, that it didn't mean anything. But deep down, she knew that wasn't true. This was big. Bigger than her project. Bigger than anything she'd ever faced.

Nyomi took a shaky breath and glanced around the room, hoping to ground herself in the here and now. The projects were impressive, some of them massive and elaborate, with moving parts and flashing lights. A group of students huddled around a robotic arm that was meticulously stacking blocks in perfect alignment, while another project involved a holographic display of the solar system, with each planet spinning in perfect harmony.

Somehow, these feats of engineering seemed ordinary compared to the secret that weighed heavy on Nyomi's mind.

She caught a glimpse of Callie across the room, already immersed in conversation with a group of students from their chemistry class. Callie's project—a robotic dog that could respond to voice commands—was a hit with everyone, her energetic personality pulling people in. Callie's enthusiasm had always been infectious, but today, it grated against Nyomi's nerves.

She could feel her heart pounding in her chest, each beat a reminder that she was holding something back, something she didn't know how to control. Her palms were sweaty as she fumbled with the edges of her display board, trying to focus on her project and not the thoughts spiraling through her mind.

You can do this. Just focus. Don't think about it. Don't let it control you. But it was too late. It had already taken over.

As the minutes ticked by, the tension inside Nyomi only grew. She could feel it creeping up her spine, tightening in her chest. The gym's noise, the excited voices, the clatter of machines, the low murmur of conversation— felt like it was closing in on her, pressing against her until she thought she might snap.

She had felt like this before. The first time she'd brought the butterfly to life, that same pressure had built up inside her, as if something deep within was straining to break free. Now, with the crowd around her, the noise, the anticipation— it was happening again.

"Nyomi! Hey, over here!"

Callie's voice broke through the fog of Nyomi's thoughts. She looked up to see her best friend bounding toward her, a wide grin on her face. Callie's dark curls bounced with every step, her eyes bright with excitement.

"You've got to see this!" Callie grabbed her arm, tugging her toward a project at the far end of the gym. "There's this kid—Thomas, I think his name is? His project is insane. I swear, he's some kind of genius."

Nyomi let herself be pulled along, too dazed to resist. She had heard of Thomas Hale before, of course—everyone had. He was the quiet kid, always keeping to himself, never really interacting with anyone. She'd seen him around school, noticed him in the hallways, but they'd never spoken. He had always been a background figure, someone who blended into the shadows.

But today, Thomas wasn't in the background.

They reached his display, and Nyomi's breath caught in her throat.

Thomas stood at his booth, his hands moving fluidly as he adjusted a series of sleek glass panels that seemed to glow with an inner light. His project was a device that involved light refraction—at least, that was what the sign said—but there was something otherworldly about the way the light bent and twisted through the panels. It wasn't just a reflection of scientific principles. There was something more. Something deeper.

Nyomi stared at the display, mesmerized. The light shimmered in a way that made her skin tingle, a sensation that was eerily familiar. The way it danced and flickered reminded her of the shimmer she had seen on her drawings, just before they had come to life.

Thomas glanced up, and for a moment, their eyes met. His expression was calm, almost serene, but there was a flicker of something in his gaze— something knowing, something that made Nyomi's heart skip a beat. He knew. He knew something.

"Pretty cool, huh?" Callie said, oblivious to the tension that suddenly filled the air. "I have no idea how it works, but it's definitely going to win. I mean, look at it!"

Nyomi swallowed hard, her throat dry. Thomas was still watching her, his dark eyes steady and unreadable. She felt a shiver run down her spine. There was something about him, something in the way he carried himself, that felt... off. As if he was hiding something, just like she was.

Callie continued talking, animated and excited, but Nyomi barely heard her. Her mind was spinning, trying to make sense of what she was seeing, of the strange connection she felt to Thomas's project. It wasn't just scientific. It was... something else. Something she couldn't explain.

"I—uh—I should get back to my project," Nyomi muttered, taking a step back.

Callie frowned, clearly disappointed, but nodded. "Okay, but don't hide out over there all day! This is supposed to be fun!"

Fun. Nyomi almost laughed at the word. There was nothing fun about what was happening to her. Nothing fun about the way her powers seemed to be slipping further out of her control with every passing second.

She turned and hurried back to her booth, her heart racing. The noise of the gym seemed to swell around her, a constant, suffocating buzz that pressed in on all sides. She could feel her pulse quickening, her skin prickling with the same strange energy that had filled the air the night she had brought the butterfly to life.

As she reached her display, Nyomi grabbed the edges of the table, trying to steady herself. She closed her eyes, taking slow, deep breaths, willing the tension to fade.

Focus. Just focus. You can control this. You can.

But as much as she tried, she couldn't shake the feeling that something inside her was slipping. The same pressure that had built up when she was drawing was here now, pushing at the edges of her mind, demanding to be released. Her thoughts raced in a chaotic spiral, jumping from one fear to the next.

What if someone saw? What if they found out? What if I lose control again?

Her hands trembled as she ran her fingers over the materials for her project, her heart pounding so loudly she could barely hear the noise around her. The smooth, biodegradable packaging felt familiar, grounding her momentarily, but even as she touched it, she saw something out of the corner of her eye—a faint shimmer, a flicker of light along the edges.

Her breath caught in her throat. No.

Not here. Not now.

She blinked, trying to steady her vision, but the shimmer remained, faint but unmistakable. Her heart raced as she glanced around, half-expecting someone to have noticed. But the students and judges were all caught up in their own projects, their own demonstrations. No one was looking at her.

She was losing control.

Panic surged in her chest as she tried to pull her hands away from the project materials, but it was as if they were glued to the table. Her fingers tingled with the same strange warmth she had felt when she'd brought the butterfly to life, when she'd drawn the leaf. The warmth spread up her arms, quickening her pulse, making her vision blur.

Nyomi squeezed her eyes shut, trying to push the feeling down, trying to focus on anything but the rising panic in her chest. She couldn't let this happen. Not here. Not in front of everyone.

But the more she tried to suppress it, the stronger it became.

Her breathing grew shallow as the pressure inside her mounted, a wave of fear and energy that threatened to burst through the carefully constructed walls she'd built around herself. She could feel the magic—her magic— pushing at the edges of her consciousness, demanding to be released.

No. No, no, no. Not here. "Nyomi!"

Callie's voice cut through the noise, startling Nyomi out of her spiraling thoughts. She looked up to see her best friend bounding toward her again, her wide smile full of excitement.

"You've got to come see this other project! It's got these—" Callie stopped mid-sentence, her smile faltering as she studied Nyomi's face. "Hey, are you okay?"

Nyomi forced a smile, trying to steady her shaking hands. "Yeah, I'm fine. Just... nervous, I guess."

Callie frowned, her brow furrowing with concern. "You don't look fine.

You're shaking."

Nyomi's pulse quickened. "I'm just... I haven't eaten much. It's no big deal."

But Callie wasn't convinced. "You've been acting weird for days now.

What's really going on?"

Nyomi's throat tightened. She opened her mouth, searching for the right words, but nothing came out. How could she explain what was happening to her? How could she tell Callie about the magic, about the things she had brought to life? Callie would never believe her. And even if she did, what would she think? That Nyomi had lost her mind?

"I'm fine," Nyomi said again, her voice unconvincing. "I'm just tired."

Callie crossed her arms, clearly not buying it. "Nyomi, come on. We've been friends forever. I can tell when something's bothering you. You can talk to me."

Nyomi's heart ached at the sincerity in Callie's voice. She wanted to tell her. She wanted to open up, to spill everything, to let someone else carry the weight of this terrifying secret. But the words stuck in her throat, tangled in fear and doubt.

"I just..." Nyomi hesitated, her hands still trembling. "I don't know how to explain it."

Callie's expression softened, her eyes filled with concern. "Hey, whatever it is, we'll figure it out. You don't have to go through this alone."

Nyomi swallowed hard, her emotions swirling. She wanted so badly to confide in Callie, to let her in. But the fear of what she might say, of how she might react, held her back. It was too risky.

"I" Nyomi's voice cracked, and she shook her head, looking away. "I can't."

Callie blinked, clearly taken aback. "What do you mean, you can't?

Nyomi, I'm your best friend."

"I know." Nyomi's voice was barely above a whisper. "I just... I can't explain it."

The hurt in Callie's eyes was like a punch to the gut. She reached out, her hand hovering in the air between them, but Nyomi took a step back, the panic rising again in her chest. She couldn't do this. Not here. Not now.

Callie dropped her hand, her shoulders slumping. "Okay. But... whenever you're ready, I'm here. Don't shut me out, okay?"

Nyomi nodded, guilt gnawing at her insides. "Thanks."

But even as she said the words, she knew that wasn't enough. Callie had always been there for her, always been the one person she could rely on. And now, when she needed her most, Nyomi was pushing her away.

The weight of her secret pressed down harder than ever.

Callie offered a small smile and turned to leave, but before she could take more than a few steps, a sudden gust of wind rushed through the gymnasium.

Nyomi froze.

The wind seemed to come from nowhere, swirling around her in a soft, almost imperceptible breeze. Papers fluttered, hair lifted, and a few students glanced up, confused by the strange, out-of-place gust.

Nyomi's heart pounded in her chest as she realized what was happening. The wind was hers.

Her magic. It was slipping again, leaking out in small, uncontrolled bursts, responding to her emotions. Her pulse quickened, her breath coming in shallow gasps as she tried to tamp it down, to force the magic back into its cage.

But the harder she fought it, the stronger it became.

"Nyomi?" Callie's voice was barely audible over the rush of wind. She looked back, her face full of confusion.

"I—I need to go," Nyomi stammered, panic rising in her chest.

Without waiting for a response, she turned and fled the gym, the sound of her footsteps echoing in her ears as she pushed through the double doors and into the hallway.

She didn't stop running until she reached the empty corridor outside, her heart pounding, her skin tingling with the leftover remnants of the magic she had barely managed to contain.

CHAPTER 4: WHEN SCIENCE COMES TO LIFE

The sound of footsteps echoed against the polished floor as Nyomi hurried down the empty hallway, her heart pounding like a drum in her chest. The farther she moved from the gymnasium, the quieter the world seemed to become—yet the thrum of magic beneath her skin only grew louder. She didn't dare stop, not until the air around her was still again, until the strange energy coursing through her had calmed.

She reached a small alcove near the school's exit doors and pressed her back against the wall, taking shallow breaths. Her pulse raced with a mixture of fear and excitement. She'd almost lost control. Again.

The wind—her wind—had appeared in the gym. It had felt different this time, though. Stronger. More insistent. The same unsettling power that had brought her drawings to life now wanted something more. But what?

Her hands shook as she rubbed her arms, trying to shake off the sensation, trying to gather her thoughts. She had to get herself under control before things escalated any further.

But deep down, Nyomi knew she was only delaying the inevitable.

Back at the Science Fair

After a few minutes, Nyomi forced herself to head back toward the gym. As much as she wanted to run, to disappear, she couldn't leave. Her project was still there, and so was Callie. If she disappeared now, people would start asking questions, and that was the last thing she needed.

She pulled open the gym doors and slipped back inside, bracing herself for the noise. The moment she stepped into the room, the cacophony of voices and machines hit her all at once—a sensory overload that made her head spin. The gym was as chaotic as ever, with students huddled around their projects, teachers chatting with the judges, and spectators wandering from one display to the next.

But beneath the surface, Nyomi could sense the tension. It wasn't just the noise or the crowd. It was the magic—the energy that pulsed beneath her skin, the same energy that had filled the air just moments ago. It was still there, waiting.

Waiting for her.

She swallowed hard and made her way back to her booth, trying to keep her head down, hoping no one had noticed her sudden exit. Callie was nowhere to be seen, probably caught up in someone else's project. Nyomi was grateful for the brief moment of solitude.

Her hands shook as she adjusted the display materials for her biodegradable packaging project. She glanced at the judges near the far end of the room—they were slowly making their way toward her section, their eyes sharp with interest and judgment.

I just need to get through this, she told herself, taking a deep breath. One more presentation, and then I can leave. Just focus.

But the pressure didn't let up. If anything, it grew stronger. The closer the judges came, the more Nyomi felt the magic stirring inside her, pushing at the edges of her control. It was as if the energy was alive, writhing beneath her skin, desperate to break free.

She could feel it in her fingertips—the same tingling sensation she'd felt when she brought the butterfly to life. Her eyes flicked down to her project, her heart skipping a beat as she noticed a faint shimmer along the edges of the materials. It was subtle, almost imperceptible, but it was there.

No, no, no...

Nyomi quickly glanced around, panic swelling in her chest. No one seemed to have noticed yet. The students nearby were too engrossed in their own projects, the teachers too busy with the judges. But she knew it wouldn't be long before someone saw.

She took a shaky breath and tried to calm herself, tried to push the magic back down, to contain it. But the more she fought it, the stronger it became. The shimmer intensified, spreading across the surface of the packaging, and Nyomi could almost feel the magic reaching out, like invisible tendrils weaving through the air.

Her pulse quickened, and a wave of fear washed over her. It's happening again.

The judges were just a few booths away now, nodding approvingly at a robotics project that had students gathered around it. Nyomi's panic deepened. If they saw the magic—if anyone saw—it would be over. She couldn't let that happen.

Desperate to stop it, Nyomi gripped the edges of the table, closing her eyes and focusing on steadying her breath. She tried to block out the noise, the crowd, the pressure mounting inside her. She tried to imagine herself calm, in control, like she had been before everything changed.

But the magic wasn't listening.

Suddenly, the hum of the machines around her grew louder —louder than it should have been. Nyomi's eyes snapped open just in time to see the lights flicker, dimming for a moment before flaring back to life with an almost blinding intensity.

Her heart raced as the shimmer along her project's surface grew brighter, pulsing in rhythm with her panicked breaths. The biodegradable packaging began to shift, the materials warping and twisting as if they were alive.

The crowd didn't notice at first. But then a student across the aisle let out a gasp, pointing at a nearby project—a robotic arm that had suddenly started moving on its own. The arm jerked and twitched, its mechanical fingers curling and uncurling with unnatural speed. The student stepped back, eyes wide with confusion.

"What the—?"

Nyomi's stomach dropped.

Before she could react, the chaos spread.

The lights in the gym flickered again, and more machines began to whirr to life. Projects that had been sitting idle just moments before now buzzed with unnatural energy—lights blinked erratically, robotic limbs twitched, and small motors revved without anyone touching them.

The noise level spiked as students began to notice. Gasps and murmurs filled the air, followed by confused shouts as one by one, the projects started behaving in ways they shouldn't. A holographic display of the solar system flickered wildly, the planets spinning out of control. A drone that had been sitting on a nearby table suddenly shot into the air, zipping around the room with no one at the controls.

Nyomi's breath came in short, sharp bursts as she watched the chaos unfold around her. The gym was a swirling mass of noise and light, a sensory overload that sent her mind reeling.

She could feel the magic growing stronger, feeding off her fear, her panic. It was everywhere now, seeping into the air, latching onto the projects around her like a living thing.

And she couldn't stop it.

Her hands gripped the edge of the table so tightly her knuckles turned white, but it wasn't enough. The magic was slipping out of her control, spreading through the room like wildfire.

This is my fault.

The realization hit her like a punch to the gut. She had done this. Her magic had caused this. The projects were coming to life because of her, and there was nothing she could do to stop it.

"Nyomi?"

The voice cut through the noise like a knife, pulling her back to the present.

She turned and saw Thomas standing just a few feet away, his dark eyes fixed on her. His expression was calm—too calm, given the chaos swirling around them—but there was something in his gaze, something that made her heart race even faster.

He knew.

The thought was like a flash of lightning in her mind. Thomas knew what was happening. He had seen the magic, sensed it somehow. His eyes locked onto hers, and for a moment, it was as if the rest of the room disappeared. The noise, the lights, the chaos—all of it faded into the background.

Only Thomas remained, standing in the middle of the storm, watching her with that same steady, knowing gaze.

"I think it's time to leave," Thomas said softly, his voice barely audible over the noise.

Nyomi's pulse quickened. How did he know? How could he possibly know what was happening? But there was no time to question it. She had to get out of there—before things got any worse.

She nodded, her throat tight, and without another word, she turned and bolted for the exit.

The noise of the gym faded behind her as Nyomi sprinted down the hallway, her breath coming in ragged gasps. Her heart pounded in her chest, and the magic still buzzed beneath her skin, pulsing with a life of its own.

She didn't stop running until she reached the school's back entrance. The door slammed shut behind her as she stumbled outside into the cold evening air. The wind bit at her skin, but it wasn't enough to shake the panic that still gripped her.

Nyomi leaned against the brick wall, her body trembling with exhaustion. Her hands were still shaking, the adrenaline pumping through her veins. She couldn't get the image of the gym out of her mind—the flickering lights, the robotic limbs jerking to life, the chaos she had caused.

What have I done?

Her stomach churned as she replayed the events over and over again. It had been her fault. Her magic had done this. And if Thomas hadn't been there—if he hadn't seen her, hadn't pulled her out of the gym when he did

—who knows what could have happened?

She took a deep breath, trying to calm her racing heart. But the questions wouldn't stop. Why had Thomas helped her? How had he known what was happening? And why wasn't he as shocked or confused as everyone else?

She couldn't shake the feeling that Thomas knew more than he was letting on.

As if on cue, the door behind her creaked open, and Thomas stepped outside. His expression was still calm, but there was a tension in his posture, a quiet intensity that made Nyomi's skin prickle.

For a moment, they stood in silence, the cool wind swirling around them. Nyomi didn't know what to say—what could she say? She was still reeling from everything that had happened.

Finally, Thomas spoke. "You need to be more careful." Nyomi blinked, caught off guard by his tone. "What?"

Thomas sighed, running a hand through his hair. "Whatever it is you're doing... you're losing control."

Nyomi's heart skipped a beat. "How—how do you know?"

Thomas glanced down at his hands, his expression unreadable. "Let's just say... I've seen something like this before."

Nyomi's mind raced, trying to make sense of his words. He had seen something like this before? What did that mean? Was he like her? Did he have the same kind of power?

But before she could ask, Thomas straightened and met her gaze, his eyes sharp. "You need to get a handle on it, Nyomi. Before things get worse."

Nyomi's breath caught in her throat. Worse? How could things possibly get worse?

"I don't—" she started, but the words caught in her throat. She didn't know what to say. Didn't know how to explain what was happening to her, let alone how to control it.

Thomas seemed to understand her hesitation. He stepped closer, his voice soft but firm. "You can't keep running from this. It's part of you. You have to face it."

Nyomi swallowed hard, her mind spinning. Thomas was right. She couldn't keep running. She couldn't keep pretending that this wasn't happening, that her magic wasn't real. But the thought of facing it, of trying to control it, terrified her.

"I don't know how," she whispered, her voice trembling.

Thomas studied her for a long moment, his gaze steady. "Then you'll have to learn."

Nyomi's heart pounded in her chest as his words sank in. He wasn't offering help, wasn't giving her answers. But he was telling her the truth, and that truth hit her like a cold wave of reality.

She couldn't keep ignoring her powers. She couldn't keep pretending that this wasn't happening. The magic inside her was growing, and if she didn't learn to control it—if she didn't figure out what it was—then she would lose herself completely.

The fear gnawed at her, but there was something else now, too. A spark of determination, a glimmer of hope.

Thomas turned to leave, but before he stepped away, he paused, glancing back at her. "I'll see you around, Nyomi."

And just like that, he was gone, disappearing into the darkness.

Nyomi stood there for a long time, staring after him, her mind still reeling. The magic buzzed beneath her skin, pulsing with quiet intensity. It wasn't going away.

But maybe—just maybe—Thomas was right. Maybe she could learn to control it.

The evening sky melted into shades of dusky pink and purple, casting a soft glow over the quiet clearing where Nyomi and Thomas sat, side by side. The energy of the day had faded, replaced by the gentle, humming stillness of twilight. With a deep breath, Nyomi opened her sketchbook, its pages now filled with intricate lines and shapes that held more than just graphite—they held possibility, each sketch pulsing with the latent power she had only begun to understand.

Thomas watched her in silence, his calm presence a steadying force beside her. Unlike everyone else, he didn't pepper her with questions or shower her with reassurances. He simply sat, eyes thoughtful, as she experimented, testing her power's edges and letting herself push just a little further each time. There was something comforting about his quiet confidence, the way he seemed to accept this world she was discovering without hesitation.

Her fingers moved over the paper, tracing the outline of a delicate feather she'd just drawn. She focused, drawing her breath deep into her lungs, feeling the energy tingle in her fingertips. Slowly, the feather began to lift, its edges shimmering with a faint light, hovering just above the page. The familiar thrill bubbled up inside her, tempered now by Thomas's steady gaze, grounding her.

The feather floated, its soft edges curling as though caught by a breeze, and for the first time, she felt in control—not just of the feather but of the power that moved through her. Thomas nodded slightly, his face calm, but she could see the hint of a smile in his eyes, a shared understanding that made her feel seen in a way she hadn't before.

As the sun dipped below the horizon, Thomas's calm presence beside her felt reassuring. Together, they tested boundaries she hadn't dared explore alone, and slowly, her fears melted into a focused determination. She could do this. With Thomas by her side, she might finally unlock the secrets of her power. As darkness settled around them, she knew one thing: she wasn't alone anymore.

A quiet peace settled over her as she closed her sketchbook, the feather drifting gently back to the page, a perfect symbol of the magic that had brought her and Thomas together. She felt a warm glow inside, a sense of shared purpose that she had never experienced before. The weight of her secret, the fear of facing it all by herself, lifted just a little.

They sat in silence, watching as the first stars appeared, their tiny points of light flickering against the deepening sky. For a moment, everything felt right, like the world had shifted into place. Thomas didn't break the silence, didn't try to label what they were discovering; he simply let it unfold, allowing her the space to grow into her power at her own pace.

Finally, as the last light faded, Nyomi turned to him. "Thank you... for being here. For helping me," she said, her voice barely more than a whisper.

Thomas gave her a small nod, his expression soft but resolute. "We're just getting started, Nyomi," he replied. "Whatever this power is, we'll figure it out together."

With those words echoing in her mind, Nyomi felt a new sense of hope bloom within her, fragile yet fierce. She had spent so long feeling different, alone in her struggle to understand this strange magic, but now, with Thomas by her side, the journey didn't feel so daunting. Together, they would explore this mystery, unraveling its secrets one step at a time.

She packed up her sketchbook and pencil, the night settling around them like a blanket. And as they made their way back down the path, she couldn't help but feel that this was only the beginning. There would be challenges, perhaps dangers, but she knew now that she had someone she could trust. Someone who understood.

In the quiet of the evening, as they walked side by side, Nyomi looked up at the stars, feeling more alive—and more connected—than she ever had before.

Nyomi sat across the dining room table from her parents, their voices filling the space as they went back and forth, each word carrying a mix of disappointment and concern. Her father's brow furrowed as he spoke, the usual gentle tone of his voice edged with frustration. Her mother leaned forward, her gaze unwavering, her hands clasped tightly in front of her. They both seemed to be searching for the right words to get through to her, as if somehow, they could redirect her with enough logic and persistence.

"… You're so talented, Nyomi," her mother said, her tone pleading. "But art isn't going to carry you through life. You need to focus on things that will give you stability, something to fall back on. You know how competitive it is to make a living from art."

Her father chimed in, his voice measured but firm. "We just want what's best for you, Nyomi. There are other, more practical options. Science, math, something that will always have opportunities for someone as bright as you."

Nyomi listened quietly, the words drifting over her like a familiar tide. She had heard it all before, the well-meaning arguments and the soft reprimands disguised as encouragement. But tonight, something inside her felt different. She no longer felt the usual ache of self-doubt or the sinking guilt that often accompanied these conversations.

Instead, she felt a quiet strength building within her—a new sense of clarity that had grown in the spaces between her moments with Thomas, in the nights spent bringing her art to life and understanding her power. There was something about discovering her abilities, about feeling that magic in her hands, that had changed her. It had shown her that she could create a reality from her dreams, a truth that was uniquely her own.

Nyomi braced herself as she faced her parents, their voices sharp with concern. But inside, she felt an unshakable resolve, a quiet confidence she hadn't known before. She'd found something that mattered—something no one could take from her.

"Mom, Dad... I understand what you're saying," she began, her voice steady. "And I know you're worried about me. But I need you to trust me. I've found something that means more to me than anything else ever has. I know it doesn't make sense to you, but I can't give this up. It's who I am."

Her parents exchanged a glance, their faces softening, but she could see the worry lingering in their eyes. She didn't expect them to understand fully, not yet. But this was a start—her first step in claiming her own path.

Her mother sighed, reaching across the table to place a gentle hand on hers. "We just want to make sure you're secure, Nyomi. That you're safe."

"I know, Mom. And I appreciate it, I really do," she replied, squeezing her mother's hand before letting go. "But this is something I have to do. I need to see where it leads me."

The conversation eventually drifted to a quiet close, her parents relenting, if only for now. Their acceptance wasn't complete, but it was enough. She had stood her ground, and for the first time, she felt that they had truly listened.

Later that night, Nyomi climbed the stairs to her room, feeling a mix of relief and exhilaration. As she closed her door behind her, she felt the weight of her parents' expectations finally ease, loosening its grip on her heart. She glanced around her room, her eyes falling on her sketchbook and the soft glow of the evening sky filtering through her window.

She knew this path wouldn't be easy. There would be more questions, more doubts, perhaps even more arguments to come. But tonight, as she returned to her room, she realized that for the first time, her path was her own. She had carved it out with her own hands, fueled by her dreams, her determination, and the quiet magic that flowed through her fingertips.

Sitting down at her desk, she opened her sketchbook and traced the lines of her latest drawing, her fingers tingling with that familiar pulse of energy. She felt alive, grounded in a way that she never had before, and she knew that whatever challenges lay ahead, she was ready.

With a quiet smile, Nyomi picked up her pencil, ready to continue her journey. Because no matter where it led, she was certain of one thing: she was finally free to follow her heart.

CHAPTER 5: THE POWER OF IMAGINATION

Nyomi couldn't stop thinking about the science fair. She replayed the chaos over and over again in her mind—the flickering lights, the robotic limbs jerking to life, the strange energy that had gripped the room. But most of all, she replayed the look on Thomas's face. That calm, steady gaze, filled with a knowing she couldn't shake.

He knew. He had to know something about her powers, about the magic that had slipped out of her control in that moment of panic. But how? And why wasn't he afraid? Why had he helped her?

Those questions haunted her long after the science fair had ended, long after she'd returned to her room and tried to sleep. But sleep had eluded her that night, her mind too full of unanswered questions and the fear that her powers were growing beyond her control.

The next morning, Nyomi woke with a sense of dread settling deep in her chest. She had hoped the feeling would fade, that maybe she could chalk up the events of the science fair to stress or exhaustion, but the buzzing under her skin remained, a constant reminder that the magic was still there, just beneath the surface.

In the days that followed, Nyomi couldn't escape Thomas's presence. He was everywhere—watching her from across the courtyard at lunch, standing quietly by the lockers after class, sitting a few rows behind her in chemistry. His quiet attention was unnerving, but he never approached her again after that brief conversation outside the gym.

He didn't need to. His presence alone was enough to make her skin crawl with anticipation, with the growing suspicion that he was somehow connected to the strange energy inside her. He seemed to be observing her, waiting for something. But what?

Nyomi found herself stealing glances at him, too. She hadn't noticed Thomas much before the science fair—he had always been on the edges of things, quiet and reserved, almost invisible. But now, she couldn't stop noticing him. There was something about the way he moved, the way his eyes seemed to see more than he let on.

The first time she caught him watching her was in chemistry class. She had been trying—really trying—to focus on the lecture, to force herself to act normal. But her mind kept drifting back to the shimmer she'd seen on her project, the way the materials had twisted and warped under the influence of her magic.

The thought made her stomach twist with anxiety. She couldn't afford to lose control again. Not here. Not where everyone could see.

As she sat there, her hands fidgeting with her pencil, she felt it again—a faint, familiar tingling in her fingertips, like the magic was just waiting for an excuse to slip free. She gripped the pencil tighter, willing the sensation to fade.

That's when she saw him.

Thomas was sitting a few rows behind her, his dark eyes fixed on her with quiet intensity. His expression was unreadable, but there was something in the way he watched her—something that made her pulse quicken.

He wasn't just watching. He was studying her.

Nyomi's breath caught in her throat, and she quickly looked away, her heart pounding. What was he seeing? Did he know what was happening inside her? Did he sense the magic, just as she could feel it buzzing beneath her skin?

The thought terrified her. But at the same time, it fascinated her. Thomas wasn't reacting with fear or confusion like everyone else at the science fair had. He wasn't running away or asking questions. He was just... watching.

Nyomi clenched her fists, trying to steady her breathing. She had to stay calm. She had to keep it together. But the more she tried to push the magic down, the more it seemed to rise, like a tide swelling inside her, demanding to be acknowledged.

I have to control this, she thought, her hands trembling. I can't let anyone see.

But Thomas had already seen. He had been there, right in the middle of the chaos, and somehow, he hadn't been surprised.

The bell rang, and Nyomi jumped, her pencil slipping from her hand and clattering to the floor. She bent down to pick it up, her fingers brushing against the cool metal of the desk leg. When she sat back up, Thomas was gone.

But the feeling of being watched lingered.

The Internal Conflict

As the days passed, Nyomi's anxiety only grew. She couldn't shake the feeling that her powers were slipping further out of her control, no matter how hard she tried to suppress them. And worse, part of her didn't want to suppress them.

That was the part that scared her the most.

There was something thrilling about the magic, something exhilarating about the way it hummed beneath her skin, just waiting for her to release it. It wasn't just fear she felt when she thought about the butterfly coming to life or the leaf fluttering from the page. There was excitement, too. Wonder. The same wonder that had filled her when she first started drawing, when art had been her escape from the pressures of school and her parents' expectations.

But now, art was something more. It was a doorway to another world, a world where her imagination could shape reality, where the things she created could come to life.

The thought sent a shiver down her spine.

But with that wonder came dread. Because if she couldn't control it—if she couldn't stop it—what would happen next? What if she brought something into the world that she couldn't undo? What if she hurt someone?

That fear gnawed at her constantly, making her jittery and tense, her mind racing with possibilities she couldn't even begin to understand.

Tension with Callie

And then there was Callie.

Callie had always been Nyomi's rock, the one person who could pull her out of her head, who could make her laugh even when everything felt like it was falling apart. But now, even Callie's presence felt like too much. Her energy, her optimism, her endless excitement—it grated against the anxiety building inside Nyomi, making it harder to hold everything together.

"Nyomi, are you even listening?"

Callie's voice cut through Nyomi's thoughts, snapping her back to the present. They were sitting in the library after school, working on their science fair reports—well, Callie was working. Nyomi hadn't been able to focus for more than a few minutes at a time.

"Sorry," Nyomi muttered, rubbing her temples. "I'm just... distracted."

Callie frowned, her brow furrowing with concern. "You've been distracted for days now. What's going on?"

Nyomi's heart skipped a beat. She couldn't tell Callie. She couldn't tell anyone. But Callie was her best friend—she deserved some kind of explanation. Something. Anything.

"I'm just... tired," Nyomi said, the lie slipping out before she could stop it. "The science fair, school, my parents. It's all just a lot right now."

Callie sighed, leaning back in her chair. "Yeah, I get that. But you've been acting really weird. Like, you keep zoning out, and you've barely touched your sketchbook all week. That's not like you."

Nyomi swallowed hard, her fingers curling into fists under the table. She wanted to tell Callie the truth. She wanted to explain what had happened at the science fair, to confess that she was scared, that she didn't know how to control what was happening to her. But the words stuck in her throat, tangled in fear and doubt.

"I'm fine," she said again, her voice quieter this time. "I just need some time to figure things out."

Callie gave her a long, searching look, her eyes filled with concern. "Okay, but if you need to talk, I'm here, okay? I don't want you to feel like you have to go through whatever this is alone."

Nyomi nodded, forcing a smile. "Thanks."

But even as she said the words, she felt the distance between them growing. Callie's concern was genuine, but it only made Nyomi feel more isolated. How could she talk to her best friend when she couldn't even begin to explain what was happening? How could she confide in Callie when she didn't fully understand it herself?

The weight of her secret pressed down on her, heavier than ever.

The final straw came the next day during their science class.

Callie had been working on her science fair project after hours, putting the finishing touches on her robotic dog. It was an impressive piece of work

—far more advanced than anything Nyomi could have imagined putting together. The dog could respond to basic voice commands, wag its tail, and even sit on command.

The whole class had been buzzing about it for days, and today, Callie was giving a demonstration to the class.

"Okay, Rover," Callie said, grinning as she stood in front of the class, holding a small remote in her hand. "Sit."

The robotic dog's ears twitched, and then, after a brief pause, it sat down, its metal legs clinking softly against the floor.

The class erupted in applause, and Callie beamed, her cheeks flushed with excitement.

Nyomi tried to smile, but her heart wasn't in it. She was happy for Callie—really, she was—but the noise, the energy, the excitement in the room—it was too much. Her skin tingled with the same strange energy she'd felt at the science fair, the magic stirring inside her, just beneath the surface.

As Callie continued the demonstration, the robotic dog performed perfectly—until it didn't.

One moment, the dog was responding to commands flawlessly, and the next, its movements became erratic. Its head jerked to one side, then the other, and its tail began to wag uncontrollably, faster and faster.

Callie frowned, tapping at the remote. "That's weird. I didn't program it to do that."

The class murmured in confusion, but Nyomi's heart was pounding in her chest. She felt it—the magic. It was in the air again, just like at the science fair. And this time, it wasn't confined to her project. It was leaking out, slipping into the room, into Callie's project.

No. Not again.

She closed her grip, her nails digging into her palms as she tried to control it, tried to push the magic back down. But it was already too late. The robotic dog was twitching uncontrollably now, its movements erratic and jerky.

"Rover, stop!" Callie shouted, her voice tinged with panic.

But the dog didn't stop. Its head jerked violently to the side, and then, without warning, it lunged forward, its metal paws clattering against the floor as it barreled toward the front of the classroom.

The students scrambled out of the way, shouting in surprise as the dog crashed into one of the desks, sending papers and books flying.

Nyomi's breath came in short, shallow gasps as she watched the chaos unfold. She knew this was her fault. The magic—her magic—had caused this. And she had no idea how to stop it.

But then, out of the corner of her eye, she saw Thomas.

He was standing near the back of the room, his arms crossed over his chest, his expression calm and steady. But there was something in his eyes, something that sent a shiver down Nyomi's spine.

He knew. He definitely knew. And he was watching her closely.

Thomas didn't move, didn't speak, but his gaze never left her, even as the robotic dog finally came to a sputtering halt in the middle of the room, its limbs twitching one last time before going still.

Callie stood frozen at the front of the classroom, her face pale with shock. "I—I don't know what happened," she stammered, her voice shaky. "It wasn't supposed to do that."

The teacher rushed over, his face tight with concern as he inspected the dog. "It's probably just a malfunction," he said, trying to reassure the class. "Everyone, calm down. Let's get back to our seats."

But Nyomi could barely hear him. Her mind was racing, her heart pounding in her chest. She felt sick, her stomach twisting with guilt and fear.

She had caused this. The magic was growing stronger, slipping further out of her control. And Thomas knew. He had to know.

As the class settled back down, Nyomi sank into her seat, her hands trembling in her lap. She could feel Thomas's eyes on her, watching, waiting.

And for the first time, Nyomi realized that maybe—just maybe— Thomas wasn't just an observer. Maybe he was something more.

CHAPTER 6: DREAMERS AND MAKERS

The gymnasium hummed with excitement, the atmosphere thick with anticipation as the science fair reached its peak. All around her, students were buzzing with the thrill of competition and the magic of invention. Nyomi, however, stood in the center of the chaos, her heart pounding in her chest, feeling as though she was barely keeping herself tethered to reality.

Projects flickered and hummed around her. Robotic arms moved with impossible precision, holographic displays shimmered with unnatural brilliance, and mechanical creatures roamed freely. But something had changed in the air —something Nyomi could feel in her bones. It was the magic.

Her magic.

It was everywhere now, flowing through the room like an invisible current, feeding off the excitement and creativity of the students. The projects that had once been still were now alive, moving and shifting in ways that defied logic. Dreams were manifesting before her eyes, and she couldn't stop it.

Nyomi clenched her fists at her sides, her palms slick with sweat. The buzzing in her ears grew louder, a constant hum that matched the growing chaos around her. She could feel the magic thrumming beneath her skin, pulsing in time with her racing heartbeat, and no matter how hard she tried, she couldn't control it.

All she could do was watch as the world around her came to life.

The Chaos of Imagination

At first, it had started small. A few flickering lights here and there, the hum of machines growing louder. But now, it was unstoppable. Thomas's light refraction project glowed with a strange intensity, the glass panels shifting and warping in ways that should have been impossible. His project seemed to reflect light not just from the room but from the very air itself, bending and twisting rays of color into shapes that hovered in mid-air. They looked like butterflies—just like the one Nyomi had drawn—and they flitted around the gym with a grace that defied explanation.

Other projects were coming to life, too. A solar system hologram that had once spun in slow, predictable circles was now a swirling vortex of planets and stars, each one pulsing with energy. The robotic dog Callie had been so proud of earlier in the week was darting around the room, barking excitedly, its metal paws clanging against the floor.

Students and teachers were starting to notice.

"What's happening?" someone shouted from across the room.

"Is this part of the fair?" another student asked, their voice tinged with confusion and awe.

Nyomi's pulse quickened as she watched the chaos unfold. Her magic was everywhere now, threading its way through the room, taking hold of every dream, every idea, and bringing it to life. She could feel it in the air, thick and powerful, like a living thing.

It was beautiful. And terrifying.

A part of her wanted to revel in it, to let the magic run wild and see what it could do. But the other part—the part of her that was scared, the part that feared she was losing control—was screaming for her to stop it.

She didn't know how.

Her breath came in short, panicked bursts as she backed away from the projects, her eyes darting around the room. She could feel the magic growing stronger, surging through her veins like a storm ready to break.

"Nyomi."

The voice was quiet, but it cut through the noise and chaos like a knife. Nyomi turned and saw Thomas standing a few feet away, his dark eyes locked onto hers. He was calm—too calm for the madness swirling around them. The light from his project cast strange, shifting shadows across his face, but his expression was unreadable.

"You need to breathe," Thomas said softly, his voice steady and sure.

Nyomi blinked, her heart still racing. "I—I can't stop it," she stammered, her voice trembling. "It's too much."

Thomas stepped closer, his gaze never leaving hers. "You're not supposed to stop it."

The words hung in the air between them, heavy and filled with a meaning Nyomi didn't fully understand. She shook her head, her hands trembling at her sides. "But I—this is all my fault. I'm causing this."

Thomas studied her for a long moment, his expression softening. "You're not causing it. You're bringing it to life."

Nyomi's breath caught in her throat. "What do you mean?"

Thomas glanced around the gym, his eyes flicking over the projects that were now moving on their own, defying the laws of science and logic. "This is what happens when dreams and imagination are given the freedom to exist. You're not just creating things, Nyomi. You're making them real."

Nyomi stared at him, her mind spinning. Could that really be what was happening? Was her magic not just an uncontrollable force, but a manifestation of something deeper —her imagination, her dreams?

But if that was true, then what did it mean? Was she losing herself to the magic, or was she discovering something new about herself?

Thomas seemed to sense her turmoil. He stepped closer, his voice low and gentle. "You're not losing control. You're just learning what you're capable of."

Nyomi swallowed hard, her chest tightening with a mix of fear and awe. She wanted to believe him, but the chaos in the room—the projects running wild, the looks of confusion and fear on her classmates' faces—told her otherwise.

"I don't know how to control it," she whispered, her voice barely audible over the noise.

Thomas tilted his head slightly, his gaze piercing. "It's not about control.

It's about understanding."

Nyomi frowned, confusion flickering across her face. But before she could ask what he meant, the lights in the gym flickered again, and the noise level spiked.

Callie's voice rang out above the chaos, her tone tinged with panic. "Nyomi! What's going on?"

Nyomi turned and saw her best friend rushing toward her, her eyes wide with confusion and fear. The robotic dog that had been sitting at Callie's project table was now running in circles, its movements erratic and unpredictable.

"I don't know!" Nyomi shouted back, her voice shaking. "I can't stop it!"

Callie reached her, grabbing her arm. "Is this—are you doing this?" Nyomi froze, her stomach twisting with guilt and fear. She didn't know how to answer. She didn't want to lie to Callie, but how could she explain what was happening when she didn't fully understand it herself?

"I—" Nyomi's voice faltered, and she glanced at Thomas, who was still standing nearby, watching her closely.

Callie followed her gaze, her brow furrowing. "Thomas? What's going on?"

Thomas's expression remained calm, but there was a flicker of something in his eyes—something that made Nyomi's pulse quicken. He knew more than he was letting on. He had always known.

"I think it's time you told her," Thomas said quietly, his gaze shifting back to Nyomi.

Nyomi's heart pounded in her chest. She had kept this secret for so long, hidden it from everyone—even Callie. But now, with the magic spiraling out of control, with her powers on full display for everyone to see, she realized that she couldn't hide it anymore.

She couldn't hide who she was anymore.

Taking a deep breath, Nyomi turned to Callie, her hands shaking. "I—I think this is me. My powers. I don't know how, but... I think I'm causing all of this."

Callie blinked, her expression a mix of confusion and disbelief. "Powers? What are you talking about?"

Nyomi opened her mouth to explain, but before she could speak, one of the nearby projects—a model of a wind turbine —began spinning wildly, the blades whipping through the air with a force that sent papers flying across the room.

The gym descended into chaos as students scrambled to control their projects, but it was no use. Everything was out of control. Dreams were running wild, imagination given free rein to manifest in ways that defied reason.

Nyomi's heart raced as she watched the madness unfold, the weight of her secret pressing down on her. She could feel Callie's eyes on her, waiting for an explanation, but she didn't have the words.

How could she explain something she didn't even understand herself?

Thomas's Backstory: A Glimpse of Understanding

Amid the chaos, Thomas remained still, his gaze focused on Nyomi. There was something different about him—something calm, almost knowing. He didn't seem surprised by any of it. In fact, he seemed to be waiting for it.

"Nyomi," Thomas said softly, stepping closer. "You're not the first to experience this."

Nyomi's eyes widened, her breath catching in her throat. "What do you mean?"

Thomas glanced around the gym, his expression unreadable. "You're not the first person to discover you have powers like this. I've seen it before."

Nyomi stared at him, her mind racing. "You've seen it? Where?"

Thomas hesitated, his gaze shifting to the flickering lights above. "It was a long time ago. Someone I knew—someone close to me—had abilities like yours. She struggled with them, just like you are now. But she learned to control them."

Nyomi's pulse quickened. "How? How did she control them?"

Thomas met her gaze, his expression softening. "She didn't try to suppress them. She accepted them. She learned that her powers were tied to her emotions, her imagination. The more she fought them, the stronger they became. But when she embraced them, when she allowed herself to feel, she found peace."

Nyomi's heart pounded in her chest as Thomas's words sank in. Could it really be that simple? Was her power not something to be feared, but something to be embraced?

Before she could respond, the noise in the gym grew louder, and Nyomi's eyes darted to Callie, who was still watching her with a mixture of confusion and concern.

"Nyomi," Callie said softly, her voice trembling. "What's happening?"

Nyomi swallowed hard, her hands shaking. She could feel the magic building inside her, a storm of energy waiting to be unleashed. But Thomas's words echoed in her mind.

Embrace it.

For the first time, Nyomi didn't try to push the magic down. She didn't try to control it. Instead, she closed her eyes and let herself feel—the fear, the excitement, the wonder. She let the magic flow through her, accepting it for what it was.

And in that moment, something shifted.

The noise in the gym faded, the chaotic energy settling into a quiet hum. The projects that had been moving wildly just moments before slowed to a gentle, rhythmic pulse. The lights flickered once, then steadied, casting a warm, golden glow over the room.

Nyomi opened her eyes, her breath catching in her throat.

The magic was still there, but it was no longer out of control. It was calm. It was hers.

She glanced at Thomas, who gave her a small nod, his expression softening. "See? You're not losing control. You're finding it."

Nyomi's heart swelled with a mixture of relief and awe. For the first time since the butterfly had come to life, she didn't feel afraid of her powers. She felt... at peace.

But as the room settled, her gaze drifted back to Callie, who was still standing beside her, her face pale with confusion.

"Nyomi," Callie whispered, her voice shaking. "What... what just happened?"

Nyomi took a deep breath, her chest tightening with guilt. She had kept this secret for so long, hidden this part of herself from her best friend. But now, there was no hiding. There was only the truth.

"I think I have magic," Nyomi said quietly, her voice trembling. "I don't know how or why, but... it's real."

Callie stared at her, her eyes wide with disbelief. "Magic? Nyomi, that's

—"

"I know," Nyomi interrupted, her voice soft but firm. "I know it sounds crazy. But it's the truth. I've been trying to control it, trying to keep it hidden, but... I don't think I can anymore."

For a long moment, Callie said nothing. The silence stretched between them, heavy and filled with unspoken words. Nyomi's heart pounded in her chest, waiting for her friend to react—for better or worse.

Finally, Callie let out a long breath and shook her head. "I don't understand any of this," she said quietly. "But I trust you."

Nyomi's breath caught in her throat. "You do?"

Callie nodded, her expression softening. "You're my best friend, Nyomi.

Whatever this is, we'll figure it out together."

A wave of relief washed over Nyomi, and for the first time in days, she felt like she wasn't alone.

But as the chaos in the gym subsided, as the projects slowly returned to normal, Nyomi knew that this was only the beginning. There was so much she didn't understand about her powers, so much she still had to learn. But with Callie by her side—and with Thomas's quiet guidance—she knew she could face whatever came next.

Researching the Unknown The following days were a blur of questions and quiet contemplation. Nyomi couldn't shake the feeling that her magic was growing, that there was something deeper she had yet to uncover. Thomas had given her a glimpse of understanding, but there was so much more she needed to know.

So, late one night, when the house was silent and her parents were asleep, Nyomi sat down at her desk with a notebook and a pen. She flipped open her laptop and started researching—searching for any mention of magic, supernatural events, or unexplained phenomena that might help her make sense of what was happening to her.

Her fingers flew across the keyboard as she delved into old myths, legends, and ancient texts. Stories of people with powers like hers—people who could bring their dreams to life, who could shape reality with their imagination.

One story, in particular, caught her attention.

It was an old legend, passed down through generations. It spoke of a group of dreamers—people with the ability to manifest their deepest desires and fears into the real world. They were called the Makers, and they were said to have shaped the world with their imagination, creating beauty and chaos in equal measure.

But there was a warning, too. The Makers' powers were tied to their emotions, and if they lost control—if their fears and insecurities overtook them—their creations could become dangerous, even destructive.

Nyomi's heart pounded as she read the words, the weight of the legend sinking in.

Is that what I am? A Maker?

The thought both thrilled and terrified her. If it was true—if she was one of these dreamers—then her powers were more than just a random fluke. They were part of something much bigger, something ancient.

But with that power came responsibility. She had to learn to control it, to understand it. Otherwise, she risked losing herself to the magic, just like the Makers in the legend.

Nyomi closed the notebook and sat back in her chair, her mind racing. There was so much more to uncover, so much she didn't know. But for the first time, she felt a sense of purpose, a drive to understand her powers, not just for herself, but for the people she cared about.

Because if she was a Maker, then she had the power to shape the world. And she wasn't going to let it slip away.

Nyomi's thoughts spiraled as she slipped into the library after school. The usual solace she found in the rows of books and the dusty quiet seemed fleeting, as if her nerves were too raw to be soothed. She clutched her sketchbook against her chest, trying to gather herself, trying to shake the feeling that she was unraveling.

The empty rows beckoned her, and she moved toward the back of the library. This was her safe space, tucked away from prying eyes and hushed conversations. But when she turned the corner of a dimly lit aisle, her heart jumped.

Thomas Hale sat in the far corner, his head bent over an old book. The sight of him seemed to slow time, and for a moment, Nyomi was suspended between the urge to retreat and the pressing need to understand the connection between them. Before she could make her choice, Thomas looked up, as if sensing her presence.

His calm, steady gaze met hers, and he gave a faint nod.

She hesitated, but he closed his book and gestured to the empty seat beside him. Her feet moved before her mind caught up, drawn by curiosity that overpowered her nerves.

"Didn't expect to see you here," Thomas said, his voice quiet, almost conspiratorial.

Nyomi sat down, feeling the weight of her sketchbook in her lap. "Yeah, me neither. I just... needed a quiet place to think."

He gave a small, knowing smile. "Seems like you have a lot to think about."

Nyomi nodded, unsure of what to say. She'd tried to convince herself it was all in her head, but now, face-to-face with Thomas, the magic in her veins seemed undeniable. She studied him for a moment, trying to make sense of the calm certainty in his eyes.

"Thomas... how did you know?" she finally asked, her voice barely above a whisper.

Thomas looked away, his fingers tracing the edges of his book. "You're not the only one who's... different." He hesitated, glancing around as though deciding how much to reveal. "In my family, certain things are passed down—gifts, you could call them. Sometimes we're born with them, and sometimes they choose us when we're ready."

Nyomi's pulse quickened. "So... your family has powers too?"

He shook his head slightly. "Not exactly the same kind, but yes. The strange things we carry—well, they're more than just coincidences or tricks of the mind."

Nyomi leaned forward, her curiosity piqued. "Then, have you always known you had these... abilities?"

Thomas let out a soft laugh, his expression distant. "Not really. When I was young, my grandmother used to tell me stories about the world beyond what most people see. She'd show me little things—a light that danced between her fingers, a way she'd know what someone was thinking before they spoke. I thought they were just her way of keeping me entertained. But then one day, I started seeing things, feeling things I couldn't explain."

He paused, his gaze sharpening. "It's not easy, Nyomi. Power like this— it doesn't come without a cost. My family's spent years learning to manage it, to make sure it doesn't consume us."

Nyomi shivered. A quiet dread coiled in her chest as she realized that her powers weren't some strange accident. There were rules, limits—things she didn't understand.

Thomas watched her carefully, reading the fear in her face. "That day at the science fair... you weren't in control, were you?"

She swallowed, her voice barely a whisper. "No. I didn't mean for any of it to happen. I just... panicked."

Thomas sighed, glancing at his hands. "That's what worries me. Power like yours—it doesn't wait for you to be ready. You have to meet it halfway, learn to control it before it controls you."

Nyomi looked down at her sketchbook, feeling the weight of his words. Thomas was right; she couldn't keep hiding from this. But the idea of wielding something so potent, something that could bring her drawings to life, terrified her.

"But... how?" Her voice trembled. "How do I learn to control something like this?"

Thomas held her gaze, his eyes intense. "By understanding it. And by practicing. You can't avoid it, Nyomi. Whatever this is, it's part of you now. And if you don't face it..." He trailed off, his meaning clear.

Her throat tightened. "What happens if I don't?"

He glanced away, his jaw tight. "In my family, there were... incidents. People who didn't learn to control their gifts—who lost themselves to it." He looked at her, his expression softening. "I'm not saying that's what will happen to you, but I've seen what can happen when power goes unchecked."

Nyomi's stomach twisted with fear, but something else stirred too—a spark of determination. She didn't want to lose herself to something she didn't understand. And she didn't want to hurt anyone. Her gaze fell on her sketchbook, the blank page seeming to call to her.

"I don't know if I can do it," she whispered.

"You don't have a choice," Thomas replied, his tone gentle but firm. "If you want to control it, you have to start somewhere. Test it, practice it. Find out where it comes from and what it can do."

Nyomi looked up, her eyes meeting his. She nodded, the weight of his words settling in. There was no going back now. Whatever this power was, it had chosen her, and she had to face it head-on.

They sat in silence for a moment, the gravity of her decision hanging in the air. Thomas gave her a small, encouraging nod, as if to say, You're not alone in this. And somehow, that made all the difference.

"I'll try," she said finally, her voice barely audible but filled with resolve.

Thomas gave her a reassuring smile. "That's all you need to start. But just know—you don't have to do this alone."

Nyomi nodded, feeling a strange sense of comfort in his presence. For the first time, she wasn't completely terrified of the magic within her. She was beginning to see it for what it was—a challenge, yes, but also a gift.

The school bell echoed through the library, pulling them both back to reality. Thomas stood, giving her a final nod before disappearing down the aisle, leaving Nyomi alone with her thoughts. She looked down at her sketchbook, tracing her fingers over the blank page. A flicker of excitement sparked within her, mingling with the fear.

It was time to learn.

As she rose to leave, a familiar figure blocked her path at the library exit

—Callie, her best friend, wearing an expectant look on her face.

"Where have you been?" Callie asked, her voice carrying a mix of concern and frustration. "I've been looking everywhere for you."

Nyomi hesitated, glancing down at her sketchbook before meeting Callie's gaze. "I... I needed some time alone."

"Alone? You've been acting weird lately, Nyomi. Don't tell me you're skipping out on life now too," Callie said, folding her arms. "Come on, let's go grab some coffee. I'll help you figure out the science fair fiasco."

The tension between them was subtle, but Nyomi could feel it—a distance growing with every secret she kept. But this time, she nodded, deciding to go along, if only to keep Callie from asking more questions.

She left the library beside her best friend, clutching her sketchbook a little tighter. The world outside seemed sharper, more vivid, as if her senses were heightened. Each step felt like an affirmation that she would face whatever lay ahead, one way or another.

As they walked through the hallways, Nyomi felt the weight of Thomas's words settle on her shoulders. She couldn't help but feel a growing divide between her and Callie, knowing that she carried a secret too strange, too powerful to share. Yet Callie's presence grounded her in the everyday world, reminding her of who she was outside of her powers.

But as they walked toward the café, her thoughts drifted back to the library, to Thomas's calm, steady guidance, and the way he seemed to understand what no one else could. She was no longer just a girl with a dream and a sketchbook; she was something more, something that defied the mundane and beckoned her to explore the unknown.

Determined, Nyomi resolved that whatever it took, she would learn to control her gift. And she would start tonight.

CHAPTER 7: A NEW BEGINNING

The senior center was a world apart from the high school. The moment Nyomi stepped through its doors, the familiar, high-energy buzz of adolescent chatter and clanging locker doors faded, replaced by a soft hum that seemed to slow time itself. The center's hallways were wide and spotless, filled with the quiet shuffle of slippers on linoleum floors and the occasional clink of a distant television or the muted sound of soft music playing in the activity room. Even the air felt different here—thicker somehow, with a subtle scent of old books, worn leather, and the medicinal tang that seemed to accompany places like this.

Nyomi hesitated just inside the entrance, clutching her volunteer badge in her hand. She wasn't sure what she'd expected, but the quiet felt both comforting and intimidating. There was a stillness here, a peacefulness that she hadn't experienced in the noisy, chaotic world of high school. She was used to the constant buzz of movement, the chatter of classmates, and the rush between classes. But here, everything was slower, more deliberate.

For a moment, she wasn't sure if she belonged here at all.

The volunteer coordinator, a kind-looking woman named Karen, noticed her hesitation and smiled warmly. "Welcome, Nyomi. It's great to have you here." Karen's voice was gentle, almost soothing, as if she knew exactly how to speak in this quiet, contemplative place. "I know this can feel a bit intimidating, but you'll get the hang of it. It just takes a little patience and a lot of empathy."

Nyomi managed a small smile, nodding. "Thank you. I'm... I'm excited to be here."

But as Karen led her down the hallway, explaining the daily routines and activities that filled the residents' days, Nyomi's excitement was quickly overshadowed by nerves. She had volunteered for this position in the hopes of finding a way to use her powers for something good, to make a difference in people's lives. But now, standing in the quiet halls of the senior center, the enormity of what she'd signed up for began to sink in.

First Impressions and Uncertainty Karen showed her around the center, introducing her to the different areas—the activity room, the dining hall, the garden courtyard where residents often gathered for fresh air. The center was well-maintained, with cheerful paintings on the walls and cozy furniture arranged in small clusters to encourage conversation. It was a far cry from the fluorescent-lit classrooms and crowded hallways of high school.

But despite the welcoming atmosphere, Nyomi couldn't shake the feeling of being out of place. The residents, most of whom were in their seventies or eighties, moved at a different pace, one that Nyomi struggled to match. They spoke in low, measured tones, their words often accompanied by long pauses that left her feeling awkward and unsure of how to respond. It was a strange feeling, this sense of stillness, and Nyomi found herself missing the familiar chaos of her school, the loud laughter of her friends, and even the sharp edge of Thomas's gaze as he watched her from across the room.

Her first day was a blur of introductions and small tasks— serving tea in the activity room, helping organize a few books in the library, and assisting with an art class that the center held for residents who enjoyed painting. But each task left her feeling more unsure than the last.

In the art class, she'd accidentally handed one resident the wrong brush, and he'd scolded her for not paying attention. During tea service, she'd spilled a few drops on a woman's blanket, earning a sharp glare in return. And when she'd tried to strike up a conversation with one of the residents in the library, the woman had simply nodded politely and turned back to her book, leaving Nyomi standing there, feeling foolish.

By the end of the day, she felt exhausted—not from the work itself, which was physically easy compared to the bustle of high school, but from the emotional strain of trying to connect with people who seemed to exist in a world of their own. It was like trying to bridge a gap between two different realities, and she couldn't help but wonder if she was failing.

As she left the center that evening, her thoughts were a jumble of self- doubt and frustration. She had come here with the hope of using her powers to help people, to bring something positive into their lives. But now, she wasn't even sure if she could get them to like her, let alone help them.

Struggling to Connect

The next few days were much the same. Nyomi arrived each morning, trying her best to settle into the routine and find her place among the residents and staff. But no matter how hard she tried, she couldn't seem to break through the invisible barrier that separated her from the people she was trying to help.

In the dining hall, she served meals to residents who barely acknowledged her presence, their focus on the food in front of them or on the soft murmurs of conversation around the room. In the garden, she helped set up chairs for a small gathering, but when she tried to join in on the conversation, she was met with polite nods and short, distant answers that left her feeling like an outsider.

It wasn't that the residents were unkind—most of them were polite, even friendly in a quiet, reserved way. But they seemed to move through their days with a sense of detachment, as if they were existing in a world that Nyomi could only glimpse from a distance. She tried to smile, to engage, to make herself approachable, but each attempt felt like it fell flat.

One afternoon, as she was helping a resident named Mr. Jameson organize his chessboard, he glanced at her with a sharp look.

"You don't have to pretend to be interested, you know," he said, his tone gruff but not unkind. "I've been playing this game longer than you've been alive. You probably think it's boring."

Nyomi felt her cheeks flush, embarrassed. "No, I... I'm interested, really. I just don't know much about chess."

Mr. Jameson raised an eyebrow, his expression softening just a little. "Well, it's not for everyone. But if you're going to help me, at least learn the basics."

Nyomi managed a small smile, grateful for the hint of warmth in his voice. It was a small connection, a tiny crack in the wall that separated her from the residents. But it wasn't enough to ease the nagging doubt that lingered in the back of her mind.

As the days went on, Nyomi found herself questioning her decision to volunteer at the center. She had come here with the hope of using her powers for good, of bringing something positive into the lives of the people who lived here. But she didn't know how to do that, didn't know if her powers even had a place in this quiet, contemplative world.

Every night, she lay awake, her mind racing with questions. She wanted to believe that her powers could be a force for good, that she could use them to help people in ways that went beyond the ordinary. But the senior center was a place of routines and familiarity, a place where change was slow and measured, and Nyomi's magic felt out of place in that world.

Her thoughts often drifted back to the science fair, to the way her powers had brought dreams and ideas to life. She had seen the wonder in people's eyes, the joy that her magic had brought, even if only for a moment. But here, in the senior center, that same magic felt almost intrusive, like a bright light in a room filled with soft shadows.

One afternoon, as she was helping in the activity room, she caught sight of Mrs. Hargrove, an elderly woman with a gentle smile and eyes that seemed to hold a thousand memories. Mrs. Hargrove was sitting alone, her hands folded in her lap, her gaze distant as she stared out the window.

Without thinking, Nyomi walked over and sat down beside her. "Hi, Mrs. Hargrove. How are you today?"

Mrs. Hargrove looked at her, her smile faint but kind. "Oh, I'm just fine, dear. Just thinking."

Nyomi hesitated, unsure of what to say. She wanted to connect with Mrs. Hargrove, to understand the world she was seeing through that distant gaze. But words felt inadequate, too clumsy to bridge the gap between them.

"Do you... do you ever think about the past?" Nyomi asked softly, her voice barely above a whisper.

Mrs. Hargrove's gaze softened, her eyes filling with a mixture of warmth and sadness. "All the time, dear. It's all I have left, really. The memories."

Nyomi felt a pang of sorrow, a deep ache that seemed to resonate with something inside her. She thought about her powers, about the way they could bring dreams and memories to life. For a fleeting moment, she wondered if she could use that magic here, to give Mrs. Hargrove a chance to relive a memory, to hold onto something precious for just a little longer.

But the thought terrified her. She didn't know if she could control it, didn't know if it was even possible to use her powers in such a delicate way. And the last thing she wanted was to hurt someone, to bring chaos into a world that was already fragile.

So instead, she sat with Mrs. Hargrove in silence, letting the quiet moments stretch between them like a shared memory.

Introducing Mr. Jameson and Mrs. Hargrove As the days passed, Nyomi grew more familiar with the residents, learning their names and their routines, slowly becoming a part of their world. She met Mr. Jameson, the retired firefighter who spent his afternoons in the courtyard, a cigarette clutched between his fingers as he watched the world go by with a stoic expression.

Mr. Jameson was a man of few words, his gaze sharp and unyielding, but there was a kindness beneath his rough exterior, a gentleness that showed itself in fleeting moments. Nyomi learned that he had lost several close friends in a fire years ago, a tragedy that had left him scarred in ways that went beyond the physical. He rarely spoke of it, but the weight of that loss was always there, a silent presence that seemed to follow him wherever he went.

Mrs. Hargrove, on the other hand, was a quiet, introspective woman who spent most of her time by the window, her gaze lost in the past. She rarely spoke of her memories, but there was a sadness in her eyes, a longing for something that had been left behind in the years gone by.

Nyomi found herself drawn to them both, sensing a connection that went beyond words. They were dreamers, in their own way, people who had lived and loved and lost, their lives shaped by memories that had become part of who they were. And as she spent more time with them, Nyomi began to feel a growing desire to help them, to bring something good into their lives, even if she didn't yet know how.

But her powers remained a mystery, a force that she couldn't fully control, and the fear of what might happen if she let them loose in the senior center kept her from acting on that desire.

Small Failures and Awkward Moments In her first week at the center, Nyomi had her fair share of small failures and awkward moments. She spilled a pitcher of water in the dining hall, accidentally handed Mr. Jameson the wrong medication, and fumbled with the bingo cards during the weekly game. Each mistake left her feeling more out of place, more unsure of her ability to connect with the residents.

But slowly, she began to find her footing.

She learned to listen, to sit quietly with the residents and let them speak on their own terms, to let the silence settle between them without feeling the need to fill it with words. She learned to be patient, to move at their pace, to respect the routines and rhythms that defined their days.

And gradually, the residents began to warm to her.

Mrs. Hargrove started sharing small stories, bits and pieces of her life that felt like fragments of a distant dream. Mr. Jameson taught her the basics of chess, his gruff demeanor softening as he showed her the moves and strategies that had become second nature to him.

It was a slow process, a quiet journey of learning and growth. But with each day, Nyomi felt a little more at home, a little more connected to the world of the senior center.

One evening, as Nyomi lay in bed, her thoughts drifted to the residents she had met, to the quiet, unspoken stories that filled the center. She thought about Mrs. Hargrove's longing for the past, about Mr. Jameson's silent grief, about the memories and dreams that seemed to linger in the air, like whispers waiting to be heard.

And in that moment, she felt a spark of something new—a deeper purpose, a desire to use her powers not just for herself, but for others. She didn't yet know how, didn't yet understand the full extent of her abilities, but she knew that she wanted to help. She wanted to bring something beautiful into the lives of the people she had come to care about.

It was a small spark, a fragile hope. But as she closed her eyes and drifted off to sleep, she felt a sense of peace, a quiet certainty that she was on the right path.

And for the first time, she wasn't afraid of her powers. She was ready to embrace them, to learn what they could do, and to bring a little magic into the world of the senior center.

The coffee shop was warm and buzzing with the late afternoon crowd. Callie sipped her iced latte, her gaze fixed on Nyomi with a mixture of concern and curiosity. Nyomi could feel her friend's questions lingering in the air, but she was too preoccupied with the quiet hum of magic beneath her skin to address them. It was as if a part of her had come alive, her senses sharper, her awareness heightened since her conversation with Thomas.

But Callie wasn't one to let things go easily.

"So, what's up with you?" Callie finally asked, leaning forward with her elbows on the table. "You've been acting so... distant lately. You disappear all the time, and you don't even tell me what's going on."

Nyomi felt her pulse quicken. She hadn't expected Callie to be so direct, but she knew her friend too well to be surprised. Callie was the kind of person who confronted things head-on, and Nyomi could tell she wasn't going to let this go without an answer.

"I know, I'm sorry," Nyomi replied, fidgeting with the sleeve of her jacket. "It's just... I've had a lot on my mind."

Callie raised an eyebrow. "A lot on your mind? That's the best you've got? Come on, Nyomi, I'm your best friend. I can tell when something's seriously off."

Nyomi hesitated, her thoughts swirling. Thomas's words echoed in her mind—You don't have to do this alone. But the idea of revealing even a hint of her secret felt dangerous, like stepping too close to the edge of a cliff.

Still, Callie deserved something more than vague apologies.

"There are things going on that I... don't really know how to explain," Nyomi started cautiously, studying Callie's face for a reaction. "Things that... aren't normal."

Callie tilted her head, her expression shifting from concern to intrigue. "Aren't normal, like... weird dreams? Or family drama? Or... something else?"

Nyomi's heart pounded as she weighed her next words carefully. "More like... things that happen when I don't expect them to. Things that I'm not sure I can control."

Callie's eyes narrowed slightly. "You mean like... supernatural stuff?" she asked, her tone laced with skepticism but also an underlying curiosity.

Nyomi swallowed, choosing her words carefully. "Maybe... yes. I don't know how to describe it exactly, but lately I've been noticing things. Things I thought were just in my head, but they're not. They're... real."

The look on Callie's face was hard to read—somewhere between fascination and disbelief. Nyomi braced herself, waiting for her friend to laugh it off or dismiss it as nonsense. But instead, Callie just stared, her gaze intense and searching.

"Nyomi, are you... okay?" she asked gently. "You're not, like... losing it or anything, right?"

Nyomi let out a shaky laugh, unsure whether to be relieved or frustrated. "I know how it sounds. Honestly, I'd probably think the same thing if you told me. But I swear, Callie, I'm not crazy. Something... changed, and I don't know why. Or how."

Callie bit her lip, tapping her fingers against her coffee cup as she processed Nyomi's words. "Okay, so... give me an example. If you're saying something's changed, then... what does that look like?"

Nyomi hesitated, her fingers brushing against her sketchbook. Part of her wanted to tell Callie everything, to show her the truth and see if she'd believe it. But another part of her held back, remembering Thomas's warning. *Power like yours—it doesn't wait for you to be ready. You have to meet it halfway, learn to control it before it controls you.*

Taking a deep breath, Nyomi decided to test the waters. She opened her sketchbook to a blank page and tapped her fingers along the edge, willing herself to focus.

"Imagine I drew something here," she began, keeping her voice steady. "What if I told you that this drawing could... I don't know, come to life somehow?"

Callie's eyebrows shot up. "Like, it could move on its own? Like magic?"

Nyomi nodded slowly, her heart racing. "Yeah. Like magic."

For a moment, Callie was silent, her eyes studying Nyomi with newfound intensity. Nyomi could see the gears turning in her friend's mind, the way Callie seemed to be considering, weighing her options before speaking.

"I mean, magic would be amazing and all," Callie said, a hint of a smile on her lips. "But come on, Nyomi. You're an artist. If this is some new art project you're doing, I totally support it. But if you're serious about this... I need to know you're not just imagining things."

Nyomi's stomach twisted. She wanted Callie to believe her, to see the truth, but it was clear that without evidence, her words were nothing more than a strange story.

"Just forget I said anything," Nyomi mumbled, closing her sketchbook with a sigh. "It probably does sound crazy."

But Callie didn't drop it. She leaned forward, her tone softening. "Hey, I didn't say I didn't believe you. I just... I don't understand it, that's all. You've been my best friend for years, and I've never seen you act like this. If there's something real going on, if you're going through something, then I want to be there for you. I just... need you to let me in."

Nyomi's chest tightened at the sincerity in Callie's voice. The weight of her secret felt unbearable, but the fear of losing Callie's trust was even stronger. She glanced down at her sketchbook, her fingers itching to open it, to show Callie a glimpse of the truth.

Maybe, just maybe, she could share a little more.

"There's a part of me that wants to show you everything," Nyomi admitted, her voice barely a whisper. "But I don't know if I'm ready. I don't even know if I understand it myself yet."

Callie nodded, a look of determination in her eyes. "Then let me help you figure it out. Whatever this is, we'll face it together. And if it really is magic..." She paused, her eyes shining with excitement. "Then that's amazing. And a little terrifying."

Nyomi felt a rush of relief, and for the first time in days, she allowed herself to smile. Maybe she didn't have to carry this burden alone. Maybe, with Callie by her side, the unknown wouldn't feel quite so daunting.

The two of them sat in silence for a while, sipping their drinks and allowing the weight of their conversation to settle. Callie's unwavering loyalty gave Nyomi a sense of courage she hadn't felt before. Perhaps she could trust her friend with the truth, bit by bit. She didn't have to tell her everything now, but maybe one day, when she was ready.

As they finished their coffee, Callie glanced at her phone and winced. "Yikes, it's getting late. We should probably head out before your mom starts texting me, wondering where you are."

Nyomi laughed, feeling lighter than she had in weeks. "Yeah, she's probably already planning her interrogation."

Callie nudged her playfully as they stood to leave. "Don't worry. I'll just tell her we were having a deep conversation about life and the universe. She can't argue with that."

As they walked out of the coffee shop, the cool evening air greeted them, carrying a hint of something electric. Nyomi's thoughts drifted back to Thomas's warning, to the importance of learning control. She knew she couldn't put off her powers any longer. Tonight, she would try. She'd take the first step toward understanding what she was capable of.

The walk home felt surreal, as if Nyomi were caught between two worlds—the ordinary one with Callie by her side, and the strange, magical realm that had begun to take shape in her life. Her steps felt weightier, her purpose clearer. The conversation with Thomas, her hints to Callie, the bubbling energy inside her—it all aligned to one single truth: she had to confront this.

When she finally reached her room, Nyomi shut the door behind her, feeling the quiet settle around her like a blanket. She pulled out her sketchbook, her hands trembling as she flipped to a blank page. She knew what she had to do, but the fear of what might happen held her back, keeping her pencil poised above the paper.

She thought of Thomas's words—Power like yours... you have to meet it halfway. And she thought of Callie, the way her friend's belief had given her strength.

Taking a deep breath, Nyomi lowered her pencil to the page. She began to draw, letting her hand move instinctively, letting the image take shape without overthinking. A delicate bird, small and unassuming, emerged on the paper. She focused on it, on the details of each feather, on the sense of life she wanted to bring to it.

The air in her room seemed to grow thick, and the faint hum of magic she had come to recognize stirred within her. Her heartbeat quickened, her fingers tingling as the bird seemed to shimmer, the lines of its wings pulsing with a quiet glow. She held her breath, willing herself to stay calm, to channel her focus, just as Thomas had urged her.

And then, ever so softly, the bird's wings lifted from the page.

A mix of fear and wonder washed over her as she watched it flutter, tentative but alive, hovering just above her hand. She felt the energy buzzing through her, but this time, it wasn't wild or erratic. It was hers, a part of her she could touch and guide.

Nyomi's gaze softened as she watched the bird, feeling a new certainty settle within her. She didn't know where this journey would take her, but she was ready to learn.

And as the bird fluttered out the open window, disappearing into the night, Nyomi felt the first spark of control settle into place. She was ready for whatever came next.

CHAPTER 8: DEPTHS OF CONNECTION AND SELF-DISCOVERY

Nyomi settled into her third week at the senior center with a newfound awareness of her surroundings. Each day, she tried to approach her role with patience, attempting to connect with the residents and understand the routines they clung to. The challenges were constant— moments of failure, misunderstandings, and the persistent feeling that she wasn't quite equipped for this work. Yet, each day she stayed, compelled by the faint hope that her presence could bring a flicker of warmth into the lives of those around her.

Thomas's unannounced appearances became more frequent, though each time his presence seemed incidental, he was careful to avoid drawing attention. He would stand in the corner of the activity room or watch her from across the dining hall, a subtle but grounding presence. One afternoon, as Nyomi cleared tables after lunch, she finally gathered the courage to confront him.

"What are you doing here, Thomas?" she asked quietly, glancing over her shoulder to ensure no one else was listening. "You're not a volunteer, so why keep coming?"

Thomas met her gaze with a calm smile. "I guess you could say I've been... assigned."

Nyomi raised an eyebrow, confused. "Assigned?"

"Think of it as an obligation," Thomas said, his tone uncharacteristically serious. "My family... we have a history of being close to people like you, those who have gifts." He paused, his expression softened by a trace of something Nyomi hadn't seen before. "I once knew someone with abilities like yours. She struggled with them, too, didn't know how to control them."

Nyomi's curiosity surged. "What happened to her?"

Thomas's gaze dropped to the floor. "She learned—eventually. But not without hardship. Not without mistakes." His voice dropped, filled with a mixture of regret and determination. "I'm here because I want to help you avoid some of those mistakes."

The gravity of his words sank in, and Nyomi felt a flicker of understanding. Thomas's presence, his subtle guidance, wasn't just out of casual curiosity. He had seen firsthand the struggles of someone with powers like hers, and he was here to help her navigate the journey.

Nyomi's Ethical Dilemma: The Question of Power and Vulnerability

That evening, Nyomi sat by the small window in her room, gazing out at the night sky. Her fingers traced circles along the edge of her notebook as she thought about what Thomas had shared. It gave her comfort to know he understood her struggle, that he wasn't just an observer but someone who had a stake in her well-being. Still, the sense of responsibility pressed heavily on her, especially when she thought of using her powers around the residents.

She flipped open her notebook, finding a blank page where she could organize her thoughts.

"Is it right to use my powers here? These people have lived long lives, filled with memories and hardships of their own. Who am I to interfere with their past, their pain? Even if my intentions are good, is it enough?"

Her hand trembled slightly as she wrote. She remembered the science fair, the moment when everything spiraled out of control. The unintended chaos her powers had caused. She had seen the wonder in people's faces that day, but she'd also seen fear. Here, in the senior center, she couldn't afford to make such a mistake.

"What if I bring back a painful memory? What if my powers do more harm than good?"

She closed her notebook, her thoughts a tangle of hope and fear. The urge to help the residents, to ease the grief she saw in their eyes, was strong. But so was the fear of losing control, of accidentally hurting someone who had already endured enough.

The next day, as Nyomi sat with Mrs. Hargrove in the garden, she noticed a peculiar sensation. A gentle warmth began to tingle in her fingertips, a soft heat that seemed to rise from somewhere deep within her. She glanced at her hands, watching as the skin seemed to shimmer faintly under the afternoon sun.

Mrs. Hargrove was talking about her late husband again, her voice filled with nostalgia and quiet sorrow. Nyomi's heart ached for her, the connection between them growing as she listened intently. And as the warmth in her hands intensified, she realized that her powers seemed to respond to this empathy, to the emotions she felt as she listened to Mrs. Hargrove's memories.

This realization startled her, and she pulled back, clasping her hands together to muffle the sensation. The warmth subsided, leaving her with a strange sense of both relief and longing. Was this the "tell" she had been searching for? The physical manifestation of her powers, triggered by the depth of her emotions?

As she helped Mrs. Hargrove back inside, Nyomi resolved to experiment more, to understand this connection between her feelings and her abilities. But she would have to be careful. Each use of her powers would have to be measured, intentional, controlled.

Observing Mr. Jameson's Silent Grief

Her observations of the residents deepened over the next few days, her gaze lingering on Mr. Jameson whenever he was nearby. He spent most of his time alone, sitting by the window or in the courtyard, his eyes focused on something far beyond the walls of the center.

One afternoon, she saw him turn over a small, tarnished medal in his hands, his fingers tracing the worn metal with a reverence that was almost painful to watch. She approached him cautiously, her voice barely above a whisper.

"Is that a medal from your firefighting days?"

Mr. Jameson glanced up, his gaze sharp but not unkind. He held up the medal, the engraved words barely visible from years of wear. "Yeah. Earned this one a long time ago, before..." He trailed off, his eyes growing distant as his thumb brushed over the edge of the medal.

Nyomi felt a surge of empathy, an urge to reach out and offer him comfort. But her hands tingled with that familiar warmth, and she hesitated. The intensity of his grief, his attachment to the past, made her cautious. Could her powers offer him peace, or would they only reopen old wounds?

She clenched her fists, her emotions a tangle of compassion and fear. She wanted to help him, to ease the weight of his memories, but the consequences of using her powers remained unknown, too unpredictable.

A Call from Callie: Friendship and Distance

That evening, as Nyomi was preparing for bed, her phone buzzed. She glanced at the screen, surprised to see Callie's name. They hadn't spoken much since Nyomi started volunteering, the distance between them widening with each passing day.

"Hey, stranger!" Callie's cheerful voice filled the line. "You've been practically invisible lately. What's going on?"

Nyomi hesitated, unsure of how to explain the whirlpool of emotions and responsibilities that had taken over her life. "I'm... just busy, I guess. The senior center is a lot of work."

Callie's voice softened. "Are you okay? I feel like you're hiding something from me. We used to tell each other everything, remember?"

Nyomi's chest tightened with guilt. She wanted to tell Callie the truth, to share the weight of her secret, but fear held her back. "I'm okay, really. Just... it's complicated."

There was a pause, then Callie's voice perked up again. "Well, maybe you need a break! How about coming to the art club this Friday? We miss you, and I bet a little creativity would do you good."

Nyomi forced a smile, though Callie couldn't see it. "Maybe... I'll think about it."

After hanging up, Nyomi sat in silence, her thoughts tangled. She missed Callie, missed the comfort of her friend's optimism and laughter. But the distance between them felt inevitable, the secret of her powers forming a barrier she couldn't break. Telling Callie would mean sharing everything—the responsibility, the fear, the weight of her abilities—and she wasn't sure if she was ready for that.

The next morning, Nyomi slipped into the art room at the senior center during a rare moment of solitude. She found a blank sheet of paper and a pencil, her hands trembling as she prepared to test her powers in a controlled setting. She thought of a butterfly—something small, delicate, and safe. If her powers responded to emotion, then focusing on calm, gentle thoughts might allow her to control them.

As she began to sketch, a faint warmth spread through her fingertips, and she held her breath, concentrating on that sensation. The lines on the paper seemed to shimmer, almost as if the butterfly was ready to lift off the page.

But then her concentration wavered, a surge of anxiety breaking through her focus. The warmth vanished, leaving only the faint outline of a butterfly on the page.

Nyomi let out a shaky breath, her heart pounding. Control was harder than she had thought. The brief moment of connection, of magic, had felt like balancing on the edge of a cliff, one misstep away from losing herself to the unknown.

Yet, despite the difficulty, she felt a renewed determination. She was learning, slowly, to harness her powers. It would take time, patience, and discipline, but she was willing to put in the effort.

Reflections in Her Journal: Power and Consequences

That night, Nyomi returned to her journal, her thoughts heavy as she recounted the day's events. She wrote about Mr. Jameson, about his silent grief and the hint of his past she had glimpsed. Her heart ached for him, but the fear of causing harm kept her from reaching out.

"My powers can bring comfort, but they can also amplify pain," she wrote, her pen pressing harder against the paper. "If I'm not careful, I could hurt someone instead of helping. And that's the last thing I want."

As she closed her journal, she felt a sense of clarity settle over her. She was beginning to understand the boundaries of her powers, the balance between compassion and control. Her magic was not just a gift—it was a tool, one that required respect and caution.

A few days later, Thomas approached her in the courtyard, his expression unusually serious. "You're making progress," he said quietly, nodding toward the activity room where Mrs. Hargrove was sitting, a peaceful smile on her face.

Nyomi glanced at him, a mixture of gratitude and frustration in her gaze. "I want to help them, Thomas. I really do. But... I'm afraid. What if I cause more harm than good?"

Thomas considered her question, his gaze thoughtful. "Magic amplifies what's already there, Nyomi. If your intent is pure, if your heart is in the right place, then you have little to fear. But you must always respect the boundaries of those you wish to help."

Nyomi nodded, his words echoing the thoughts she had written in her journal. "So it's about intent. About empathy."

"Exactly," Thomas replied. "Magic is a connection, a bridge between souls. Use it wisely, and it can bring light. But misuse it, even unintentionally, and it can deepen shadows."

As Thomas's words sank in, Nyomi felt a sense of purpose solidify within her. She would be cautious, mindful of the power she wielded, and she would only use it when she was certain it could bring comfort.

A Moment of Decision with Mr. Jameson

One afternoon, as Nyomi sat in the courtyard, she watched Mr. Jameson sitting alone, his eyes focused on the faded medal in his hands. A memory surfaced, a conversation she had overheard between two staff members about the fire that had taken the lives of Mr. Jameson's fellow firefighters. His grief was a constant presence, a wound that hadn't healed.

She felt the warmth in her fingertips, the familiar shimmer that signaled her powers awakening. This time, she didn't pull back. She approached him slowly, her voice soft.

"Mr. Jameson," she said, hesitating for a brief moment. "Would you like to talk about... them? Your friends?"

He looked up at her, his eyes filled with a vulnerability she hadn't seen before. And as he spoke, his voice trembling with the weight of memories, Nyomi felt the magic flow through her, a gentle force that connected their souls.

In that moment, she understood her purpose—not to change the past, but to honor it, to bring peace to those who had carried their burdens alone for far too long.

CHAPTER 9: BUILDING TRUST

The early morning light filtered into the Riverview Senior Center, casting a gentle glow through the hallways and reflecting off the polished floors. Nyomi stepped through the entrance with a new sense of purpose. Over the past weeks, this place had begun to feel like a second home—a space where she could make a difference, where her Butterfly Touch became more than just a strange talent she barely understood. It was now a lifeline, a connection that allowed her to truly see people, to reach into the quiet places in their hearts and bring comfort.

Every morning, she slipped into a comfortable routine: a cup of coffee with Sarah before the residents stirred, helping the kitchen staff with breakfast, then moving through the hallways, her steps guided by the needs and rhythms of the residents. The Butterfly Touch had become like a compass, guiding her to moments when her power felt natural and meaningful.

Yet, Nyomi was aware of the journey ahead. Every day was a test of patience, compassion, and self-control—qualities she was only beginning to cultivate. She reminded herself to tread carefully, to let the warmth of her powers flow only when necessary and to respect the lives of those she touched.

Gaining the Residents' Trust

Her connection with the residents grew in small, consistent ways. She took time to learn their habits, their stories, and the little preferences that brought them joy. Mrs. Hargrove, for instance, liked her tea with precisely three drops of honey. Mr. Oswald, an aviation enthusiast, preferred his newspaper folded a certain way, allowing him to skip to the stories about aerospace technology without fuss. Nyomi honored these small details, knowing they were tokens of respect for the rich lives the residents had led before arriving here.

One morning, she noticed Mrs. Hargrove sitting in the courtyard garden, her eyes lingering on the petals of a wildflower. Without a word, Nyomi gathered a small bouquet of similar flowers from a nearby patch and brought them to her.

"These reminded me of the ones you liked," she said, handing the bouquet to Mrs. Hargrove with a soft smile.

The elderly woman's eyes brightened, her hands trembling as she took the bouquet. She inhaled deeply, her gaze turning wistful. "These remind me of the garden I used to have," she murmured. "My husband and I used to pick wildflowers together every spring. He'd laugh, call them weeds, but he'd always bring me some anyway."

Nyomi felt the familiar warmth building in her fingertips, the gentle nudge of her powers urging her to connect. She placed a steady hand over Mrs. Hargrove's and allowed the warmth to subside, respecting the sanctity of the memory itself.

Mrs. Hargrove smiled, her eyes glistening. "Thank you, dear. It's like you brought him back for a moment."

These small gestures were victories, each one building her confidence and deepening the bonds she was forming. Her powers weren't just a mysterious force anymore; they were becoming a way to connect with others, to reach into the invisible spaces where words couldn't tread.

Building a Connection with Sarah

Nyomi often observed Sarah, the senior center's nurse, moving through her duties with focused precision. Sarah was in her early thirties, her hair always pulled back into a tight ponytail, her expression no-nonsense and impenetrable. There were rumors among the staff about Sarah's past—that she had once been a combat medic, a fact that explained her stoic demeanor and cautious attitude.

One day, Nyomi was helping an elderly man, Mr. Cline, into his seat in the dining hall. Mr. Cline groaned in pain as he sat, his hand clutching his side. "Easy there," Nyomi murmured, steadying him with a gentle hand on his shoulder.

When she looked up, she found Sarah watching her with narrowed eyes. A brief moment passed before Sarah nodded approvingly. "Good job, kid," she muttered before moving on.

That was the first indication of trust from Sarah, and Nyomi held onto it like a fragile token. In the following days, their interactions grew. Sarah observed her more closely, her wariness gradually softening into something like respect. When Nyomi handled minor injuries, prepared meals, or comforted residents, she would catch Sarah's glance—a quiet acknowledgment of her efforts.

One afternoon, as Nyomi was helping restock medical supplies, Sarah approached her, leaning against the doorframe. "You're pretty good with them," Sarah said, her tone cautious but sincere.

Nyomi looked up, surprised. "Thank you," she replied. "I... I just try to listen."

Sarah studied her for a moment before nodding. "That's rare. Most people just do the basics, stick to routines, but you're different. You care."

Nyomi felt a flicker of warmth at Sarah's words. "They deserve it," she said, choosing her words carefully. "They've lived full lives, seen so much. I want to... I guess I want to honor that."

Sarah's expression softened, her guarded gaze revealing a hint of understanding. "Just remember, working with people—especially people who've known loss—it's tough. Takes a lot of patience and a steady heart."

Nyomi nodded, her respect for Sarah growing with each conversation. In Sarah's cautious, guarded manner, she saw a woman who had experienced deep pain and loss—a woman who chose to protect herself by keeping her heart sheltered.

From that day on, Sarah began to trust Nyomi in small but meaningful ways. She invited her into tasks, occasionally asked her opinion on resident care, and even let her handle certain responsibilities. Their connection deepened through shared moments and unspoken respect, a quiet bond built on trust and mutual understanding.

Routine Struggles and Growing Responsibilities

Nyomi's routine became a rhythm that anchored her days. She spent mornings helping serve breakfast, then moved to the activity room where residents gathered for games, crafts, and conversation. In these quiet moments, as she helped residents with puzzles or chose colors for a paint- by- numbers kit, she found the space to listen—to truly hear the stories they wanted to share.

Many residents recounted fragments of their pasts: lost loves, grand adventures, childhood memories. Each story was a glimpse into a life that had been rich and vibrant, a reminder that these were people with full histories and deep emotions. Listening became her way of connecting, her way of letting the residents know she saw them for who they truly were.

But there were practical challenges as well. One week, the center's food supplies ran low, forcing Nyomi to take matters into her own hands. She visited nearby grocery stores, negotiating with managers and asking for donations. Though most were wary of giving away food without proper documentation, her persistence eventually paid off. She secured a few small donations and even convinced a local charity to provide regular supplies.

As she returned to the center, carrying bags of groceries, she ran into Sarah. The nurse looked at the bags, raising an eyebrow. "You're doing all this yourself?" she asked, her voice carrying a hint of disbelief.

Nyomi nodded, her arms aching from the weight of the groceries. "I thought it might help. They deserve good food."

Sarah's expression softened, a flicker of admiration crossing her face. "You've got a good heart, Nyomi. Not many would go to these lengths."

Nyomi smiled, feeling a surge of pride. Sarah's approval felt like a milestone, a sign that she was earning her place here, step by step.

Building Trust with Small Gestures

Over the following days, Nyomi's gestures of kindness became more intentional and personalized. She made a habit of remembering the little things that mattered to each resident: the way Mrs. Hargrove liked her tea, Mr. Oswald's favorite newspaper sections, and even the stories that resonated with them. Each small act of attentiveness created a quiet bond, drawing the residents closer to her, bit by bit.

For Mr. Jameson, however, it was different. The retired firefighter kept to himself, spending long hours in the courtyard, staring off into the distance with a solemn expression. Nyomi had tried speaking with him a few times, asking gentle questions about his past, but he responded with brief, curt answers, his eyes never quite meeting hers.

One day, she found him sitting on a bench, a small, faded photo in his hands. She approached slowly, sensing the weight of the memory held within that single image. It was a picture of a group of young men in firefighting gear, their faces filled with pride and purpose.

Nyomi took a deep breath, her voice soft as she spoke. "Were they your friends?"

Mr. Jameson's hand tightened around the photo, his jaw clenched. "Yes," he replied after a long pause, his voice barely a whisper. "They were."

Her heart ached at the sorrow in his tone. "It must have been difficult to lose them."

He looked up, his eyes flashing with a mixture of anger and pain. "You don't know anything about it," he said, his voice harsh. "You're just a kid."

Nyomi took a step back, the sting of his rejection sharp and unexpected. She wanted to reach him, to help him find peace, but his pain was a fortress she wasn't sure how to breach.

Still, she didn't give up. Each day, she greeted him with a quiet "Good morning" and continued her small gestures—bringing him an extra cup of coffee, offering to read him the day's headlines, or simply sitting nearby in comfortable silence. It wasn't much, but she hoped that her patience would eventually earn his trust.

Testing the Boundaries of the Butterfly Touch

As Nyomi continued her routine at the center, she became more attuned to the residents' emotions, sensing moments when her Butterfly Touch wanted to reach out, to connect. Each time she felt the warmth in her fingertips, she paused, asking herself whether it was the right moment to use her power.

She'd begun to understand that the Butterfly Touch wasn't just a magical gift; it was a responsibility, one that required discernment and self-restraint.

One evening, as she sat in her room, she opened her sketchbook and began to draw, letting her thoughts drift to her experiences at the center. Each resident's story, each memory, felt like a piece of a puzzle she was only beginning to comprehend. The warmth of her powers flickered faintly as she sketched, almost like a whisper, as if her abilities were responding to the emotions stirred by each stroke of her pencil.

She closed her eyes, focusing on the sensation. The warmth began in her chest, a gentle, pulsing energy that radiated through her fingertips. In those moments, she felt as though she could reach into someone's heart, touch their memories, and bring them comfort. But a question lingered in her mind: Was there a limit to what her powers could handle?

Her thoughts drifted to Mr. Jameson, whose grief felt like a wall she couldn't penetrate. She wanted to ease his pain, to help him find peace, but she worried that delving too deeply might overwhelm her. The weight of his emotions felt heavy, a burden she wasn't sure she was ready to bear.

Nyomi sighed, setting her sketchbook aside. She closed her eyes, concentrating on containing the warmth within her, holding it back like a river restrained by a dam. The energy resisted, a gentle pressure building in her chest, but she managed to keep it in check. A quiet resolve settled within her: she would use her Butterfly Touch only when she was certain it was right. She had to respect the boundaries of her power, to wield it carefully.

As she drifted off to sleep that night, she made a promise to herself—to approach each moment with caution, to honor the lives she touched without overstepping.

Guidance from Thomas: The Balance of Power

The next morning, Nyomi arrived at the center to find Thomas waiting outside. He leaned against the wall, his gaze distant yet focused, as though he were lost in thought.

"Thomas?" she said, surprised to see him.

He looked up, a faint smile tugging at the corners of his mouth. "Just checking in. Thought you might want to talk."

Nyomi felt a mixture of curiosity and apprehension as she approached him. "About what?"

"Your powers," he replied, his tone serious. "You're starting to feel the toll, aren't you?"

Nyomi froze, her heart pounding. She hadn't spoken to anyone about the strain she felt after using her Butterfly Touch, the quiet exhaustion that lingered after connecting with someone's memories. "How... how did you know?"

Thomas sighed, his gaze shifting to the sky. "I had a friend once— someone with a gift like yours. She wanted to help people, but she didn't set boundaries. She thought she could handle anything, that she could keep giving without taking a break. But eventually, it became too much."

"What happened to her?" Nyomi asked, her voice barely a whisper.

Thomas's expression softened, a hint of sorrow in his eyes. "She lost herself in the process. Her powers consumed her, and in the end, she couldn't control them anymore."

Nyomi swallowed, fear prickling at the edges of her thoughts. "Do you think... that could happen to me?"

"It could," Thomas said quietly. "If you don't learn to set limits. The Butterfly Touch is powerful, but it's not limitless. If you overuse it, it could hurt you—or worse, it could hurt the people you're trying to help."

She nodded, absorbing his words. "Thank you, Thomas. I'll be careful."

He placed a reassuring hand on her shoulder, his gaze steady. "Remember, the power is part of you, but it doesn't define you. It's a tool, a gift. Treat it with respect, and it'll serve you well."

With that, he turned and walked away, leaving Nyomi with a sense of both caution and reassurance. His words lingered in her mind, a reminder of the responsibility she carried.

Callie's Concern: Balancing Two Worlds

Later that week, Nyomi received a call from her best friend, Callie. She hadn't seen much of Callie since she started volunteering at the center, and a pang of guilt tugged at her heart as she answered the phone.

"Hey, stranger!" Callie's voice was warm, but there was a hint of concern in her tone. "You've been so busy. I barely see you anymore."

Nyomi sighed, glancing around her room at the notes she'd been keeping about the residents. "I know. I'm sorry. The senior center has been... intense."

"Intense how?" Callie asked, her curiosity piqued.

Nyomi hesitated, struggling to find the right words. "It's just... there's so much to do, so many people who need help. I feel like I'm finally making a difference, you know?"

Callie was silent for a moment. "I get that, but don't forget about us— the people who love you. You can't lose yourself in all this. You need balance."

Nyomi felt a surge of gratitude for her friend's words. Callie had always been her grounding force, the one who reminded her of who she was outside of her powers. "Thanks, Callie. I needed that."

"Anytime," Callie replied. "And don't be a stranger. Come hang out with us soon. We miss you."

Nyomi promised she would, feeling a renewed commitment to balance her life between her responsibilities at the center and her friendships outside of it.

A Moment of Reflection and Doubt

That evening, as she sat in her room, Nyomi felt a flicker of doubt creeping in. She had used her powers several times in the past few weeks, each time feeling the strain a little more acutely. She wondered if she was pushing herself too hard, if she was letting the Butterfly Touch become a burden rather than a blessing.

Opening her journal, she began to write, capturing her thoughts in a series of questions and reflections:

Is it possible to use my powers too much? Am I risking my own well- being to help others? How do I know when it's safe to use the Butterfly Touch, and when it's too much?

The words flowed from her pen, a release of the worries that had been building inside her. As she read over her reflections, she felt a sense of clarity. Her powers were a gift, but they came with limitations. She would need to navigate those boundaries carefully, learning to discern the right moments to use them and the moments to hold back.

Slowly Gaining Mr. Jameson's Trust

The next day, Nyomi resumed her efforts to reach Mr. Jameson. She greeted him with a warm "Good morning" as usual, offering him his favorite cup of coffee. He accepted it with a nod, his expression unreadable.

Instead of pressing him with questions, Nyomi took a different approach. She began to share small stories from her own life—memories of her family, moments from her childhood, snippets of her own struggles. She spoke without expecting a response, letting her stories create a bridge between them, hoping he would feel the sincerity in her words.

Days passed, each one marked by her gentle persistence. She continued to bring him coffee, to sit nearby in silence, to share pieces of herself in the hope that he might feel comfortable enough to do the same.

One afternoon, as they sat in the courtyard, Mr. Jameson surprised her by speaking first.

"My friends," he said quietly, his gaze fixed on the sky. "We went through a lot together. Fires, rescues... things I can't even talk about."

Nyomi listened, her heart swelling with gratitude. It was a small step, but it was a sign that her patience was beginning to pay off. Mr. Jameson was starting to trust her, to see her as someone who genuinely cared.

"I can't imagine what that must have been like," she said softly, respecting the weight of his words. "But I'm here if you ever want to share more."

He didn't respond, but his expression softened, a hint of peace settling over his features. It was enough—a small victory that filled Nyomi with a renewed sense of purpose.

A New Layer of the Butterfly Touch

In the quiet moments between helping residents, Nyomi found herself contemplating the nature of her Butterfly Touch. Each time she used it, it seemed to adapt and respond to the emotions and needs of those around her. There were times when the warmth in her hands felt strong, as if her powers were urging her to reach out, and other times when it felt faint, almost hesitant. She began to realize that her powers were not just a tool she could wield at will; they were linked to her emotions, to her empathy, and to the connection she had with each resident.

One afternoon, she sat with Mrs. Montgomery, a retired nurse who often spoke of her days working in a hospital during the war. The stories she shared were filled with both pride and sorrow, tales of lives saved and lost, of moments of courage and heartbreak.

As Mrs. Montgomery described a particular night when she had stayed up tending to a wounded soldier, Nyomi felt the familiar warmth of the Butterfly Touch stirring in her hands. This time, however, she noticed something different. The warmth wasn't urging her to connect in the usual way. Instead, it felt softer, like a gentle pulse, almost as if it were mirroring Mrs. Montgomery's feelings of compassion and resilience.

Nyomi placed her hand over Mrs. Montgomery's, focusing on the sensation. Her vision blurred slightly, and for a moment, she could see the hospital as Mrs. Montgomery had described it—the dim lights, the quiet determination on her face as she cared for her patients, the way she moved with a grace and strength that seemed to transcend time.

When the vision faded, Mrs. Montgomery's hand was still in hers, and her eyes were misty. "Thank you, dear," she murmured, a smile playing on her lips. "You've made me feel young again, if only for a moment."

Nyomi realized that the Butterfly Touch wasn't just about reliving memories; it was about connecting to the essence of a person's experiences, to the emotions that shaped them. And as she held Mrs. Montgomery's hand, she felt a new layer of her powers unfolding—a realization that her Butterfly Touch could bring comfort in ways she hadn't fully understood before.

Mr. Jameson's First Gesture of Trust

Each day, Nyomi continued her patient attempts to reach Mr. Jameson, never pushing, simply being there for him in quiet companionship. One day, as she brought him his morning coffee, she noticed a subtle change in his demeanor. His gaze, usually distant and guarded, softened as he looked at her.

"Thank you," he said, his voice quieter than usual. He hesitated, as if weighing his words, before adding, "It's nice...

having someone around who listens."

Nyomi smiled, touched by his words. "You're welcome, Mr. Jameson.

I'm glad to be here."

He looked down at his coffee, his hands wrapped around the cup. After a pause, he glanced at her, his expression a mixture of reluctance and vulnerability. "Do you... have time to sit for a bit?"

Her heart swelled with gratitude. "Of course," she replied, taking a seat beside him.

For the first time, he began to share glimpses of his past, speaking of the years he spent as a firefighter, of the camaraderie and sense of purpose he had found in his work. He spoke of the fires he had fought, the lives he had saved, and the ones he couldn't. And as he spoke, Nyomi listened with her whole heart, her presence a silent reassurance that he didn't have to carry his memories alone.

When he finished, there was a calm in his expression that Nyomi hadn't seen before. "Thank you for listening," he murmured, his voice barely above a whisper.

"You're always welcome to share, Mr. Jameson," she replied, her words filled with sincerity. And in that moment, she knew that their bond had deepened, that he had begun to trust her in a way that felt both fragile and profound.

A Challenge with the Butterfly Touch: Reaching Emotional Limits

As Nyomi continued using her powers, she began to notice a pattern. Each time she connected with a resident's memories, she felt a sense of peace and fulfillment, but she also felt a growing sense of fatigue, a weight that seemed to settle in her chest after each use. She realized that her powers, though gentle and comforting, were taking a toll on her, that the emotional weight of each connection lingered within her long after the experience ended.

One afternoon, she attempted to use her Butterfly Touch to help soothe a difficult memory for Mrs. Hargrove. The elderly woman had been struggling with the loss of her husband, and Nyomi wanted to bring her comfort by reconnecting her to a happier memory. As she placed her hand over Mrs. Hargrove's, she felt the warmth of her powers surge, responding to the depth of the woman's grief.

But this time, something was different. The emotions were overwhelming, the sadness so intense that it felt like a wave crashing over her, pulling her under. Nyomi struggled to maintain her focus, but she felt her strength wavering, her heart pounding with the weight of Mrs. Hargrove's sorrow.

She pulled her hand away, gasping for breath, her body trembling. Mrs. Hargrove looked at her with concern, her own pain momentarily forgotten. "Are you all right, dear?"

Nyomi forced a smile, nodding. "Yes, I'm fine. Just... just a bit tired."

But as she left Mrs. Hargrove's room, she couldn't shake the feeling of exhaustion that had settled over her. She realized that her powers had limits, that there were memories and emotions too intense for her to handle. And as she returned to her room that evening, she resolved to be more cautious, to respect the boundaries of her powers, knowing that her own well-being was just as important as the comfort she offered others.

A Warning from Thomas: The Dangers of Overusing Her Powers

That evening, Thomas visited her again, his expression serious as he looked at her. "I can see it's starting to weigh on you," he said quietly, his gaze filled with concern.

Nyomi sighed, feeling the weight of the day's events pressing down on her. "It's just... there's so much pain here, so many memories that need healing. I want to help, but it's harder than I thought."

Thomas nodded, his voice gentle yet firm. "That's why it's important to set limits. Your powers are a gift, but they're not limitless. And if you push yourself too far, you risk losing yourself in the process."

She looked at him, a mixture of gratitude and fear in her eyes. "How do I know when it's too much?"

"You'll feel it," he replied. "The weight in your heart, the exhaustion in your soul. Those are signs that you need to pull back, to rest. Remember, your powers are meant to bring comfort, not to consume you."

Nyomi nodded, taking his words to heart. She understood now that her powers were both a blessing and a responsibility, that she would need to navigate their boundaries carefully if she wanted to use them wisely. And as Thomas left, she felt a renewed sense of purpose, a commitment to honoring her powers without letting them control her.

A Growing Bond with Sarah

In the weeks that followed, Nyomi's relationship with Sarah continued to deepen. They shared quiet moments of camaraderie, moments when Sarah would confide in her about her experiences as a combat medic. Each story was a glimpse into the resilience and courage that had shaped Sarah's life, and Nyomi listened with respect, drawing strength from her mentor's wisdom.

One afternoon, as they were cleaning up after lunch, Sarah paused, her gaze distant. "You remind me of someone I used to know," she said quietly.

Nyomi looked at her, sensing the weight behind her words. "Who was it?"

Sarah hesitated, her expression pained. "A friend from the war. She had a heart like yours—kind, compassionate, always willing to help. But she pushed herself too far, didn't know when to pull back. In the end, it broke her."

Nyomi felt a chill run down her spine, her mind flashing back to Thomas's warnings. "What happened to her?"

Sarah sighed, a sadness filling her eyes. "She wanted to save everyone, to heal every wound. But there are limits to what we can do, no matter how much we care. She lost herself trying to give too much."

Nyomi nodded, feeling a new sense of responsibility settling over her. She understood now that her powers required balance, that her compassion would need to be tempered with caution if she wanted to continue helping others without losing herself.

From that day on, Sarah began to rely on Nyomi in more practical ways, trusting her with tasks and responsibilities she hadn't before. It was a subtle shift, but Nyomi felt the weight of Sarah's trust, a quiet validation of her efforts to make a difference.

Experimenting with Control: Switching Off the Butterfly Touch

Determined to understand her powers better, Nyomi decided to experiment with controlling the Butterfly Touch, testing whether she could limit or "switch off" the warmth in her hands. She realized that her powers seemed to respond to her emotions, to the depth of empathy she felt in each moment. But she wondered if she could control that response, to choose when to use her powers and when to hold back.

One evening, as she sat in her room, she closed her eyes and focused on the warmth in her chest, the familiar pulsing energy that guided her Butterfly Touch. She concentrated on containing it, on keeping it dormant, as if placing a barrier around her heart. It was like holding back a wave, a force that resisted her efforts, but with enough focus, she felt the warmth subside, settling into a quiet calm.

When she opened her eyes, she felt a sense of relief, a newfound confidence in her ability to control her powers. She understood now that the Butterfly Touch was not something that controlled her; it was a part of her, a gift she could wield with intention and respect.

Finding Balance Between Her Two Worlds

As Nyomi continued her work at the center, she made a conscious effort to reconnect with her life outside. She spent time with Callie, joined her friends for outings, and even attended a school event. Each experience felt like a reminder of the world she had nearly forgotten, the life that had shaped her before she discovered her powers.

One evening, as she sat with her friends at a cafe, she felt a sense of joy and relief, a reminder that she was still herself, still a teenager with dreams and friendships that mattered. She realized that her powers, while a part of her, did not define her. She could still laugh, still find joy in the ordinary moments of life.

And as she balanced her two worlds, she felt a sense of peace, a quiet certainty that she was on the right path—a path that honored both her gifts and the life she cherished.

Final Reflections: A Journal Entry

That night, Nyomi opened her journal and wrote:

Today, I learned that my powers have limits, that there are moments when I must choose to hold back. I learned that my compassion is both my strength and my responsibility, that I must wield it with care. I learned that I am more than my powers, that I am still Nyomi, a girl with friends, with dreams, with a heart that wants to help.

And as I continue on this journey, I promise to honor both sides of myself, to embrace the balance between my gifts and the life I want to live.

As she closed her journal, she felt a sense of clarity, a renewed commitment to the path she was forging—one that honored both the magic within her and the love that surrounded her.

CHAPTER 10: STORIES FROM THE HEART

The days at Riverview Senior Center fell into a familiar rhythm, but each new interaction brought something different. Every resident had a story, each life an intricate tapestry of moments woven with joy, sorrow, resilience, and dreams left behind. Nyomi had begun to feel that she was not just a volunteer, but a quiet witness to the lives these people had lived, to the triumphs and heartbreaks that defined them.

Through her Butterfly Touch, she could glimpse their memories, connecting to a time when they were vibrant and full of hope. It was a gift, a rare privilege, but with each memory, Nyomi felt the weight of the emotions, the complexity of the lives she touched. Her empathy was growing, transforming her from a listener to a healer, someone who could ease the burden of memories long hidden.

As Nyomi continued to connect with each resident, she began to understand that her power wasn't just about reaching into the past. It was about understanding the depth of human resilience and the strength it took to live a full life. And with each story, her own heart grew, her understanding of empathy deepening in ways she had never expected.

Mr. Jameson: A Memory of Bravery and Loss

One afternoon, Nyomi found Mr. Jameson sitting by the window, staring out at the garden with an expression that seemed distant yet intense. The lines on his face spoke of years of experience, of battles fought and wounds carried in silence. She approached him gently, bringing his favorite cup of coffee and sitting beside him without a word.

After a moment, he looked at her, his eyes softening. "You know, I used to be a firefighter," he said, his voice gruff but carrying a hint of pride.

Nyomi nodded, listening intently. "I remember you mentioned that. It must have been challenging."

Mr. Jameson sighed, a heavy weight in his gaze. "It was. But there was something about it—the sense of purpose, the knowledge that I was helping people. That's what kept me going, even when things got tough."

Nyomi reached out, placing her hand gently over his. She felt the warmth of her powers responding, the familiar pulse of the Butterfly Touch stirring within her. Closing her eyes, she allowed the connection to deepen, feeling herself being drawn into one of his memories.

Suddenly, she was transported into the past, standing beside Mr. Jameson in the midst of a raging fire. Flames crackled around them, the heat intense, the air thick with smoke. She could feel his determination, his unwavering focus as he pushed forward, searching for survivors. His heart beat with both fear and courage, a relentless drive to save lives.

As the memory unfolded, Nyomi watched as Mr. Jameson and his team rescued a young family trapped inside. The relief on their faces, the gratitude in their eyes—it was a moment that filled Mr. Jameson with pride, a reminder of the lives he had touched.

But then, the memory shifted. Nyomi felt a wave of sorrow wash over her as Mr. Jameson recalled the times when he couldn't save everyone, when the flames were too fierce, too unrelenting. She saw the weight he carried, the faces of those he had lost etched deeply into his memory.

When the vision faded, Nyomi opened her eyes, her heart heavy with the emotions she had witnessed. Mr. Jameson's gaze was distant, his expression somber.

"Thank you for sharing that with me," Nyomi whispered, her voice filled with sincerity. "I can't imagine the strength it took to keep going, to carry those memories."

Mr. Jameson nodded, his eyes glistening with unshed tears. "It wasn't easy. But it was worth it, knowing I could make a difference, even if just for a few."

As she sat with him, Nyomi felt a deep sense of admiration for the man beside her. His bravery, his resilience—it was a reminder of the courage it took to face life's challenges, to keep going even when the weight of the past felt overwhelming.

And as she left him that day, she carried his story with her, a quiet inspiration that strengthened her own resolve.

Mrs. Montgomery: The Nurse's Healing Touch

The next day, Nyomi spent time with Mrs. Montgomery, a retired nurse who often shared stories from her days working in a hospital. Mrs. Montgomery's eyes would light up as she spoke of her patients, of the countless lives she had tended to with compassion and skill.

One afternoon, as they sat in the courtyard, Mrs. Montgomery spoke of a particular night during the war, when the hospital had been overwhelmed with wounded soldiers. Her voice wavered as she recalled the chaos, the desperation of that night.

"I remember the fear in their eyes," Mrs. Montgomery murmured, her gaze distant. "They were so young, so full of life. And there I was, just a girl myself, trying to hold them together, to keep them from slipping away."

Nyomi reached out, sensing the sorrow in her words, the weight of the memories she carried. She placed her hand over Mrs. Montgomery's, feeling the warmth of her powers stirring, and allowed herself to connect.

In an instant, she was transported into Mrs. Montgomery's memory. The scene around her shifted, becoming a bustling hospital filled with wounded soldiers. She could feel the urgency in the air, the tension as nurses and doctors moved swiftly from bed to bed, administering care.

Mrs. Montgomery was there, younger and determined, her face set in a look of fierce concentration as she worked tirelessly to tend to each patient. Nyomi could feel her compassion, her unwavering dedication as she soothed frightened soldiers, offering words of comfort in the midst of their pain.

As the memory unfolded, Nyomi witnessed moments of connection between Mrs. Montgomery and her patients—small gestures of gratitude, quiet words of hope. Each interaction was a testament to the healing power of compassion, a reminder that even in the darkest times, kindness could bring light.

When the memory faded, Nyomi opened her eyes, her heart filled with a profound respect for the woman beside her. "You saved so many lives," she whispered, her voice trembling with emotion. "Your strength... your compassion... it's incredible."

Mrs. Montgomery smiled, a tear slipping down her cheek. "It wasn't easy. But in those moments, I knew I was doing something meaningful. I was giving them hope, even if only for a little while."

Nyomi nodded, feeling the weight of the memory settle in her chest. Mrs. Montgomery's resilience, her dedication—it was a lesson in the power of empathy, in the difference a single person could make in the lives of others.

Mr. Oswald: A Dream of Freedom

A few days later, Nyomi found herself sitting with Mr. Oswald, a former pilot with a passion for aviation. He often spoke of his days in the air, of the freedom he felt as he soared above the clouds. His eyes would light up as he described the thrill of flight, the sense of adventure that had filled his youth.

"Flying... it was like nothing else," Mr. Oswald said, his voice filled with nostalgia. "Up there, everything felt so small, so insignificant. It was just me, the sky, and the endless horizon."

Nyomi smiled, her heart touched by the excitement in his voice. "It sounds incredible. Like you were free from everything."

He nodded, a wistful look in his eyes. "It was. Those were the best days of my life."

Sensing his longing, Nyomi reached out, placing her hand gently over his. She felt the familiar warmth of her powers, the gentle pull of his memory drawing her in.

In an instant, she was transported to the cockpit of a plane, the roar of the engines filling her ears as Mr. Oswald guided the aircraft through the open sky. She could feel the exhilaration in his heart, the sense of freedom that filled him as he soared above the world.

The sky stretched out before them, a vast expanse of blue and white, the clouds like soft pillows beneath the plane. Nyomi could feel the joy in Mr. Oswald's heart, the thrill of being weightless, untethered from the worries and constraints of life below.

As the memory unfolded, she saw moments of adventure and camaraderie—the friendships he had forged with his fellow pilots, the laughter they shared, the challenges they faced together. Each memory was a testament to the freedom he had found in the skies, a reminder of the dreams that had shaped his life.

When the vision faded, Nyomi opened her eyes, her heart filled with a sense of wonder. "Thank you for sharing that with me," she whispered, her voice filled with gratitude. "I feel like I was up there with you, soaring through the sky."

Mr. Oswald chuckled, his eyes twinkling with joy. "It was a good life.

And remembering it... well, it makes me feel young again."

As she left him that day, Nyomi felt a renewed sense of awe for the lives she was touching. Each story, each memory, was a reminder of the beauty and resilience of the human spirit, a testament to the dreams and experiences that made each person unique.

The Weight of Responsibility

With each memory she touched, Nyomi felt the weight of her powers growing heavier. She was learning to master her abilities, to use them with precision and care, but the emotional toll was beginning to build. Each memory left an imprint on her heart, a fragment of the resident's life that lingered long after the connection ended.

There were days when she felt overwhelmed, when the memories became a tapestry of emotions that filled her mind, making it difficult to focus on her own thoughts. She began to realize that her empathy, while a gift, was also a burden—a responsibility that required strength and resilience.

One evening, as she sat alone in her room, she opened her journal and began to write:

Today, I witnessed moments of courage and sorrow, of dreams and memories that shaped lives. Each story is a piece of the human heart, a reminder of the resilience it takes to live fully. But with each memory, I feel the weight of my powers growing. It's as if their emotions are becoming part of me, a quilt of experiences woven together.

How do I carry this responsibility? How do I honor their memories without losing myself?

As she closed her journal, she felt a quiet resolve settling within her. She understood now that her powers were not just about comfort and healing; they were a bridge to understanding, a way to honor the lives of those around her. And as she continued her journey, she promised herself that she would carry each memory with care, that she would let each story strengthen her own heart.

Nyomi felt her role deepening each day at Riverview Senior Center. She had become more than just a volunteer to many of the residents; she was a confidante, a presence they could trust. Her Butterfly Touch had evolved from a mysterious power to a skill she wielded with intention, each connection an experience that brought comfort and clarity to those she helped. But with each memory she touched, Nyomi found herself growing more aware of the gravity of her powers, the emotional toll they exacted.

A Memory of Lost Dreams with Mrs. Hargrove

One quiet afternoon, Nyomi noticed Mrs. Hargrove sitting alone in the garden, her gaze fixed on a small, delicate flower struggling to bloom. There was a sadness in her eyes, a longing that seemed to reach back through time.

Nyomi approached her gently, sensing that Mrs. Hargrove was lost in thought. "It's beautiful, isn't it?" Nyomi said, nodding toward the flower.

Mrs. Hargrove sighed, her expression wistful. "Yes, it is. It reminds me of my daughter... she had the gentlest soul. Always finding beauty in the simplest things."

Nyomi's heart softened at her words, and without a second thought, she reached out, placing her hand over Mrs. Hargrove's. The warmth of her powers stirred, the Butterfly Touch responding to the deep emotions hidden within the memory.

In an instant, Nyomi was drawn into the past, standing in a sunlit garden filled with flowers in full bloom. She could see a young woman kneeling among the blossoms, her smile radiant, her laughter filling the air. Nyomi could feel Mrs. Hargrove's pride and joy, the love that filled her heart as she watched her daughter.

But then the memory shifted, the colors fading, and Nyomi sensed a sorrow beneath the surface. She saw a hospital room, dimly lit, the young woman lying in a bed, her face pale and her breathing shallow. The grief in Mrs. Hargrove's heart was overwhelming, a loss that had left an unhealed wound.

When Nyomi returned to the present, her eyes were misty, her heart heavy with the sorrow she had witnessed. Mrs. Hargrove looked at her, her own eyes glistening with unshed tears.

"Thank you, dear," she whispered, her voice trembling. "It's been so long since I let myself remember her like that."

Nyomi nodded, her voice soft. "She was beautiful. And she's still with you, in every memory, every flower."

Mrs. Hargrove smiled, a bittersweet expression. "You're right. She always loved flowers. Maybe that's why I come here —to feel close to her again."

As she left Mrs. Hargrove, Nyomi felt the weight of the memory settle within her, a quiet ache that reminded her of the fragility of life and the resilience it took to carry on. She realized that her powers weren't just about revisiting the past; they were about helping people find peace, even in moments of sorrow.

Mr. Jameson's Gratitude and a Lesson in Resilience

Over the weeks, Mr. Jameson had grown more open with Nyomi, his gruff exterior softening as he allowed her to see the man beneath the silence. She noticed him seeking her out in the mornings, a small gesture that spoke volumes about the trust he had come to place in her.

One day, as they sat together in the courtyard, he turned to her, his expression unusually serious. "You know, I never thought I'd feel this way again," he said, his voice low. "After losing so many people... I didn't think I had anything left to share."

Nyomi looked at him, her gaze filled with empathy. "But you do, Mr. Jameson. Your story, your experiences—they matter. They're part of you, and they deserve to be heard."

He nodded slowly, his eyes softening. "I think I forgot that somewhere along the way. But talking to you... it's reminded me of who I was, of what I stood for."

Nyomi reached out, placing a gentle hand on his shoulder. "You're still that person, Mr. Jameson. Your courage, your resilience—it's all still there. And I'm honored to know that side of you."

He looked away, a hint of emotion in his eyes. "Thank you, Nyomi. I don't say it enough, but thank you."

As she left him that day, Nyomi felt a sense of pride and gratitude. Mr. Jameson's resilience, his ability to carry on despite the losses he had endured, was a testament to the strength of the human spirit. And as she walked down the hallway, she felt his story become a part of her own, a reminder of the bravery it took to keep going, even when life felt overwhelming.

Mrs. Montgomery's Journey of Healing

Mrs. Montgomery had always been open with Nyomi, sharing stories of her days as a nurse, the moments of triumph and heartbreak she had witnessed. But there was one story she had never shared, one that lingered in the corners of her memory like a shadow.

One evening, as they sat together in the quiet of the activity room, Mrs. Montgomery looked at Nyomi, her expression somber. "There's something I've never told anyone... something that's haunted me for years."

Nyomi nodded, her gaze steady. "You can tell me, Mrs. Montgomery.

I'm here to listen."

The elderly woman took a deep breath, her hands trembling slightly. "During the war, there was a young soldier... barely eighteen, just a boy. He came in with a wound, nothing too serious, but he was so frightened. I sat with him, held his hand, and promised him he'd be all right."

Nyomi placed her hand over Mrs. Montgomery's, feeling the warmth of her powers responding to the depth of her sorrow. She allowed the connection to deepen, feeling herself drawn into the memory.

In an instant, she was in a bustling hospital, standing beside Mrs. Montgomery as she tended to the young soldier. Nyomi could feel the compassion in her heart, the determination to bring comfort in the face of fear. She watched as Mrs. Montgomery held the boy's hand, her voice gentle, her presence a source of reassurance.

But then, the memory shifted, and Nyomi felt a wave of guilt and sorrow. The boy had died later that night, his fear unrelieved, and Mrs. Montgomery had never forgiven herself for not being able to save him.

When the memory faded, Nyomi opened her eyes, her heart aching with the weight of Mrs. Montgomery's guilt. She looked at the elderly woman, her voice filled with empathy. "You did everything you could, Mrs. Montgomery. You gave him comfort, even in his final moments. That was a gift, one that he carried with him."

Mrs. Montgomery's eyes filled with tears, her expression softening. "Thank you, dear. I needed to hear that... after all these years, I needed to let go."

As Nyomi hugged her, she felt a sense of closure, a peace that settled over them both. Mrs. Montgomery's journey of healing had come full circle, a reminder that even in moments of loss, there was room for forgiveness and grace.

Mr. Oswald's Final Flight

One morning, as Nyomi prepared to leave the center, Mr. Oswald stopped her, his gaze filled with a quiet determination. "I want you to see something," he said, his voice firm.

Curious, Nyomi followed him to the garden, where he pulled a small, worn photograph from his pocket. It was a picture of him as a young man, standing beside a plane, his face filled with pride and excitement.

"That was my first flight," he said, his voice soft. "The moment I knew that flying was what I was meant to do."

Nyomi reached out, placing her hand over his, allowing the Butterfly Touch to connect with the memory. She was transported to the past, standing in the open sky as Mr. Oswald took to the air for the first time. She felt his exhilaration, the thrill of freedom as he soared above the clouds, the world unfolding beneath him like a vast, limitless canvas.

As the memory faded, Nyomi opened her eyes, her heart filled with a sense of wonder. "You were incredible, Mr. Oswald. Your passion, your spirit—it's still alive, even now."

He looked at her, a gentle smile on his face. "Thank you, Nyomi. I needed to remember that part of myself, to know that my dreams were real."

As they shared a moment of silence, Nyomi felt a deep sense of gratitude for the lives she was touching, for the memories she was privileged to witness. Each story was a reminder of the resilience and beauty of the human spirit, a testament to the dreams that had shaped each resident's life.

A Growing Sense of Responsibility

With each memory she touched, Nyomi felt her powers becoming both a blessing and a burden. She was learning to master her abilities, to use them with care, but the weight of the emotions she absorbed was beginning to build.

In quiet moments, she found herself reflecting on the lives she had touched, the stories that had become a part of her. She realized that her powers required both strength and humility, that empathy was her greatest gift but also her greatest challenge.

One evening, as she sat alone, she opened her journal and wrote:

Today, I witnessed moments of courage, of heartbreak, of dreams fulfilled and dreams lost. Each memory is a piece of a person's heart, a reminder of the resilience it takes to live fully. But with each memory, I feel the weight of my powers growing, the responsibility becoming heavier.

How do I carry this gift without losing myself? How do I honor their stories while staying true to my own?

As she closed her journal, Nyomi felt a sense of resolve. She knew that her powers were more than just a tool; they were a bridge to understanding, a way to honor the lives of those around her. And as she continued her journey, she promised herself that she would carry each story with respect, letting each memory strengthen her own heart.

A Final Reflection and Acceptance

In the weeks that followed, Nyomi continued to work at the center, balancing her role as both a healer and a friend. She had learned to approach each memory with reverence, to let each story become a part of her without overwhelming her own sense of self.

Through her Butterfly Touch, she had witnessed the strength and vulnerability of the human spirit, the beauty of lives lived fully. She had seen courage in Mr. Jameson's resilience, compassion in Mrs. Montgomery's healing touch, and freedom in Mr. Oswald's dreams of flight.

And as she looked out over the garden one evening, watching the sun set over the flowers, Nyomi felt a sense of peace. She understood now that her powers were not just about reliving the past; they were about connecting with the essence of each person, about honoring the lives they had led.

As she closed her eyes, she made a silent promise to herself—to carry each story with gratitude, to let each memory be a lesson in empathy and resilience. And as she opened her eyes to the fading light, she knew that her journey was just beginning, that the lives she touched would shape her own path in ways she had yet to discover.

CHAPTER 11: A SUMMER OF TRANSFORMATION

The days grew longer and warmer as summer at Riverview Senior Center neared its end. With each sunrise, Nyomi felt the season slipping away, but her bond with the center and the people within it only grew stronger. She had arrived here uncertain, unsure of what she could offer or who she was becoming, yet now, just a few weeks later, she found herself feeling like an integral part of the community, someone the residents and staff relied on and looked forward to seeing every day.

Her mornings began with a familiar routine: a quiet coffee with Sarah, a smile and greeting to each resident, small gestures that had become second nature. The residents knew her now—not just as a volunteer, but as a friend, a confidante, a gentle presence they could count on.

But it was more than that. Nyomi had become the heart of Riverview, a steady source of comfort and warmth. Her Butterfly Touch had allowed her to witness their stories, to honor their memories, and through that connection, she had woven herself into the very fabric of their lives.

Indispensable to the Community

One morning, as Nyomi entered the dining hall, she noticed the lively energy filling the room. Several residents greeted her with smiles, calling her over to their tables, each wanting a moment of her time. Mr. Oswald waved her over, a familiar sparkle in his eyes.

"Good morning, Nyomi," he said, holding up his newspaper. "I saved a spot for you right here." He patted the seat beside him, a gesture that warmed her heart.

She took the seat, glancing around at the bustling room. Over the weeks, she had formed a unique bond with each resident, each connection as varied and intricate as the individuals themselves. Mrs. Hargrove often sought her out in the garden, asking for help with planting new flowers; Mr. Jameson greeted her every morning with a nod and a quiet "Thank you," a testament to the trust they had built.

And then there was Mrs. Montgomery, who always made a point of saving a cup of tea for Nyomi, a small ritual that had become a part of their mornings together.

"Have you thought about staying on with us?" Mrs. Montgomery asked that morning, her voice hopeful. "The place wouldn't be the same without you."

Nyomi felt a surge of emotion at the words. She hadn't considered how much she meant to the residents, how deeply she had embedded herself into their lives.

Mr. Oswald chuckled, his eyes twinkling. "You can't leave us now, Nyomi. Who else will listen to my stories about flying?"

Nyomi laughed, feeling a warmth settle in her chest. She realized that she had become more than just a visitor to these people; she was part of their daily lives, a constant presence that had brought light into their routines. And as the summer drew to a close, she felt the bittersweet weight of saying goodbye, of knowing that her time here had changed her— and them—in ways she hadn't anticipated.

Reflecting on Her Journey

As the last days of summer approached, Nyomi found herself reflecting on her time at Riverview. She remembered the uncertainty she had felt when she first arrived, the hesitation she had about using her powers. She had been unsure of her abilities, fearful of overstepping or causing unintended harm.

But each moment here had taught her something, shaping her into the person she was now. She recalled her first true connection with Mrs. Hargrove, when she had allowed the Butterfly Touch to soothe the woman's heartache. That experience had shown her the gentle power of her abilities, the way they could bring comfort without causing disruption.

Then there were the memories she had shared with Mr. Jameson, the moments of silence and trust that had gradually blossomed into a friendship. She thought of Mrs. Montgomery's stories, of the compassion and healing that had defined her life as a nurse. Each memory, each connection, had been a lesson in empathy and resilience, a reminder of the strength it took to live fully.

As she sat in the garden, her journal open on her lap, she began to write:

This summer has taught me more than I ever could have imagined. I've learned that my powers are not just a gift, but a responsibility—a bridge to understanding the lives around me. Each story, each memory, has become a part of me, woven into my heart.

I came here to help, to bring comfort, but I realize now that I have received so much in return. I am stronger, more compassionate, and more connected to the world than ever before.

As she closed her journal, Nyomi felt a quiet sense of fulfillment. She had grown in ways she hadn't expected, finding her own strength in the memories and lives of those she had touched. And as she looked out at the garden, she felt ready to move forward, to carry these lessons with her into the future.

A Defining Moment with Sarah

Sarah had become a steady presence in Nyomi's life, a mentor and friend who had guided her through the complexities of working with people who carried the weight of the past. Their bond had grown through shared experiences, through moments of quiet understanding and mutual respect.

One evening, as they finished up the day's work, Sarah surprised Nyomi by inviting her out to the garden for a quiet chat. The two of them sat side by side, the warm evening air filled with the scent of flowers, the soft hum of crickets in the background.

"I wanted to thank you, Nyomi," Sarah began, her voice soft but sincere. "You've done something incredible here. I don't know if you realize it, but you've changed this place."

Nyomi looked at her, her heart swelling with emotion. "I don't know... I feel like they've changed me just as much."

Sarah smiled, a hint of admiration in her gaze. "That's what makes you special, Nyomi. You have this way of connecting, of listening. It's something rare."

They sat in silence for a moment, the weight of Sarah's words settling over them. Then, after a pause, Sarah spoke again, her tone more serious.

"When I first came here, I didn't think I'd stay long," she admitted, her gaze distant. "I was so used to moving, to not putting down roots. But this place... it grew on me. And so did you."

Nyomi felt a rush of gratitude, a deep appreciation for the woman beside her. "Thank you, Sarah. You've taught me so much... more than you realize."

Sarah nodded, her eyes softening. "And you've reminded me of why I do this. Why it matters to connect, to care. You're going to do amazing things, Nyomi. Just remember to carry that heart of yours with you, wherever you go."

In that moment, Nyomi felt their bond solidify, a quiet, unspoken understanding that would remain with her long after she left Riverview. Sarah had become more than a mentor; she was a friend, someone who had seen her at her most vulnerable and had guided her with compassion and wisdom.

As they sat together under the fading light, Nyomi felt a sense of peace, a calm that came from knowing she had left a mark on this place—and that it had left a mark on her, too.

The Farewell: A Community's Gratitude

On her last day at Riverview, the residents and staff gathered to bid Nyomi farewell. The dining hall was filled with smiles, laughter, and the soft murmur of gratitude as each person shared a memory, a moment that had meant something to them.

Mrs. Hargrove held her hand tightly, her eyes misty. "You brought me peace, Nyomi. I'll always be grateful for that."

Mr. Oswald gave her a warm embrace, his voice filled with pride. "You reminded me of who I was, of the dreams I once had. Thank you."

Mr. Jameson, usually reserved, gave her a small, rare smile. "I don't say this often, but... you've done good here, kid. Don't ever forget that."

As she moved through the room, receiving hugs and kind words, Nyomi felt a profound sense of fulfillment. She had come here hoping to make a difference, but she hadn't anticipated the depth of connection she would find, the way this place had become a part of her.

When it was time to go, Sarah walked her to the door, her expression filled with pride and warmth. "Take care of yourself, Nyomi. And remember—you're always welcome here."

Nyomi nodded, a bittersweet smile on her face. "Thank you, Sarah. For everything."

As she stepped outside, she looked back one last time, the faces of the residents and staff etched in her memory, a collection of lives that would remain with her forever. She had found her place here, her purpose, and as she walked away, she felt ready to face whatever lay ahead, carrying the strength and lessons of Riverview with her.

Reflections on Growth

As the summer came to a close, Nyomi spent time reflecting on her journey, on the lessons she had learned and the ways she had changed. She felt more grounded, more connected to the world around her. She had grown in empathy, in courage, and in her understanding of her own power.

Looking back, she saw each moment as a stepping stone, a part of the path that had led her here. She knew now that her powers were not just a gift, but a bridge to connection, a way to honor the lives she touched.

And as she looked toward the future, she felt a quiet confidence, a sense of purpose that would guide her on her next journey. Riverview had been her beginning, the place where she had found her strength and her calling, and she knew that she would carry it with her, wherever she went.

As Nyomi's last week at Riverview approached, the reality of her departure settled over her like a bittersweet weight. She found herself lingering in her interactions with the residents, savoring each memory they shared, each smile and nod that had become a part of her daily life. The center had shaped her in ways she hadn't anticipated, and with each passing day, she became more aware of the profound impact these experiences had left on her heart.

A Morning with Mr. Oswald: Dreams Beyond the Sky

On one of her final mornings, Nyomi found Mr. Oswald waiting by the large window in the activity room, gazing out at the clear sky. She approached him, noticing a wistful expression on his face.

"It's a perfect day for flying," he said, his voice carrying a hint of longing.

Nyomi smiled, nodding. "Would you take me with you, if you could?"

He chuckled, his eyes twinkling. "Oh, I'd take you soaring above the clouds, show you the world from up high. There's a freedom up there that's hard to describe."

She placed a hand on his arm, sensing his desire to relive those days. With a gentle touch, she activated her Butterfly Touch, allowing the warmth to flow from her fingertips. In a soft, dreamlike vision, she found herself alongside Mr. Oswald, piloting a plane high above the earth, his spirit alive with excitement. The sky stretched endlessly around them, a vast blue horizon filled with possibility.

As the vision faded, Mr. Oswald took a deep breath, his gaze softening. "Thank you, Nyomi," he whispered. "You've given me my wings back, if only for a little while."

The moment left Nyomi filled with gratitude, both for the memories he had shared with her and for the resilience he had shown. He had faced so many challenges, yet he continued to find joy in the simplest things. In his smile, she saw the courage it took to keep dreaming, even when life seemed to have taken away so much.

A Visit with Mrs. Hargrove: Finding Peace

Later that day, Nyomi joined Mrs. Hargrove in the garden. They sat together in silence, surrounded by flowers that Mrs. Hargrove had carefully tended to over the summer. Nyomi admired the way each bloom seemed to reflect a piece of the woman's heart, a testament to her nurturing spirit.

"I think of her sometimes," Mrs. Hargrove said suddenly, her voice quiet. "My daughter. It's like she's still here, in these flowers, in the beauty she saw in the world."

Nyomi felt the familiar warmth of her powers in her hands, the gentle pull of Mrs. Hargrove's memory. She placed a hand over Mrs. Hargrove's, allowing herself to connect to the woman's past. In a soft vision, she saw the two of them—mother and daughter—tending to a garden together, laughter filling the air as they worked side by side. The love between them was palpable, a bond that had transcended time.

When the vision faded, Mrs. Hargrove's eyes were filled with tears, but a gentle smile softened her face. "Thank you, dear," she whispered. "You've helped me remember her the way she was. Happy, vibrant... just like these flowers."

As Nyomi hugged her, she felt the peace radiate from Mrs. Hargrove's heart. She had given the woman a precious gift—a chance to reconnect with a loved one who had never truly left her side.

A Day with Mrs. Montgomery: The Legacy of Healing

The next afternoon, Nyomi spent time with Mrs. Montgomery in the activity room, helping her organize books and materials for a weekly crafting session. Mrs. Montgomery was in high spirits, her laughter filling the room as she recounted stories of her time as a nurse.

"You know, I never thought I'd be here, in a place like this," Mrs. Montgomery said, her eyes twinkling. "But life has a funny way of surprising you."

Nyomi smiled, sensing that Mrs. Montgomery had something more she wanted to share. "What do you mean?" she asked, her curiosity piqued.

Mrs. Montgomery sighed, a thoughtful look crossing her face. "I spent so many years caring for others, so many nights by their bedsides, helping them find peace in their final moments. I thought I'd end up just like them, in a quiet room, without anyone left to remember me."

She looked at Nyomi, her gaze filled with gratitude. "But then you came along, dear, and you've reminded me that there's still so much beauty left to experience."

Nyomi felt a surge of emotion at her words. "It's an honor to be here with you, Mrs. Montgomery. You've shown me the power of healing, of kindness. It's something I'll carry with me always."

The older woman patted her hand, her smile soft. "You have a gift, Nyomi. Don't ever let anyone tell you otherwise."

In that moment, Nyomi felt a sense of validation, a quiet assurance that her journey was just beginning. She realized that Mrs. Montgomery's legacy of healing was something she could carry forward, a way to honor the lives she had touched.

Sarah's Surprise and A Final Moment of Connection

As Nyomi wrapped up her tasks one evening, Sarah approached her, a rare smile on her usually composed face. "Come with me," she said, leading Nyomi to the quiet of the garden. There, beneath the soft glow of lantern lights, Sarah had set up a small table with a pot of tea, a simple but heartfelt gesture.

"I thought we could have one last tea together," Sarah said, her tone gentle.

Nyomi felt a lump form in her throat as she sat down, the weight of the moment settling over her. "Thank you, Sarah. For everything."

Sarah poured the tea, her hands steady but her gaze thoughtful. "You've done more than I could have imagined, Nyomi. I knew you had potential, but seeing the way you connect with the residents... it's something rare. I don't say this often, but I'm proud of you."

Nyomi felt a warmth spread through her chest, a sense of validation she hadn't realized she had been waiting for. "I've learned so much from you, Sarah. Your strength, your compassion—it's changed me."

They shared a quiet moment of companionship, sipping tea under the stars. For the first time, Nyomi felt like an equal to Sarah, a person who had earned her respect and friendship through shared experience and mutual trust.

When they parted ways that evening, Nyomi knew that she and Sarah would always share a bond, one built on the journey they had walked together, a journey of healing, growth, and friendship.

The Farewell Gathering: A Community United

On her final day at Riverview, Nyomi entered the dining hall to find it decorated with streamers and balloons, a lively celebration organized by the staff and residents in her honor. The room was filled with laughter and smiles, each face reflecting the joy and gratitude Nyomi had brought into their lives.

Mrs. Hargrove handed her a small bouquet of flowers, a token of the garden they had tended together. "You'll always have a place here, dear," she said, her voice filled with emotion. "Whenever you need a reminder of what you've done, just think of these flowers."

Mr. Jameson approached her with a rare smile, handing her a worn firefighter badge, a symbol of his past. "You've earned this," he said quietly. "You brought me back to myself, helped me remember the man I used to be."

Mrs. Montgomery gave her a warm hug, pressing a small locket into her hand. "For you," she whispered. "A reminder that you carry the strength of those you've helped."

Each resident, each staff member, offered her a token, a memory of their time together. As she held these gifts in her hands, Nyomi felt a deep sense of fulfillment, a realization that she had left an indelible mark on this place—and it had left a mark on her as well.

Final Reflections: Embracing Her Growth

That evening, as she sat in her room, Nyomi looked back on her summer at Riverview, her heart filled with gratitude and pride. She remembered the uncertain girl who had arrived here, unsure of her powers, of her place in the world. She had grown into someone stronger, someone who understood the depth of her empathy and the responsibility that came with her gifts.

Each resident, each memory, had taught her something invaluable. Mr. Oswald's dreams had reminded her of the courage to soar, Mrs. Hargrove's love had shown her the power of memory, Mrs. Montgomery's healing touch had reinforced the beauty of compassion, and Mr. Jameson's resilience had inspired her to carry on, even in the face of pain.

As she wrote in her journal, she felt a sense of closure, a readiness to face whatever lay ahead. She knew that her journey was only beginning, that Riverview had been the first step in a path that would lead her to new challenges and new connections.

This summer has changed me in ways I never expected. I have seen courage, resilience, love, and loss, and each moment has become a part of who I am. I will carry these memories with me, let them shape me, and honor the lives I have touched.

As she closed her journal, Nyomi felt a quiet resolve, a certainty that her powers were more than just a gift—they were a bridge to the lives around her, a way to connect and understand. And as she prepared to leave Riverview, she knew that she was ready for whatever came next, her heart strengthened by the lives she had touched and the lessons she had learned.

A Final Goodbye

On the morning of her departure, Nyomi took one last walk through the center, each hallway and room filled with memories of the summer. She stopped by the garden, inhaling the scent of flowers she and Mrs. Hargrove had tended, feeling a bittersweet warmth in her chest.

As she turned to leave, Sarah approached her, a proud smile on her face. "You'll do great things, Nyomi. I know it."

Nyomi hugged her tightly, a final moment of connection with the mentor who had guided her with strength and compassion. "Thank you, Sarah. I'll never forget this place—or the people I've met."

With a last wave to the residents and staff gathered to see her off, Nyomi walked away, her heart full, her mind brimming with memories, and her spirit ready for whatever lay ahead.

The last few days of summer at Riverview Senior Center were filled with a unique blend of warmth and sadness. Every corner of the center reminded Nyomi of moments shared, stories uncovered, and lives that had touched her own in ways she hadn't expected. The hallways, once unfamiliar, now felt like a second home, each resident a member of a new family she hadn't known she was missing.

As she prepared to leave, Nyomi felt a need to spend time with each resident who had become a part of her heart. Each goodbye carried its own weight, a piece of herself that she would leave behind, just as they had left their memories with her.

A Memory of Love and Laughter with Mrs. Hargrove

On her second-to-last day, Nyomi sought out Mrs. Hargrove in the garden, where they had spent so many afternoons together. The older woman was seated near her favorite roses, gently trimming away the withered petals, her hands moving with the ease of someone who had tended to gardens for a lifetime.

When she noticed Nyomi, Mrs. Hargrove smiled, her face lighting up with a warmth that never failed to touch Nyomi's heart. "I was hoping you'd stop by. I have something for you."

Nyomi sat down beside her, curiosity sparkling in her eyes. Mrs. Hargrove reached into her gardening apron and pulled out a small, intricately carved wooden butterfly. Its wings were painted in shades of blue and lavender, delicate and vibrant.

"I made this with my husband," Mrs. Hargrove said softly, her voice carrying a trace of nostalgia. "We used to carve little things like this together—flowers, birds, butterflies. He loved butterflies."

Nyomi took the butterfly, her fingers tracing the delicate curves of the wings. "It's beautiful," she whispered, her heart swelling with emotion. "Thank you, Mrs. Hargrove."

Mrs. Hargrove patted her hand, a bittersweet smile on her face. "You brought back so many memories, dear. Every time I see these flowers, I'll think of you, and all the memories you helped me remember."

Nyomi felt the familiar warmth of her Butterfly Touch stirring within her, and she reached out, gently placing her hand over Mrs. Hargrove's. This time, the vision was gentle, a memory of a summer day in the past when Mrs. Hargrove and her husband had worked side by side in the garden, laughter and love filling the air.

As the vision faded, Nyomi saw tears in Mrs. Hargrove's eyes, but there was a peace there too, a quiet acceptance that had come from the memories they had shared.

"Thank you for everything," Nyomi said, her voice barely above a whisper. "You've taught me so much about love, about cherishing the moments we have."

Mrs. Hargrove nodded, her gaze soft. "Remember that, dear. Life is precious, and love is what makes it worthwhile. Carry that with you."

As Nyomi hugged her tightly, she felt the weight of their shared moments settle in her heart, a gift she would carry forward, a reminder of the beauty of connection.

An Afternoon with Mr. Oswald: Dreams of Freedom

Later that day, Nyomi found Mr. Oswald sitting in the activity room, leafing through an old album filled with photographs of his time as a pilot. He looked up when she entered, a smile breaking across his face.

"Ah, my favorite co-pilot," he greeted her, his voice filled with affection. "Come, sit with me. I've got something to show you."

Nyomi sat beside him, leaning in as he pointed to a photograph of himself as a young man, standing proudly beside a small plane. His eyes were alight with excitement, the thrill of adventure.

"This was taken right before my first solo flight," he said, a hint of pride in his voice. "There's nothing like that feeling—the freedom, the open sky, knowing that you're in control of your own path."

Nyomi smiled, feeling a pang of sadness that he no longer had that freedom. "It must have been incredible."

He nodded, his gaze distant. "It was. But life has its seasons, and I'm grateful for every moment I had up there."

After a pause, he looked at her, his expression turning serious. "Nyomi, you've given me a second chance to relive those days, to feel that freedom again. You've shown me that our dreams don't die; they live on in the people we share them with."

Tears prickled in Nyomi's eyes as she took his hand. "Your dreams are still alive, Mr. Oswald. Every story, every memory— it's a part of you that will never fade."

He squeezed her hand, his voice soft. "Thank you, Nyomi. You have a rare gift. Use it wisely, and don't let anything hold you back."

As they shared a quiet moment, Nyomi felt a sense of resolve building within her. Mr. Oswald had faced the end of one chapter in his life with grace and acceptance, and his words were a reminder that she, too, could carry her dreams forward.

Mr. Jameson's Farewell: A Test of Trust

As her final day approached, Nyomi found herself wanting to spend time with Mr. Jameson, the man who had once been so distant but had come to trust her in a way that felt profound. She found him sitting alone in the courtyard, his gaze fixed on the horizon, a quiet strength in his posture.

When she sat beside him, he didn't say anything at first, but she could feel his presence, steady and unwavering.

"Leaving soon, aren't you?" he finally said, his voice gruff but tinged with a sadness she hadn't expected.

Nyomi nodded, her heart heavy. "Yes, but I'll carry all of you with me." He looked at her, his gaze penetrating. "You've done something here, Nyomi. Something no one else has. You've made us feel... seen, understood."

Nyomi felt a lump in her throat as she reached out, placing her hand on his shoulder. "Thank you for trusting me, Mr. Jameson. It means more than you know."

After a long pause, he reached into his pocket, pulling out a worn leather notebook. "This was mine when I first joined the force," he said quietly. "I used it to keep track of every fire, every rescue, every lesson I learned. I want you to have it."

Nyomi accepted the notebook, her fingers brushing over the faded cover. It was a piece of his history, a part of the man he had been, and she felt honored to be entrusted with it.

"Thank you, Mr. Jameson," she whispered, her voice filled with emotion. "I'll take care of it, just as I'll carry your strength with me."

As they sat together in silence, Nyomi felt the weight of his story settle in her heart, a reminder of the resilience it took to keep going, to honor the past without letting it define the future.

An Evening with Mrs. Montgomery: The Power of Healing

On her last evening, Nyomi found Mrs. Montgomery in the quiet of the library, surrounded by books that had become like friends to her. The older woman looked up with a smile, motioning for Nyomi to join her.

"I thought we could read together one last time," Mrs. Montgomery said, her voice soft. "You know, these books have been my comfort, my way of finding peace."

Nyomi settled beside her, and they began to read, the words flowing between them like a gentle river. As they turned the pages, Mrs. Montgomery began to share stories of the patients she had cared for, the lives she had touched, the moments of healing that had brought her purpose.

"You've given me something precious, Nyomi," she said, her gaze filled with gratitude. "A chance to remember the good I've done, to see the lives I've touched."

Nyomi felt the warmth of her Butterfly Touch in her hands, and she gently placed her hand over Mrs. Montgomery's, allowing the connection to deepen. In a vision, she saw Mrs. Montgomery in a bustling hospital, her face filled with compassion as she tended to patients, offering comfort in their moments of need.

When the vision faded, Mrs. Montgomery looked at her, a tear slipping down her cheek. "Thank you, dear. You've helped me find peace."

As they hugged, Nyomi felt the strength of Mrs. Montgomery's legacy, a healing force that would remain with her, a reminder of the power of compassion.

A Final Evening with Sarah: A Bond Solidified

On her last evening, Sarah invited Nyomi out to the garden, where they shared a quiet dinner under the stars. The two of them sat in comfortable silence, their bond having grown beyond words, a friendship built on shared experience and mutual respect.

After a while, Sarah looked at her, a smile softening her usual stoic expression. "I don't know how you did it, Nyomi, but you've left a mark on this place. On all of us."

Nyomi felt her heart swell with emotion. "You've been a huge part of that, Sarah. I don't know if I could have done any of this without you."

Sarah reached out, squeezing her hand. "Promise me you'll keep in touch, that you'll let us know where life takes you."

"I promise," Nyomi said, her voice steady. "And thank you, for everything."

They sat together under the stars, a quiet companionship that needed no words, and in that moment, Nyomi knew that Sarah was more than a mentor

—she was family.

A Final Goodbye

The next morning, as Nyomi prepared to leave, the residents and staff gathered to see her off, each offering her a piece of their heart, a memory to carry with her. Mrs. Hargrove gave her a small bouquet of flowers, a reminder of the garden they had shared. Mr. Oswald handed her an old aviator's pin, a symbol of the freedom he had cherished. Mr. Jameson offered her a final nod, a gesture that spoke of respect and gratitude.

Sarah embraced her, whispering, "Go do great things, Nyomi. And remember, you'll always have a place here."

With a last wave, Nyomi left Riverview, her heart full of memories, her spirit stronger than ever. She walked away knowing that she had left a piece of herself here, just as they had given her pieces of their lives to carry forward.

As she stepped into the next chapter of her life, she felt ready, her heart a quilt of stories and experiences that would guide her wherever she went.

CHAPTER 12: A NEW SCHOOL YEAR

The first day back at Riverside High felt surreal to Nyomi. The familiar hallways, once an intimidating labyrinth of faces and voices, now seemed smaller, less overwhelming. She noticed things she hadn't before—the nervous glances of younger students clutching their schedules, the hurried strides of teachers balancing coffee and lesson plans, and the buzzing energy that filled the air as everyone settled back into the rhythm of a new school year.

For the first time, she didn't feel like she was just another student blending into the crowd. She walked with a quiet confidence, her steps surer, her gaze steadier. Riverview Senior Center had changed her. The lessons she had learned there, the resilience she had witnessed in the residents, had become a part of her, woven into the fabric of who she was.

As she walked to her locker, Nyomi's thoughts drifted back to the summer. She could still feel the warmth of Mrs. Hargrove's hand in hers, the weight of Mr. Jameson's worn notebook, the freedom in Mr. Oswald's dreams of flight. Each memory felt like a guidepost, a reminder that she was capable of much more than she had ever believed. And as she stood in the bustling hallway, she realized that she was ready to make this school year different, to carry forward the confidence and empathy she had gained.

The Decision to Mentor New Students

That morning, as Nyomi sat in homeroom, her teacher, Ms. Greene, made an announcement about a new mentorship program. "As you know, we have a large group of new students this year, and we're looking for volunteers to help them transition smoothly into Riverside High," Ms. Greene explained, scanning the room. "If you're interested in mentoring, please sign up after class."

Nyomi's heart quickened at the mention of mentoring. She remembered how lost and unsure she had felt on her first day of high school, wishing for someone to guide her through the unfamiliar territory. But more than that, she thought of Riverview and the connections she had built over the summer. She had learned the power of empathy, of reaching out and offering support. And now, she felt compelled to extend that compassion to others who might need it.

When class ended, Nyomi made her way to Ms. Greene's desk, where a sign-up sheet was waiting. She hesitated for only a moment before writing her name in bold letters.

As she walked away, she felt a surge of purpose. She was ready to give back, to be the person she had needed when she first arrived at Riverside. Mentoring wasn't just a responsibility; it was an opportunity to put her newfound confidence and empathy into action, to use what she had learned to make a difference in the lives of others.

A New Perspective on Riverside High

In the days that followed, Nyomi found herself viewing Riverside High with fresh eyes. The things that had once felt daunting—crowded hallways, social cliques, the endless assignments—now seemed smaller, less significant. She no longer felt weighed down by the need to fit in or meet others' expectations. Instead, she moved through the school with a quiet assurance, her focus on the people around her, on the chance to make a genuine connection.

Her interactions with her classmates took on a new depth as well. She found herself listening more intently, noticing the subtle emotions behind people's words and expressions. When her friend Callie mentioned feeling overwhelmed by her classes, Nyomi sensed the underlying anxiety and offered words of encouragement, drawing on her experiences at Riverview.

One afternoon, as she walked past the library, she noticed a group of new students huddled together, their faces a mixture of excitement and nerves. She smiled, remembering how she had felt on her first day, the uncertainty that had filled her. But now, with her newfound purpose, she saw herself in a different light—a source of support, a steady presence who could offer guidance.

First Mentorship Meeting: New Responsibilities

A week later, Nyomi attended her first meeting for the mentorship program. She found herself seated with a small group of freshmen, each one looking at her with a mix of curiosity and trepidation. Among them were Maya, a shy girl with dark, expressive eyes; Ethan, a rebellious boy with a skateboard resting against his chair; and Sofia, a poised girl who held her head high, exuding a sense of quiet ambition.

As Nyomi introduced herself, she noticed the subtle differences in each student's demeanor. Maya seemed hesitant, her gaze flickering nervously between Nyomi and the floor. Ethan wore a bored expression, his arms crossed as if daring someone to break through his tough exterior. Sofia, meanwhile, sat with perfect posture, her gaze direct and unwavering, a hint of challenge in her eyes.

"Hi, everyone. I'm Nyomi," she began, her voice calm and welcoming. "I know high school can feel overwhelming, especially when everything's new. I've been where you are, and I want you to know that I'm here to help with anything you need."

As she spoke, Nyomi felt the warmth of her confidence guiding her words. She remembered the lessons from Riverview, the importance of listening, of seeing beyond surface-level impressions. With each word, she felt her connection to the group deepening, her empathy guiding her interactions.

The meeting continued, with each student slowly opening up about their hopes, fears, and challenges. Maya admitted that she struggled with making friends and often felt out of place. Ethan scoffed at the idea of school altogether, saying he'd rather be out skating than sitting in a classroom. Sofia, in contrast, expressed a strong desire to succeed, mentioning her family's frequent moves and her need to prove herself academically.

As they spoke, Nyomi listened intently, drawing on the patience and compassion she had cultivated over the summer. She offered Maya gentle encouragement, reassuring her that it was okay to feel nervous and that friendships would come in time. She shared with Ethan her own memories of feeling restless and disconnected, showing him that he wasn't alone. And with Sofia, she emphasized the importance of balance, reminding her that academic success didn't have to come at the cost of personal connections.

By the end of the meeting, Nyomi could sense a shift in the group. The students' initial wariness had softened, replaced by a tentative trust, a willingness to let her guide them through the unfamiliar territory of high school.

Growing Responsibility and New Insights

In the following weeks, Nyomi's role as a mentor began to expand. She found herself spending more time with her group, helping them navigate both academic and social challenges. She met with Maya after school to talk about joining clubs and making friends, encouraging her to find activities that resonated with her interests. With Ethan, she attended a skateboarding club event, showing him that there were ways to blend his passion with school. And for Sofia, she offered a quiet support, helping her manage her workload and reminding her to take breaks and enjoy the journey.

Through these interactions, Nyomi felt a deepening sense of purpose. Her experiences at Riverview had taught her the value of connection, of truly seeing people for who they were, and she was applying those lessons here, in the hallways and classrooms of Riverside High.

But with this responsibility came a new awareness—a realization that her powers, while subtle, were guiding her in ways she hadn't fully understood before. She felt the warmth of the Butterfly Touch stirring at unexpected moments, a gentle nudge that reminded her of her empathy, her ability to sense the needs and emotions of those around her. She wasn't actively using her powers, but they had become a part of her, woven into the fabric of her interactions.

As she walked through the halls, Nyomi felt a quiet confidence, a sense of purpose that carried her forward. She was no longer just a student; she was a mentor, a guide, someone who could make a difference in the lives of others.

Subtle Interactions with Thomas: A Quiet Presence

In the midst of her busy school routine, Nyomi occasionally caught sight of Thomas, the quiet, observant student who had crossed paths with her in the past. He seemed to appear and disappear in the hallways, always watching her with a look that was both curious and knowing.

One afternoon, as Nyomi was helping Maya find her way to the science lab, she noticed Thomas leaning against the wall, his gaze fixed on her. He didn't say anything, but his expression held a hint of intrigue, as if he knew more about her than he let on.

Their eyes met briefly, and Nyomi felt a strange sensation—a flicker of awareness, as if Thomas could sense the changes within her, the quiet strength she had gained over the summer. She wondered if he knew about her powers, if he somehow understood the depth of her empathy, her ability to connect with others.

Later that day, as she was leaving school, she saw Thomas again, this time near the entrance. He gave her a slight nod, a subtle acknowledgment that sent a shiver down her spine. She couldn't shake the feeling that he was watching her, observing her growth with an interest that went beyond casual curiosity.

As the days went by, Thomas's presence became a familiar, if mysterious, part of her routine. He never approached her directly, but his quiet observation was a reminder that her journey was far from over. She sensed that he was waiting, watching to see how her powers would continue to unfold, as if he held answers to questions she hadn't yet asked.

A New Sense of Purpose and Connection

As the school year progressed, Nyomi continued to balance her responsibilities as a mentor with her own studies and friendships. She felt a growing sense of purpose, a quiet determination that guided her interactions and decisions. She had become someone her peers could rely on, someone who offered a steady presence in the sometimes chaotic world of high school.

Her experiences at Riverview had given her a foundation of empathy, a strength that allowed her to connect with others on a deeper level. She found herself offering support to students outside her mentorship group as well, noticing when someone seemed withdrawn or overwhelmed, offering a kind word or a listening ear.

Each day brought new challenges, but Nyomi faced them with a sense of resilience that came from her summer at Riverview. She had learned to see beyond the surface, to understand the complexities of human experience, and she carried that knowledge with her, letting it shape her interactions and relationships.

And through it all, she felt the quiet presence of Thomas, a reminder that her journey was ongoing, that there were still mysteries to uncover, powers to explore, and connections to build.

In the days that followed her decision to become a mentor, Nyomi threw herself wholeheartedly into the role. She wanted to make a difference, to be the person who could guide these new students through the maze of high school with the same compassion and support she had once needed. Each interaction with her mentees—Maya, Ethan, and Sofia—provided her with unique challenges, insights, and opportunities for growth.

Helping Maya Find Her Voice

Nyomi quickly noticed that Maya often faded into the background, her quiet demeanor making it easy for her to be overlooked. Whenever Nyomi tried to engage her in conversation, Maya would respond in a barely audible voice, her gaze fixed on the floor.

One day after school, Nyomi invited Maya to join her in the library for a casual study session. As they settled at a table by the window, Nyomi sensed Maya's nervousness, the way she fidgeted with her pencil, her shoulders hunched.

"Maya, I know it can be hard to feel comfortable in a new place," Nyomi said gently, hoping to put her at ease. "When I first started here, I felt like I didn't fit in at all."

Maya glanced at her, a flicker of interest in her eyes. "Really?" she whispered, her voice barely above a whisper.

Nyomi nodded, smiling warmly. "I know how it feels to be uncertain, to feel like everyone else has it all figured out. But I learned that sometimes, all it takes is one person who really sees you, who believes in you, to make you feel like you belong."

Maya seemed to consider this, her expression softening. After a moment, she spoke, her voice a little louder. "I... I like drawing. I used to draw all the time, but... I haven't done it since I moved here. I guess I just didn't think anyone would care."

Nyomi's heart swelled with empathy. She remembered her own love for art, the way it had been her escape, her way of expressing herself when words felt inadequate. "You know, the art club is looking for new members. If you'd like, I could go with you to the next meeting."

Maya's face lit up with a shy smile, a spark of excitement shining in her eyes. "That... that would be nice. Thank you, Nyomi."

In that moment, Nyomi felt a deep sense of fulfillment, knowing that she had helped Maya take a small but significant step toward finding her place. It reminded her of the importance of being seen, of the simple power of connection.

Guiding Ethan Toward Purpose

Ethan, on the other hand, presented an entirely different challenge. He had a rebellious energy that made him resistant to authority, and he often showed up to their mentorship meetings with a scowl, his arms crossed defiantly.

One afternoon, Nyomi found him in the skate park behind the school, practicing tricks on his skateboard. She watched him for a few moments, admiring the focus and skill he demonstrated with each trick, before approaching him.

"Hey, Ethan," she greeted, giving him a friendly wave. "I didn't know you were into skateboarding."

He shrugged, glancing at her briefly before resuming his practice. "It's the only thing I'm good at. And it doesn't involve sitting in a boring classroom all day."

Nyomi chuckled, sensing his frustration. "You know, there's a skateboarding club here at school. They do competitions and events. Maybe you could check it out?"

Ethan raised an eyebrow, his expression skeptical. "A school club? No offense, but that sounds lame."

Nyomi smiled, undeterred by his resistance. "I get it, but think about it this way: being part of the club could give you a place to practice, to meet others who share your passion. Plus, you'd have a chance to show off your skills in competitions."

For a moment, Ethan didn't respond, his gaze thoughtful as he considered her words. Finally, he gave a small nod. "Maybe I'll check it out. But no promises."

Nyomi's smile widened. She knew that getting through to Ethan would take time, but this was a start, a small opening that held the potential for growth. As she walked away, she felt a renewed sense of purpose, a quiet pride in knowing that she had planted a seed, that she was helping him find direction.

Supporting Sofia's Ambition

Sofia was, in many ways, the opposite of Maya and Ethan. She was confident, ambitious, and driven by a desire to excel in every aspect of her life. But Nyomi sensed an underlying tension in her, a pressure that seemed to weigh heavily on her shoulders.

One evening, after a mentorship meeting, Sofia approached Nyomi, her expression serious. "I want to ask you something," she said, her tone direct. "How do you handle it when you're not... good enough?"

Nyomi looked at her, surprised by the vulnerability in her question. "What do you mean?"

Sofia hesitated, her gaze dropping. "I've always been the top student, always succeeded at whatever I set my mind to. But here... everything feels different. It's like I have to prove myself all over again, and I'm scared that I won't be able to keep up."

Nyomi felt a pang of empathy, understanding the weight of Sofia's ambition and the pressure she placed on herself. She reached out, placing a comforting hand on Sofia's shoulder. "It's okay to feel that way, Sofia. You don't have to be perfect all the time. It's enough to do your best, to allow yourself to grow at your own pace."

Sofia looked at her, a hint of relief in her expression. "But what if my best isn't good enough? What if I fail?"

Nyomi smiled gently. "Then you learn from it and keep going. Failure isn't the end—it's a part of the journey. You're capable of amazing things, but it's okay to give yourself grace along the way."

As Sofia processed her words, Nyomi saw a shift in her expression, a softening that suggested a release of some of the pressure she had been carrying. In that moment, Nyomi felt a profound sense of fulfillment, knowing that she had helped Sofia see the strength in vulnerability, the beauty of growth.

Throughout her time as a mentor, Nyomi occasionally crossed paths with Thomas, each encounter stirring a sense of curiosity. He seemed to appear at the edges of her vision, always watching, always observing. His gaze held a quiet intensity, a look that suggested he saw more than he let on.

One afternoon, as Nyomi was helping Ethan in the library, she noticed Thomas standing by the shelves, a book in his hands. His eyes were fixed on her, a thoughtful expression on his face.

When their eyes met, Thomas gave her a slight nod, as if acknowledging her efforts. It was a subtle gesture, but it sent a shiver down her spine. She couldn't shake the feeling that he was aware of her powers, that he understood something about her that no one else did.

Another time, during lunch, Nyomi spotted Thomas sitting alone at a table by the window, his gaze following her as she moved through the cafeteria. His expression was inscrutable, but there was a hint of intrigue in his eyes, a quiet curiosity that made her wonder what he knew, what he was searching for.

Their interactions were brief, often wordless, but each one left her with a lingering sense of mystery. Thomas's presence was a reminder that her journey was far from over, that there were still layers to her powers, and perhaps even to her own identity, that she had yet to uncover.

Reflections on Growth and Responsibility

As the weeks went by, Nyomi found herself reflecting on the changes within her, the ways her time at Riverview had shaped her into the person she was now. She felt a newfound strength, a resilience that had come from witnessing the courage of the residents, from seeing their stories and understanding the beauty of their journeys.

Each interaction with her mentees was a chance to apply what she had learned, to offer them the support and compassion that had once been shown to her. She realized that her powers, while subtle, were a guiding force, an extension of her empathy and intuition. She didn't need to actively use the Butterfly Touch; it was already a part of her, woven into the way she connected with others.

But with this strength came a sense of responsibility, a weight that she carried with quiet pride. She knew that her role as a mentor was more than just a title—it was a calling, a chance to make a real difference. And as she walked through the familiar hallways of Riverside High, she felt a sense of purpose, a readiness to face whatever challenges lay ahead.

A New Challenge with Ethan: Facing Rebellion

One afternoon, Nyomi received a call from the school counselor, who informed her that Ethan had been involved in an incident. He had skipped class and been caught sneaking off campus with a group of students.

When Nyomi confronted him later that day, Ethan's demeanor was defiant, his arms crossed as he avoided her gaze.

"Why, Ethan?" Nyomi asked, her voice calm but firm. "I thought you were starting to find your place here."

Ethan shrugged, a hint of frustration in his eyes. "Maybe I don't want a place here. Maybe I'm just fine on my own."

Nyomi took a deep breath, sensing the anger beneath his words, the walls he had built to protect himself. She reached out, her voice gentle. "You don't have to push everyone away, Ethan. I know it's scary to let people in, but you're not alone. I'm here, and so are others who care about you."

For a moment, Ethan's expression softened, a flicker of vulnerability crossing his face. But he quickly looked away, his walls back up. "I don't need anyone, Nyomi. I'm fine on my own."

Nyomi felt a pang of sadness, knowing that breaking through to Ethan would take time. But she was determined to be there, to offer him a steady presence, just as she had done with the residents at Riverview. She knew that trust couldn't be forced—it had to be earned, one small step at a time.

A Moment of Encouragement with Maya

With Maya, Nyomi's progress was more visible. She had accompanied Maya to the art club's first meeting, encouraging her to share her work and connect with other students who shared her interests. Maya had been nervous at first, but Nyomi's presence had given her the confidence to open up, to show a side of herself that she had kept hidden.

One afternoon, as they walked out of the art room together, Maya turned to Nyomi, her face bright with excitement. "Thank you for encouraging me, Nyomi. I... I think I finally feel like I belong here."

Nyomi's heart swelled with pride, knowing that Maya's words were a testament to her growth, a reflection of the quiet courage it took to step out of her comfort zone. "You did this, Maya. I just helped you see what was already there."

Maya smiled, a newfound confidence shining in her eyes. "I'm glad I met you, Nyomi."

In that moment, Nyomi realized that her journey was no longer just about her own growth. It was about lifting others, about helping them find their own strength and resilience. Each connection, each moment of support, was a reminder that her role as a mentor was a gift, a way to honor the lives she had touched at Riverview by continuing their legacy of compassion.

Final Reflection: Embracing Her Purpose

As the first semester progressed, Nyomi settled into her role with a sense of fulfillment and purpose. She had become more than just a student at Riverside High; she was a mentor, a guide, a quiet presence that offered strength and support.

Her interactions with Thomas remained a mystery, each encounter leaving her with more questions than answers. But she sensed that he was waiting, watching her journey with an interest that hinted at something deeper, something she had yet to understand.

And as she continued to walk the halls of Riverside High, Nyomi felt a quiet certainty that she was on the right path. She was growing, evolving, carrying forward the lessons of Riverview with a heart that was open, compassionate, and ready to face whatever lay ahead.

In the quiet moments, when she reflected on her journey, she knew that her purpose was more than just a role—it was a calling, a path that would lead her to new challenges, new connections, and a deeper understanding of herself and her powers.

CHAPTER 13: THE WEIGHT OF RESPONSIBILITY

As the semester unfolded, Nyomi became increasingly invested in the lives of her mentees. Each of them—Maya, Ethan, and Sofia—had their own unique struggles, and Nyomi found herself drawn to their stories, her empathy intensifying with every interaction. Mentorship was proving to be as much a journey of self-discovery as it was a responsibility, challenging her in ways she hadn't anticipated.

Maya's shyness remained a challenge. She often sat silently during mentorship meetings, her gaze focused downward, her shoulders tense. One day, after a meeting, Nyomi invited Maya to join her for a walk around campus. She wanted to understand the quiet girl's insecurities, to find a way to ease her into the world of Riverside High.

As they strolled through the courtyard, Nyomi spoke gently, "You know, Maya, I used to be really shy too. It took me a long time to feel comfortable speaking up."

Maya's eyes flickered with interest, though she kept her gaze on the ground. "Really?" she murmured. "I thought you... always seemed so confident."

Nyomi chuckled softly. "Not always. But I realized that sometimes, it's okay to be nervous. Everyone feels that way once in a while."

She noticed a slight softening in Maya's posture and decided to use her Butterfly Touch, but in the subtlest way she could manage. She placed her hand lightly on Maya's shoulder, allowing a gentle warmth to radiate, a quiet reassurance that would let Maya feel seen, understood.

Maya relaxed visibly, her shoulders loosening. She looked up at Nyomi, a small, grateful smile on her face. "Thanks, Nyomi. It... helps to know I'm not the only one."

As they walked back to class, Nyomi felt a sense of accomplishment but also an awareness of the delicate balance she had to maintain. Her powers were a gift, but they had to be used thoughtfully, with respect for each person's boundaries.

Ethan's Guarded Heart

Ethan, however, continued to be a challenge. His rebellious spirit and refusal to conform made it difficult for Nyomi to connect with him. But there were small moments, glimpses of vulnerability beneath his tough exterior, that gave her hope.

One afternoon, after he had stormed out of a group activity, Nyomi found him sitting alone by the skate park, his skateboard propped up beside him. She approached quietly, knowing that pressing too hard would only make him withdraw further.

"Ethan," she said softly, "I know you're frustrated. But I'm here to listen if you want to talk."

Ethan shrugged, looking away. "It's nothing. I just don't fit in here. I never have."

Nyomi felt a pang of empathy, remembering her own struggles with belonging. She sat down beside him, letting the silence stretch between them before she spoke. "Sometimes, fitting in isn't the goal. Sometimes, it's about finding the people who see you for who you are."

Ethan glanced at her, his expression skeptical. But Nyomi saw a flicker of curiosity in his eyes, a faint crack in his guarded heart. She resisted the urge to use her powers outright, instead allowing her empathy to guide her words, to create a space where he felt safe to let his guard down.

"I know it feels like no one understands," she continued, her voice steady. "But I see you, Ethan. I know there's more to you than what everyone else sees."

For a moment, he seemed to waver, as if considering her words. But he quickly masked his emotions, giving a small, noncommittal shrug. "Whatever," he muttered, though his tone lacked its usual edge.

As she walked away, Nyomi felt both hopeful and uncertain. She was learning that being a mentor wasn't about fixing people; it was about creating connections, building trust one small moment at a time.

Sofia's Ambition and Vulnerability

Sofia was, in many ways, Nyomi's most confident mentee. Her drive was unrelenting, her ambition clear. But there were times when Nyomi sensed a fragility in her, a weight of expectation that threatened to overwhelm her.

One evening, Sofia came to Nyomi, her expression troubled. She had received a grade on a major exam that fell below her usual standards, and she looked devastated.

"I don't understand, Nyomi," she said, her voice shaking. "I worked so hard, but it wasn't enough. I feel like I'm failing."

Nyomi placed a comforting hand on her shoulder, her powers responding with a gentle, calming warmth. "Sofia, you're allowed to have setbacks. It doesn't define who you are or what you're capable of."

Sofia's gaze softened, and she looked at Nyomi with a mixture of gratitude and relief. "But what if... what if I can't keep up? What if I'm not good enough?"

Nyomi smiled gently. "You're more than just your achievements, Sofia. You have resilience, strength, and kindness. And those qualities will carry you through, even when things don't go as planned."

As Sofia nodded, Nyomi felt a quiet pride. She was learning that her role as a mentor was not just to guide her mentees but to help them see their own worth, to believe in themselves in ways they hadn't before.

Reflecting on Her Own Growth

As Nyomi walked home that evening, she found herself reflecting on her own journey. She remembered the residents at Riverview—Mrs. Hargrove's gentle wisdom, Mr. Oswald's adventurous spirit, Mrs.

Montgomery's resilience. Each of them had taught her something valuable, lessons she now carried into her role as a mentor.

In her journal that night, she wrote:

Riverview changed me. I see people more clearly now, not just for who they are but for who they're trying to become. It's a gift, this ability to connect, but it's also a responsibility. I want to honor it, to use my powers carefully and with purpose.

As she closed her journal, she felt a renewed sense of commitment, a promise to herself to continue growing, to be the mentor her mentees deserved.

Controlling Her Powers Through Meditation

The next morning, Nyomi decided to set aside time to focus on her powers, to explore the boundaries of her Butterfly Touch and gain better control. She found a quiet spot in the park, closed her eyes, and began to meditate.

She focused on the warmth within her, the sensation that accompanied her powers. With each breath, she imagined that warmth expanding, then contracting, a gentle ebb and flow that she could direct. She practiced letting the energy build, then releasing it, honing her ability to control its activation.

After several minutes, she felt a deeper connection to her powers, a newfound awareness of how they responded to her emotions and intentions. She knew that this control would be essential, not just for her own growth, but for the respect and trust of those around her.

A Cryptic Encounter with Thomas

Later that week, Nyomi ran into Thomas in the library. He was leaning against a shelf, his gaze focused on her as she helped Maya find a book. There was a knowing look in his eyes, a subtle awareness that sent a shiver down her spine.

When Maya left, Thomas approached, his expression inscrutable. "You have an interesting way with people," he remarked, his tone neutral yet filled with an underlying curiosity.

Nyomi looked at him, uncertain. "What do you mean?"

He shrugged, a slight smirk on his face. "You seem to... see people differently. It's not something everyone can do."

Nyomi felt her heart race, wondering how much he knew. "I just try to help," she replied carefully, her gaze steady.

Thomas nodded, his eyes thoughtful. "Helping others is a gift. But be careful—it can be a heavy weight to carry if you don't set boundaries."

With that, he walked away, leaving Nyomi with a sense of both intrigue and caution. His words echoed in her mind, a cryptic reminder that her journey was far from over, and that there were still mysteries she had yet to understand.

The Weight of Responsibility

As the weeks went by, Nyomi began to feel the weight of her responsibilities. Balancing her own schoolwork with her mentorship duties was proving to be more challenging than she had anticipated. She often stayed up late, working on assignments long after everyone else had gone to bed.

One evening, after a particularly exhausting day, she confided in her teacher, Ms. Greene, during a free period. "Sometimes, I wonder if I'm doing enough. It feels like there's so much to balance, and I'm not sure I can handle it all."

Ms. Greene looked at her kindly. "Nyomi, being a mentor isn't about being perfect. It's about being there, offering support even when things aren't easy. You're doing more than enough."

Nyomi felt a wave of relief at her teacher's words. She realized that she didn't have to carry the weight of everyone's struggles alone; she could be a guide, a friend, without needing to have all the answers.

Reflections on Empathy and Purpose

That night, as she lay in bed, Nyomi found herself reflecting on the nature of empathy, of what it meant to truly see and understand others. Her powers were a part of her, but they didn't define her. They were a tool, a way to connect, but it was her heart, her compassion, that made her a mentor.

She made a silent promise to herself: to use her powers wisely, to honor the trust of those she helped, and to continue growing, even when the path ahead seemed uncertain.

In the following days, Nyomi's interactions with Thomas grew more frequent. Each time, he would offer subtle hints, cryptic advice that hinted at a deeper understanding of her journey.

One afternoon, as they passed each other in the hallway, he stopped her briefly. "You're going to face challenges, Nyomi.

But remember, you're not alone. There are others like you— people who understand."

Nyomi looked at him, a mixture of surprise and curiosity in her expression. "Do you mean... people with powers?"

Thomas's smile was enigmatic. "Maybe. Or maybe just people who know what it's like to feel deeply, to see the world differently. Just remember, empathy is a strength. Don't let anyone make you believe otherwise."

As he walked away, Nyomi felt a new sense of resolve. She knew her journey was far from over, that there were still lessons to be learned, mysteries to uncover. But with each step, she was becoming more certain of who she was, and the path she was meant to walk.

As Nyomi continued her mentorship journey, she found herself deeply invested in each of her mentees. Maya's self-doubt, Ethan's resistance, and Sofia's perfectionism were challenges she related to, yet each struggle was unique. Her empathy guided her, but it also weighed on her, forcing her to confront her own limitations and the boundaries of her powers.

Maya's shyness and fear of failure were apparent in her quiet demeanor and reluctance to speak up in group settings. Nyomi observed Maya's hesitancy to join discussions, often watching her wring her hands or glance nervously around the room. During one mentorship meeting, Maya seemed particularly tense, her eyes cast down as if she wished she could disappear.

After the meeting, Nyomi walked alongside Maya, breaking the silence gently. "I noticed you seemed a bit anxious today," she said softly. "It's okay to feel that way. I get nervous too, especially when I feel like I'm not meeting expectations."

Maya's expression softened slightly, though she still avoided eye contact. "I just... I'm afraid of saying the wrong thing, of people judging me."

Nyomi placed a reassuring hand on Maya's shoulder, allowing a warm, subtle pulse of the Butterfly Touch to flow through her. She focused on sending a wave of calm, a small gesture of encouragement without intruding on Maya's emotions. "I think you're braver than you realize, Maya," she said. "The fact that you keep showing up here, even when you feel scared—that takes strength."

Maya looked up at her, a hint of gratitude in her eyes. "Thank you, Nyomi. I... I've never thought of it that way."

As they parted ways, Nyomi felt a mix of pride and humility. She was learning that mentorship didn't always require grand gestures—sometimes, it was enough to simply offer a quiet presence, to be a steady source of encouragement.

Navigating Ethan's Guarded Walls

Ethan continued to be both a puzzle and a challenge. His rebellious attitude and reluctance to engage made it difficult for Nyomi to break through to him. But every so often, she would catch a glimpse of vulnerability—a flicker of doubt or a brief moment of hesitation. It was enough to keep her trying.

One afternoon, after Ethan skipped a mentorship meeting, Nyomi found him in the library, his skateboard leaning against his chair as he stared out the window. She approached him cautiously, sitting across from him without a word.

After a few moments, he looked at her, raising an eyebrow. "You're not going to give up on me, are you?"

Nyomi shook her head, smiling. "Nope. But I'm here to listen, whenever you feel ready to talk."

Ethan shrugged, glancing away. "I don't get why you even care. I'm not... like everyone else here."

Nyomi sensed the weight of his words, a hint of loneliness beneath his defiance. She reached out, letting the Butterfly Touch activate gently, filling the space between them with a comforting warmth. "Maybe you don't fit into the same mold as everyone else. But that doesn't mean you don't belong here."

For a moment, Ethan seemed to consider her words. He looked at her with an expression that held both gratitude and frustration, as if he wanted to trust her but wasn't quite ready to let his guard down. "Maybe," he muttered, his voice softening.

As he left, Nyomi felt the bittersweet satisfaction of a small breakthrough. She was beginning to understand that mentoring wasn't a straight path—it was filled with stops and starts, with victories and setbacks.

Sofia was a star student, driven and ambitious, but Nyomi noticed how hard she was on herself, how her confidence wavered whenever she faced even the smallest setback. One afternoon, Sofia approached her, her face clouded with frustration.

"I bombed a test," she admitted, her voice trembling. "I studied so hard, but I... I just wasn't good enough."

Nyomi reached out, placing a gentle hand on Sofia's arm. She allowed a faint wave of the Butterfly Touch to pass through, offering reassurance without pushing too hard. "Sofia, you're more than just your grades. One test doesn't define you, and it's okay to stumble sometimes."

Sofia looked at her, her expression softening. "But what if I can't keep up? What if I'm not as strong as I thought?"

Nyomi smiled, her own experiences at Riverview echoing in her mind. She remembered Mrs. Montgomery's resilience, the way she had carried herself with quiet strength despite her struggles. "Strength isn't about being perfect all the time. It's about learning from mistakes, picking yourself back up. You have that strength, Sofia—you just need to trust yourself."

As Sofia nodded, Nyomi felt a surge of confidence. Her experiences at Riverview had given her wisdom to share, and she was learning how to apply those lessons in ways that resonated with others.

Later that evening, Nyomi found a quiet corner in the park and closed her eyes, centering herself in a meditative state. She focused on the warmth within her, the familiar energy of the Butterfly Touch. With each breath, she visualized the warmth expanding and contracting, practicing the control she had started to develop.

She reflected on her powers, the moments they activated on their own versus when she consciously chose to use them. She wanted to be intentional, to ensure her empathy respected each person's boundaries. As she meditated, she thought of Riverview—the compassion she had learned from the residents, the understanding that true connection was a gift that required both care and restraint.

As she opened her eyes, she felt a renewed sense of purpose. Her powers were part of who she was, but they were also a responsibility, a tool she needed to wield with respect.

In the following days, Nyomi noticed Thomas watching her more closely. He seemed to appear at the edges of her vision, observing her interactions with Maya, Ethan, and Sofia. His gaze held a quiet intensity, a hint of understanding that both intrigued and unsettled her.

One afternoon, after she had helped Maya with a project, she caught Thomas's eye. He approached her, his expression thoughtful.

"You have a way with people," he said, his tone cryptic. "It's like you see something most people miss."

Nyomi looked at him, studying his expression. "What do you mean?"

Thomas shrugged, but his eyes held a hint of knowledge. "Just that... empathy is a rare gift. But it can be heavy too, especially if you don't set boundaries."

Nyomi felt a shiver run through her. There was something in his words, a subtle acknowledgment that he knew more about her than he let on. "Do you... know what that's like?" she asked cautiously.

He gave her a small, enigmatic smile. "Maybe. Or maybe I've just seen it in others. Either way, it's something you'll need to understand—because it's only going to get more complicated."

As he walked away, Nyomi felt a mixture of curiosity and unease. Thomas's words lingered in her mind, a reminder that her journey was far from over and that there were challenges she had yet to face.

That evening, Nyomi sat down with her journal, feeling the need to put her thoughts into words. She wrote about Riverview, about the residents who had taught her so much— Mrs. Montgomery's resilience, Mr. Oswald's adventurous spirit, Mrs. Hargrove's kindness. Each memory felt like a guidepost, a reminder of the values she wanted to carry forward.

Riverview changed me in ways I'm only beginning to understand, she wrote. I want to honor the lives of the people I met, to use what I've learned to help others. But it's hard sometimes, balancing empathy with boundaries, learning when to step in and when to step back.

As she closed her journal, she felt a renewed sense of purpose, a quiet determination to grow, to honor the gifts she had been given and the people who had touched her life.

Over the next few weeks, Nyomi saw small signs of progress in her mentees. Ethan began to show up more consistently, even if he still maintained his tough exterior. One afternoon, he approached her after a meeting, shifting awkwardly.

"Hey," he muttered. "Thanks for... not giving up on me. I know I'm not easy to deal with."

Nyomi smiled, touched by his honesty. "Everyone deserves someone who believes in them, Ethan. I'm glad you're here."

Ethan gave her a small nod, a flicker of gratitude in his eyes. She knew that trust was a gradual process, built on moments like these, and she was honored to be a part of his journey.

Similarly, Sofia continued to open up, especially after facing another academic setback. She sought Nyomi's support, sharing her fears and frustrations, and Nyomi encouraged her to see her value beyond her achievements.

"You're resilient, Sofia," she said gently. "Strength isn't about never falling—it's about getting back up, about learning and growing."

Sofia smiled, a look of appreciation in her eyes. "Thank you, Nyomi. I feel like... I'm starting to understand that."

Each interaction left Nyomi feeling both proud and humbled. She was growing alongside her mentees, learning that empathy was not just about understanding others but also about embracing her own vulnerabilities and strengths.

One afternoon, Nyomi spoke with her teacher, Ms. Greene, about the challenges of being a mentor. She voiced her concerns about balancing empathy with boundaries, about the emotional toll of helping others.

Ms. Greene smiled warmly. "Empathy is a beautiful thing, Nyomi. But remember, you're allowed to set limits, to protect your own energy. Helping others doesn't mean you have to give up a part of yourself."

Nyomi nodded, feeling reassured. Her conversations with Ms. Greene and Thomas had helped her see empathy not as a burden, but as a strength

—a guiding force that could help her grow without losing herself.

A few days later, Thomas approached her again, his expression serious. "There's more to this journey than you realize, Nyomi," he said quietly. "Your powers... they're going to be tested, and you'll have to make choices. But remember, you're not alone."

Nyomi looked at him, feeling a mixture of gratitude and curiosity. "Do you... have powers too?"

Thomas smiled cryptically. "Maybe. Or maybe I just understand the weight of responsibility. Either way, you'll see soon enough."

As he walked away, Nyomi felt both reassured and intrigued. She knew her path was only beginning, that there were challenges she hadn't yet encountered. But with the guidance of those around her—and the lessons of Riverview—she felt ready to face whatever lay ahead.

The autumn weeks at Riverside High passed in a blur of mentorship meetings, classes, and quiet, reflective moments where Nyomi grappled with the weight of her growing responsibilities. Each day brought new challenges with her mentees—small victories and setbacks that filled her with both pride and doubt. She was beginning to see how empathy could be both a blessing and a burden, how the desire to help could sometimes lead to exhaustion if not balanced with self-care.

Nyomi's own academic workload was intensifying. Between exams, essays, and her mentorship duties, she often found herself staying up late, caught between her drive to excel and her commitment to her mentees. One evening, as she struggled through an essay, she felt the strain of it all.

In that moment, her mind drifted to Riverview Senior Center, and a wave of calm washed over her as she remembered Mr. Oswald's words on resilience. "Life's a journey, Nyomi. You don't have to conquer it all at once. Sometimes, it's about taking one step at a time." She took a deep breath, allowing his advice to settle within her, reminding herself that she didn't have to do everything perfectly.

But as comforting as the memory was, the pressure of her commitments continued to weigh on her. One afternoon, she sought out Ms. Greene, her teacher, for advice. As they sat in Ms. Greene's quiet office, Nyomi found herself voicing her worries.

"It's just... hard sometimes," she admitted, her voice barely above a whisper. "I feel like I need to be there for my mentees, but I also need to keep up with my own work. And I don't want to let anyone down."

Ms. Greene listened with a sympathetic expression, her gaze warm and encouraging. "Empathy is a beautiful gift, Nyomi, but you're allowed to set boundaries. Helping others doesn't mean you have to sacrifice your own well-being. Find balance, and remember that your growth is just as important as theirs."

Nyomi nodded, feeling a sense of relief. Her teacher's words reminded her that it was okay to prioritize herself, that her journey didn't have to come second to her responsibilities. She left the office with a renewed commitment to finding balance, understanding that her empathy could be a strength without overwhelming her.

Later that evening, Nyomi decided to dedicate time to practicing control over her powers. She found a quiet spot in her room, lit a candle, and closed her eyes, focusing on the gentle warmth that she knew as her Butterfly Touch. She visualized the energy within her, a soft, glowing light that pulsed in sync with her heartbeat. With each breath, she imagined the light expanding, then contracting, honing her ability to direct it consciously.

As she meditated, she reflected on moments when her powers activated without her intention—when her empathy had taken over and she had sensed emotions she wasn't prepared to handle. She thought of Maya's anxiety, Ethan's defensiveness, Sofia's self-doubt. In each case, her powers had responded automatically, amplifying her empathy and connecting her deeply to their struggles.

But tonight, she was determined to find control. She practiced visualizing the energy stopping when she chose, resting dormant within her until she consciously called it forth. The process was challenging, requiring focus and patience, but with each breath, she felt her confidence growing. She was learning that her powers didn't have to define her actions; she could wield them with intention, allowing her empathy to enhance her mentorship without overwhelming her.

In the following weeks, Nyomi's mentorship with Maya blossomed. They began meeting regularly after school, with Maya slowly opening up about her struggles with self-doubt. One afternoon, as they worked on a project together in the library, Maya admitted her insecurities in a soft, trembling voice.

"Sometimes, I feel like I'm just... invisible," Maya whispered, her gaze downcast. "Like no one really sees me or cares about what I have to say."

Nyomi reached out, placing her hand gently over Maya's, allowing the Butterfly Touch to activate in a subtle, supportive way. She focused on sending warmth, a silent message that Maya's presence mattered.

"Maya, I see you," she said softly. "You're thoughtful and kind, and you have a voice that deserves to be heard. You don't have to be loud to make an impact."

Maya's eyes brightened, and she gave a small smile. "Thank you, Nyomi. I've never had someone say that to me before."

The moment felt like a victory, a sign that Maya was beginning to believe in herself. As they continued their project, Nyomi felt a surge of pride and gratitude, knowing that her empathy had created a safe space for Maya to grow.

Breaking Down Ethan's Guarded Heart

Ethan remained a challenging mentee, his rebellious nature and defensive attitude making it difficult for Nyomi to connect with him. But over time, she noticed small changes in his behavior—subtle signs that he was starting to trust her, even if he didn't fully understand why.

One afternoon, she found him in the art room, experimenting with spray paints on a canvas. He looked up as she entered, giving her a half-hearted nod.

"Didn't expect you to be here," he muttered, focusing back on his work.

Nyomi approached, watching as he added splashes of color to the canvas. "You're really talented, Ethan," she remarked, her tone genuine. "Your art has a lot of energy and depth."

Ethan shrugged, though there was a flicker of pride in his expression. "It's just something I do. Keeps me busy."

Nyomi let the Butterfly Touch activate in a subtle way, radiating warmth and encouragement without overwhelming him. "Art can be powerful," she said gently. "It's a way of expressing things words can't capture. Maybe... you could show others what you're capable of."

He didn't respond immediately, but his posture relaxed slightly, his guarded expression softening. "Maybe," he muttered, though his tone held less resistance.

As she left the art room, Nyomi felt a small sense of accomplishment. Ethan was beginning to trust her, inch by inch, and she was learning that building trust was a gradual process, one that required patience, empathy, and resilience.

Sofia's Struggles with Perfectionism

Sofia's ambition and drive to excel were both admirable and intense. But Nyomi sensed the toll it was taking on her, especially after a recent exam where Sofia didn't achieve the grade she'd hoped for. When she approached Nyomi after school, her frustration was evident.

"I studied for hours," Sofia admitted, her voice filled with disappointment. "I did everything I could, but it still wasn't enough."

Nyomi placed a comforting hand on her shoulder, allowing a gentle wave of the Butterfly Touch to pass through, offering reassurance. "Sofia, you're more than just a grade. You're strong, dedicated, and incredibly capable. One test doesn't define your worth."

Sofia looked at her, her expression softening as she absorbed Nyomi's words. "It's just... hard. I feel like I have to prove myself constantly, like if I'm not perfect, then I'm failing."

Nyomi nodded, remembering Mrs. Montgomery's resilience and the quiet strength she had found in accepting her limitations. "Perfection isn't the goal, Sofia. Growth is. And sometimes, growth means stumbling, learning, and trying again."

As they talked, Nyomi felt a sense of fulfillment, a quiet pride in knowing that her guidance had helped Sofia see her worth beyond achievements. She was beginning to realize that mentorship wasn't about solving problems—it was about walking alongside her mentees, helping them find strength within themselves.

Thomas's Presence and Cryptic Guidance

In the midst of her busy schedule, Nyomi continued to notice Thomas's watchful presence. He seemed to observe her interactions with her mentees,

his gaze thoughtful and intense, as if he saw something others didn't.

One day, as she left a meeting with her mentees, Thomas approached her, his expression contemplative. "You're carrying a lot on your shoulders," he remarked, his tone laced with subtle empathy. "It's admirable, but... be careful not to lose yourself in the process."

Nyomi looked at him, intrigued by his insight. "Do you... understand what that's like?"

Thomas gave her a faint smile, his eyes reflecting a hint of shared understanding. "I know what it's like to feel deeply, to carry other people's burdens. It can be both a gift and a challenge."

Nyomi felt a shiver of recognition, as if he had touched on something she hadn't yet fully acknowledged. "How do you handle it?" she asked quietly.

Thomas shrugged, his expression distant. "It's a journey. You learn as you go, finding balance between compassion and self-preservation. But remember, empathy is a powerful force —one that can guide you, if you let it."

His words lingered with her long after he left, a reminder that her path was one of both growth and responsibility.

Thomas's quiet understanding and cryptic advice added a layer of mystery to her journey, as if he was somehow part of the challenges she would face in the future.

A Moment of Reflection

That evening, Nyomi returned to her journal, feeling the need to process her thoughts. She wrote about Riverview, the lessons she had learned from the residents, and the ways those lessons continued to shape her interactions with her mentees.

Riverview taught me so much—about resilience, kindness, and the importance of connection. Each resident had a story, a strength they shared with me, and now I'm beginning to see those same qualities in the people around me. I want to honor their legacy by using what I've learned to help others, but it's not always easy.

As she closed her journal, she felt a renewed sense of purpose, a commitment to continue growing and to use her powers responsibly. She knew her journey was far from over, but with each step, she felt more certain of her path, more connected to the people who had shaped her.

Foreshadowing from Thomas

The next day, Thomas approached her again, his expression more serious than usual. "There are challenges ahead, Nyomi. You'll face choices that will test your empathy and your powers in ways you haven't yet imagined."

Nyomi felt a surge of curiosity and apprehension. "Do you mean... with my mentees?"

Thomas shook his head, his gaze distant. "This is bigger than any one person. But you're not alone—you have allies, even if you don't see them yet."

As he walked away, Nyomi felt a mixture of anticipation and determination. She knew that her journey was far from over, that there were mysteries and challenges awaiting her.

But with her empathy, her resilience, and the support of those around her, she felt ready to face whatever lay ahead.

CHAPTER 14: MAYA'S STORY

Nyomi had noticed Maya around school before—always seated by herself in the cafeteria, her eyes focused on a book, her shoulders hunched as if to shrink into invisibility. Maya seemed to embody an invisible line that kept her separated from others. Nyomi recognized the signs because she had once felt the same way, like a puzzle piece that didn't quite fit.

As Nyomi walked across the cafeteria to where Maya sat, she could feel the girl's tension as if it were her own. She moved slowly, cautiously, hoping to avoid startling her. "Hey, Maya," she greeted gently, trying to make her voice as warm as possible. "Mind if I join you?"

Maya looked up, clearly surprised. She hesitated before giving a slight nod, her gaze darting down to her book as Nyomi took a seat.

For a few minutes, neither of them spoke, and Nyomi observed her carefully. Maya clutched her book like a shield, her fingers curled tightly around its edges. There was a familiar ache in her eyes, an uncertainty that Nyomi recognized. She waited a moment before speaking again.

"Looks like a good book," Nyomi remarked, nodding toward the cover.

Maya smiled faintly, relaxing a little. "It is," she replied softly. "I... I guess I just really like getting lost in stories. It's easier than dealing with... things."

Nyomi's heart went out to her. "I totally get that. Stories are like escape hatches—safe places where you can just be yourself. Have you ever thought about writing your own?"

Maya's face flushed, her eyes widening. "Oh... well... I've thought about it, but... I don't think I'd be any good. No one would read what I write, anyway."

There it was—the hesitation, the fear of not being enough. Nyomi felt her Butterfly Touch respond, as if her very gift could sense the potential within Maya. Nyomi closed her eyes briefly, reaching out with her power, and was gifted with a fleeting vision—a bookstore, a crowded table with stacks of books, and a line of fans waiting to meet Maya, who was smiling with an infectious sense of joy and fulfillment.

Nyomi opened her eyes, giving Maya a gentle smile. "You know, I think you might surprise yourself. Sometimes all it takes is one step toward something you're passionate about. You might find it's more fulfilling than you could have ever imagined."

Maya's gaze softened, and for a moment, her shoulders relaxed, as if Nyomi's words had lifted a small weight off her.

Maya's Dream to Write

Over the next few days, Nyomi continued to spend time with Maya, learning about her and gently coaxing her out of her shell. They talked about their favorite authors, shared book recommendations, and soon enough, Maya began opening up about the stories she had written in her notebooks —tales she had never dared to share with anyone else.

"It's silly, really," Maya said one day, tucking her hair behind her ear. "I've had this dream of being a writer since I was little. But it's just... something I do for fun, you know? I could never be a real writer."

"Why not?" Nyomi asked, her tone encouraging but curious. "Why couldn't you be a real writer?"

Maya looked down, her cheeks pink. "Because... I don't think I'm good enough. Real writers... they're different. They're brave. They put their ideas out into the world and... I don't think I could ever do that."

Nyomi reached across the table and squeezed Maya's hand gently. "You're braver than you think. Writing takes courage, but so does sharing who you are with others. The fact that you're even talking about it shows that you have that courage inside you. Sometimes, we just need a little reminder."

Maya's eyes met Nyomi's, a flicker of hope there. "Do you really think so?"

Nyomi nodded, sensing that this was the right moment to give Maya a glimpse of her potential. She concentrated, letting her Butterfly Touch work its magic, creating a vision that would show Maya what she could achieve if she embraced her dreams.

The world around them shimmered as Nyomi closed her eyes and guided Maya into a vision. They stood in a large, bustling bookstore, its walls lined with bookshelves reaching to the ceiling. In the center of the room was a table stacked high with copies of a book—Maya's book, with her name emblazoned across the cover.

Maya gasped, taking in the scene. She looked down at her hands and saw a pen held between her fingers, poised over the page of an open book. Before her stood a line of readers, each holding a copy of her book, eager for her signature.

"Is this... really happening?" Maya whispered, her voice filled with awe.

Nyomi nodded. "It's as real as you want it to be. This is what you could accomplish, Maya. This is what you're capable of."

As Maya signed books, she felt a profound sense of joy and fulfillment wash over her. It was as if she were tapping into a part of herself she had always kept hidden. Each reader she met thanked her, some sharing how her words had touched their lives, helped them see the world in a new way, or inspired them to pursue their own dreams.

The vision faded, but the feeling lingered as Maya returned to the present. She looked at Nyomi, her eyes shining. "That was... incredible.

I've never felt anything like that before."

"You can make it real," Nyomi said softly. "That feeling you had? It's a part of you. And if you want it badly enough, you can make it come true."

Maya swallowed, determination flickering in her eyes. "Maybe... maybe I could try."

The Writing Club

The next day, Nyomi brought up the school's writing club again, suggesting it might be a good place for Maya to start sharing her work. But Maya hesitated, fear shadowing her face.

"I don't know... I don't think I'm ready. What if they don't like what I write?" she asked, her voice wavering.

Nyomi gave her a reassuring smile. "Everyone has to start somewhere, Maya. The club isn't about being perfect—it's about sharing your love for stories with others who understand. Besides, you won't be alone. I'll be there with you."

After a long pause, Maya took a deep breath. "Okay. I'll... I'll try. But just once."

That Friday, Maya walked into the writing club meeting with Nyomi by her side. She looked around, taking in the room filled with students discussing their latest stories and projects. Her hands trembled as they found seats, but Nyomi offered her a reassuring nod.

The club leader, Liam, welcomed Maya warmly, making her feel a little more at ease. When it came time to share ideas, Maya hesitated, glancing at Nyomi for encouragement. Nyomi squeezed her hand, silently urging her to take the plunge.

Finally, Maya raised her hand and shared a story idea about a hidden village where the boundaries between dreams and reality blurred. The other club members listened intently, and when she finished, they responded with genuine interest, asking her questions and giving her ideas to explore.

Maya's face glowed with excitement, and Nyomi felt a surge of pride as she watched her friend begin to open up. It was a small step, but it was one filled with courage.

Over the following weeks, Maya continued to attend the writing club, growing bolder with each meeting. She shared more of her work, each story revealing a piece of her heart that had been hidden away. The club members offered her encouragement and feedback, helping her refine her voice and explore new ideas.

For the first time in her life, Maya felt seen and valued. Her words mattered, and she began to believe that her stories could make a difference. She even began to make friends within the club, forming bonds with students who shared her passion.

One day, as they walked home from a club meeting, Maya turned to Nyomi, her eyes filled with gratitude. "Thank you, Nyomi. I don't know if I could have done this without you."

Nyomi smiled, feeling a warmth spread through her chest. "You're the one who found the courage to step forward, Maya.

I just gave you a little nudge."

Maya's confidence had blossomed, and seeing her friend's transformation filled Nyomi with a deep sense of purpose. She realized that her Butterfly Touch wasn't just a gift; it was a tool that could help people uncover their dreams and live with courage.

That night, Nyomi sat alone in her room, reflecting on her journey with Maya. Helping her friend find her voice had opened Nyomi's eyes to the true power of her gift. It wasn't just about magic; it was about helping others realize their potential.

Nyomi picked up her sketchbook and began to draw. As the lines formed into the shape of a butterfly, she thought about the journey she had been on and the people she had helped along the way. Each line of the butterfly's wings represented a story, a dream, a hope that she had nurtured.

In that quiet moment, Nyomi felt a profound sense of peace. She knew that her gift was meant to be shared, to inspire others to believe in themselves and pursue their dreams.

She closed her sketchbook, a sense of determination settling over her. She would continue to use her Butterfly Touch to make a difference, helping others see the beauty within themselves and the possibilities that lay before them.

That evening, after Maya's first club meeting, Nyomi sat alone, a quiet stillness enveloping her room. She flipped through her sketchbook, absentmindedly tracing the lines of a drawing she had made of a butterfly. The delicate wings reminded her of Maya's journey and, unexpectedly, of her own.

Growing up, Nyomi had often felt like she was trapped in a cage made of expectations and self-doubt. Her parents had always encouraged academic achievements, pushing her to prioritize math and science over her art. It had taken her years to summon the courage to admit, even to herself, that art was her calling. Watching Maya's transformation felt like reliving her own struggles in a way she hadn't anticipated.

Nyomi took a deep breath and let herself sink into the memory. She remembered her own feelings of isolation, the moments when she had felt invisible, convinced that her dreams weren't valid in a world that seemed to only value logic and practicality. In helping Maya, she realized she was also healing parts of herself.

Helping others unlock their dreams makes my own feel more possible, Nyomi thought, a gentle smile forming on her lips. Her Butterfly Touch wasn't just about bringing drawings to life; it was about unlocking the potential in others and witnessing the beauty that unfolded when people believed in themselves.

A Writing Club Project and Overcoming Self-Doubt

The following week, the writing club announced an exciting new project: each member would draft a short story for an upcoming school publication. The project was meant to showcase each writer's unique voice, a way for students to express their personalities through stories.

Maya's face lit up with excitement, but as she read over the assignment details, her expression clouded with worry. "I don't know if I can do this, Nyomi," she whispered. "Writing something for myself is one thing, but for the whole school to see... what if it's terrible?"

Nyomi gave her a reassuring look. "Maya, you're not alone in feeling nervous. Every writer has moments of self-doubt. But you've got a story to tell, and this is your chance to share it. You don't have to be perfect—you just have to be real."

Maya swallowed, her fingers trembling slightly. "I... I don't know what to write about. Nothing in my life is all that interesting."

Nyomi closed her eyes, letting her Butterfly Touch show her glimpses of Maya's untold stories. In her mind's eye, she saw a vibrant, small-town world, filled with family gatherings, summer bonfires, and moments that seemed ordinary but were filled with hidden magic.

"What about a story that blends reality with a touch of magic?" Nyomi suggested. "Something close to your heart, with a little bit of fantasy thrown in. You've got so much inside you, Maya. I know you'll find the right story to tell."

Maya nodded slowly, her uncertainty melting into a spark of inspiration. She started jotting down notes, her ideas flowing more freely, as Nyomi watched her with pride.

A few days later, Maya arrived at the club meeting, visibly upset. She held a printed copy of her story, her fingers gripping the edges of the paper tightly. Nyomi noticed her distress immediately and moved closer.

"Maya, is everything okay?" she asked gently.

Maya shook her head, her voice quivering. "I... I let my older brother read my story last night. I thought he'd understand, but he just laughed and said it was childish. He didn't think anyone would want to read it."

Her words hung heavy in the air, and Nyomi's heart ached for her friend. She could see how deeply Maya had internalized the criticism, her earlier confidence shattered. Nyomi knew that wounds inflicted by loved ones often cut the deepest.

"Not everyone will understand what we create," Nyomi said softly, her hand resting on Maya's shoulder. "But that doesn't mean it isn't valuable. Sometimes, the people closest to us have a hard time seeing our dreams clearly."

Maya took a shaky breath, her eyes glistening. "But... what if he's right? What if no one else will get it either?"

Nyomi reached into her backpack and pulled out her sketchbook. She flipped to a page filled with sketches of butterflies, each one unique, beautiful, and intricate in its own way. "Look at these," she said. "They're all different, and some are more detailed than others. Some people might love one drawing and not care for another. But that doesn't mean each one isn't special. Your story is like that—it's your unique expression, and it will resonate with the people who are meant to see it."

With her Butterfly Touch, Nyomi created a small vision for Maya. In it, she saw a girl standing in front of a crowd, her story being read aloud, and the audience was captivated. She let Maya experience the vision briefly, allowing her to feel the joy of connecting with others through her story.

Maya's face softened, and a tiny smile broke through her sadness. "Maybe... maybe you're right. I'll keep working on it."

Maya's Writing Club Presentation

The day came for each member to share a draft of their short story with the group. Maya had revised hers several times, and though she was still nervous, she was determined to read it aloud. As she stood before her peers, she glanced at Nyomi, who nodded with encouragement.

Maya began to read, her voice trembling at first, but gradually growing stronger. Her story was about a young girl who discovers a hidden world in her backyard, a place where dreams come to life, and where each person's unique spirit animal protects them. Her words painted a vivid world filled with colors, sounds, and emotions that mesmerized the group.

When she finished, the room was silent for a moment before it erupted in applause. Her fellow club members began to comment, praising her creativity and the vividness of her descriptions. The feedback filled Maya's heart with a warmth she hadn't known before. She finally felt accepted, seen, and valued.

As they left the meeting, Maya turned to Nyomi, her face glowing. "I can't believe they liked it. I didn't think anyone would understand."

Nyomi smiled, her heart swelling with pride. "You've shown them who you are, Maya. And it's beautiful. Your story has touched them because you had the courage to share it."

Nyomi's Reflections on the Impact of Her Butterfly Touch

That evening, as she reflected on Maya's journey, Nyomi felt a shift within herself. The joy she had felt watching Maya come out of her shell had left a lasting impact, one that went beyond friendship. Nyomi realized that her Butterfly Touch was more than a simple gift; it was a way to bring people closer to their dreams, to remind them of the beauty within themselves.

She picked up her pencil and began sketching again, this time drawing Maya standing proudly, surrounded by a crowd of people captivated by her words. It was a symbol of Maya's journey, a reminder of the courage it took to follow one's heart.

Nyomi wondered how many more lives she could touch with her gift, how many dreams she could help bring to life. For the first time, she saw her Butterfly Touch not just as magic, but as a purpose—one that went beyond herself.

Maya's Continued Success and Transformation

In the weeks that followed, Maya's confidence continued to blossom. She began contributing to school projects and participating more actively in class discussions. Her once-frequent hesitations grew rare, replaced by a quiet self-assuredness that Nyomi admired deeply.

One day, Maya approached Nyomi with a surprising announcement. "I think... I think I want to enter a writing competition. It's local, but it's a chance to share my work with even more people. I just... I want to try."

Nyomi grinned, thrilled by her friend's courage. "That's incredible, Maya! You're so ready for this."

Maya's eyes sparkled, though a shadow of doubt lingered. "I still feel nervous. I keep hearing my brother's voice in my head, telling me it's all silly. But I want to prove to myself that my words matter."

Nyomi took her hands, squeezing them warmly. "Then do it for yourself, Maya. No one else's opinion matters. If this is your dream, you owe it to yourself to go after it."

Maya nodded, her resolve strengthening. She began working on her submission, throwing herself into her writing with a dedication that amazed even her. She was no longer the timid girl who hid behind a book; she had become someone brave, someone who dared to put her dreams into words.

Nyomi's Reflections on the Power of Dreams

As Maya prepared her entry for the competition, Nyomi sat at home, reflecting on the transformation she had witnessed. Helping Maya had illuminated a truth that Nyomi hadn't fully grasped before: dreams were powerful, and they could change lives, not only for the dreamers but for those around them.

The journey with Maya had shown Nyomi that courage wasn't always loud; sometimes, it was quiet, like the slow unfurling of a flower. It was the willingness to step forward despite fear, to risk failure for the sake of self- expression. And in guiding Maya, Nyomi had found her own sense of purpose, a realization that perhaps her Butterfly Touch was part of a larger path.

She opened her sketchbook and drew a butterfly emerging from a cocoon, symbolizing the journey Maya had taken. The image felt right—a reflection of transformation, growth, and the courage it took to reveal one's true self.

As Nyomi added the final touches to the sketch, she felt a peace settle over her. She knew that her journey as a mentor was only beginning. There were other dreams to nurture, other people to encourage. And with her Butterfly Touch, she could help others find the strength to spread their wings.

The following week, the writing club met with an exciting new theme for their upcoming stories: "Moments of Magic." Liam, the club's leader, encouraged members to explore moments of wonder in their work, urging them to write about something extraordinary that could happen in an ordinary world.

When Maya heard the theme, her eyes lit up with excitement, but Nyomi could see a flicker of hesitation as well. As everyone settled in to brainstorm ideas, Nyomi leaned over to Maya.

"That theme sounds perfect for you," Nyomi whispered with a smile. "You're so good at creating magic with words."

Maya blushed, fidgeting with her notebook. "I have a few ideas, but... I don't know if they're good enough. I keep second-guessing myself."

Nyomi placed a comforting hand on Maya's shoulder. "How about I show you a little something to spark your confidence?"

With Maya's quiet nod of consent, Nyomi closed her eyes and focused her Butterfly Touch. She crafted a vision of Maya reading aloud from her story, her words painting vivid scenes for an audience spellbound by her imagination. Nyomi let the vision show Maya how her words created worlds, bringing joy and wonder to the listeners as her tale unfolded.

As the vision faded, Maya looked at Nyomi with wide, shining eyes. "That was... amazing. I didn't know my words could have that kind of power."

Nyomi smiled softly. "You have a gift, Maya. Your stories matter, and this theme is the perfect chance to show it. Just let yourself believe."

With a newfound confidence, Maya began scribbling ideas in her notebook, the fear that had held her back now replaced by a quiet determination. Nyomi watched her friend write, feeling a deep sense of satisfaction. Helping Maya was like watching a flower bloom—a delicate yet powerful transformation that filled her with joy.

Overcoming Writer's Block

A few days later, Maya approached Nyomi in the hallway, looking worried. "I'm stuck," she admitted, clutching her notebook tightly to her chest. "I started writing my story for the club, but I can't seem to finish it. Every time I try, the words just... stop."

Nyomi nodded thoughtfully, sensing Maya's frustration. She knew that writer's block could be daunting, especially when self-doubt crept in. "Let's take a walk," Nyomi suggested. "Maybe a change of scenery will help."

They strolled around the campus, and Nyomi gently prompted Maya to talk about her story. Maya described a scene where her main character, a young girl, finds a glowing key in her grandmother's attic that unlocks a hidden door. But each time Maya tried to write the next part, she felt blocked, as if the magic she had created wasn't enough to carry the story forward.

As they walked, Nyomi felt the familiar tingle of her Butterfly Touch, and an idea came to her. "Close your eyes for a moment," she encouraged Maya. "Imagine yourself as the main character in your story. What do you see?"

Maya hesitated, then closed her eyes. Nyomi activated her Butterfly Touch, showing Maya a vision of herself holding the glowing key, walking through a door that opened onto a world filled with luminous gardens, floating lanterns, and shimmering lakes. The vision captured the essence of wonder, a place where magic was real and alive, beckoning Maya's character to explore further.

When Maya opened her eyes, she was beaming, her previous worry replaced by excitement. "I know exactly what to write next," she said, gripping her notebook with renewed enthusiasm. "Thank you, Nyomi. That vision—it felt so real."

Nyomi laughed softly. "That's because it is real—at least, as real as you make it. Just remember, Maya, the magic is already inside you. All you have to do is let it out."

Reading Day at the Club

As the "Moments of Magic" assignment deadline approached, the writing club held a reading day for everyone to share their drafts. The room buzzed with excitement as each member took a turn reading their stories aloud, their voices bringing their unique worlds and ideas to life.

When it was Maya's turn, she stood up with her story in hand, glancing at Nyomi for encouragement. Nyomi gave her a reassuring nod, silently conveying her belief in Maya's ability to captivate the room.

Maya cleared her throat and began to read. Her story unfolded with vivid descriptions of the mysterious attic, the magical key, and the fantastical world that her character discovered. As Maya spoke, Nyomi saw a transformation in her friend's expression—her voice grew stronger, her words more confident, as if she were stepping into her own power.

When Maya finished, the room was silent for a moment, and then everyone burst into applause. The club members offered compliments and enthusiastic feedback, praising Maya's creativity and storytelling skills.

Liam approached her afterward, giving her a warm smile. "Maya, that was incredible. You have a real talent for creating worlds. I hope you keep writing—your stories deserve to be shared."

Maya blushed, overwhelmed by the positive response. She looked at Nyomi with gratitude, mouthing a silent "thank you." Nyomi smiled back, feeling a sense of pride and fulfillment. This moment was Maya's, a testament to her bravery and the power of believing in her dreams.

One evening, Maya and Nyomi decided to have a late-night writing session at Nyomi's house. They sat together in her room, surrounded by notebooks, snacks, and the soft glow of a desk lamp.

Maya tapped her pen against her notebook thoughtfully. "It's strange... for so long, I was afraid of putting my stories out there. Now, I can't imagine not writing. It's like... like it's a part of me."

Nyomi nodded, understanding exactly what she meant. "That's how you know it's something you were meant to do. Writing is your way of sharing a piece of yourself with the world."

As they talked, Nyomi felt a surge of energy within her. She sensed that this was the perfect moment for one last vision, one that would show Maya the path she could walk if she continued to believe in herself. Closing her eyes, Nyomi reached out with her Butterfly Touch, creating a vision that was both vibrant and inspiring.

In the vision, Maya was seated at a table in a packed bookstore, surrounded by stacks of her own published books. Fans lined up, eagerly waiting for her to sign their copies, and Maya's face glowed with pride and happiness. She chatted with her readers, listening as they shared how her stories had touched them, inspired them, or brought them comfort.

When the vision faded, Maya looked at Nyomi, her eyes wide with awe. "That was... was that really me? Signing books?"

Nyomi nodded, her expression gentle. "That could be you, Maya. That's the future waiting for you, if you keep following your passion. Believe in yourself—you have a gift, and the world needs your stories."

Tears glistened in Maya's eyes, and she wiped them away, laughing softly. "I used to think that dreams like that were impossible. But with you here... it feels like anything is possible."

The Announcement of Maya's Story

The day finally came when the school published the writing club's stories in an anthology that would be shared with the student body. Maya's story was featured prominently, with a beautiful illustration that captured the essence of her magical world.

As she held the printed copy in her hands, Maya's face lit up with joy. She turned to Nyomi, unable to contain her excitement. "It's real," she whispered, almost in disbelief. "My story... it's in here. People are going to read it!"

Nyomi squeezed her shoulder, her pride evident. "Yes, they are. And they're going to love it, Maya. This is just the beginning for you."

Later that day, Nyomi watched as students gathered around Maya to congratulate her, some of them expressing how much they had enjoyed her story. She saw Maya talking animatedly, sharing details about her writing process and answering questions about her characters. It was a far cry from the shy, reserved girl who had once sat alone with her books, too afraid to share her voice.

That evening, Nyomi found herself alone, sitting by her window and gazing out at the stars. Helping Maya had shown her so much more than she could have imagined about her Butterfly Touch. This journey hadn't just been about magic—it had been about friendship, courage, and the quiet power of believing in oneself.

In guiding Maya, Nyomi had found a deeper understanding of her own purpose. She realized that her gift could help others find the courage to face their dreams, just as it had helped her see the beauty within herself.

As she sat there, a sense of peace and fulfillment washed over her. She knew her journey was far from over, but for now, she felt content. Helping Maya had been her own moment of magic, a reminder that true purpose often lay in the connections we forged and the dreams we helped to nurture.

With a smile, Nyomi closed her eyes, whispering a quiet promise to herself. She would continue to use her Butterfly Touch to help others, to inspire them to see their own potential, and to believe that anything was possible.

CHAPTER 15: ETHAN'S STRUGGLE

Nyomi had noticed Ethan around school for months. He was hard to miss, with his unkempt hair, worn leather jacket, and an expression that seemed to dare anyone to approach him. He was a figure of defiance in a school where most students tried to fit in, where conformity often felt like a survival strategy.

Ethan skipped classes frequently, and when he did show up, it was often to disrupt. Teachers would sigh and shake their heads, clearly exasperated with him. Nyomi had heard rumors of a difficult home life, but nothing concrete. All she knew was that Ethan kept everyone at arm's length and wore his isolation like armor.

One day, Nyomi found herself in the courtyard during lunch, sketching quietly under the shade of a large oak tree. Out of the corner of her eye, she spotted Ethan sitting alone at the far end, absently tossing rocks into a patch of dirt, his gaze unfocused.

Taking a deep breath, Nyomi decided to approach him. She'd helped Maya find her courage; maybe she could do the same for Ethan. But as she walked over, Ethan glanced up and scowled.

"What do you want?" he muttered, his voice laced with hostility.

Nyomi hesitated, searching for the right words. "I just thought you might want some company."

Ethan scoffed. "Not interested. I don't need anyone, least of all someone who thinks they can 'fix' me."

His words stung, but Nyomi refused to give up. "I'm not here to fix anyone, Ethan. I just thought you might like to talk."

He narrowed his eyes, a bitter smile tugging at the corner of his mouth. "Talk? About what? How everything in my life is falling apart? You wouldn't understand."

Without another word, Ethan stood up and strode away, leaving Nyomi standing alone, her heart heavy. She'd sensed the pain behind his words, a raw and unspoken hurt that reminded her of the loneliness she'd felt before finding her own path.

Learning About Ethan's Background Over the next few days, Nyomi couldn't shake the image of Ethan's bitter expression and his words: You wouldn't understand. She wanted to help, but she realized that approaching him without understanding his situation would be pointless.

One afternoon, Nyomi found herself in the library, browsing through the shelves when she noticed Mrs. Gallagher, a kind teacher who taught English and seemed to know each student's story as if they were characters in one of her novels.

"Mrs. Gallagher," Nyomi said, her voice low. "Can I ask you something?"

The teacher looked up from her book and smiled warmly. "Of course, dear. What's on your mind?"

Nyomi hesitated, wondering how much she should say. "It's about Ethan. I... I tried to talk to him the other day, but he seemed really upset. I just... I feel like there's something more going on."

Mrs. Gallagher's face softened. "Ethan's had a rough time, Nyomi. His parents are going through a difficult divorce, and he's caught in the middle. From what I understand, they've been fighting over custody, and it's taken a toll on him. He acts out because it's easier than facing the pain he feels inside."

Nyomi felt a pang of sympathy. The more she learned, the more she realized how heavy Ethan's burden must be. It wasn't just teenage rebellion

—it was the fallout from a broken home, a life splintered by circumstances beyond his control.

"Thank you, Mrs. Gallagher," Nyomi said softly. She knew now that reaching Ethan would require patience and understanding, and maybe—just maybe—her Butterfly Touch could help him see a way forward.

A Confrontation with Ethan The next day, Nyomi decided to try again. She spotted Ethan loitering by the bike racks after school, kicking at the ground in a way that suggested he was itching for something to release his frustration.

She approached him carefully, calling out his name to avoid startling him. "Ethan!"

He turned, rolling his eyes when he saw her. "Didn't I tell you to leave me alone?"

"I know," Nyomi replied calmly, refusing to back down. "But I also know that you're going through a lot right now. You don't have to go through it alone."

Ethan scoffed, his expression hardening. "What makes you think you know anything about me?"

Nyomi held his gaze, her voice steady. "I don't know everything, but I do know what it feels like to feel trapped, like the world is caving in around you. Sometimes... we just need someone who understands."

For a brief moment, something flickered in Ethan's eyes— something raw and vulnerable. But it vanished as quickly as it had appeared, replaced by anger. "You don't get it, Nyomi. No one does. Just leave me alone. I don't need your pity."

He turned and walked away, his shoulders hunched, a storm of emotions radiating from him. Nyomi felt a wave of frustration but resolved not to give up. She knew she'd need to try a different approach, one that could help him see that his pain didn't have to define him.

Using the Butterfly Touch to Understand Ethan That night, Nyomi sat alone in her room, thinking about Ethan and his seemingly impenetrable walls. She knew there had to be a way to reach him, to show him that he wasn't alone. Her Butterfly Touch had helped others see their potential, and maybe, just maybe, it could help Ethan confront the things he was running from.

Taking a deep breath, Nyomi closed her eyes and focused on Ethan, letting her Butterfly Touch guide her. She felt her surroundings shift, the world becoming dreamlike and surreal as she entered his mindscape.

In the vision, she saw Ethan skating down an endless road, the sky dark and heavy with storm clouds. He was moving fast, almost recklessly, as if trying to escape something unseen. Nyomi noticed the tension in his posture, the way he glanced back over his shoulder as if something were chasing him.

Suddenly, the road twisted and fragmented, turning into a chaotic labyrinth. Shadows loomed around him, representing the fear and uncertainty he couldn't outrun. Nyomi watched as

Ethan's pace faltered, his movements growing more frantic. His escape was a loop, leading him nowhere.

With a surge of empathy, Nyomi reached out, projecting a vision of herself standing at the end of the road, waiting for him with open arms. She wanted him to see that he didn't have to face his fears alone.

The vision ended, and Nyomi opened her eyes, her heart heavy with the weight of what she'd seen. She understood now—Ethan wasn't defiant because he wanted to be difficult; he was lost, desperate to escape the things that haunted him. If she could show him a way out, perhaps he'd find his own path forward.

Encouraging Ethan to Join the Skateboarding Club The following day, Nyomi approached Ethan after school. He was sitting alone near the parking lot, his skateboard beside him, and for the first time, he didn't glare at her. Instead, he looked tired, worn down.

"Hey," Nyomi greeted, sitting down next to him. He didn't reply, but he didn't tell her to leave either.

"I saw you skating the other day," she said, keeping her tone casual. "You're really good. Have you ever thought about joining the school's skateboarding club?"

Ethan raised an eyebrow, clearly skeptical. "A club? You think I'm the 'join a club' type?"

Nyomi smiled. "Maybe not, but it could be a way to channel some of that energy. Skating might give you a place to escape, but it could also be a way to connect. You don't have to face everything alone."

Ethan scoffed, but his expression softened slightly. He looked away, considering her words. After a long pause, he muttered, "I'll think about it."

It wasn't a full commitment, but it was a start, a crack in the walls he'd built around himself. Nyomi felt a glimmer of hope, knowing that even a small step was progress.

Ethan's First Day with the Skateboarding Club The next week, Ethan showed up at the skateboarding club, looking uncertain and out of place. The other club members welcomed him, though he remained distant, reluctant to engage fully. Nyomi watched from a distance, offering silent encouragement.

Ethan skated with the group but kept mostly to himself, his eyes wary, as if expecting rejection at any moment. But as the session went on, he began to relax, letting his focus shift from his internal turmoil to the rhythm of his movements.

One of the club leaders approached him, complimenting his skills and inviting him to join a practice session. Ethan hesitated, glancing at Nyomi, who gave him a supportive nod. Tentatively, he accepted, joining in the drills and starting to open up, if only slightly.

Ethan's Frustration with the Skateboarding Club A few days later, Ethan attended another skateboarding club meeting. The club members were friendly and open, often exchanging tips and tricks on techniques or cheering each other on. But while the other skaters seemed at ease, Ethan struggled to shake off his guarded demeanor.

During the session, the club leader, Tyler, suggested they all try a new trick: an ollie down the three-stair by the bleachers. One by one, the skaters attempted it, some landing smoothly, others stumbling, but all getting back up to try again. When it was Ethan's turn, he hesitated, feeling all eyes on him.

He took a breath, rolling toward the stairs, but his mind flashed with self-doubt. His foot slipped as he kicked down, and his board skidded out from under him, sending him sprawling onto the concrete. The other skaters rushed over, offering him a hand, but Ethan pushed them away, scowling.

"Back off. I don't need help," he muttered, dusting himself off. He grabbed his skateboard and walked away, his frustration evident.

From the sidelines, Nyomi watched, her heart aching. She knew this wasn't just about the trick—Ethan was grappling with feeling vulnerable and exposed. She let him have his space, deciding it would be better to approach him later when he had cooled down.

A Late-Night Conversation with Nyomi That evening, Nyomi found Ethan sitting alone near the park, where he often went after school. She approached quietly, taking a seat beside him on the bench without saying a word. The silence stretched between them, but it wasn't uncomfortable. Finally, Ethan broke it.

"Why do you keep following me around?" he asked, his tone softer than usual. "Don't you have better things to do?"

Nyomi shrugged. "Maybe. But I think you're worth the effort. Besides, you're not the only one who's felt like an outsider."

Ethan frowned, his gaze focused on the ground. "Yeah? And what do you know about that?"

Nyomi took a deep breath, choosing her words carefully. "I know what it feels like to have something important to you that no one else understands. It's like carrying a weight you can't put down, one that keeps you at a distance from everyone else. For me, it was my art. For you... maybe it's skating."

He looked at her, a flicker of surprise in his eyes. "It's just skating," he muttered, as if trying to convince himself.

"Maybe it's more than that," Nyomi suggested gently. "Maybe it's something you can rely on when everything else feels out of control."

Ethan's face softened slightly, and for a moment, Nyomi thought he might open up. But he quickly closed off, his walls going back up. "Whatever. I don't need advice from you."

Nyomi sighed but didn't push him. She knew he needed time to trust her, and she was willing to be patient. She'd seen glimpses of the pain he was hiding, and she was determined to help him, even if it took a while.

Using the Butterfly Touch to Create a Vision for Ethan The next day, Nyomi decided to try something different. She had seen Ethan's struggle firsthand, and she wanted to give him a glimpse of the potential she saw within him—a potential he seemed unable to see for himself.

After school, she found him sitting on the low wall by the skate park, staring off into the distance. She approached him and said, "Can I show you something?"

He eyed her suspiciously but didn't protest. Nyomi reached out, letting her Butterfly Touch flow gently, creating a vision just for him.

In the vision, Ethan stood on a sunlit street, his skateboard under his feet as he raced forward. The path was smooth, the air clear, and he was surrounded by a group of skaters who cheered him on. He landed each trick with ease, the thrill of success lifting his spirits. He was smiling—a wide, genuine smile that Nyomi hadn't seen before.

As the vision faded, Ethan blinked, his expression softening. "What... was that?" he asked, his voice barely above a whisper.

"It's what I see in you," Nyomi replied. "Someone who's strong, resilient, and capable of doing great things. You don't have to face everything alone, Ethan. There are people who want to support you—you just have to let them in."

Ethan looked away, but Nyomi could tell her words had reached him. The vision had shown him a version of himself he hadn't believed was possible, and it was slowly chipping away at the walls he'd built around his heart.

Ethan's Breakthrough with the Club Over the next few weeks, Ethan continued attending the skateboarding club. He was still quiet, still kept to himself, but he began to try more tricks, pushing himself to improve. The other club members noticed his dedication and began to offer tips and encouragement, which he accepted with only a slight hesitation.

One afternoon, Tyler, the club leader, suggested a friendly competition. "Whoever lands the cleanest ollie down the three-stair gets to pick the next spot for a skate session," he announced with a grin.

Ethan's heart pounded as he took his turn. He'd been practicing this trick ever since his first failed attempt, determined to land it cleanly. As he rolled toward the stairs, he felt a surge of confidence—a belief in himself that had been slowly building thanks to Nyomi's encouragement.

He kicked down, his body moving instinctively, and the board landed smoothly beneath him. The club erupted into cheers, and for the first time, Ethan felt a genuine sense of belonging.

Tyler clapped him on the back. "Nice work, Ethan. You get to choose the next spot!"

A small smile crept onto Ethan's face. He glanced at Nyomi, who stood nearby, giving him an approving nod. For the first time, he felt like he wasn't just skating to escape—he was skating for the joy of it, and for the friendships he was beginning to form.

Ethan Opens Up to Nyomi That evening, as they walked home together, Ethan seemed different—lighter, as if a weight had been lifted from his shoulders. They walked in silence for a while before he finally spoke.

"My parents," he began hesitantly, "they're going through a divorce. It's been going on for months, and... I just feel like I don't belong anywhere. Like no matter what I do, I'm just... in the way."

Nyomi listened quietly, her heart aching for him. She reached out, placing a comforting hand on his shoulder. "You're not in the way, Ethan. You're just caught in something that's out of your control. And that doesn't make it any easier, but it doesn't make you any less important."

Ethan swallowed, nodding slowly. "Skating... it's the only thing that feels right. When I'm on my board, I don't have to think about anything else."

Nyomi smiled gently. "Then let it be your escape, but don't let it be your cage. You can use it to express yourself, to connect with others. And you don't have to do it alone."

For the first time, Ethan didn't argue or push back. Instead, he nodded, his expression thoughtful. Nyomi knew he was beginning to understand, to realize that there were people who cared about him.

Ethan's Newfound Confidence As the days went by, Ethan continued to attend the skateboarding club, each session a new opportunity to push his limits and grow. His skills improved, and so did his confidence. He started laughing more, even sharing jokes with his teammates, something he hadn't done in a long time.

One afternoon, Tyler announced that they'd be organizing a skate demo at the school's spring festival. It would be an opportunity for the club to showcase their skills and hopefully recruit more members. Ethan looked nervous but excited, and Nyomi could see the fire in his eyes—a desire to prove to himself that he could succeed, that he could belong.

The Skate Demo and a Heartfelt Thanks On the day of the spring festival, the skateboarding club gathered by the bleachers, setting up ramps and preparing for the demo. Ethan felt a mix of excitement and nerves, but Nyomi's steady presence calmed him.

When it was his turn, he stepped onto the ramp, taking a deep breath as he pushed forward. He performed each trick with precision, the cheers from the crowd fueling his confidence. By the end of the demo, he was beaming, his heart racing with pride.

After the performance, Ethan found Nyomi by the edge of the crowd. Without a word, he pulled her into a quick, awkward hug, his face flushed with emotion.

"Thank you, Nyomi," he murmured, his voice choked with gratitude. "I don't know where I'd be without you. You helped me find something worth holding on to."

Nyomi smiled, touched by his words. "You found it yourself, Ethan. I just reminded you that you could."

As they stood there, Ethan felt a sense of peace he hadn't known in a long time. For the first time, he felt like he belonged—not just in the skateboarding club, but within himself. And he knew that whatever challenges lay ahead, he would face them with a newfound strength, and with friends who believed in him.

In the weeks that followed, Ethan continued to grow, his journey of self- discovery inspiring others around him. He learned to trust, to open up, and to embrace the support of his friends, all while finding freedom in the art of skateboarding. His connection with Nyomi remained strong, a friendship born from understanding and compassion.

Through Ethan, Nyomi had deepened her understanding of her own gift. Her Butterfly Touch wasn't just a magical ability —it was a means of healing, of helping others see their worth and realize their potential. She knew there were others who might need her guidance, and she felt ready to continue using her gift to make a difference.

As they moved forward, both Nyomi and Ethan knew that they would face new challenges, but with each other's support, they felt ready to take on whatever came next, their friendship a beacon of hope and strength.

Ethan's Backstory and Family Dynamics As Nyomi spent more time with Ethan, she learned bits and pieces about his life, mostly through fleeting comments or offhand remarks. One afternoon, while they were sitting on the school lawn after a skateboarding session, Ethan opened up unexpectedly.

"My parents... they were never really happy," he began, his gaze fixed on the grass. "I mean, I don't even remember them laughing together. But they always stayed together for my sake—or so they said."

Nyomi listened quietly, sensing that he was finally letting go of things he'd been holding inside for a long time.

"When they told me they were getting divorced, I thought, 'Good. Maybe now everyone will be happier.' But instead, it's been a nightmare. They're fighting over who gets custody of me like I'm some... prize or something."

He clenched his fists, his voice tightening with anger. "And it's not just that. They're using me to hurt each other. Mom says Dad's unreliable, and Dad says Mom's too controlling. I feel like... like I'm being torn in two."

Nyomi placed a comforting hand on his arm. "I'm so sorry, Ethan. That sounds incredibly hard. No one should feel like they're stuck in the middle."

Ethan took a deep, shuddering breath. "That's why I started skipping class and acting out. It's like, if they're going to tear everything apart, why should I even try? What's the point?"

Nyomi squeezed his arm gently. "Sometimes, when everything feels out of control, it helps to focus on something you can control—like your own happiness. Skating, connecting with others, finding things that make you feel whole... maybe that can be your way of holding onto yourself."

Ethan nodded slowly, as though her words were starting to make sense. He looked at her with a flicker of gratitude. "Thanks, Nyomi. I don't think anyone's ever... really listened before."

Deeper Connections at the Skateboarding Club With each skateboarding session, Ethan grew more comfortable around his teammates. He started sharing tips, laughing with them, and joining in on friendly challenges. The club became a refuge—a place where he could be himself, free from the chaos of his home life.

One day, after a particularly fun practice, Tyler, the club leader, slapped Ethan on the back and said, "You know, you've got some serious talent. Ever thought about entering competitions?"

Ethan's eyes widened. "Me? In a competition?"

"Why not?" Tyler replied with a grin. "You've got the skills, and I think it'd be awesome to have you represent the club. Plus, it's a good way to focus your energy."

Ethan glanced over at Nyomi, who nodded encouragingly. "It could be a great opportunity, Ethan. You're not just skating to get away from things anymore. You're skating because you love it."

The idea of a competition sparked something in him—a sense of purpose he hadn't felt in a long time. For the first time, he considered that his passion for skating might actually lead him somewhere.

"Alright," he said with a shy smile. "I'll think about it."

Nyomi's Reflection on Mentorship That evening, Nyomi sat in her room, sketchbook open but untouched, her thoughts drifting to Ethan. Helping him find his way through his struggles had taught her more than she'd expected about her own journey. She'd initially seen her Butterfly Touch as a simple gift, a way to bring art to life. But over time, she realized it was a tool for connection and healing, a way to reach out to people who felt lost.

She thought back to Maya, who had flourished under her encouragement, and to Ethan, whose walls were slowly coming down. She'd started to understand that her gift was about more than creating visions—it was about helping people see what was already inside of them.

"Maybe that's my purpose," she whispered to herself. "To help others find their strength."

The thought filled her with a warm sense of peace. She knew that she would continue using her Butterfly Touch to guide others, to help them see the beauty and potential within themselves.

A New Vision for Ethan's Future As Ethan grew more involved in the skateboarding club, Nyomi could see his confidence blossoming. But she sensed that he still had doubts—uncertainties about his future and whether he could truly escape the shadow of his parents' divorce.

One afternoon, after practice, Nyomi decided to offer him a new vision. She approached him, gently placing a hand on his shoulder. "Ethan, can I show you something?"

He looked at her curiously, then nodded. "Sure."

Nyomi focused her Butterfly Touch, creating a vision of Ethan a few years in the future. In the vision, he was at a skate park, surrounded by a group of young kids who watched him with admiration. He was coaching them, helping them learn tricks, and cheering them on as they found their own confidence.

When the vision faded, Ethan's face softened, his eyes filled with wonder. "Was that... me? Teaching kids?"

Nyomi smiled. "Yes. I see you as someone who can inspire others, just like you're learning to inspire yourself. You have the ability to make a difference, Ethan—to be someone that others look up to."

He took a deep breath, the idea sinking in. For the first time, he began to see his passion for skating as something that could not only bring him peace but also help others.

Preparing for the Competition As the weeks passed, Ethan decided to take Tyler's advice and enter a local skateboarding competition. He practiced every day, pouring his energy into perfecting his tricks.

Nyomi often stayed after school to watch him, cheering him on and offering support.

One day, as he landed a particularly difficult trick, he skated over to her, his face beaming with pride. "Did you see that?" he asked, breathless.

Nyomi grinned. "You nailed it! I knew you could."

Ethan's smile faltered slightly, his gaze dropping. "I just... I hope my parents show up. I know it's a long shot, but part of me hopes they'll come and see that I'm... worth something."

Nyomi's heart ached for him, and she placed a reassuring hand on his shoulder. "No matter what happens, Ethan, you're already proving to yourself that you're worth it. You're doing this for you, not for anyone else."

He nodded, his determination rekindled. "Yeah. You're right. This is my chance to show myself what I'm capable of."

The Competition Day and a Moment of Doubt The day of the competition arrived, and Ethan's nerves were palpable.

The skate park buzzed with excitement as skaters from different schools gathered, each hoping to make a name for themselves.

Ethan glanced around, scanning the crowd, but his parents were nowhere to be seen. A wave of disappointment washed over him, and for a moment, he wondered if it was even worth competing.

Sensing his hesitation, Nyomi approached him, her voice gentle. "You're not alone, Ethan. You've got your friends here, and you've got me. This moment is yours, regardless of who shows up."

He took a deep breath, nodding slowly. "Thanks, Nyomi. I... I needed to hear that."

With renewed determination, he stepped onto the ramp, ready to show everyone, but most importantly himself, what he could do.

Ethan's Performance and the Celebration Ethan's performance was flawless. He landed every trick with precision, his movements a blend of power and grace. The crowd cheered, and his teammates from the skateboarding club erupted with excitement, congratulating him as he finished his run.

Tyler clapped him on the back. "That was incredible, Ethan! You owned that ramp!"

Nyomi beamed with pride, watching as Ethan soaked in the applause. She saw in his eyes a new confidence, a sense of belonging that hadn't been there before. This was more than a competition—it was a turning point, a moment where he embraced his own potential.

After the competition, the club celebrated with pizza at a local hangout. As they laughed and shared stories, Ethan felt a sense of camaraderie that he hadn't experienced in a long time. He glanced over at Nyomi, and for the first time, he realized just how much she'd helped him find his way.

A Heartfelt Conversation with Nyomi Later that evening, as they walked home, Ethan turned to Nyomi, his expression sincere. "I don't think I ever thanked you properly... for everything."

Nyomi smiled softly. "You don't have to thank me, Ethan. I'm just glad I could help you see how strong you are."

He looked down, his voice barely a whisper. "I've never really had anyone believe in me like you do. And I think... I think that's what I needed most."

Nyomi placed a comforting hand on his shoulder. "We all need someone to believe in us, Ethan. Sometimes, that belief gives us the strength to believe in ourselves."

They walked in silence for a moment, the weight of the conversation settling around them. Ethan felt a sense of peace he hadn't known before— a peace that came from accepting himself and the journey he was on.

Ethan's Final Reflection and Newfound Purpose In the days following the competition, Ethan continued to reflect on his journey. He had started skating to escape, to find a way out of his pain. But now, it had become something more—a passion, a purpose, a source of pride.

One afternoon, as he practiced at the skate park, a young kid approached him, wide-eyed and eager. "Hey, can you show me how to do that trick?" the boy asked, pointing at Ethan's skateboard.

Ethan grinned, feeling a surge of warmth. "Sure thing, kid. Let's start with the basics."

As he coached the boy, he realized that he was becoming the person Nyomi had shown him in her vision—a mentor, someone who could guide others the way she had guided him.

The thought filled him with gratitude and a renewed sense of purpose.

Ethan looked across the park, spotting Nyomi sitting on a bench, sketchbook in hand. She waved, her smile bright and full of pride. In that moment, Ethan knew he wasn't just a kid with a broken family and a rebellious streak. He was someone with strength, with resilience, and with a future he could shape.

And for that, he would always be grateful.

Ethan's Reflection on the Competition and Its Aftermath The weekend after the skateboarding competition, Ethan found himself back at the skate park, sitting on the edge of a ramp with his board resting across his knees. The echoes of the crowd's cheers and the sense of accomplishment still lingered, but beneath that, he felt a quieter, more personal satisfaction—a sense of pride in himself that he'd rarely experienced.

He ran a hand through his hair, his gaze focused on the empty park as he thought back to the competition. I did it, he thought, almost in disbelief. I actually did it.

As he sat there, a thought crossed his mind: What if he could use this feeling to carry him through other areas of his life? The skateboarding club had become a sanctuary, a place where he felt like he could belong, but he wondered if he could bring this newfound confidence into his relationships, too—especially with his family.

A pang of sadness tugged at him as he remembered his parents' absence from the competition. Despite the personal growth he had achieved, the void of their support still hurt. But the realization filled him with a strange new resolve. I can't control them, he thought, but I can control how I move forward.

Ethan took a deep breath, letting the cool afternoon air fill his lungs. For the first time, he felt ready to confront the reality of his family situation and decide what he wanted for his own future.

A Quiet Conversation with Nyomi Later that day, Ethan met up with Nyomi by the school's library. She was sitting on the steps, flipping through her sketchbook, and she looked up with a bright smile as he approached.

"Hey, Ethan! How are you feeling after the big day?"

Ethan shrugged, a small smile tugging at his lips. "Honestly? It still feels kind of surreal. But... I think I'm starting to understand what you've been telling me all along—that I don't have to let my past hold me back."

Nyomi nodded, her eyes warm with understanding. "You've come a long way, Ethan. I'm really proud of you."

He looked down, a flicker of vulnerability crossing his face. "Do you think... Do you think people can really change? I mean, do you think I can keep moving forward, even if things with my family stay the same?"

Nyomi reached out, resting a gentle hand on his shoulder. "I think change is possible for everyone. And you've already proven that you're capable of it. Whatever happens with your family, you have the strength to build your own future. You've already started doing it."

Ethan took a deep breath, feeling a newfound sense of determination. "Thank you, Nyomi. I... I don't know if I would've made it this far without you."

Nyomi squeezed his shoulder gently. "You're the one who did the work, Ethan. I just reminded you of what was already inside you."

He felt a wave of gratitude wash over him. For the first time, he realized that Nyomi's presence in his life had been more than a source of encouragement—she had helped him see his own worth and had shown him that he wasn't as alone as he'd thought.

Bonding Moments with the Skateboarding Club As the weeks went on, Ethan became even closer with his skateboarding teammates. They began to rely on each other, not only for tips and techniques but also as friends. The bonds he was forming felt solid, a foundation of support that he could lean on.

One afternoon, the club organized a trip to a skate park in a nearby town. They piled into Tyler's van, joking and laughing the entire way there. For Ethan, the trip felt like more than just a fun outing—it was a celebration of his newfound confidence and a chance to build deeper connections.

At the park, Ethan found himself in conversation with Sam, one of his teammates, who had been in the club for years. Sam shared stories about his own challenges growing up, explaining how skateboarding had given him an outlet.

"Honestly, man," Sam said, adjusting his helmet, "we all got our stuff to deal with. But out here, none of it matters. It's just you, the board, and the moment."

Ethan nodded, feeling the truth of Sam's words. "Yeah... I think that's what I love about it. For the first time, I feel like I'm where I belong."

They shared a fist bump, a silent acknowledgment of the journey each of them was on. As they skated together, Ethan felt a profound sense of camaraderie—a feeling that had once felt out of reach but now filled him with a deep sense of belonging.

A New Vision for Ethan's Future One afternoon, Nyomi invited Ethan to the quiet garden behind the school, a place they'd often visited when they needed to talk without interruption. She had something special planned, something that would help Ethan see just how far he'd come.

As they sat together on a bench beneath the shade of a large oak tree, Nyomi turned to him, her expression gentle but purposeful. "Ethan, I want to show you something. One last vision."

He looked at her with curiosity, nodding. "Alright. Show me."

Nyomi reached out with her Butterfly Touch, letting her magic flow through her. In a moment, the world around them transformed into a dreamlike vision of the future. Ethan saw himself at a skate park, surrounded by young skaters who looked up to him with admiration. He was teaching them, guiding them with patience and confidence, and their faces lit up with excitement and gratitude.

In the vision, Ethan could see the joy in his own expression as he watched them succeed, as he helped them find the same sense of belonging that had once eluded him. He was a mentor, a role model—someone who had learned to transform his struggles into strength.

As the vision faded, Ethan blinked, his heart pounding with emotion. "Is that... is that really what you see in me?"

Nyomi nodded, her voice soft. "Yes. You've come so far, Ethan. And now, you have the power to help others the way you've learned to help yourself. That's the kind of future you deserve."

He looked away, a hint of tears in his eyes. "I... I don't even know what to say. I never thought that could be me."

"It already is," Nyomi said gently. "You just have to believe in it."

Confronting His Parents The following weekend, Ethan decided to confront his parents about the divorce. He knew he couldn't change the past, but he felt ready to express his feelings and set boundaries for himself.

They met in the living room of his mother's house, the tension thick in the air as they sat down to talk. Ethan took a deep breath, feeling the weight of Nyomi's words and the support of his friends behind him.

"Mom, Dad... I need to say something," he began, his voice steady but firm. "I know you're both going through a lot, but so am I. And I can't keep feeling like I'm caught in the middle. It's not fair."

His parents exchanged a glance, surprise in their eyes as they listened. Ethan's father shifted uncomfortably, but his mother reached out, her hand resting gently on his.

"I love you both," Ethan continued, "but I can't keep carrying this weight. I need to focus on my own life, my own future. And that means setting boundaries. I need you to respect that."

The silence that followed was heavy, but Ethan felt a surge of relief. He had finally voiced the things he'd been holding inside for so long, and it felt like a weight had lifted from his shoulders.

His mother nodded slowly, her eyes softening. "Ethan... I'm so sorry. I didn't realize how much this was hurting you."

His father cleared his throat, nodding as well. "We both want what's best for you, son. We'll do our best to respect your wishes."

Ethan felt a wave of gratitude, and though he knew there would still be challenges, he felt more empowered than ever to face them.

A Final Celebration with Friends As summer approached, the skateboarding club organized a small celebration at the park to mark the end of the school year. They set up ramps, brought snacks, and invited friends and family to watch them perform their best tricks.

Ethan was at the center of the action, his energy infectious as he led the group through a series of impressive moves. His friends cheered him on, and he felt a sense of pride and joy that he could share with those who had supported him.

After the event, Ethan sat on a picnic table with Nyomi, Tyler, Sam, and a few other club members. They laughed, shared stories, and reminisced about the year's ups and downs. For Ethan, it felt like he was finally surrounded by people who understood him, who valued him for who he was.

As the sun began to set, Tyler raised a soda can in a toast. "To friendships, to growth, and to a summer filled with epic skating!"

They all clinked their cans, laughter filling the air. Ethan looked around, his heart swelling with gratitude. He had found a family here—a community that had become a part of him.

Turning to Nyomi, he grinned. "I don't know how I got so lucky to have you as a friend. Thanks for everything."

Nyomi smiled back, her eyes shining. "You found your own strength, Ethan. I just helped you see it."

They shared a quiet, meaningful look, the kind that needed no words. For both of them, it was a moment of closure, a promise of friendship that would last beyond high school, beyond the skate park—a bond forged in understanding, growth, and mutual support.

CHAPTER 16: SOFIA'S AMBITION

Sofia sat at her desk, surrounded by neatly organized stacks of textbooks, notes, and color-coded index cards. The muted hum of the desk lamp filled the silence as she bent over her latest assignment, tapping her pencil in rhythmic, precise beats against the page. Her planner lay open to the current week, its every inch filled with tasks, deadlines, and goals. The sight of it usually filled her with a sense of accomplishment, a confidence that she was on track. Today, however, the tightly packed calendar looked daunting, even confining.

The truth she kept to herself was that she was exhausted. Her mind, which usually raced eagerly from one challenge to the next, felt like it was trudging through sand. Every page turned in her textbooks weighed her down, and each equation felt like a mountain instead of the satisfying puzzle she usually enjoyed solving. Yet she pushed on, dismissing her fatigue as weakness, a feeling she had trained herself to overcome.

She was on the brink of something great, after all. Her grades were the highest they'd ever been, and she was closer than ever to the top position in her class. Her parents' pride was palpable, something that, as much as she hated to admit, drove her as much as her own ambition did. She knew they believed she was destined for success, that she'd be someone who could set a standard others aspired to reach.

But beneath all that, another feeling simmered. It was a feeling she was less comfortable acknowledging, one that made her question if something was missing in her well-organized life.

She thought of Nyomi. In the short time since they'd become study partners, Nyomi had somehow found ways to slip past her barriers. They shared a passion for learning, a curiosity that often led to late-night texts and enthusiastic discussions. With Nyomi, studying felt like a game they both understood, a language only the two of them could speak.

Nyomi had even nudged her to join their study group, suggesting it would "bring a little fun" to their otherwise solitary work. The idea unsettled Sofia. She couldn't help thinking that time spent with friends would weaken her focus. There was no denying that friendships would require her to relax her schedule and make room for unplanned interruptions, things that could chip away at her carefully laid plans. Nyomi's warmth and ease around others sometimes made her feel like she'd lost a map to a world she didn't know she needed.

Sofia tapped her pencil faster. She knew she was missing out on something—she saw it when she watched others laugh together in the cafeteria, saw it in the way Nyomi's eyes sparkled when they talked about more than just formulas and study techniques. Her heart squeezed as she remembered times she'd had friends and felt part of something bigger than herself. It was a strange, unsettling thought that she pushed down as quickly as it surfaced. She'd been fine on her own so far, she reminded herself. In fact, she'd done better than fine.

"Friendships just complicate things," she muttered, flipping to the next page of her textbook with a little too much force.

But as the words slipped out, they felt hollow. Nyomi's voice echoed in her mind, gentle yet persistent, like a quiet stream that eroded rock over time. Nyomi didn't seem to believe that ambition and friendships were mutually exclusive. She'd said so once when Sofia brought it up, lightly mentioning that sometimes people in your life could help keep you grounded, help you go further. The thought had confused Sofia back then, and it still did now.

A knock on her door startled her. Sofia's mother stepped in, her expression a familiar mix of pride and caution. "How's it going?" she asked, her gaze landing on the neat rows of textbooks.

"Fine," Sofia replied automatically. "Just a lot to cover."

Her mother smiled approvingly. "That's my girl. Hard work pays off.

Remember, all of this is for your future."

Sofia nodded, her chest tightening slightly. Her mother's words were comforting, but they also reinforced the silent truth between them—that her time was best spent on things that directly served her goals. If she was to live up to the legacy her parents expected of her, she couldn't afford to get sidetracked. Social events, casual friendships, even things like a weekend outing felt like distractions.

"Let me know if you need anything," her mother said, closing the door softly.

The moment her mother was gone, Sofia slumped back in her chair, rubbing her temples. She hadn't told her parents about Nyomi, or the study group, or the moments she'd stolen just to talk about things other than academics. It felt like a private rebellion, something fragile that she didn't want to disturb with their well-meaning advice.

She knew she was supposed to be happy. Her success in school was proof that her approach worked, that her life was heading exactly where it needed to go. But sometimes, as she watched Nyomi and others talking freely and laughing without reservation, a small voice in the back of her mind questioned what she was missing. She didn't know how to reconcile that curiosity with her ambition, or if she even wanted to.

Nyomi's Influence and Shared Love for Learning Sofia wasn't sure why, but she found herself looking forward to her next study session with Nyomi. It was a strange feeling— usually, study time was simply that: time to study. With Nyomi, though, she felt something different. There was a lightness in their conversations, a natural ease that she'd grown to appreciate, even if it was slightly unnerving.

That Saturday, Sofia settled into her seat across from Nyomi in the corner booth of a quiet coffee shop. They'd chosen the spot for its long hours and peaceful ambiance, knowing that they could slip into hours of uninterrupted focus. The quiet clink of coffee cups, the hum of light chatter, and the scent of espresso surrounded them, creating a cozy backdrop for their study.

As they organized their materials, Sofia could see Nyomi's curiosity spark. Nyomi glanced up with a half-smile, her fingers dancing across her notebook's cover.

"Have you ever thought about joining the science club, Sofia?" she asked, her voice casual but her gaze intent.

Sofia's pencil stilled on the edge of her notebook. "The science club?" She shook her head slightly, unsure how to answer. The idea had never crossed her mind—clubs, like friendships, felt like an indulgence that might lead her astray from her true goals.

"Yeah! I mean, they do some interesting projects. Last year, they collaborated on this really cool experiment for the spring fair. And the best part?" Nyomi's eyes twinkled. "The whole thing was a group effort. They learned from each other, you know?"

Sofia raised an eyebrow, trying to mask her discomfort. "I don't know... I feel like that would just... take time away from studying."

Nyomi shrugged, unbothered. "Maybe. Or maybe it would make studying feel... different. More energizing."

Sofia wasn't convinced. "But what if you end up relying on others? It might be fun, sure, but if it means losing focus..." Her voice trailed off as she saw Nyomi's gentle expression, full of patience and a little curiosity.

"Is focus only about the time you spend on something?" Nyomi asked quietly, her fingers tracing absent circles on the cover of her notebook. "Sometimes I feel like connections with other people help me focus, like they bring out ideas I wouldn't have thought of alone."

Sofia fidgeted, half-listening and half unsure of what to make of Nyomi's words. Focus had always been something she achieved alone, with her planner, her textbooks, and a strong dose of discipline. The idea that connecting with people might add to her concentration felt contradictory, almost like a test question with no correct answer.

But Nyomi didn't press her. Instead, she flipped open her notebook, letting their conversation settle back into the comforting rhythm of shared study. They went over equations, concepts, and problems, Nyomi offering insights that often surprised Sofia with their simplicity and brilliance.

After about an hour, Nyomi paused, glancing around with a slight frown. "You know what would be a perfect addition to this? A big coffee," she said, grinning. "Be right back." She hopped up and joined the line at the counter, leaving Sofia momentarily alone.

While she waited, Sofia flipped through her notes, trying to make the most of the brief break. But her mind kept drifting back to what Nyomi had said earlier. Nyomi seemed to live in a world where friendships and study weren't opposites but pieces of a whole. Didn't it ever make her lose her focus? Sofia wondered, watching as Nyomi chatted with the barista.

The question lingered in Sofia's mind, tugging at her carefully ordered priorities. She looked down at her notebook, feeling a flicker of envy at the thought of enjoying her studies as much as Nyomi did, of having something or someone to enrich her learning beyond her solitary pursuit.

Nyomi returned, sliding a large latte in front of Sofia, her own drink in hand. "Surprise!" she said brightly. "It's my go-to 'brain fuel.' Just try it; it's amazing."

Sofia blinked, a little thrown off by the unexpected gesture. She didn't often drink lattes, preferring the control that water or black coffee provided. Still, she took a tentative sip, surprised by the warm sweetness, a hint of vanilla lingering on her tongue.

"Thanks, Nyomi," she murmured, offering a small smile.

"No problem!" Nyomi said, taking her seat. "Consider it a reward for being one of the few people who understand the thrill of molecular geometry."

Sofia laughed softly, her guard lowering just a little. They continued studying, the latte a small, comforting presence on the table beside her. It was a simple gesture, yet it stirred something in her—a quiet realization that maybe, just maybe, a small break for connection didn't have to threaten her ambition.

After another hour, Nyomi stretched, closing her notebook with a satisfied sigh. "You know, Sofia, I think it's really cool how much you care about doing well. And I get it. I feel that way too. But I don't think our friends are a distraction. I mean, sometimes they keep us grounded, make us feel like we're not alone in the craziness, you know?"

Sofia looked down, considering her words. "I don't know... it just feels like I can't have both. Like... if I do something just for the sake of friendship, I'll lose my edge."

Nyomi didn't laugh or try to argue. Instead, she simply said, "Maybe there's a way to do both, though. I think friendships and success can grow together, each adding something to the other."

Sofia listened, both drawn to and unsettled by the idea. Part of her wanted to believe Nyomi, to think that she could make room for friendship without losing her focus. But another part of her, the part shaped by years of striving to be the best, pushed back. Friendships took time and energy—two things she couldn't risk losing.

As the day wrapped up, Nyomi leaned across the table, her eyes warm with understanding. "Listen, I don't think you need to change who you are to make friends, Sofia. And I don't think you need to sacrifice your goals either. I just think... there might be ways to enjoy both without giving anything up."

Sofia nodded, her chest tightening slightly. Nyomi's words stirred something in her, a quiet, persistent thought that maybe she didn't have to be alone to succeed. It was a gentle shift, like the faintest light breaking through dark clouds. And while it was small, it was enough to leave her wondering.

The Butterfly Touch Vision – Sofia's Potential Future

As the sun began to set, painting the sky in hues of pink and gold, Sofia gathered her notebooks and began packing up. She was about to offer a quick goodbye to Nyomi when Nyomi's hand gently brushed her shoulder.

"Hey, before you go... there's something I want to share with you," Nyomi said, her gaze warm but a little serious.

Sofia raised an eyebrow. "What is it?"

"It's hard to explain. But... just trust me." Nyomi smiled softly, her expression both comforting and mysterious. "I call it the 'Butterfly Touch.' It's a kind of... vision, I guess. A way to see things a bit differently."

Sofia blinked, uncertain. "A vision?"

Nyomi nodded, her fingers tracing soft, invisible patterns on Sofia's shoulder. "Sometimes, when we're too close to something, we miss the bigger picture. This will show you a possible future—a glimpse of what things could be if you let both your ambition and friendships flourish."

Sofia hesitated, her heart beating a little faster. It felt surreal, even a bit unbelievable, but the warmth in Nyomi's gaze gave her the courage to nod.

"Alright," Sofia whispered.

Nyomi closed her eyes, her hand resting lightly on Sofia's shoulder. A soft warmth radiated from her touch, spreading through Sofia's skin and filling her with a sense of calm. The room around them blurred slightly, and Sofia felt a strange sensation, as if she were drifting between waking and dreaming. Colors swirled, shifting and blending, until an entirely new scene took shape.

Sofia found herself standing in a bustling campus courtyard, vibrant with energy and filled with groups of people laughing and talking. She recognized the scene instantly—it was a prestigious university, the kind she had always dreamed of attending. Students moved around her, textbooks in hand, laughter ringing through the air. The environment pulsed with ambition and excitement, the very essence of the life she'd envisioned for herself.

But as she looked closer, she realized she wasn't standing alone. A group of friends surrounded her, faces familiar yet older, more confident. She spotted Nyomi among them, along with a few other classmates from school. They were smiling, chatting animatedly about classes, upcoming projects, and shared plans.

In the vision, Sofia watched herself laugh along with them, her posture relaxed, her expression radiant with joy. She seemed... different. Happier, more at ease, as though the weight of her ambitions had lightened. She held a textbook under one arm, but her focus was on her friends, not just on her studies.

A sudden pang of surprise hit her as she realized that she was still succeeding—more than succeeding, in fact. The vision shifted, and she saw herself presenting a groundbreaking research project, her professors watching with admiration and respect. Her classmates cheered for her, their pride evident as they clapped and shouted encouragement.

Another shift in the vision revealed a quiet night in her dorm room, where she was studying alone by a small desk lamp. Yet even in solitude, the room felt full of warmth. Her friends' laughter echoed faintly from down the hall, a reminder that she wasn't truly alone. She felt grounded, supported by a network of people who believed in her and celebrated her achievements as if they were their own.

And then, as if sensing her lingering doubts, the vision shifted one last time. This time, she saw herself struggling. Exams were approaching, deadlines loomed, and stress etched lines into her face. Her room was filled with textbooks and papers, the signs of a student working through the pressures of ambition. But this time, she wasn't alone in the struggle. Her friends appeared beside her, offering support, encouragement, and laughter to lighten the heavy load. They were her anchors, pulling her back from the edge of burnout, reminding her that success wasn't just about solitary achievements, but also about the strength found in companionship.

The warmth of Nyomi's hand brought Sofia back to the present, the vision fading like mist in the morning light. Sofia blinked, feeling disoriented yet strangely peaceful.

"Nyomi... that was..." Sofia struggled for words, her heart still racing from what she had seen. "Was that really a possibility?"

Nyomi nodded, her gaze gentle. "It's one of many possibilities. There's no one right way to live out your ambition, Sofia. But sometimes, the paths we fear most are the ones that make us the strongest."

Sofia stared down at her hands, the memory of the vision vivid and alive in her mind. She saw the potential for both success and companionship, a life where she didn't have to choose one over the other. It was a life where she could feel the fulfillment of achievement while also leaning on others for support and finding strength in shared experiences.

"A life with friends..." Sofia murmured, more to herself than to Nyomi. She let out a long breath, a mixture of relief and uncertainty in her exhale. "It's so different from how I thought it would be."

Nyomi reached over, squeezing Sofia's hand gently. "You don't have to do it all alone, Sofia. And you don't have to lose your ambition. Just... don't forget to make room for the people who care about you. They'll be there to help lift you higher, not hold you back."

Sofia swallowed, her throat tight with emotion. She had spent so long believing that success was something she had to build alone, that friendship was a risk to her dreams. But the vision showed her something different— an image of a life where she wasn't only successful but also fulfilled, with friends by her side every step of the way.

The weight of her decision settled on her shoulders, but it felt lighter than before. She looked at Nyomi, a quiet gratitude in her gaze.

"Thank you, Nyomi," she whispered. "For showing me... for letting me see that."

Nyomi smiled, giving her hand one last squeeze before letting go. "You've always had this within you, Sofia. Just remember, ambition is beautiful, but it shines brightest when it's shared."

Sofia nodded, the vision replaying in her mind like a promise. It wouldn't be easy—she knew that. But the image of that future, of her surrounded by friends while also reaching her goals, was too powerful to ignore.

For the first time, she felt as if a door had opened, revealing a path she hadn't dared to imagine before. She could still be the best, still achieve everything she'd worked for. But now, the idea of sharing that journey didn't feel like a distraction—it felt like a gift.

Resisting Social Invitations After their study session, Sofia couldn't shake the memory of the vision Nyomi had shown her. It lingered, vivid in her mind, coloring her thoughts and casting new light on her meticulously planned life. Part of her felt energized, inspired by the possibility of having both success and connection, just as she'd seen. But as the days passed, another part of her grew hesitant, wary of the unfamiliar territory she was about to tread.

One Friday evening, Nyomi texted her: Nyomi: Hey! A bunch of us are going to get coffee and hang out tomorrow. Nothing fancy, just a little break. You should totally come with us!

Sofia's immediate instinct was to refuse. She glanced around her room, noting the stack of books and study materials spread across her desk. She had plans—she always did. This weekend, she was supposed to finish her advanced chemistry assignment and go through another set of practice problems for calculus. Her mind buzzed with reminders of her commitments, of the importance of staying on top of her work.

But then she remembered the vision—herself surrounded by friends, laughing, at ease. In that life, she seemed capable of balancing it all, of enjoying moments like the one Nyomi was offering without sacrificing her goals. Was it really possible?

Her fingers hovered over her phone, unsure of what to type back.

Sofia: Thanks for inviting me! But I have a lot of studying planned for tomorrow...

She hesitated, the ellipsis blinking on the screen as she watched her unfinished message. Would it hurt to try? It was just coffee. Just a few hours away from her studies.

Before she could reconsider, Nyomi's reply appeared.

Nyomi: You can bring your notes, you know! Who says we can't mix a little studying with hanging out?

Sofia's lips curved into a faint smile despite herself. Nyomi's effortless optimism and warmth made her wonder, just for a moment, if a balance might really be within her reach.

Taking a deep breath, she decided to give it a try.

Sofia: Alright... I'll come. Just for a little while, though! Nyomi: Yay! Trust me, you won't regret it.

The next morning, Sofia arrived at the café where Nyomi and a few of their friends had gathered. She entered cautiously, her fingers tightly gripping the straps of her bag as her gaze swept the cozy space. Laughter and conversation filled the air, a hum of warmth and camaraderie she rarely experienced outside of study groups or classroom discussions.

Nyomi waved her over enthusiastically from a large table near the window. Beside her sat Thomas, Callie, and a few others from their chemistry class. Sofia recognized them, of course—she shared classes with most of them—but the casual setting felt new and unfamiliar. It was strange to see these people, usually so focused on coursework, talking and laughing together like they didn't have a single deadline in the world.

"Hey, Sofia! So glad you could make it!" Nyomi greeted her, beaming.

Sofia forced a smile, setting her bag on an empty chair as she took a seat between Nyomi and Callie. Thomas gave her a nod and a small smile, and Callie immediately started telling a story about a funny mishap in her art class that morning. Sofia listened politely, unsure how to join in without shifting the conversation back to academics.

Nyomi seemed to sense her discomfort and leaned over, nudging her gently. "It's okay, you know. You don't have to have something clever to say. Just... relax."

Sofia exhaled slowly, letting herself sink back into the chair. It was harder than she'd expected, letting her mind wander, detaching herself from the mental checklist of tasks waiting back at her desk. But as the minutes passed, she found herself slowly easing into the rhythm of the group.

The conversation turned to their favorite movies and hobbies, and to her surprise, Sofia discovered that Thomas shared her interest in classic science fiction novels. They fell into an animated discussion about their favorite books, each talking over the other in their enthusiasm. She hadn't had a conversation like this outside of schoolwork in ages, and it felt... nice. The tension in her shoulders melted as she laughed, genuinely enjoying herself.

Before she knew it, an hour had passed. She glanced at her watch, a prick of guilt piercing her thoughts. She had promised herself she'd only stay for a short while. Her mind jumped to the assignments awaiting her at home, the notes she'd intended to review this morning.

She rose from her seat, brushing imaginary dust from her clothes. "I should get going," she said, her voice a little too brisk. "I have some studying to do."

Nyomi looked at her, a flicker of understanding in her eyes. "Of course," she said, her tone light and easy. But there was something else, too

—a gentle persistence. "But hey, remember, it's okay to take a break sometimes. You're allowed to have fun."

Sofia managed a small smile, nodding in thanks before heading to the door. As she left, she could feel Nyomi's words following her, lingering in her mind with a quiet insistence.

Back in her room, she settled down at her desk, opening her textbook and reaching for her notes. But the usual focus was absent. Instead, her thoughts drifted back to the café, to the warmth of her friends' laughter, the ease of being part of something simple and enjoyable. For the first time in a while, her books didn't hold her attention.

Instead, she found herself wondering what might have happened if she'd stayed just a bit longer.

Academic Struggles Amid Emotional Growth When Monday arrived, Sofia settled into her usual seat in the chemistry lab, her notebook and pens aligned with precision on the table. She glanced around, mentally preparing herself for the day's lesson, when a voice broke through her concentration.

"Sofia!" Nyomi waved from across the room, beaming as she made her way over. She plopped into the seat beside her, a familiar warmth lighting her eyes. "So, are you still alive after joining us this weekend?"

Sofia managed a small smile. "Barely," she joked, though part of her meant it. The coffee outing had been a refreshing break, but it left her feeling slightly behind. She'd spent most of Sunday catching up on the work she had planned for the weekend, fighting an unsettling twinge of guilt as she struggled to concentrate.

"Good, because I was thinking—maybe next time, we could do a little study picnic? Get some work done but also relax outside." Nyomi's eyes sparkled with enthusiasm.

Sofia hesitated, the word next time sending a ripple of unease through her. She liked Nyomi and her friends, and the idea of blending study with relaxation seemed tempting. But she couldn't ignore the faint guilt gnawing at her—guilt over the time she could have spent solely on her studies.

"I'll... think about it," Sofia said, trying to keep her tone light. She didn't want to disappoint Nyomi, but another part of her wondered if this social involvement was starting to cost her more than she'd realized.

Just as she finished speaking, Mr. Calloway, their chemistry teacher, strode into the room, his usual brisk energy filling the space. He launched right into the day's lesson, scribbling equations and chemical reactions across the whiteboard.

Sofia tried to focus, her pen poised to take notes, but her mind kept drifting. She replayed the conversation from the café, Thomas's quiet excitement about science fiction novels, Nyomi's laughter echoing around the table. She remembered the relaxed atmosphere, the feeling of belonging. It felt foreign but deeply comforting, like a warmth she hadn't known she'd missed.

She forced herself back to the present, her gaze snapping to Mr. Calloway's notes. But even as she wrote, her thoughts felt fragmented, her attention slipping with each word. She was behind the others in the lesson, her mind still tangled in her memories of Saturday.

"Focus, Sofia," she whispered to herself, trying to shake off the lingering warmth of those moments. But the tighter she clung to her determination, the more her focus eluded her.

After the lecture, Mr. Calloway handed out a surprise quiz, a quick assessment on the material they'd covered over the past two weeks. Normally, quizzes didn't faze Sofia. She'd made it a habit to review her notes meticulously, often ahead of time, ensuring she was ready for anything. But today, as she read the first question, her mind drew a blank.

Her pulse quickened as she stared at the problem, struggling to pull the information from her memory. The answers were there, buried under layers of scattered thoughts, but no matter how hard she tried to focus, she couldn't grasp them. It felt like her mind was slipping through her control, and frustration bubbled within her.

How could this be happening? she thought, her pencil trembling slightly in her hand. She'd always prided herself on being prepared, on having an unbreakable concentration. But now, for the first time, it felt like her focus was crumbling.

When the bell rang, she handed in her quiz, fighting the urge to glance at Mr. Calloway's reaction. The pages felt heavier than usual in her hands, the gaps she'd left stark reminders of her divided attention.

As she left the classroom, Nyomi caught up with her, her usual smile fading as she noticed Sofia's tense expression. "Hey, you okay?"

Sofia forced a shrug, trying to appear unfazed. "It's nothing. Just... had a hard time with the quiz."

Nyomi's face softened with understanding. "It happens to the best of us, you know. One quiz doesn't define you."

Sofia clenched her jaw, feeling a prick of irritation mixed with shame. "I guess. It's just... I've never had that problem before," she admitted, her voice low. "I always do well on quizzes."

Nyomi looked at her with a quiet compassion, as though she could see the storm brewing behind Sofia's carefully maintained calm. "Sofia, maybe it's just a rough day. Sometimes our brains need a break too, you know?"

Sofia shook her head, the guilt resurfacing, sharper now. "Or maybe I'm letting myself get distracted," she muttered, her gaze fixed on the floor. "Maybe I should have spent more time studying this weekend."

Nyomi's hand touched her shoulder, grounding her with a gentle pressure. "You can't study every minute of every day, Sofia. It's okay to need a balance. And besides, you've been working so hard. Don't you think you deserve to let yourself breathe?"

Sofia's chest tightened, her eyes stinging with the frustration she fought to suppress. Nyomi's words resonated with a part of her that wanted to believe, that wanted to embrace the possibility of enjoying life without feeling guilty. But her ambition tugged her back, reminding her of the path she'd set for herself, the endless hours of study and sacrifice that had brought her this far.

"I don't know," she said softly, her voice barely above a whisper. "I feel like I'm losing focus, like I'm... not myself."

Nyomi smiled gently, her hand still resting on Sofia's shoulder. "Maybe it's not about losing focus, but about finding a new kind of balance. You're not giving up on your goals, Sofia. You're just finding a way to be happy while you reach them."

The words settled over her like a blanket, comforting yet unfamiliar. Sofia wanted to believe them, but doubt held her back, like a shadow lurking at the edge of her mind. She felt like she was standing at a crossroads, torn between the drive that had always guided her and a new, fragile hope that maybe, just maybe, she could live a life where her ambitions and friendships coexisted.

For the rest of the day, Sofia tried to focus on her classes, pushing herself to concentrate as she usually did. But the slip in her focus from that morning nagged at her, an uncomfortable reminder of how easily her perfect rhythm could be disrupted. She felt as if she were on unstable ground, as though she might stumble if she took another step forward.

That evening, she sat alone at her desk, her textbooks spread before her, each one a reminder of the high expectations she'd set for herself. But her mind kept drifting, replaying the warmth of her friends' voices, the relaxed moments she'd shared with them over coffee.

Sighing, she rubbed her temples, trying to will herself back into her usual focus. Yet every time she picked up her pen, the words on the page blurred, her concentration slipping through her fingers like sand.

Maybe Nyomi was right. Maybe balance wasn't about sacrificing her ambition. Maybe it was about making room for the things that brought her joy, the moments that reminded her she wasn't alone in her journey.

But as much as she wanted to believe that, the fear of letting her focus waver, even slightly, held her back. For Sofia, success had always meant relentless dedication, the single-minded pursuit of her dreams. To veer even a little from that path felt like a risk, one that could unravel everything she'd worked so hard for.

She closed her textbook, her thoughts tangled in doubt and confusion. Her fingers brushed over the vision Nyomi had shown her in her mind's eye, the memory of that balanced future tempting yet daunting. She knew she had a choice to make, but the fear of failure loomed, casting a shadow over the decision she was struggling to make.

Flashback – Pressure from Sofia's Parents That night, as Sofia sat alone in her room, her thoughts turned to a memory that had always lingered at the edges of her mind, a quiet reminder of what was expected of her. It was a conversation from nearly two years ago, during her first year of high school. Her parents had sat her down in their living room, their faces filled with both pride and seriousness.

Her father had started with a warm smile, his hand resting on her shoulder. "Sofia, we're so proud of everything you've achieved so far. Your grades, your dedication—they're everything we hoped for. But as you get older, things are going to get more challenging. Colleges will look at every score, every achievement. Your future depends on the choices you make now."

Her mother nodded, her expression softer but equally focused. "You're so bright, Sofia, and you have such incredible potential. But potential needs commitment. Success requires sacrifice. You may need to put some things aside, to choose your priorities carefully."

Sofia had nodded, feeling the weight of her parents' words settle over her. She'd always felt a responsibility to make them proud, to be the person they believed she could become. They had never openly discouraged her from making friends or participating in other activities, but the message was clear—her future, her success, her entire worth rested on her academic achievements.

Her mother had continued, her tone gentle but firm. "Remember, Sofia, these years will shape your future. Every hour you spend studying, every effort you put into your work—it all matters. And while there will be temptations to socialize, to get distracted, just remember what's most important."

At the time, Sofia had nodded eagerly, feeling a surge of pride and resolve. She'd promised herself that she would live up to their expectations, that she wouldn't allow herself to fall behind or be swayed by things that didn't serve her goals. Friendship, she had decided, was secondary. If it didn't help her get closer to her dreams, it simply wasn't worth the time.

Yet now, sitting alone in her room with her books and notes spread before her, that memory weighed heavily on her heart. She felt torn, as if two different versions of herself were battling for control. One part clung to her parents' words, the promises she'd made to them and to herself to always prioritize her academics. But another part of her, a part that had only recently awakened, yearned for connection, for something beyond the pages of her textbooks.

She closed her eyes, recalling the vision Nyomi had shown her—the future where she had achieved her goals but was also surrounded by friends, supported by people who cared about her. It was a version of herself she hadn't dared to imagine, a possibility that had always felt out of reach. Yet seeing it, even as a vision, had stirred something deep within her, a longing she couldn't ignore.

Her phone buzzed softly, pulling her out of her thoughts. It was a text from her mother.

Mom: Hope you had a productive day, sweetheart! We're so proud of how focused you are. Keep up the great work—everything you're doing is leading to a bright future.

Sofia stared at the message, feeling a familiar mix of pride and pressure tighten in her chest. She knew her parents loved her deeply and wanted what was best for her, but their belief in her potential had become a silent expectation, a reminder that her value lay in what she could achieve. It left little room for anything else.

She texted back a quick, reassuring reply—Thanks, Mom! I'm studying hard.—before placing her phone face-down on her desk. The silence in her room felt heavier now, filled with the weight of choices she hadn't yet made.

She thought of Nyomi's words, her gentle encouragement to find balance, to allow herself the freedom to connect with others without sacrificing her goals. Could she really have both? The idea seemed almost too good to be true, like a dream she was afraid to reach for, fearing it might slip through her fingers.

But something about the memory of that vision lingered, a quiet promise that perhaps, she didn't have to choose one or the other. Maybe, just maybe, there was a way to honor her parents' expectations while also honoring her own need for connection.

The thought was tentative, like the first breath of dawn. But it was there, a small glimmer of hope, and it gave her the strength to believe that balance might not be as impossible as she'd once thought.

Parental Concern about Social Activities The next evening, as Sofia was deep into her physics notes, her phone buzzed with a call from her mother. She took a deep breath, bracing herself. Though they rarely called unless it was important, the timing felt... significant, as if her parents had sensed that something was shifting in her.

"Hi, Mom," Sofia answered, keeping her voice steady, prepared for the usual questions about her schoolwork.

"Sofia, sweetheart! How's everything going?" Her mother's tone was warm, and yet Sofia could already detect the underlying curiosity, the probing edge that usually led to a conversation about her studies.

"It's good. Just going over some notes for physics," Sofia replied, keeping her answer brief.

"That's great. We're so glad you're staying on top of things. You know, with your schedule being so demanding, it's more important than ever to keep your focus," her mother continued, her words carrying a familiar weight.

Sofia nodded automatically, even though her mother couldn't see her. "I know, Mom. I've been putting in extra time to make sure I'm ready for the exams coming up."

"Good," her mother said, the approval evident in her voice. There was a slight pause before she continued, her tone softening just a little. "You've been spending a bit more time with friends lately, haven't you?"

Sofia's heart skipped a beat, her fingers instinctively tightening around her phone. She felt a surge of self-consciousness, as if her parents had somehow seen her moments at the café, witnessed the slight detour she'd taken from her usual routine. How had they noticed?

"Um... a little bit, I guess," Sofia replied, trying to sound nonchalant. "Just a coffee break here and there."

Her mother's voice remained gentle, yet there was an undercurrent of caution. "It's wonderful that you're making friends, Sofia. Really, it is. But remember, you have your priorities, and with all the goals you've set for yourself... well, we don't want you to lose sight of them. You've worked so hard, and you're so close."

Her father's voice chimed in from the background, steady and reassuring. "Just keep in mind, Sofia, that friends come and go. But what you're building, the future you're working toward, that's lasting. Once you're in college and achieving all those dreams, everything else will fall into place."

Sofia's stomach twisted, a mix of emotions swirling within her— gratitude for their pride, guilt for wanting more than their expectations, and a creeping sense of unease. They had always taught her that success was about endurance, discipline, and an unswerving commitment to her goals. She had adopted that belief as her own, had built her life around it, yet now it felt strangely heavy, as if it might tip over the fragile balance she was trying to find.

"I understand," Sofia said quietly, her voice barely above a whisper. She could feel her parents' approval as though it were a tangible weight resting on her shoulders. It was what she had always wanted, what she had worked so hard to earn. But now, that approval felt complicated.

"Just remember, sweetheart," her mother said softly, "we believe in you. We know you'll achieve amazing things. Just don't let distractions get in the way of that."

"Of course," Sofia replied, a faint hint of resignation in her tone. She felt like she was trying to hold two versions of herself together—one who had followed this path her entire life, and another who was just beginning to discover that maybe there could be more.

They said their goodbyes, and Sofia ended the call, staring at her phone for a long time afterward. The message was clear: any time not devoted to her studies, any time spent socializing, was a potential risk to her success. And yet, her heart felt torn. She had tasted something different in those hours at the café with Nyomi and the others, something that had made her feel alive in a way her solitary hours of studying couldn't replicate.

She looked down at her notes, the carefully highlighted passages and meticulously organized formulas. They represented years of effort, of unwavering dedication to the path her parents had set for her. But now, in the silence of her room, they felt incomplete, like pieces of a puzzle that were missing something essential.

Her mind drifted back to the vision Nyomi had shown her—the future where she had achieved her dreams without sacrificing friendships, where she had found success while also feeling connected, supported, understood. That life seemed impossibly distant, yet it lingered in her heart, a quiet reminder that perhaps, success didn't have to come at the cost of connection.

But her parents' voices echoed in her mind, their words pressing down on her as she struggled to reconcile the conflicting paths before her. Friends come and go, they'd said. But the memory of Nyomi's warmth, of the easy laughter they'd shared, suggested otherwise. It hinted at something lasting, something real.

Sofia turned back to her books, trying to push away the doubts, the quiet longing that tugged at her heart. She reminded herself of her goals, the dreams her parents had instilled in her, the path that she had always known.

But somewhere within her, a small, fragile hope began to take root—a hope that maybe, just maybe, she could create her own path, one that honored her ambition as well as her need for connection.

Decision-Making Conflict – To Study or Socialize?

A few days later, as Sofia settled into her routine of after-school study, her phone buzzed with a notification. She glanced down, seeing a message from Nyomi.

Nyomi: Hey! A few of us are heading to the park tomorrow. Just a chill afternoon to take a break. You should join us!

Sofia felt a familiar twinge of hesitation. She'd promised herself to stay on top of her study schedule, especially after the slip-up during that last quiz. She had spent hours making up for it, reviewing every concept and reworking every formula she'd struggled with. Tomorrow, she planned to dedicate the afternoon to a full review of her calculus notes. She needed the time to stay sharp, to keep herself on track.

But then her thoughts wandered back to her time at the café with Nyomi and the others. She remembered the laughter, the easy camaraderie, and the warmth of being part of a group. She had felt lighter, more relaxed, and in a way, more like herself than she'd been in a long time. That afternoon had been a rare escape from the relentless drive of her daily schedule, a glimpse into a different way of living.

Sofia's fingers hovered over the screen, her mind playing out the possibilities. If she joined them tomorrow, she'd miss precious study hours, and falling behind wasn't an option— not with the exams approaching. Her parents' words echoed in her mind, urging her to stay focused, to avoid "distractions." The fear of letting them down, of deviating from the carefully planned path they'd laid out for her, held her back.

But then, Nyomi's voice drifted into her memory: "Maybe it's not about losing focus, but about finding a new kind of balance."

Sofia took a shaky breath, her thumb hovering over the keyboard. She wanted to go, to let herself enjoy an afternoon outside, to be part of the world beyond her textbooks. Yet, she couldn't ignore the anxiety twisting in her stomach at the thought of abandoning her schedule, even for a few hours.

Finally, she typed a response, her heart heavy with reluctance.

Sofia: Thanks for inviting me, but I think I'll have to pass. I have a lot of studying to do.

She hit "send" before she could second-guess herself, feeling a strange sense of relief mixed with disappointment. Rationalizing her decision, she reminded herself of her goals, her parents' expectations, and the future she'd been working toward her whole life. This wasn't the time to get distracted, she told herself firmly. She needed to stay focused, to keep pushing herself forward.

A few minutes later, her phone buzzed again.

Nyomi: Aw, are you sure? It'll be fun! But I get it—study hard, okay?

We'll miss you!

Sofia's chest tightened at the last line: We'll miss you! It was a simple phrase, but it carried a warmth that unsettled her. Her friends wanted her there. They valued her presence, her company, in a way that her academic achievements alone couldn't provide. For a moment, she wondered if she'd made the wrong choice, if maybe she should have allowed herself that brief escape.

The next day, as she sat at her desk, her calculus notes spread in front of her, she found herself glancing out the window. The sunlight filtered through the blinds, casting warm patterns across her desk, and she imagined her friends laughing together in the park, enjoying the freedom of the weekend.

She tried to focus on her notes, to lose herself in the numbers and equations, but her mind kept drifting, drawn to the thought of her friends. The formulas on the page blurred, her concentration fraying as the emptiness of her room pressed down on her. The usual quiet that helped her think now felt suffocating, a reminder of the choice she'd made.

As the afternoon wore on, a hollow feeling settled in her chest, a sense of being left out, as if she were watching her friends from a distance, separated by a barrier of her own making. She knew this was her decision, a necessary sacrifice for the sake of her goals, yet it left her feeling strangely isolated, as though she were chasing her dreams alone.

For the first time, the thought troubled her. She had always believed that sacrifice was a sign of dedication, that true success required giving up things others took for granted. But now, as she sat alone, her thoughts drifting back to the laughter she had heard at the café, she wondered if there was a cost to this single-minded focus—if she was losing something valuable in her relentless pursuit of excellence.

Her phone buzzed with another message, a photo from Nyomi: her friends gathered at the park, laughing and leaning on each other, their faces lit with joy. Nyomi's text followed: Nyomi: Wish you were here!

Sofia's heart twisted as she looked at the photo, a longing tugging at her heart that she couldn't ignore. She'd made her choice, but for the first time, she wondered if she was really happy with it.

The room around her felt quieter than ever, the walls pressing in as she tried to return to her studies. But the words on the page were just that— words. They lacked the meaning and purpose she had always associated with her studies. And for the first time, she questioned whether success, in all its solitary glory, was truly worth the moments she was missing.

She tried to shake off the feeling, reminding herself of her goals, her parents' expectations, and the vision of her future that had driven her for so long. But the image of her friends laughing together lingered in her mind, a bittersweet reminder of the life she was leaving behind in her quest for perfection.

With a sigh, she returned to her books, her heart heavy, the echoes of laughter haunting her as she worked alone.

A Risky Choice for Friendship The following week, Sofia found herself in the library, buried under a mountain of textbooks and notes, determined to catch up on her chemistry assignments. The library was quiet, the air thick with the familiar scent of paper and ink, her preferred environment for uninterrupted focus. She had fallen into her usual rhythm, scanning each line of her notes with practiced concentration, when her phone buzzed softly beside her.

It was a message from Nyomi.

Nyomi: Hey! Last-minute idea, but we're all going to the new art exhibit downtown this evening. You should totally come with us!

Sofia glanced at the message, feeling an immediate tug of interest. She'd heard about the exhibit—a mix of science-inspired art installations that sounded fascinating. Normally, an outing on a school night was unthinkable, especially with her schedule so tightly packed. But the thought of spending an evening with her friends, experiencing something new and engaging, stirred a quiet excitement in her. It would be a break from her usual routine, a small escape from the relentless drive she'd always placed on herself.

She glanced at her notebook, her mind racing through her commitments. Her chemistry notes weren't finished, and she had planned to get a head start on her calculus review. But the pull to go out, to let herself enjoy a few hours away from her studies, was strong. Just this once, she thought, she could allow herself to do something different. After all, the exhibit wasn't just a distraction; it was an experience that could enrich her understanding of science in a unique way. That's how she rationalized it, at least, telling herself it was a calculated risk.

Before she could change her mind, she typed a quick response. Sofia: Okay, I'll come! What time?

Nyomi's reply came almost instantly, filled with enthusiasm.

Nyomi: Yay! We're meeting at 6. It's going to be amazing!

When Sofia arrived at the art exhibit, her friends were already there, admiring a sculpture that resembled a swirling galaxy, each detail painstakingly crafted from tiny metal fragments that shimmered in the low lighting. Thomas waved her over, grinning, and Callie gave her a cheerful thumbs-up, clearly thrilled she'd decided to join them.

Nyomi beamed, her excitement infectious as she leaned in to whisper, "I'm so glad you're here. This place is incredible, right?"

Sofia nodded, taking in the intricate details of each exhibit, the way science and art blended to create something both thought-provoking and beautiful. As they moved through the gallery, she felt a lightness she hadn't experienced in a long time. The pressure of her unfinished assignments faded, replaced by a sense of wonder and connection as she shared in her friends' awe at each display.

They spent hours wandering through the exhibits, discussing everything from the physics behind a kinetic sculpture to the symbolism woven into an abstract painting. Sofia felt herself relax, her usual tension melting away as she laughed with her friends, feeling, for once, fully present in the moment.

It was late by the time they all headed home, and Sofia knew she had stayed longer than she'd intended. A small flicker of worry pricked at her as she thought about the unfinished assignments waiting in her bag. She'd need to make up for the lost time, but as she walked back with Nyomi, she didn't regret her choice. The evening had been a rare reprieve, a moment of freedom that felt worth the potential consequences.

But the next morning, reality hit hard. Sitting in chemistry class, she realized she hadn't completed her review notes. Mr. Calloway announced a pop quiz, and Sofia's stomach dropped. She opened her notebook, skimming her notes frantically, but the gaps in her understanding were glaring. She hadn't studied as thoroughly as she usually did, and it showed.

As she worked through the questions, her mind scrambled to remember the details she'd skimmed over, but her answers came slowly, hesitantly. Each question felt like a hurdle, a reminder of the hours she'd chosen to spend elsewhere.

When she handed in the quiz, her hands shook slightly, a mixture of frustration and disappointment bubbling within her. She was used to excelling, to feeling the confidence of knowing she was prepared. But now, that confidence was replaced by a gnawing uncertainty.

After class, Nyomi caught up with her, her expression curious. "How was the quiz? You did okay, right?"

Sofia forced a small smile, brushing a stray hair behind her ear. "It was... fine," she replied, though the tightness in her voice betrayed her worry. "I just... didn't feel as prepared as usual."

Nyomi's gaze softened, her understanding evident. "Sometimes, we don't do as well as we hope. It doesn't mean you're not capable, Sofia."

Sofia nodded, biting her lip as she tried to process the conflicting emotions inside her. She had enjoyed the evening with her friends—truly enjoyed it—but now, facing the consequences, doubt seeped into her mind. Had she made the wrong choice?

"It's just... I've never let myself slip like this before," Sofia admitted, her voice low. "I feel like I'm letting myself down. I should have stayed home and studied."

Nyomi gave her a reassuring smile, resting a gentle hand on her arm. "Sofia, you're allowed to have an off day. One quiz doesn't define you. You're still the same brilliant person, whether you get a perfect score or not."

Sofia exhaled slowly, the tension in her chest loosening just a bit. "Maybe you're right. But it's hard not to feel... like I've failed somehow. Like I've compromised my goals just by taking one night off."

Nyomi's gaze held a quiet intensity. "Failure isn't just about the scores we get, Sofia. Sometimes, failure is letting fear keep us from experiencing life. You did something out of the ordinary, something that made you happy. That's not a failure. It's just a part of growing."

Sofia considered Nyomi's words, a sense of relief mingling with her uncertainty. She wanted to believe that balance was possible, that she didn't have to be perfect all the time to achieve her dreams. But a part of her still clung to the belief that every choice mattered, that even a single slip-up could unravel everything she'd worked for.

As they walked down the hallway together, Sofia found herself reflecting on the vision Nyomi had shown her. The balanced life, the friendships, the sense of fulfillment beyond academic achievements—it felt distant, but maybe not impossible. She realized that she might have to make sacrifices in both directions, that success wasn't a single, unbroken line but a series of choices and recalibrations.

She looked over at Nyomi, who had been nothing but supportive, and felt a spark of gratitude. Perhaps she didn't have to carry the weight of her goals alone. Perhaps, even with moments of doubt and missteps, she could find a way to honor both her ambition and the connections that made her feel alive.

As they parted ways, Sofia felt a sense of determination building within her. She wasn't certain of the path ahead, but maybe that was okay. She was learning, step by step, that ambition didn't have to be isolating—that it could grow alongside friendships, each choice a part of her journey.

And for the first time, the future didn't feel like a narrow, lonely road. It felt wide and open, filled with possibilities she was only beginning to explore.

Building Trust Through Shared Study Sessions The following week, Sofia and Nyomi met again for one of their usual study sessions in the quiet corner of the campus library. Sofia was still shaken by her recent quiz performance, a nagging feeling of inadequacy lingering even as she tried to reassure herself that one slip wouldn't ruin her overall record. She wanted to push harder, to make up for what she saw as lost time, but Nyomi's presence brought a calming energy that kept her from spiraling into her usual stress-driven focus.

They started with their notebooks open, each girl flipping through pages of meticulously organized notes. For a while, they worked in comfortable silence, the only sounds coming from the scratch of their pens and the occasional rustle of pages. Sofia found herself slowly relaxing, the familiar rhythm of studying grounding her, even if the memory of the missed quiz still haunted the back of her mind.

After about an hour, Nyomi closed her textbook and stretched, letting out a soft sigh. "You know," she said, her voice casual, "I'm really glad we get to do this together. Studying alone is fine, but there's something... nice about having someone else here."

Sofia glanced up, a bit surprised. She had always seen studying as a solitary endeavor, a place where she could shut out distractions and focus entirely on her goals. The idea of enjoying study time with someone else had always seemed foreign to her, almost like an intrusion. But now, with Nyomi sitting across from her, she realized that she hadn't felt as isolated, as pressured, as she normally did when she studied alone.

"It is... different," Sofia admitted, the words feeling tentative on her tongue. "Usually, I just like being alone with my notes. But this... it's nice, too."

Nyomi smiled, her eyes warm and encouraging. "Sometimes I think that's how we stay motivated, you know? By sharing things with people who understand. When we study together, I feel like I'm more focused, not less. It reminds me why I care so much about learning."

Sofia looked down at her notebook, turning over Nyomi's words in her mind. She had always believed that motivation came solely from within, from the drive to reach her goals and prove herself. But Nyomi's approach, the idea that motivation could also come from others, from the connections that reinforced her passion, stirred something in her. It was a small, subtle shift, but it made her wonder if she had underestimated the value of sharing her journey with someone else.

They continued studying, exchanging questions and insights as they worked through problem sets together. Nyomi had a way of breaking down

complex concepts, making them feel accessible and even a little fun. And when Sofia struggled with a particular formula or question, Nyomi was quick to offer a new perspective, encouraging her without judgment.

"See? You got it," Nyomi said with a grin as Sofia finally solved a tricky problem. "Sometimes all it takes is a fresh set of eyes."

Sofia found herself smiling, a genuine sense of accomplishment warming her from within. She had always prided herself on her independence, on being able to handle any academic challenge on her own. But this moment, the simple joy of solving a problem together, felt uniquely fulfilling. She realized that sharing her successes, even small ones, made the victory feel richer, more complete.

"Nyomi," Sofia began, her voice hesitant. "Do you... do you really think that friendships can help with focus? Like, actually make you better at reaching your goals?"

Nyomi nodded, her expression thoughtful. "Absolutely. It's not about being less dedicated. It's about having people who believe in you, who remind you why you're working so hard in the first place. Sometimes, friends give us the courage to push ourselves further than we would alone."

Sofia absorbed her words, her heart aching with a longing she hadn't fully acknowledged until now. She had always believed that strength came from within, from her own determination and focus. But perhaps, she thought, strength could also come from the people who supported her, who lifted her up when the weight of her ambitions felt overwhelming.

"I don't know if I'm ready to believe that completely," Sofia admitted, a faint smile tugging at her lips. "But... I think I'm starting to see what you mean."

Nyomi reached across the table, her hand resting briefly on Sofia's in a reassuring touch. "You don't have to figure it all out right now, Sofia. Just remember, you're not alone. We're all here, and we want to see you succeed. Maybe success doesn't have to mean shutting everyone out."

Sofia felt a warmth spreading through her chest, a quiet reassurance that softened her doubts. The words resonated deeply, touching a place in her heart that had long been guarded, closed off by the fear of losing her focus, her edge. But now, with Nyomi beside her, she felt the faintest glimmer of hope that maybe, just maybe, her goals didn't have to be a solitary pursuit.

The rest of the study session passed smoothly, and as they packed up their things, Sofia felt lighter than she had in weeks. She realized that for the first time, she hadn't been plagued by the usual worries about her performance or the gnawing fear of failure. Instead, she felt grounded, supported by Nyomi's gentle encouragement and her quiet belief in their shared journey.

As they walked out of the library together, Nyomi nudged her with a playful grin. "So, about that art exhibit... any regrets?"

Sofia laughed, shaking her head. "Maybe a little," she admitted, "but I think it was worth it. I needed that break, even if it didn't go exactly as planned."

"Exactly!" Nyomi replied. "We all need those breaks sometimes. You're not a machine, Sofia. You're human, and humans need both challenge and connection."

The words stayed with her long after they'd parted ways. Sofia knew she still had a lot to learn about balance, that she was only just beginning to explore the possibility of allowing friendships into her life. But with each study session, with every shared laugh and encouraging word from Nyomi, she felt a quiet conviction growing within her.

Maybe Nyomi was right—maybe she didn't have to choose between success and connection. Maybe, in the presence of friends who believed in her, she could find a new kind of strength, one that didn't rely on isolation or sacrifice.

As Sofia walked home, she felt a renewed sense of purpose. The road ahead was still uncertain, but for the first time, she felt as if she were stepping onto it with a new kind of confidence, a quiet trust that whatever challenges came her way, she didn't have to face them alone.

Observing Nyomi's Balance The more time Sofia spent with Nyomi, the more she found herself questioning her assumptions. Nyomi was unlike anyone she'd ever known— ambitious, dedicated, and yet remarkably balanced. She managed to excel in her studies while staying connected to her friends, showing a quiet confidence that seemed to radiate from a different source, one that Sofia was only beginning to understand.

One afternoon, they'd both decided to study in a sunny spot on the lawn near the library. Sofia liked the focused quiet of the library, but Nyomi had suggested a change, saying that sometimes fresh air made it easier to concentrate. They spread their notebooks on the grass, settling into a comfortable silence as they dove into their studies.

After a while, a group of students passed by, waving and calling Nyomi's name. Sofia looked up, her eyes widening as she watched Nyomi smile and wave back, pausing her work to chat briefly. She could see that the other students were delighted to see Nyomi, their laughter and friendly banter spilling over in a way that felt effortless.

Sofia was struck by how naturally Nyomi navigated the moment. She didn't seem to see her friends as distractions; rather, they were part of the environment, a source of support that blended seamlessly into her day. Nyomi's face was radiant, her joy evident as she exchanged a few words with her friends, and yet, the moment they left, she turned back to her studies without hesitation, her focus unbroken.

It was a simple interaction, but it left Sofia quietly stunned. She had always viewed friendships as something that required complete attention, something that would pull her away from her goals if she allowed them into her life. But Nyomi made it look easy, as though her friends gave her energy rather than taking it away. It was a balance Sofia had never believed possible, a delicate harmony between focus and connection that felt as foreign as it was alluring.

"Nyomi," Sofia said slowly, still watching as Nyomi returned to her notes, "how do you... do that?"

Nyomi glanced up, a curious smile on her face. "Do what?"

Sofia hesitated, searching for the right words. "Balance everything. You have so many friends, and yet you're still one of the best students in our class. Doesn't it... ever make you feel torn? Like you're spreading yourself too thin?"

Nyomi's gaze softened, and she leaned back, thoughtful. "It took me a while to figure it out," she admitted. "I used to think I had to choose too. But eventually, I realized that the things I care about—my goals, my friends

—they're all part of what makes me... me. I wouldn't be the same without either of them."

Sofia listened, feeling a strange mix of admiration and confusion. Nyomi spoke with such quiet conviction, as if she'd found a secret Sofia had been searching for all her life. But even as Sofia felt drawn to this idea, she couldn't ignore the fear that had always held her back. She remembered her parents' words, the constant reminders to stay focused, to avoid distractions, and the nagging doubt that friendships might make her lose sight of her path.

"But aren't you afraid?" Sofia asked, her voice barely above a whisper. "That one day, you might... lose your focus? That maybe, if you don't give your all to your studies, you won't reach your goals?"

Nyomi gave her a gentle, understanding smile. "Sofia, I think we're all afraid of that, in some way. But here's the thing —friends don't take away from who you are. They remind you of who you are. They keep you grounded, help you stay connected to the things that matter. And when you're supported, when you feel loved and encouraged, that's when you're able to give your best."

Sofia considered her words, her heart aching with the weight of a realization she wasn't quite ready to acknowledge. She had spent so long believing that her worth, her success, depended on how much she could sacrifice, how willing she was to shut out anything that didn't directly contribute to her goals. But Nyomi's words suggested a different kind of strength, one rooted in connection rather than isolation.

As the day went on, Sofia found herself watching Nyomi closely, noticing the small ways she balanced her friendships with her academic pursuits. Nyomi's life seemed to flow with an ease Sofia had never known, her friendships woven seamlessly into her routine. She didn't treat them as separate from her goals, as if one had to be sacrificed for the other.

Instead, she let them coexist, supporting one another in a way that felt almost magical.

The next day, Sofia was sitting in the school cafeteria, eating lunch alone and reading over her notes, when Nyomi joined her, a warm smile lighting up her face.

"Mind if I join?" she asked, though she was already sitting down.

Sofia nodded, her heart lifting at Nyomi's presence. As they chatted, Sofia noticed her usual tension beginning to ease, the pressure to be perfect fading as she laughed at Nyomi's jokes, letting herself relax in a way she rarely allowed.

A few minutes later, Thomas and Callie joined them, turning their quiet table into a small, lively gathering. Sofia felt a flicker of discomfort, her instinct to retreat urging her to leave before the conversation could distract her from her studies. But as she watched Nyomi engage with their friends, her smile bright and genuine, Sofia felt herself pause.

Nyomi looked over at Sofia, her eyes filled with quiet encouragement. "You don't have to choose one or the other, you know," she said softly, as if sensing Sofia's hesitation. "There's room for both. Trust me."

For the rest of lunch, Sofia stayed with them, her doubts lingering but her heart feeling lighter with each passing moment. She found herself laughing with Thomas, sharing stories with Callie, and feeling a sense of connection she hadn't expected. And when she returned to her studies that afternoon, she was surprised to find her mind clear, her focus sharper than before.

As she worked through her assignments, Nyomi's words echoed in her mind, a quiet reminder that maybe, just maybe, she didn't have to choose between ambition and friendship. Perhaps, like Nyomi, she could find a way to honor both.

That evening, as Sofia packed her bag for the next day, she felt a spark of something new—a belief that her path didn't have to be narrow, that it could expand to include more than she'd ever allowed herself to imagine.

Maybe balance was possible, even for her. And maybe, with friends like Nyomi by her side, she could learn to believe it.

The Extended Vision – Both Highs and Lows A few days later, Sofia and Nyomi found themselves back in their usual spot at the library, quietly working through their respective assignments. They had fallen into a comfortable rhythm, the silence between them filled with mutual focus and a sense of camaraderie that felt new, yet natural.

As they wrapped up their study session, Nyomi looked over at Sofia with a thoughtful expression. "Hey, Sofia... do you remember the vision I showed you? The one with the future that included friendships and success?"

Sofia nodded, her heart fluttering as she recalled that vivid glimpse of a possible life—a life where she was surrounded by friends, supported and valued, yet still achieving her dreams. The vision had stayed with her, a gentle reminder of the balance she was beginning to hope for, even if she hadn't fully accepted it yet.

Nyomi's gaze softened. "There's more I can show you, if you're open to it. It won't just be the easy parts, though. I want you to see the whole picture—both the highs and the lows."

Sofia hesitated, uncertainty prickling at her. Part of her felt nervous, worried about what she might see. She'd spent so long chasing perfection, building her future around a carefully crafted image of success. The idea of glimpsing a future with both triumphs and struggles was unsettling. But deep down, she knew that if she wanted to truly understand balance, she had to be willing to face all aspects of it.

"I… I'd like that," she replied, her voice steady, though her heart beat a little faster.

Nyomi reached across the table, her fingers brushing Sofia's shoulder with a warmth that spread through her like a gentle wave. Sofia felt the world blur around her, colors shifting and merging as a new scene took shape.

In an instant, Sofia found herself in a university lecture hall, the room filled with eager students and the quiet hum of anticipation. She recognized herself, sitting among them, her expression focused but relaxed. The professor at the front of the room called on her, and she answered confidently, her voice steady as she shared her thoughts. Her classmates nodded in approval, some even smiling as if they admired her insight. She felt a surge of pride, a sense of belonging she hadn't known she'd craved.

The vision shifted, and she saw herself at a campus café, surrounded by friends, each of them chatting and laughing. She recognized Nyomi among them, along with others she hadn't met yet but seemed to know. She saw herself smiling, her eyes bright with joy as she listened to her friends, the stress of academics momentarily forgotten. It was a scene filled with warmth and connection, a reminder that her life didn't have to be solely defined by her achievements.

But then, the vision shifted again. This time, she was alone in her dorm room, textbooks spread out around her, her gaze weary and unfocused. She could feel the weight of deadlines looming, the pressure of exams, the constant tug-of-war between her desire to excel and the need for rest. The walls around her felt closer, almost suffocating, as she struggled to maintain her grades while also staying connected to her friends.

There were moments of frustration, times when she questioned whether she could really keep up with everything, whether the balancing act she was trying to master was worth it. She saw glimpses of missed study sessions, occasional lower scores, and nights spent doubting herself. Yet through it all, she felt the presence of her friends—people who encouraged her, reminded her of her worth, and helped her find the strength to keep going.

The vision shifted once more, showing a moment of triumph. She was on stage at a research symposium, her voice confident as she presented her findings to an attentive audience. Her professors watched with approval, her friends cheering from the seats, their support a quiet yet powerful force that lifted her spirits. She felt proud, not only because of her accomplishments but because of the people who had stood by her, who had been part of her journey.

As the vision continued, Sofia saw herself navigating setbacks and successes alike. There were moments when friendships grew strained under the weight of ambition, times when she had to make hard choices, when balance felt like an impossible goal. But through each challenge, she discovered new resilience, a strength that came not only from her dedication but from the support she received and gave in return.

Finally, the vision faded, and Sofia found herself back in the library, Nyomi's hand still resting lightly on her shoulder. Her chest felt tight with emotion, a mixture of hope and vulnerability as she processed the images she had just seen.

Nyomi gave her a soft, understanding smile. "Balance isn't always easy, Sofia. There will be times when it feels like too much, when you'll have to make difficult choices. But that doesn't mean you have to face it all alone. The people who care about you will be there to help, even during the hard times."

Sofia swallowed, her throat thick with a newfound understanding. She had seen both the joy and the struggle, the moments of doubt and the triumphs that came from persevering through them. It was a life filled with complexity, with both highs and lows, but it felt... real. It felt like a life she could embrace, one where she didn't have to sacrifice her connections or her ambition.

"But... what if I fail?" Sofia whispered, voicing the fear that had always haunted her. "What if I can't keep up with both? What if I lose my focus?"

Nyomi's eyes softened, her gaze unwavering. "Then you'll pick yourself up and keep going. And the people who care about you will be there to help you through. Failure isn't the end, Sofia. It's part of the journey, a reminder that we're human."

Sofia let the words settle over her, a quiet peace filling her as she absorbed the truth behind them. She realized that she had been so afraid of falling short, of disappointing herself and her parents, that she had locked herself into a rigid, unyielding path. But maybe life wasn't meant to be a straight line. Maybe it was a series of twists and turns, each challenge teaching her something new, each setback an opportunity to grow.

For the first time, she allowed herself to consider that failure wasn't a barrier to success but a part of it—a stepping stone that could lead to a richer, more meaningful life.

"Thank you, Nyomi," Sofia said softly, her voice filled with gratitude. "I think... I think I understand now. It won't be easy, but I don't want to lose myself to ambition. I want to live a life that feels... complete."

Nyomi squeezed her hand, her smile radiant. "That's all anyone can hope for. Just remember, you're not alone. And no matter what happens, you have people who believe in you—people who will be there, whether you're at your best or facing your biggest challenges."

Sofia felt a tear slip down her cheek, a mix of relief and hope swelling within her. She had spent so long fearing the complexity of balance, but now, she realized that life's messiness was what made it beautiful. She didn't have to be perfect; she just had to be willing to try, to embrace both the joys and the struggles, knowing she had friends by her side.

As they gathered their things and left the library, Sofia felt lighter, her heart filled with a new kind of determination. She knew there would be times when balance seemed impossible, when she'd falter and question her choices. But she also knew that those moments were part of the journey, part of a life that felt full and meaningful.

And for the first time, she felt ready to face that future, knowing she could navigate both ambition and connection, trusting that no matter where her path led, she would find her way.

Flashback – Parents Emphasizing Academics Over Friendships As Sofia walked home from the library that evening, her thoughts drifted back to a memory from years ago, one she hadn't revisited in a long time. She'd been thirteen, just entering middle school, and her parents had sat her down for a "serious talk" in their living room. At the time, she'd felt a mixture of curiosity and anxiety, wondering why they'd insisted on such an important conversation.

Her father had started, his voice steady but serious. "Sofia, we're so proud of how well you've done in school. Your teachers have told us how hard you work, and we can see that dedication every day."

Her mother nodded, her gaze warm but laced with a gravity that Sofia had felt even at that young age. "You're very smart, Sofia. You have a gift for learning, and that's something special. But as you get older, it's important to remember that you'll have to make choices—choices about how you spend your time and who you spend it with."

Sofia had looked at them, wide-eyed, unsure of where the conversation was going but feeling the weight of it pressing down on her. She had always sensed her parents' pride in her accomplishments, and in that moment, she felt a surge of determination to live up to their expectations.

Her father continued, his tone firm. "As you go through school, you're going to meet a lot of people, and there will be plenty of opportunities to socialize. But not everyone you meet will share your goals. You're different, Sofia. You have the potential to go far, to achieve things that not everyone will understand. It's important to stay focused on your future and not get distracted."

Her mother reached over, placing a gentle hand on her shoulder. "Friends are nice, but they come and go. Real success—academic success

—is something no one can ever take from you. The people who truly care about you will support your dreams and understand if you can't always be with them. Remember, Sofia, you're building something important, something lasting."

The words had settled over Sofia like a blanket, wrapping around her young heart and planting a seed of responsibility that had grown with each passing year. Her parents' voices had stayed with her, shaping her choices, guiding her focus. She'd spent her teenage years following their advice, prioritizing her studies, and viewing friendships as a potential risk, a distraction from the path she had chosen.

But now, as she walked home from the library, Nyomi's words echoing in her mind, she felt a faint unease as she considered the impact of that memory. She could still see the pride in her parents' eyes, the conviction in their voices as they had advised her to keep her focus on academics, and she knew that they had meant well. They had wanted her to succeed, to reach the heights they believed she was capable of. They had given her a vision of success that was clear, unyielding, and unwavering.

Yet, she couldn't help but wonder if, in following that vision, she had closed herself off from experiences that might have made her life richer, fuller. She thought about the joy she had felt in the art exhibit with her friends, the quiet strength of studying alongside Nyomi, the feeling of support that came from knowing she wasn't alone. These moments felt precious, meaningful in a way that academic success alone hadn't yet provided.

For so long, she had believed that friendships were secondary, a luxury she couldn't afford. But now, she wondered if that belief had kept her from fully experiencing life, from building connections that could have helped her, supported her, and even strengthened her resolve.

As she reached her house, she felt a newfound clarity settling over her. Her parents had given her a foundation, a strong sense of discipline and ambition, but perhaps it was up to her to decide what her path would truly look like. She realized she didn't have to abandon her goals to embrace friendship, nor did she have to sacrifice connection for success. She could carve her own path, one that honored both the ambition her parents had instilled in her and the need for balance that Nyomi had helped her discover.

That night, as she sat at her desk, preparing for her next study session, she felt a quiet resolve growing within her. She knew that balancing her parents' expectations with her newfound understanding wouldn't be easy. But for the first time, she felt ready to try.

With Nyomi's guidance and her own determination, she would find a way to honor both her dreams and her relationships, building a life that felt truly complete. And as she turned back to her notes, she felt a spark of hope—a belief that, no matter how difficult the journey, she was finally beginning to walk a path that was wholly her own.

Reflecting on Growth and Recognizing the Need for Balance The following week, Sofia found herself in a rare moment of stillness, sitting by the lake near campus. The day's studies were finished, and she had taken her notebook with her, intending to review her notes. But as she watched the late afternoon sunlight dance across the water's surface, her thoughts drifted, pulled toward the changes she'd been experiencing.

For so long, she had equated success with perfection, with a rigid dedication to her studies and an unyielding focus on her goals. But ever since meeting Nyomi, and seeing the gentle way she balanced her own ambitions with friendships, Sofia had started to question what her version of success might truly look like. Nyomi had shown her that it was possible to care deeply about both her dreams and her connections with others, and Sofia had begun to realize that this approach, while unfamiliar, felt more fulfilling.

She thought about her parents and the expectations they had instilled in her, the sense of duty that had shaped her decisions for as long as she could remember. They had taught her the importance of discipline, of pushing herself to achieve her best. She knew their intentions had been rooted in love and pride, and she respected the values they had given her. But now, as she sat by the lake, she felt a newfound understanding that her path didn't have to mirror theirs exactly. She could create her own balance, her own version of success that honored both her ambition and her need for connection.

The memory of the vision Nyomi had shown her resurfaced —a glimpse of a future where she had achieved her dreams, surrounded by friends who celebrated her victories and supported her through challenges. It wasn't a perfect life;

there were moments of struggle, times when maintaining balance felt difficult, even impossible. But it was a life that felt real, a life that allowed her to be fully herself, with all her strengths and vulnerabilities.

As she reflected, Sofia realized that balance wasn't a destination, something she could achieve and be done with. It was an ongoing journey, a series of choices she would have to make every day. There would be times when she would lean into her studies, driven by her ambition to excel, and other times when she would need to make space for the people who mattered to her. And that was okay. Balance didn't mean perfection; it meant flexibility, resilience, and a willingness to prioritize different parts of her life as needed.

She took a deep breath, feeling a sense of peace settle over her. For the first time, she felt as though she was truly embracing this idea of balance, not as a compromise, but as a way to live fully and authentically. She understood now that her path would be her own, guided by both her dreams and the relationships that enriched her life.

With renewed resolve, Sofia made a promise to herself: she would honor both her ambitions and her friendships, recognizing that each added something essential to her life. She would strive to find balance, knowing it wouldn't always be easy, but also knowing it was worth the effort. She would create a life that allowed her to pursue her goals while staying connected to the people who supported her, who reminded her of who she was beyond her achievements.

As the sun began to set, casting a warm glow across the lake, Sofia felt a quiet sense of gratitude. She knew the journey ahead would be challenging, but she also knew that she was no longer walking it alone. With friends like Nyomi by her side, and with the strength she had discovered within herself, she felt ready to face whatever came next.

In the distance, she could hear laughter—friends calling out to each other, their voices filled with joy and camaraderie. Sofia smiled, feeling a kinship with them, a reminder of the connections she was learning to embrace. She closed her notebook, allowing herself a moment of stillness, of contentment, before standing to head back, her heart filled with a newfound determination.

This journey, this balance—it was hers to create, and for the first time, she felt ready to live it fully.

Sofia's Commitment to Balance The next morning, as Sofia organized her planner and skimmed over her week's schedule, she paused, a sense of clarity settling over her. Each day had been meticulously planned out, every hour assigned to studying, assignments, and preparations for upcoming exams. She could see, now, how much pressure she'd placed on herself to keep everything perfectly aligned, every detail accounted for. But she also recognized something new—an awareness that maybe this rigid approach was part of what had made balance feel so elusive.

Sofia took a deep breath, grabbing a pen and hovering it over her schedule. This time, she made small adjustments, carving out an hour on Tuesday evening for dinner with her friends and planning a Saturday afternoon study session with Nyomi that could flow into a casual outing afterward. Each small change felt like a tiny act of rebellion, a promise to herself that she could create a life where both her goals and her connections had a place.

It wasn't that she was giving up her dedication; she would still work hard, still strive for excellence. But she would also make room for laughter, for warmth, and for the quiet joy that came from spending time with the people who cared about her. She had finally realized that balance didn't mean perfection—it meant making choices, day by day, that honored all the parts of who she was.

As she looked over her newly revised schedule, Sofia felt a small flicker of excitement. She knew it wouldn't always be easy; there would be times when her studies demanded more of her, and times when her friends needed her attention. But she was ready to embrace that ebb and flow, to trust that the people who cared about her would understand and support her choices.

Later that day, she met Nyomi in their usual study spot, a quiet corner of the library where they often spent afternoons buried in books and notes. Nyomi looked up from her notebook as Sofia settled in, her smile warm and encouraging.

"Hey," Nyomi greeted, her eyes twinkling. "Ready for another round of problem sets?"

Sofia nodded, but then hesitated, feeling the weight of what she was about to share. "Nyomi... I just wanted to say thank you. For everything. I've been so focused on my goals that I forgot how important it is to have people who support you, who... make the journey feel less lonely."

Nyomi's smile softened, and she reached across the table, giving Sofia's hand a gentle squeeze. "You don't have to thank me, Sofia. I'm just glad you're letting us be a part of your life. And you know, we're here for you, through all of it—good days and bad."

Sofia felt a wave of gratitude wash over her, a sense of belonging that went deeper than anything she had felt before. It wasn't just about the support Nyomi and her friends offered; it was about the sense of balance they helped her find, the reassurance that she didn't have to sacrifice connection to achieve her dreams.

As they settled into their studies, Sofia found herself working with a new sense of calm. The anxiety that usually gnawed at her, the constant pressure to prove herself, felt less overwhelming. She knew she would still face challenges, moments of doubt, and times when balance seemed impossible. But she also knew that she had people in her life who would stand by her, who would remind her that she didn't have to face those challenges alone.

Over the next few weeks, Sofia kept her commitment, making room in her life for both her studies and her friendships. She went to group outings, laughing and sharing moments that filled her with warmth, and spent time with her friends between classes, listening to their stories, offering her own, and feeling her world expand with each new connection. There were days when it was difficult to maintain that balance, when she felt the familiar tug of perfectionism, the urge to stay focused only on her studies. But each time that feeling arose, she remembered Nyomi's words, the vision of a life that allowed for both ambition and connection.

One evening, as she sat with Nyomi and a few other friends at a local café, Sofia found herself reflecting on how different her life felt now. It wasn't just her schedule that had changed —it was her perspective. She no longer saw friendships as obstacles or distractions; she saw them as sources of strength, as reminders of the joy and resilience that came from sharing life's journey with others.

Sofia glanced around the table, taking in the familiar faces, the warmth in their smiles, the easy laughter that flowed between them. This was the life she had always hoped for but had been too afraid to pursue, too worried that friendships might derail her dreams. Now, she realized that they enriched her dreams, gave them new meaning, and made every achievement feel more complete.

When she got home that night, she sat at her desk, her planner open in front of her. For the first time, she felt a sense of peace as she looked at her commitments, her friendships and studies woven together in a way that felt balanced, real, and true to herself.

She knew the journey wasn't over—balance was something she would have to work at continually, a practice she would refine with each passing day. But as she closed her planner, she felt a quiet assurance that she was finally on a path that honored all parts of who she was.

And with that commitment firmly in place, Sofia closed her eyes, letting the promise of a balanced life fill her with hope.

A Simple Outing Changes Sofia's Views on Friendship The following Saturday, Sofia received a message from Nyomi.

Nyomi: Hey! We're thinking of grabbing coffee and pastries at that little café by the park tomorrow morning. Nothing fancy, just a chill meetup. Want to join us?

Sofia felt a pang of hesitation. Weekends were usually her sacred study time, hours she had carefully allocated to catching up on assignments and pushing ahead in her coursework. But she remembered her commitment to balance, the promise she'd made to herself to make room for both her ambitions and her friendships.

She glanced at her planner, mentally rearranging a few tasks to make time for the outing. The decision felt bold, even a little unsettling, but there was also a thrill to it, a quiet excitement at the thought of starting her day in the company of friends.

Sofia: I'd love to. See you there!

The next morning, Sofia arrived at the café, a cozy spot nestled among leafy trees that framed the park's entrance. She spotted Nyomi, Thomas, and Callie sitting outside at a small round table, steaming mugs and plates of pastries spread out in front of them. Their laughter drifted toward her, warm and inviting, and she felt a flutter of happiness as she walked over.

"There she is!" Nyomi called, waving enthusiastically. "Sofia, we saved you a seat!"

Sofia grinned, settling into the chair they'd kept for her. The simple gesture—her friends thinking of her, saving a seat as if she were an essential part of their morning—touched her deeply. She realized how much she had missed this kind of camaraderie, the small acts of thoughtfulness that came from being part of a group.

The morning passed in a blur of laughter and conversation, their topics ranging from favorite movies to funny memories from childhood. They shared stories, teased each other, and offered advice on everything from study strategies to the best way to brew coffee. It was an unstructured, carefree time, and for once, Sofia didn't feel the familiar urge to check her watch or worry about her schedule.

She had always believed that time spent socializing would be time taken away from her goals, but as she sipped her coffee and listened to Callie recount a story about a disastrous camping trip, she felt something shift within her. This moment, this simple gathering, was adding something to her life, not taking anything away. It filled her with a warmth and lightness that study sessions alone couldn't provide, a joy that lingered long after the laughter had faded.

As they left the café, Nyomi nudged her gently. "So, how does it feel to start a Saturday with a little fun?"

Sofia smiled, her heart swelling with gratitude. "It feels… wonderful, actually. I didn't realize how much I'd missed moments like this."

Thomas grinned, throwing an arm around her shoulder in a friendly hug. "See? We're not so bad to hang out with."

They walked through the park, the sun filtering through the trees and casting a warm glow over everything. Sofia let herself relax, enjoying the simple pleasure of strolling with her friends, talking about things that weren't tied to grades, deadlines, or future plans. It was a rare break from her usual routine, a reminder that life could be beautiful in its simplicity, even without a tightly controlled schedule.

Later, as they sat on a bench by the lake, Sofia turned to Nyomi. "Thank you for inviting me. I think... I needed this more than I realized."

Nyomi's smile was gentle, understanding. "I know. And we're glad you're here, Sofia. It wouldn't be the same without you."

The words sank into her heart, filling her with a quiet joy that felt as grounding as any achievement. She had always associated happiness with academic success, with the feeling of reaching her goals, but this was a different kind of fulfillment—a deep, steady warmth that came from connection, from knowing she was valued simply for who she was.

As they eventually parted ways, Sofia felt a newfound sense of purpose. This morning had been simple, unremarkable by her old standards, but it had opened her eyes to the richness that friendships added to her life. It had shown her that balance wasn't just about making space in her schedule—it was about making space in her heart, allowing herself to be present and to savor the moments that brought her joy.

When she returned home, she sat at her desk, preparing to dive into her studies with a clearer mind and a lighter heart. She realized that this brief time with her friends hadn't detracted from her ambition; it had recharged her, grounding her in a way that made her focus feel sharper, her goals more achievable.

As she opened her textbook, Sofia felt a surge of gratitude for the morning's simplicity, for the laughter and companionship that had reminded her of the beauty of balance. She knew she still had much to learn about integrating her friendships with her ambitions, but today had shown her that it was possible—that she could have both, and that each could strengthen the other.

With renewed determination, she turned to the first page of her notes, feeling the quiet joy of knowing she was exactly where she needed to be, both in her studies and in her life.

Torn Between Joy and Guilt That evening, Sofia sat alone at her desk, her study materials spread out before her. She had intended to dive straight into her assignments after returning from the café, but the usual spark of focus was missing. Instead, her thoughts kept drifting back to the laughter she'd shared with her friends, the easy companionship, and the warmth of the morning. She could still hear Callie's contagious laughter, see Nyomi's gentle smile, and feel the comfortable presence of Thomas by her side.

But with every memory, a prick of guilt surfaced, tugging at her and reminding her of the hours she hadn't spent studying. She glanced at her planner, feeling a pang as she saw the unchecked boxes beside today's tasks. Normally, she'd be well into her weekend study goals by now, yet here she was, sitting at her desk with a mind that seemed more inclined to relive the morning than to tackle her notes.

Sofia rubbed her temples, torn between the joy she had felt that morning and the nagging voice in her mind that reminded her of her parents' expectations, the academic goals she had set for herself. She had been raised to believe that every hour mattered, that time spent away from her studies was time that could pull her off course. She couldn't help but wonder if she'd made the wrong choice, if maybe she should have stayed home instead of indulging in a carefree morning.

But then, she thought of Nyomi's words, the gentle encouragement she had offered each time Sofia hesitated to join them. "There's room for both," Nyomi had said. Sofia wanted to believe it, but years of conditioning made it hard to accept. She had spent so much of her life measuring success by her academic achievements, by the sense of accomplishment that came from mastering a subject. She wasn't sure how to balance that drive with the happiness she had felt simply being present with her friends.

Maybe this is just a one-time slip-up, she thought, trying to reason with herself. Tomorrow, I'll catch up. I'll make up for the lost time. But even as she told herself that, she felt a heaviness in her heart. She knew that she couldn't live every day this way—oscillating between moments of joy and waves of guilt, feeling as if she had to justify every second that wasn't dedicated to her studies.

For the first time, she allowed herself to question if this guilt was really necessary. She wondered if maybe, just maybe, her life could be richer with a little less pressure and a little more room for moments like today. The thought felt risky, even rebellious, but it also sparked a quiet thrill, a hope that perhaps she could find balance without sacrificing either her ambition or her relationships.

Sofia turned back to her notebook, attempting to study, but the numbers and formulas blurred before her eyes. Her mind was too preoccupied, caught between the echo of laughter from the café and the list of tasks she had yet to complete. She felt a pang of frustration, her usual clarity clouded by a mix of emotions she hadn't fully anticipated.

In that moment, her phone buzzed with a text. She glanced at the screen, surprised to see a message from Nyomi.

Nyomi: Hey, just wanted to say I had a great time today. Thanks for coming—it meant a lot to all of us to have you there.

Sofia's chest tightened, the simple message filling her with warmth and comfort. She knew Nyomi meant it, that her friends truly valued her presence. And as she read the words again, a realization dawned on her: she didn't have to choose one over the other. Her friends were her support system, not obstacles to her success. They offered her a reminder of who she was beyond her studies, a grounding force that made her journey feel more meaningful.

Taking a deep breath, Sofia replied.

Sofia: Thank you, Nyomi. I had a great time too. Honestly... I didn't realize how much I needed it.

She set her phone down, feeling a sense of calm wash over her. The guilt wasn't entirely gone, but it felt more manageable now, softened by the memory of Nyomi's reassurance. Sofia knew she would still face moments of doubt, times when she questioned whether she could truly maintain this balance. But for tonight, she allowed herself a rare moment of acceptance, a quiet trust that she was learning, step by step, how to honor both her goals and her relationships.

Turning back to her notes, Sofia found her focus returning, her mind clear and steady. She studied for the remainder of the evening, but this time, she felt a sense of lightness, a belief that she didn't have to sacrifice joy to achieve her dreams. Her friends were part of her journey, and with their support, she felt ready to pursue her ambitions with a renewed sense of purpose.

When she closed her books that night, Sofia felt a newfound peace. She was no longer torn between joy and guilt; instead, she was learning to hold both, to trust that each had a place in her life. And with that, she went to bed, feeling hopeful for the journey ahead.

Closing Vision – Strength from Friendships A few days later, Sofia found herself once again seated across from Nyomi in their favorite study corner. They had been working quietly, their usual rhythm settling them both into a calm focus. But Nyomi had noticed Sofia's occasional sighs, the way her pen hovered just a bit too long over her notebook, the faint crease in her brow. She could sense that something was still weighing on Sofia, a hesitation she hadn't yet put to rest.

After a moment, Nyomi set down her pen, tilting her head as she looked at Sofia with a gentle smile. "Sofia, do you remember the vision I showed you a while back?"

Sofia looked up, nodding slowly. "Yes... the future where I could have both. Where I didn't have to choose between success and friendships."

Nyomi's smile grew softer. "Would you like to see more of that? To see what it might look like in times of both success and struggle?"

Sofia hesitated, her heart fluttering with both excitement and apprehension. She had seen the possibilities of a balanced life, but part of her was still afraid of what might happen when things got difficult. What if balancing both goals and friendships wasn't as easy as she wanted to believe? But another part of her—a part that had grown stronger over these past weeks—wanted to know. She needed to see that this path was possible, even when it wasn't perfect.

"Yes," Sofia whispered. "I'd like to see it."

Nyomi reached across the table, her hand resting lightly on Sofia's shoulder as her fingers traced soft, comforting patterns. A warmth spread through Sofia, and soon the library around them blurred and faded, replaced by the vibrant, shifting colors of Nyomi's Butterfly Touch.

In the vision, Sofia found herself standing on a university campus, books in hand, her expression focused but content. She could feel the weight of her responsibilities, the expectations she had set for herself, but there was also a quiet confidence in her step. She saw herself moving between classes, working hard, her ambition as strong as ever. But this time, she wasn't walking alone. Beside her were friends— Nyomi, Thomas, Callie, and others she hadn't yet met, all laughing and chatting as they walked together, their presence grounding her, reminding her that she didn't have to bear the weight of her dreams alone.

The scene shifted, and she saw herself sitting in a lecture hall, listening intently as a professor discussed a complex topic. She noticed her hand darting up to ask a question, her curiosity evident. Her friends sat beside her, taking notes, and she could feel their support like a steady current, pushing her to engage fully, to give her best. It was as if their belief in her strengthened her own, giving her the courage to keep striving.

Then the vision shifted again. This time, she was alone in her dorm room, late at night, surrounded by textbooks and notes. The pressure of exams loomed over her, her gaze weary as she worked through complex problems, her fingers tapping nervously against the pages. She could feel the familiar weight of self-doubt, the creeping anxiety that sometimes accompanied her most difficult challenges.

But just as the weight felt too much to bear, there was a knock at her door. She looked up to see Nyomi and Callie entering, bringing snacks and warm smiles, their eyes filled with understanding. They didn't try to distract her or convince her to stop studying; instead, they sat beside her, offering quiet support. They shared stories to make her laugh, gave her the space to vent her worries, and when she felt ready, they encouraged her to return to her work. Their presence was a reminder that she didn't have to be perfect, that even on her hardest days, she had people who would stand by her, who believed in her, even when she struggled to believe in herself.

The vision continued, showing moments of both triumph and challenge. She saw herself presenting a research project, her friends cheering her on from the audience, their faces alight with pride. She saw herself celebrating her achievements with them, the joy of her accomplishments amplified by the warmth of their encouragement. And she saw the difficult times too— the days when her grades weren't as high as she'd hoped, the late nights when self-doubt crept in, the moments when balance felt like an impossible goal. But through each struggle, her friends were there, offering resilience and hope, reminding her that she was capable, worthy, and strong.

Finally, the vision shifted to a quieter moment. Sofia saw herself sitting on a park bench, her friends around her as they watched the sunset together. There was no rush, no pressure —just a shared stillness, a sense of belonging that went beyond words. Her ambition was still there, her goals burning as brightly as ever, but they no longer felt like solitary pursuits. She realized that her friends were woven into the fabric of her dreams, giving them depth, meaning, and purpose.

As the vision faded, Sofia found herself back in the library, Nyomi's hand still resting gently on her shoulder. Her heart was racing, her chest filled with emotion as she processed the images she had seen. She felt the weight of both joy and vulnerability, a mix of excitement and a quiet assurance that she hadn't felt before.

"Nyomi," Sofia murmured, her voice barely above a whisper, "I think... I understand now. Friendship isn't a distraction. It's a source of strength."

Nyomi nodded, her gaze warm and steady. "Exactly. Friendships don't take away from your ambition—they add to it. They give you the courage to keep going, the resilience to pick yourself up when things get hard. You don't have to face your dreams alone, Sofia. And you don't have to be perfect to be worthy of support."

Sofia felt tears pricking at her eyes, a quiet release of all the fears she had carried, the belief that her value was tied solely to her achievements. She realized now that she was more than her grades, more than the image of success she had built. She was someone worthy of love, of connection, of a life filled with both purpose and joy.

As they packed up their books and prepared to leave the library, Sofia felt a newfound determination building within her. She was ready to embrace both her ambition and her friendships, to trust that each would strengthen the other. She knew there would be challenges, moments when balance felt fragile, but she also knew that she had people who believed in her, who would remind her of her strength when she needed it most.

With Nyomi by her side, Sofia stepped out into the evening, the air cool and refreshing against her skin. She felt lighter, her heart filled with hope, knowing that she was finally walking a path that honored every part of who she was. She was ready to face the future—not alone, but with friends who would walk beside her, sharing in her journey and reminding her that she was never truly on her own.

For the first time, Sofia felt that she could truly achieve her dreams. Not just as a solo pursuit, but as part of a life filled with the warmth and support of the people who mattered most.

And with that belief in her heart, she felt ready to embrace whatever came next.

Flashback – Parents Emphasizing As Sofia walked home that evening, Nyomi's words echoed in her mind, soft yet powerful reminders that had begun to reshape her view of herself and her path. She felt lighter, as if a quiet strength had awakened within her—a strength rooted in the realization that she didn't have to choose between ambition and connection.

But as she turned the corner onto her street, a memory surfaced, unbidden but insistent. It was the same memory that had always guided her drive to succeed, shaping her choices and fears, especially about friendships.

It had been a Sunday afternoon, and she'd been eleven, sitting at the kitchen table while her mother prepared dinner and her father read nearby. She remembered her mother's gentle smile as she spoke, her father's approving nod as he listened.

"Sofia," her mother had said, setting down the vegetables she was chopping, "you're such a bright, capable girl. Your teachers have told us that you're one of the best students they've ever had. We know you have what it takes to go far."

Her father had glanced over the top of his book, a warm pride in his eyes. "You have a gift, Sofia. But to make the most of it, you'll need to stay focused. There will be things—people, distractions—that might pull you away from your goals. But remember, your dreams are worth more than any momentary distraction."

She had nodded eagerly, absorbing their words with the earnestness of a child eager to please. Her parents' approval meant everything to her, and their confidence in her abilities had lit a fire within her, a determination to be the person they believed she could become.

"You have plenty of time to make friends," her mother had added, her tone gentle but firm. "For now, focus on what's most important. You'll understand when you're older."

At the time, Sofia had accepted those words without question, letting them guide her every choice, her every interaction. She'd believed that friendships were something she could allow later, once her goals had been achieved, once she had proven her worth through academic success.

But now, standing outside her front door, Sofia felt a sense of sadness for her younger self—the little girl who had taken those words to heart, believing that her value lay solely in her accomplishments, that friendship and connection were things she would have to delay indefinitely. It was as if she had been living with one eye closed, only half-seeing the world around her, because she'd been so focused on reaching a version of success that excluded anything but academic excellence.

As she entered her home, her parents greeted her warmly, her mother asking how her day had been. For a moment, Sofia considered brushing it off with her usual "fine" and heading straight to her room. But something in her paused, a new courage urging her to share a part of herself she had always kept hidden.

"It was good," she replied, her voice calm but steady. "I studied with Nyomi, and we talked a lot about... balance. About how it's possible to work toward my goals without losing the people who matter to me."

Her mother looked at her with a mix of surprise and curiosity, and her father set down his newspaper, his gaze thoughtful. They both seemed unsure of how to respond, and Sofia felt a tremor of nerves, but she continued.

"I've been realizing that friendships aren't distractions. They give me strength. And they don't take away from my goals—they help me keep going. I know you both want what's best for me, and so do I. I just... I think there's more than one way to reach my dreams."

There was a pause as her parents absorbed her words, their expressions softening. Her mother nodded slowly, her gaze warm but a little distant, as if she were seeing Sofia with new eyes. Her father gave a small smile, pride and understanding mingling in his gaze.

"We're proud of you, Sofia," her father said quietly. "And we trust you to make the choices that feel right for you."

Sofia's heart lifted at the words, relief washing over her. She realized that she had been carrying a fear that if she chose a different path—one that allowed for friendships and connection—she would somehow lose their approval. But here they were, offering her the very validation she hadn't dared to hope for.

That night, as she lay in bed, Sofia felt a new sense of freedom settle over her, a quiet assurance that her dreams were still within reach, now accompanied by the support of her family and friends. She knew the journey wouldn't be easy, that finding balance would require daily effort, choices made with care and thought. But she was ready to embrace it, to let her path be one that honored all parts of who she was.

As she closed her eyes, she felt excitement for the future—not just for the achievements she would reach, but for the people who would share the journey with her.

And with that peace in her heart, she drifted off to sleep, ready for whatever awaited her.

CHAPTER 17: A GROWING COMMUNITY

Since Nyomi began mentoring students at Riverside High, her presence had created subtle, transformative ripples across the campus. What had once been a school environment where everyone seemed to be moving in their own directions, some silently struggling, had grown into a quiet yet undeniable sense of unity. Students who had previously walked through the halls with lowered gazes or sat alone during lunch now had people to turn to, study with, and share ideas.

Nyomi's influence was unmistakable, though she rarely drew attention to herself. She seemed to work in the background, connecting people, fostering an atmosphere of acceptance and encouragement that resonated deeply. Her friends, especially Maya, Ethan, and Sofia, had each taken parts of her approach to heart, subtly carrying on the spirit of her mentorship and encouraging others to do the same. It was as if Nyomi had created a chain reaction, one that made kindness and support a quiet but powerful force at Riverside.

In the library, where Nyomi often held her informal study groups, students were settling into study sessions with an ease and sense of purpose. Maya, Ethan, and Sofia sat around one of the large tables, their textbooks open, a collective energy between them. They weren't just there to get their assignments done; they were there to support each other, to learn, and to grow together. It was a transformation that had been slow but profound.

Maya glanced up from her notebook, a glint of determination in her eyes. She'd always had a spark, but before meeting Nyomi, it had been hidden, locked behind self-doubt and a quiet fear of failure. But with Nyomi's guidance, that spark had blossomed into a steady flame. She now approached her studies with confidence and had even started helping other students.

"Hey, Sofia, how's that calculus problem going?" Maya asked, leaning over with a look of genuine curiosity.

Sofia, who had once been hesitant to allow others into her study space, looked up and gave a small, appreciative smile. "It's coming along," she replied, showing Maya her work. "Honestly, I used to think asking for help would make me lose my focus. But now, I think it actually makes me stronger."

Ethan, sitting across from them, grinned. "Tell me about it. I've learned more from you guys in the past month than I ever did studying alone. There's something about doing this together that just... works."

They each nodded, feeling a shared sense of purpose. They knew they had grown, but they also knew they were part of something bigger—a community that was slowly expanding beyond just the three of them. As they continued working, other students came and went, some offering a quick hello, others pausing to ask questions or exchange notes. It was in these moments that Nyomi's influence was most visible, a quiet reminder that learning wasn't a solitary pursuit; it was a journey meant to be shared.

Maya's Growth and Community Impact

Maya had been one of the first students Nyomi reached out to, sensing her quiet hesitance and underlying potential. When they first started meeting, Maya had been anxious and unsure, her goals blurred by self-doubt. She often felt invisible, as if no one saw her struggles or her strengths. But Nyomi had seen her, had recognized the unique spark that Maya herself hadn't fully acknowledged.

With Nyomi's steady encouragement, Maya's world had opened. She now moved through the halls with a quiet confidence, offering smiles and greetings to classmates she might once have avoided out of shyness. Her approach to studying had transformed, too; she no longer viewed academics as something to be tackled alone. Inspired by the support she'd received, she had even begun to reach out to younger students, helping them navigate the very challenges she'd once faced.

One afternoon, Maya spotted a freshman standing in the hallway, his shoulders slumped, his gaze fixed on the open pages of a math textbook. She recognized the look in his eyes —the same look she had often seen in herself: frustration mixed with isolation, the feeling that the subject was too difficult, that asking for help might be a sign of failure.

Maya walked over to him, her voice soft but encouraging. "Hey, having a rough time with math?"

The boy looked up, relief flashing in his eyes. "Yeah... I just can't seem to get any of this. I'm not good at math, and it feels like I'll never get it."

Maya gave him a reassuring smile, nodding with understanding. "I used to feel the exact same way. But I can tell you, it's not about being 'good' or 'bad' at it. Sometimes, it's just about finding the right way to approach it— and having someone there to help."

She sat beside him, pulling out a piece of paper and beginning to break down the steps of the problem he was stuck on. Her tone was patient, her explanations clear, and she encouraged him to ask questions, making sure he felt comfortable to share his thoughts. After a few minutes, she noticed his expression change; the frustration began to fade, replaced by a tentative smile as he started to grasp the concept.

"See?" she said, smiling brightly. "You're getting it. And remember, it's okay to ask for help. We're all figuring things out as we go."

The boy nodded, his face brighter now. "Thanks... really. No one's ever explained it like that before."

In that moment, Maya felt a deep sense of fulfillment—a feeling that was different from the satisfaction of solving a problem or getting a good grade. This was something Nyomi had taught her: that true confidence came not just from succeeding individually but from lifting others as well. It was the kind of success that felt lasting, rooted in connection and kindness.

From that day on, Maya made it a habit to look out for students who seemed lost or overwhelmed. She began organizing small study groups, inviting classmates to join her and encouraging an atmosphere where questions were welcomed and support was freely given. Inspired by Nyomi's example, Maya had become a mentor in her own right, guiding others with the same warmth and understanding that had once helped her find her footing.

One evening, as she walked with Nyomi down the school hallway, Maya glanced over at her mentor, her heart filled with gratitude. "I don't think I would have ever found this part of myself if it weren't for you," she said quietly.

Nyomi gave her a gentle smile, her eyes reflecting pride and affection. "You've always had this strength, Maya. I only helped you see it. The rest is all you."

Maya's confidence continued to grow, and with it, her impact on the students around her. She had become a cornerstone of the supportive community Nyomi was building, and her journey was a reminder that true leadership came from empathy, from the desire to bring others along on the path to success.

Ethan's Progress and Bonding with the Group

Ethan had once felt like an outsider at Riverside High. He'd been the kid who sat in the back of the class, quiet and uncertain, afraid to ask questions or draw attention to himself. He struggled with his coursework, especially math and science, and his self-esteem had taken hit after hit from failed tests and missed opportunities. But since meeting Nyomi, everything had begun to change.

Nyomi's mentorship had shown him a different way to approach learning. She had a knack for making even the most daunting subjects feel approachable, breaking down complex ideas into smaller, understandable steps and encouraging him to work through his doubts without fear of judgment. For Ethan, her presence had become a lifeline, pulling him from a place of self-doubt and showing him that he was more capable than he'd ever realized.

Now, Ethan had become an integral part of Nyomi's growing community, his confidence and academic skills growing stronger with each study session. He'd learned to trust in himself, to believe that he was worthy of the friendships he'd formed and the achievements he was beginning to experience. And with this newfound belief came a surprising transformation: he had become a friend others could rely on, his empathy and understanding making him a trusted confidant and study partner.

One Friday afternoon, the group had gathered in the library for a study session. Maya was organizing her notes for a group presentation, Sofia was scribbling calculations in her notebook, and Nyomi was sitting across from them, listening to Ethan explain a complicated chemistry concept.

"So, if you think of the molecule like a puzzle," Ethan was saying, leaning forward with an enthusiasm that surprised even him, "you can kind of see how the bonds fit together. It's all about understanding the structure."

Sofia looked up, her eyes lighting with understanding. "That actually makes so much sense! I was looking at it as this abstract thing, but thinking of it as a puzzle... thanks, Ethan."

Ethan felt a swell of pride, his usual shyness replaced by a confidence that felt both new and natural. For so long, he had doubted his abilities, believing that he could never contribute something meaningful. But now, surrounded by friends who valued him, he had begun to recognize his own strengths.

As the study session continued, he noticed a classmate from his English class sitting alone at a nearby table, a frustrated expression on her face as she flipped through her notes. Without hesitation, Ethan stood up, making his way over.

"Hey, need any help?" he asked, his tone warm and encouraging.

The girl looked up, relief spreading across her face. "Actually, yeah. I'm completely lost with this essay structure, and I don't even know where to start."

Ethan sat down beside her, patiently guiding her through the steps of organizing her thoughts, breaking down each part of the essay in a way that felt manageable. It was a skill he'd learned from Nyomi, a method that had once helped him through his own struggles. Now, he found joy in passing it on, in being able to help someone else find their footing.

When he returned to his friends, Nyomi gave him an approving nod, her eyes reflecting quiet pride. "You're a natural, Ethan," she said softly. "You have a way of understanding what people need."

Ethan shrugged, a bit shy but deeply grateful. "I just... I know how it feels to struggle. And if I can help someone feel less alone, it feels worth it."

The friends around him shared knowing smiles, understanding the importance of these connections. Ethan's journey had come full circle— from being the one who needed help to being someone others could count on. He had found his place in their group, not just as a friend but as a mentor in his own right, his empathy and dedication a guiding force for others who walked the same path he had once feared.

As they wrapped up their session, Ethan looked around at his friends, a sense of belonging filling his heart. They weren't just study partners; they were a family, a community that had grown stronger through each shared challenge, each moment of encouragement. And for the first time, Ethan felt a quiet confidence that he could face whatever challenges lay ahead, knowing that he wasn't facing them alone.

Sofia's Integration and Balance

Sofia had always defined herself by her academic achievements. Her goals, her time, and even her sense of worth had been tied to her ability to excel in school. For years, she believed that her focus should be unwavering, that friendships and socializing could only serve as distractions. But ever since she'd met Nyomi, something had shifted. Nyomi had shown her that balance was possible—that ambition and connection weren't mutually exclusive, but could coexist, each enriching the other.

Now, as Sofia sat among her friends during their usual study session, she felt a deep, steady sense of belonging. The nagging worry that friendships might derail her dreams had begun to fade, replaced by the understanding that these relationships were as vital to her growth as her academic achievements. In her heart, she knew she was no longer simply working toward a goal—she was building a life that included both success and support.

Across the table, Thomas groaned as he flipped through his notes, scratching his head. "I swear, trigonometry feels like it's written in a different language sometimes. I can't make sense of half of these problems."

Sofia smiled, moving her chair closer. "Want some help? I think I've figured out a few tricks to make it easier."

Thomas gave her a grateful look, and together, they worked through the formulas and angles, Sofia breaking down the steps in a way that even surprised herself. In the past, she'd rarely offered help with schoolwork, believing that her time was best spent focusing on her own progress. But now, she found joy in supporting her friends, knowing that they would do the same for her if she needed it.

As they worked, Sofia noticed Nyomi watching her, a soft smile on her face. There was a quiet pride in her eyes, an expression that made Sofia's heart warm. Nyomi had been the one to show her that friendships didn't have to come at the expense of her goals—that they could, in fact, make her journey richer, her ambitions more meaningful.

The group continued to study, sharing laughter and encouragement, and Sofia found herself feeling lighter, as if a weight she'd carried for years was finally lifting. Her friends had become a grounding force, a source of joy that kept her steady even on the days when her studies felt overwhelming. For the first time, she felt that her dreams were shared, that the strength of her friendships would see her through even the most challenging moments.

Later that evening, after the study session had ended and her friends had gone their separate ways, Sofia stayed back with Nyomi, packing up her books in the now-quiet library. She felt a lingering sense of gratitude, not only for her friends but for the balance she'd begun to find—a balance that had seemed so elusive before.

"Nyomi," she began, her voice filled with quiet emotion, "I feel... different. I never thought I could find this kind of balance. I used to think it was one or the other—either I was focused or I was distracted. But now, it's like I'm more focused than ever because I know I have people around me who care."

Nyomi smiled, her expression gentle and understanding. "Balance isn't about perfection, Sofia. It's about making room for what matters. And you've found a way to do that."

Sofia nodded, her heart swelling with a mixture of pride and gratitude. "I just wanted to thank you... for helping me see that. For helping me find something I didn't even know I needed."

Nyomi placed a reassuring hand on her shoulder. "You've done all the hard work, Sofia. I just showed you what was already there."

As they left the library, Sofia felt a newfound confidence. She knew that the path ahead would still have its challenges, that there would be times when balance felt difficult to maintain. But with the friendships she'd built and the lessons she'd learned, she felt ready to face those challenges. She was no longer alone in her journey—she was part of a community, a growing network of support that had become a source of strength and encouragement.

Sofia was discovering that success wasn't just about individual achievements. It was about the connections she nurtured, the people who walked alongside her, and the joy that came from sharing her journey. And as she looked ahead, she knew that this balance, this sense of belonging, was something she would carry with her, wherever life might lead.

Nyomi's Role as a Community Mentor

Nyomi's influence had gradually woven itself into the fabric of Riverside High, becoming an unspoken but undeniable presence that extended far beyond her circle of friends. What had started as simple study sessions had grown into a network of support, trust, and mutual encouragement. Students who had once been shy or isolated were now part of a community where their voices felt heard, where their struggles were shared, and where their successes were celebrated.

The library was the heart of this transformation, a place where students gathered not just to study but to connect. It wasn't uncommon for Nyomi to be there, guiding study groups, helping someone through a tough topic, or just lending an ear to anyone who needed it. Her presence brought a sense of calm, an atmosphere of understanding that seemed to reassure everyone around her. She had a way of noticing the small things—who looked stressed, who needed encouragement, who might benefit from a few kind words.

One afternoon, as students filled the library for a study session before finals, Nyomi organized a group study booth. She'd prepared it in advance, laying out supplies, practice problems, and snacks—small touches that made the space inviting and open. As the students gathered, she moved around the tables, quietly encouraging them to work together, to ask questions, and to help each other. It was a simple gesture, but it spoke volumes. By creating a space for everyone, Nyomi had made it clear that they weren't just individuals striving for their own goals—they were a community, each person's success contributing to the strength of the group.

At one of the tables, Maya was helping a freshman with math, her voice patient and reassuring. Across the room, Ethan was explaining a chemistry concept to a group of classmates, his usual shyness replaced by a newfound confidence. Sofia was sitting beside Thomas, exchanging notes on a recent history assignment, her focused expression softened by the warmth of her surroundings. Everywhere Nyomi looked, she saw students connecting, reaching out, and sharing in the spirit of support that had come to define their school.

Watching this scene, Nyomi felt a quiet satisfaction. She knew that her role as a mentor had been to guide, to offer gentle nudges and a steady presence, but the true magic was in what each student had brought to the community. They had each found their own way to contribute, to strengthen one another, and to share in the joy of learning. It was a gift that would last far beyond high school—a gift of friendship, resilience, and mutual support that they would carry with them wherever they went.

At one point, a teacher, Mr. Calloway, passed by and paused at the entrance of the library, observing the scene with a look of quiet admiration. He approached Nyomi, his voice low so as not to disturb the others. "You've done something remarkable here, Nyomi," he said, a hint of awe in his tone. "I've never seen the students so engaged, so supportive of each other."

Nyomi gave a humble smile, her gaze soft. "I think they were always capable of this. They just needed a place to start."

Mr. Calloway nodded, his respect evident. "Whatever you're doing, keep it up. You've made a real difference here."

As Mr. Calloway walked away, Nyomi felt a deep sense of fulfillment. She had never sought recognition, but knowing that her efforts had helped foster this community filled her with a quiet pride. She continued moving through the room, offering guidance when needed, her presence a constant reminder of the values she had helped instill: kindness, patience, and the belief that they were all stronger together.

By the end of the study session, the students began to pack up, their faces filled with the quiet satisfaction of a productive day. Nyomi noticed Thomas lingering, watching the room with a thoughtful expression. He walked over to her, a smile tugging at his lips.

"Looks like you're running this place now," he teased, but his tone held genuine admiration. "I don't think I've ever seen this much energy in the library before."

Nyomi chuckled softly. "It's not me. It's everyone here. They've created this, each in their own way."

Thomas nodded, his gaze lingering on the students still chatting and laughing as they left the room. "It's amazing, though. You've done something here that I don't think anyone else could have."

Nyomi felt a warmth in his words, a validation that meant more than he could know. She had always believed in the power of community, in the strength that came from people supporting one another. Now, she was seeing that belief come to life, a living, breathing testament to the impact of kindness and understanding.

As the library emptied, Nyomi gathered her things, feeling a sense of peace that went beyond words. She knew that her role as a mentor was only one part of this journey, that the true strength of their community lay in each student's willingness to reach out, to share, and to uplift those around them. And as she stepped out into the crisp evening air, she felt ready for whatever challenges lay ahead, knowing that she was part of something greater than herself—a community that would endure, built on the foundation of friendship, trust, and unwavering support.

As the week drew to a close, Nyomi took a quiet moment to herself, sitting on one of the benches that lined the edge of Riverside High's small, tree-lined courtyard. From where she sat, she could see groups of students gathered in little clusters around the campus: some were laughing, others were studying, and a few were deep in conversation, their heads bent together, their expressions animated. She watched them with a sense of contentment, knowing that each one was part of a network of support that she had helped build.

For so long, Nyomi had wondered if it was possible to truly make a difference, to leave a lasting impact that would extend beyond her immediate circle. But now, as she observed the quiet resilience and strength that had blossomed in those around her, she knew that the answer was yes. The students at Riverside weren't just individuals anymore—they were a community, bound by mutual understanding, respect, and friendship. And Nyomi knew that these bonds would last, supporting them through whatever challenges lay ahead.

Her thoughts drifted to Maya, whose once-nervous energy had transformed into a quiet confidence. She'd found purpose in helping others, organizing study groups, and offering guidance to younger students. Maya had become a mentor in her own right, her empathy and kindness spreading through the school in ways Nyomi couldn't have anticipated.

Then there was Ethan, who had gone from a shy, unsure student to a friend everyone could rely on. His willingness to help others, to share his insights, and to lift those around him had earned him the respect of his peers. Nyomi had seen how his confidence had grown, how he'd stepped into a role that allowed him to support his friends and classmates.

And Sofia, who had once believed that friendships would distract her from her goals, had found a balance she hadn't thought possible. She was still driven, still focused, but she was no longer walking her path alone. She had embraced the support of her friends, understanding that success was more than just individual achievements—it was about sharing those moments with the people who mattered to her.

Each one of them had grown, their lives intertwined in ways that enriched them all. And as Nyomi looked ahead, she knew that the lessons they had learned would continue to shape them. They would face challenges, setbacks, and difficult choices, but they would do so with the strength of their friendships, the resilience they had built together.

Thomas approached her then, interrupting her thoughts with a quiet smile. He sat down beside her on the bench, looking out over the courtyard with a thoughtful expression.

"They're different now, aren't they?" he said, his voice filled with admiration. "It's like they're all... stronger, somehow."

Nyomi nodded, a soft smile on her face. "They were always strong.

They just needed to see it in themselves—and in each other."

Thomas tilted his head, glancing at her. "And you don't think you had anything to do with that?" he asked, a hint of teasing in his tone.

Nyomi laughed softly, her gaze distant. "Maybe I helped a little. But they're the ones who made the choice to change. They're the ones who chose to believe in themselves and each other."

Thomas nodded, his expression one of quiet respect. "Still, you've done something amazing here, Nyomi. I don't think any of us could have come this far without you."

Nyomi felt a warmth in his words, a sense of validation that went beyond recognition. She knew that her role had been to guide, to encourage, and to believe in them. But the journey was theirs; they had each chosen their own path, finding strength in one another, in the friendships they had built.

They sat in silence for a while, each lost in their own thoughts, watching the students as they moved through the courtyard, their laughter and voices a gentle reminder of the bonds they shared. Nyomi felt a quiet peace settle over her, a contentment that went beyond words. She knew that the work she'd done here would endure, that the friendships and connections they had built would carry them through whatever lay ahead.

Finally, Thomas broke the silence, his tone light. "So, what's next? You've built this whole community, made us all see the best in ourselves. What else could you possibly have up your sleeve?"

Nyomi smiled, a hint of mischief in her eyes. "Oh, I'm sure there are still a few surprises left," she replied, her voice soft but filled with a quiet confidence. "This is only the beginning."

As she spoke, a sense of anticipation filled her, a feeling that something new was on the horizon. She didn't know exactly what the future held, but she knew that she was ready for it—that they were all ready for it. Together, they had built a foundation of resilience and support, a community that would see them through whatever challenges they might face.

As they stood up and made their way back to the school, Nyomi felt a renewed sense of purpose. She knew that her journey wasn't over, that there were still more lives to touch, more connections to make. And with her friends by her side, she felt ready to embrace whatever lay ahead.

The courtyard grew quiet as the evening approached, the last rays of sunlight casting a warm glow over the campus. Nyomi looked back one last time, a soft smile on her face, before turning to join Thomas and the others, her heart filled with hope for the future.

CHAPTER 18: EMBRACING THE FUTURE

The school grounds were decorated with bright banners and flowers, each corner bursting with color as though spring itself had leaned down to give its blessing. The sky was cloudless, the early morning sun casting a warm glow over the campus where she had spent so much of her life. Nyomi glanced up at the long row of flags flapping gently in the breeze, each a marker of memories made and lessons learned.

Graduation was only weeks away. Soon, she'd step out into the unknown, her future sprawling before her in endless directions. And unlike before, when the world beyond high school felt impossibly big and intimidating, she found herself looking forward to it.

Nyomi's gaze drifted across the familiar hallways. She remembered a different Nyomi—a girl who once felt trapped by her abilities, whose fears seemed as insurmountable as the towering oaks that lined the school's paths. She had been afraid, yes, but as she watched the morning sun filter through the branches, painting delicate patterns on the ground, she could see how much she had changed.

It wasn't just that she had learned to control her powers. She had learned to respect them, to trust herself with something so strange and beautiful. That was a far cry from the days when she could barely look at her sketchbook without a tremor of anxiety. Now, she felt a sense of steady calm. Her magic wasn't something to fear—it was simply another part of her, a truth she had come to accept and even cherish. But it had taken her a long journey to get here.

As she walked the paths of the campus, Nyomi found herself thinking back to those first few moments when her powers had revealed themselves. The butterfly—her first creation. She had been terrified of it, not understanding why something she had drawn could come to life. It felt like a curse, a reminder of the parts of her she couldn't control. But over time, as she practiced, failed, and tried again, she learned that her magic was linked to her emotions, her intentions, her ability to stay present in the moment.

From fear to excitement, from doubt to acceptance—her relationship with her powers had shifted through each challenge she faced. Thomas had been there with her at each turn, offering quiet advice, never pushing but always guiding.

Today, she felt an unusual stillness, as if the world had paused just for her. The hum of magic rested beneath her skin, comforting and warm. She felt complete, whole, no longer fractured by the competing identities she once tried to reconcile.

Just then, she felt a presence beside her, a familiar one. Thomas. "Thinking deep thoughts again?" His voice was calm, yet there was a knowing glint in his eyes, as if he already knew what had been running through her mind.

Nyomi gave him a small smile. "Graduation, the future... and everything I didn't understand a year ago," she said. "Remember when I first told you about the butterfly? I was so scared. I couldn't see it as anything other than something I needed to hide."

Thomas nodded, his gaze steady. "Fear is the first reaction to the unknown. But look at you now. You've taken what scared you and turned it into something you can control, something you respect."

"Respect, yes. That was the hardest part," she admitted. "I had to stop treating my powers as something separate from me, something dangerous that I had to shut out."

"Exactly," he said, glancing up at the sky. "When you respect something, you see it clearly, without fear or judgment. It's a part of you, not something you have to run from."

Nyomi felt a warmth bloom in her chest, an appreciation for his presence that she couldn't put into words. Thomas had always been there—not in a way that demanded her attention, but in a way that reassured her, that reminded her she wasn't alone in this strange, magical journey.

They walked together in silence for a moment before Thomas spoke again, his voice unusually soft. "You know, there's a responsibility that comes with gifts like ours. They don't just belong to us; they belong to the world. They're meant to be used thoughtfully."

Nyomi looked up at him, sensing a weight in his words. "I've been thinking a lot about that," she said quietly. "For a long time, I wanted to forget about my powers. I didn't want the responsibility. But now... I can see that they're not a burden. They're something I can use to create, to help."

Thomas smiled, a rare expression of pride in his eyes. "That's exactly what it means to carry a gift like yours. It isn't about the power itself, but what you choose to do with it."

A breeze stirred, sending a flurry of leaves across their path, and Nyomi watched as they danced in the sunlight.

Thomas's words stayed with her, like a quiet heartbeat, underscoring the purpose she had come to accept. She could feel his understanding—though Thomas was still largely a mystery, he had shared enough for her to know that he, too, bore the weight of responsibility.

She thought back to the rules she'd created for herself over the past months. The rules—they were both boundaries and guides. Thomas had once told her that, for people like them, structure was a key to balance. Emotions could be both fuel and fire; they could create beauty or chaos, depending on how they were managed. And through her self-imposed limits, she had finally found a way to harness her powers without losing herself.

"I never thanked you for helping me find that balance," she said, glancing over at him. "The rules you helped me create, the control techniques... they've given me so much peace. I feel like I'm ready to step forward without fear."

He inclined his head slightly, as if the gratitude wasn't necessary. "I merely pointed you in the direction. You found the way on your own. Don't forget that."

She nodded, absorbing his words, feeling a deep sense of accomplishment. She knew she had her own strength to thank as much as Thomas's guidance.

The afternoon sun cast long shadows across the campus as Nyomi and Thomas walked in companionable silence. The air was filled with the soft chatter of students making their way home, yet for Nyomi, the world felt quieter, as if it, too, understood the weight of her thoughts.

After a few moments, Thomas spoke, his tone contemplative. "Do you remember when you used to tell me that you wished you could be like everyone else? That your powers were something to hide, to bury?"

Nyomi smiled wryly. "I do. It feels like a lifetime ago, but I remember. I used to think my powers were like a flaw—a crack that set me apart from everyone."

"Most people would have given up," Thomas said, studying her. "They would have buried it, denied it, and tried to live a life pretending they weren't meant for something different."

A breeze drifted past, carrying the faint scent of the blooming flowers near the old oak tree. Nyomi let his words settle over her, absorbing the truth in them. There had been times—moments when the fear outweighed the wonder—where she had wanted to shut it all down, to escape back to a simpler life where magic didn't disrupt the order of things. But she had pushed through, facing every challenge her power threw at her.

"I think it was realizing that my powers could be a choice," she said softly. "Once I understood that I could create boundaries—that my powers didn't control me, but that I controlled them—it changed everything."

Thomas gave a slight nod, his expression approving. "A lesson most people never learn," he murmured. "You found your own path. And now, you're ready to step into it with confidence."

Nyomi turned to him, feeling a surge of gratitude. "I owe a lot of that to you, Thomas. You taught me that power doesn't have to be something we fear. It's something we understand and respect. I can't thank you enough for that."

Thomas gave a small, almost imperceptible smile. "Guidance is one thing, but you're the one who decided to trust yourself. That's the real achievement, Nyomi."

She nodded, feeling the truth of his words. She had been the one to choose growth over fear, to believe in her own strength even when doubt seemed insurmountable.

As they walked, Nyomi found herself reflecting on the "rules" Thomas had helped her develop. Each rule had been crafted carefully, a safeguard to prevent her powers from spiraling out of control. She thought of the late nights spent practicing emotional focus, learning how to keep her mind calm even when her heart raced with fear or excitement. She had learned to let her emotions guide her without letting them consume her.

The first rule had been to only use her powers with intention—to never let her creations be guided by impulse. Thomas had taught her that clarity was her anchor, the grounding force that would keep her power contained.

The second rule had been to remember her purpose. Her power was a gift, but it didn't define her. She was still Nyomi Boones, an artist and a friend. This rule reminded her that her powers were a part of her, not the whole of her. And as long as she stayed rooted in that truth, she would never lose herself in the magic.

Finally, the third rule had been one that Thomas had helped her craft carefully: to never use her powers as a solution to her problems. Magic wasn't meant to be a shortcut or an escape, but a form of expression, a tool that could enhance life rather than disrupt it.

As she recalled each rule, Nyomi felt a surge of pride. These weren't just limitations—they were markers of her growth, evidence of the journey from chaos to balance.

"Do you ever miss it?" she asked, glancing at Thomas. "Having powers, I mean. Assuming you had them."

Thomas paused, his gaze drifting to the horizon. "Sometimes," he admitted, his tone thoughtful. "But it wasn't really about the power itself. It was about understanding the responsibility that comes with it. When you hold something so rare, you start to see the world differently. You see the ways you can impact it, for better or for worse."

He turned to her, his eyes filled with a depth she rarely saw. "And that's the choice you face now, Nyomi. How will you use your power?"

She let his words sink in, feeling the gravity of the question. "I want to use it to bring joy," she said softly. "To create things that make people feel something. I don't want it to be about control or power. I just want it to be... a part of me, something that makes the world a little brighter."

Thomas's expression softened, and he nodded approvingly. "Then that's all you need to remember. As long as you stay true to that purpose, your power will always be a gift rather than a burden."

They walked in silence after that, but Nyomi felt a new lightness within her, a quiet certainty that had been missing before. She knew her path now, even if it wasn't fully clear. She didn't need to control everything; she just needed to trust in the person she had become.

As they neared the edge of the campus, she saw Callie waving from a distance, her bright energy like a beacon. Nyomi felt a smile tug at her lips, grateful for the friends who had grounded her, who had seen her as Nyomi, not as someone with strange powers.

"Go on," Thomas said, nodding toward Callie. "And remember, the world is waiting for you. Make it your own."

Nyomi looked at him, feeling a swell of gratitude she couldn't put into words. "Thank you, Thomas," she said, her voice barely a whisper.

Without another word, she turned and walked toward Callie, feeling the warmth of her friend's smile as she approached.

As they walked together, Nyomi shared her thoughts about graduation, her dreams, and even her hopes for her powers.

Callie listened, her presence a reminder of the life Nyomi had beyond magic.

"I still can't believe it's almost over," Callie said with a sigh. "We're about to leave all this behind."

Nyomi nodded, glancing back at the campus. "Yeah. But I think I'm ready. For the first time, I feel like I know who I am—really know."

Callie looked at her, curiosity glinting in her eyes. "And who is Nyomi Boones?"

Nyomi hesitated, a smile forming. "An artist. Someone who believes in beauty, in possibility. Someone who doesn't need to hide."

Callie grinned, giving her a playful nudge. "That's the Nyomi I know.

Don't ever let that change."

Their laughter filled the air, light and carefree. Nyomi knew that whatever lay ahead, she would carry these moments with her—a foundation of friendship and trust that would keep her grounded.

In her heart, she felt a quiet determination. She would use her powers, yes, but she would also honor the simplicity of life, the joys and struggles that didn't require magic. She would create a life that honored both.

As she walked with Callie, the future no longer felt intimidating. It felt like a blank canvas, waiting for her to paint her story upon it.

As the afternoon faded into evening, the campus grew quiet, the distant sounds of students heading home giving way to the gentle rustle of leaves and the call of night birds settling into the trees. Nyomi wandered toward the quiet alcove near the old art building, where a bench overlooked the sprawling fields that stretched toward the horizon.

She sat down, feeling the coolness of the wood beneath her hands. She watched the sun sink lower, the sky shifting from bright blue to a palette of orange and pink, a masterpiece in itself. She found herself smiling at the beauty of it, marveling at how something so simple could stir such emotion.

Nyomi's mind drifted back to her journey, tracing the path from the first tremor of magic, the butterfly lifting from the page, to the moments of panic, to the quiet triumphs she'd celebrated in secret. Each memory was a step, a lesson that had guided her from fear to understanding, and now, to acceptance.

In the beginning, her powers had felt like a curse—a wild, unpredictable force that seemed to threaten everything she held dear. She had been terrified of it, of losing control, of becoming someone or something unrecognizable. She remembered the sleepless nights, the way she'd agonized over every slip, every small failure, as if each one were proof that she wasn't strong enough to handle what she'd been given.

But through it all, she had learned that strength wasn't about control. It wasn't about forcing things into place or fighting against herself. True strength was about trust—trusting herself, trusting her heart, and trusting the gifts she'd been given.

With a steadying breath, she pulled her sketchbook from her bag and opened it to a blank page. She traced her fingers along the smooth paper, feeling the familiar hum of magic beneath her skin, the same pulse that had once scared her but now felt like a gentle reminder of her connection to something greater.

She began to sketch, letting her pencil glide across the page without a plan, her hand moving as if guided by instinct. Lines emerged, soft and flowing, forming shapes that hinted at wings, at movement, at life. She lost herself in the act, each stroke grounding her in the present, each curve bringing her closer to herself.

When she finished, she looked down at the page. A delicate bird took shape, its wings outstretched as if caught mid-flight. Its eyes were bright and alive, a symbol of freedom, of possibility. She smiled, feeling the familiar tingle of magic, but this time, she didn't need it to come to life. The image was enough; it held all the meaning she needed.

For a long moment, she simply sat there, staring at the bird, feeling a profound sense of peace. Her powers didn't need to define her. They were part of her, yes, but she was more than magic. She was an artist, a friend, a daughter, a person who believed in the beauty of the world around her.

As she closed her sketchbook, she felt a gentle warmth in her chest, a quiet certainty that had settled there like a steady flame. She was ready. Whatever came next—whatever challenges, whatever triumphs—she would face it with an open heart and a steady hand.

The sky was a deep purple now, the last rays of sun slipping below the horizon. Nyomi stood, slipping her sketchbook back into her bag, and began walking back toward the campus gates. She could feel the pull of the future, of new beginnings waiting just beyond the familiar halls of Riverside High.

When she reached the edge of the campus, she paused, looking back one last time. It felt strange, knowing that this place would soon be a memory, a chapter in the story she was leaving behind. But she knew, deep in her heart, that she was ready to move forward.

The night air was cool and refreshing as she stepped away, the lights of the city twinkling in the distance like stars scattered across the earth. She walked toward them, each step filled with the quiet joy of someone who had found her place in the world.

As she moved forward, her mind brimming with dreams and plans, she whispered a silent promise to herself: she would embrace the future, with all its unknowns, with all its wonder.

Final Reflections

As Nyomi stepped through the campus gates, the weight of the past year felt light on her shoulders, a quiet presence rather than a burden. Every moment, every struggle she'd endured with her powers felt like stepping stones that had led her to this place of acceptance. The world around her was wrapped in twilight, the soft hush of evening settling over the city, and she found herself walking slowly, savoring each second.

Her thoughts drifted to Thomas, his steady guidance and subtle strength woven through each milestone she had reached. Thomas had been more than just a mentor—he had become a part of the foundation upon which she had built her understanding of magic and herself. He was someone who understood without needing an explanation, someone who saw her not only as a girl with powers but as someone with a choice to make, a purpose to fulfill.

She remembered the way he had spoken to her earlier that day, his words laced with both pride and a quiet warning about the responsibility she now bore. Thomas had opened her eyes to a world of possibilities and reminded her that while her powers could shape her future, they did not define her entirely. She knew he wouldn't always be there to guide her, but the lessons he'd shared—the calm wisdom he'd instilled in her—were etched into her heart.

With a soft smile, she made a silent vow to honor what he had given her by living responsibly, with purpose, and to keep herself grounded in everything he'd taught her.

As she walked, Nyomi's gaze drifted down the familiar streets that led toward home. The memories flowed easily—

long evenings spent with Callie, laughing at some shared joke, the quiet nights she had spent sketching by lamplight, trying to make sense of a power that had once seemed so overwhelming. Callie had been her tether to reality, her anchor when the pull of magic threatened to isolate her.

There were moments when she hadn't known how to share the weight of her secret with Callie, when her friend's easygoing laughter and casual joy had felt worlds away from the tangled complexities Nyomi carried. But Callie's unwavering presence had been a gift, a reminder that she could still have normalcy, laughter, and friendship in her life even as she grappled with powers that defied explanation. Callie had kept her grounded, reminded her of the simple things, the quiet joys that existed outside the realm of magic.

Nyomi made a mental note to thank her friend in her own way, to tell Callie how much she had meant to her throughout this journey. Perhaps she would paint something for her—something that captured their friendship, something that would remind Callie of the laughter, the loyalty, the unbreakable bond they shared. Her art could now hold meaning beyond mere images; it could capture emotion, memory, and truth.

With a slow exhale, Nyomi felt herself releasing any lingering fear, any small hesitation about stepping forward. Her life, for so long, had felt like a careful dance between magic and the ordinary, a balance she had struggled to maintain. But now, as she stood on the threshold of the future, she realized that there was no need to keep her worlds separate. She could carry both with her, blending them into a life that was uniquely hers.

Her powers were no longer an enigma, no longer a shadow she was forced to face alone. They were part of her, woven into the fabric of who she was. And in that realization, she found a sense of wholeness she had never felt before.

Nyomi looked up at the sky, where the first stars were beginning to appear, tiny points of light piercing the deepening blue. It felt symbolic somehow—a reminder that, like the stars, her powers were something she could carry within her, shining quietly, illuminating her path even in the darkest moments.

In her mind, she began to sketch a vision of her future. She saw herself walking confidently into a world that might never understand the depths of her abilities, a world that might never see the magic that hummed beneath her skin. But that didn't matter. What mattered was that she understood herself, that she knew her own strength, her own purpose.

She could see herself using her powers sparingly, as a quiet gift rather than a spectacle. She would create things of beauty, small moments that would bring joy, comfort, and inspiration to those around her. She would blend her magic into her art, leaving subtle traces of wonder in her work, like fingerprints only she could recognize. And in doing so, she would find her own place in the world—a place where magic and reality coexisted, a place where she could be fully herself.

As she walked down the last stretch of road toward her house, she felt a surge of anticipation. Graduation was only the beginning. She would carry the lessons, the friendships, and the memories with her into this new chapter, using them as the foundation upon which she would build her future.

She reached her front steps and paused, looking up at the familiar windows, each one glowing softly in the dim light. This home had been her sanctuary, a place where she had both hidden from and embraced her powers. Soon, she would step beyond it, into a world that might never know the truth of her journey. But she was ready.

With one last glance at the night sky, Nyomi whispered a silent promise to herself. She would face the unknown with courage, with hope, and with the knowledge that her journey had only just begun.

And as she opened the door and stepped inside, a sense of calm certainty filled her heart. She was ready for whatever lay ahead.

Final Night at Home

Nyomi closed the door quietly behind her, the familiar scent of home washing over her—faint traces of lavender from her mother's candles, the rich, earthy smell of books lining the shelves, and the comforting warmth of a place filled with countless memories. Her eyes roamed the small hallway, taking in each detail, each little piece of the life she was about to leave behind.

Her family was out for the evening, giving her the house to herself. She felt a surge of appreciation for this rare solitude, a final gift of quiet before tomorrow's ceremony. Tomorrow would be a day of celebration and change, but tonight was hers alone. She could feel the weight of it, the gravity of this last evening in the place that had been both a refuge and a boundary.

She slipped off her shoes and made her way to her room, pushing open the door and stepping into the space that had seen her through every twist and turn of the past year. Her sketchbooks were stacked on her desk, a testament to the journey she had taken with her powers. She ran her fingers over the worn covers, each one holding sketches and stories of moments that had once felt like secrets, like whispers only she could hear.

Taking one of the books, she sat on the edge of her bed and opened it to a familiar page—the butterfly. Her very first creation, the one that had changed everything. She could still remember that night vividly: the flickering lamplight, the quiet desperation in her heart, the breathless moment when the butterfly had lifted from the page. That single, miraculous moment had opened a door she never could have anticipated, one that had led her here.

But the butterfly was different now. Where once it had symbolized her fears, her doubts, it now felt like a promise fulfilled. She traced the delicate lines with her finger, a soft smile spreading across her lips. This butterfly was a reminder of how far she had come, of the fears she had faced and overcome. It no longer held any trace of fear—it was simply part of her story, a part of who she was.

Setting the sketchbook aside, she stood and crossed the room to the small shelf above her desk. She had arranged a few keepsakes there, little tokens of the people who had shaped her journey. A small bracelet Callie had given her on her birthday, a hand-carved wooden owl from Thomas, a photo of her family taken during a long-ago camping trip. Each item held a memory, a reminder of the connections that had kept her grounded.

One by one, she held each item, feeling a swell of gratitude. She thought of Callie and the countless hours they had spent together, sharing secrets and laughter, comforting each other through heartbreaks and setbacks. Callie had been her steadfast friend, someone who loved her without needing to understand the intricacies of her magic. And Thomas—quiet, watchful Thomas, who had entered her life like a shadow and become a guiding light. He had taught her to embrace her powers, to see them as a gift rather than a burden. He had been her mentor, her friend, and, in many ways, her inspiration.

Nyomi placed the keepsakes carefully back on the shelf, letting her gaze linger on them as she felt a quiet resolve settle within her. These people, these memories, would travel with her wherever she went. They were woven into her very being, each one a thread in the tapestry of her life.

She spent the next hour gathering a few belongings, things she would need as she left for the next chapter of her life. Clothes, art supplies, a few books. It was a simple ritual, but each item she placed in her bag felt like a piece of herself, a reminder of who she was and who she was becoming.

As she zipped up her bag, a thought struck her, and she turned to her sketchbook, flipping it open to the blank pages near the back. Taking up her pencil, she let her hand move freely, capturing the moment in soft, careful lines. She sketched her room, the view from her window, the glow of her lamp on the desk. Each line was a memory, a piece of the place that had shaped her, and by the time she finished, she felt a gentle peace settle over her.

She closed the sketchbook and set it gently in her bag, feeling the weight of it—a comforting weight, one that anchored her to everything she loved, everything that had brought her here.

A Final Quiet Goodbye

The house was dark and still as Nyomi made her way to the front door. She paused there, her hand resting on the doorknob, and took a deep breath, letting herself savor the silence, the familiarity of her surroundings. The hallway, the quiet hum of the refrigerator, the creak in the floorboards beneath her feet—all these little things were pieces of a life she was leaving behind, a life she would carry forward in her heart.

A single tear slipped down her cheek, not out of sadness, but out of a deep appreciation, a recognition of everything that had brought her to this moment. She whispered a quiet goodbye to the walls, the memories, the girl she had been in this place.

And with a final, steadying breath, she opened the door and stepped out into the night.

The air was cool and crisp, filled with the scent of blooming flowers and freshly cut grass. She looked up at the stars, feeling a sense of connection to the vastness of the universe, a reminder that she was a part of something larger than herself.

Her heart was full, brimming with the knowledge that she was ready. Ready to take the next step, to embrace the future, to become the person she had been striving to be.

With one last look back, she closed the door softly behind her, stepping forward into the night, into the future, with a heart full of gratitude and a spirit unbound.

EPILOGUE: A LIFE IN FULL COLOR

Years had passed since Nyomi left her childhood home, but the memories remained with her, woven into the fabric of her life like threads in a beloved tapestry. She was no longer the uncertain girl who had stumbled upon her powers with equal parts wonder and fear. She had grown into a woman who understood her gifts, who held her magic close to her heart yet let it shine through her art, her work, and the life she had built.

She stood in her studio, a bright and airy space filled with the soft afternoon light that streamed through large, arched windows. The walls were adorned with her paintings, each one capturing a piece of her journey, each stroke infused with a quiet magic that seemed to breathe from the canvas. Some pieces were vibrant and full of life, others gentle and subdued, but each one held a part of her story.

Her hands were smudged with charcoal as she worked on her latest piece, a painting of a delicate, sprawling landscape she had dreamed of—a place where magic felt as natural as the trees and rivers and sky. She had spent hours on it, bringing the vision to life with soft, gentle brushstrokes, capturing the beauty of the world as she saw it: a world filled with wonder, with hidden depths and quiet power.

As she added the final details, her thoughts drifted back to those who had shaped her path, the people whose voices and laughter were woven into every piece she created.

Callie's letters arrived like clockwork, each one filled with the same effervescent energy she had carried through high school. She had traveled the world, her love for discovery drawing her to places Nyomi could only imagine. They had promised to meet once a year, each reunion a joyful celebration of their unbreakable friendship. And though Callie had always lived a life without magic, she understood Nyomi in a way that went beyond words, a friend who loved her for who she was, not for what she could do. And then there was Thomas.

Thomas had become something of a mentor, though his presence was like a shadow, subtle and guiding. He would appear unexpectedly, always just when Nyomi felt she needed guidance, his words reminding her of her purpose, of the balance she had worked so hard to achieve. His role in her life had shifted as she grew more independent, his once-frequent guidance now replaced by occasional, meaningful conversations that carried weight and wisdom.

Nyomi had once asked him about his own life, his own journey, but Thomas had only smiled and told her that his path was one of observation and patience, that he found joy in helping others uncover their own truths. She knew she would never know all the mysteries he held, but that didn't matter. Thomas had taught her the importance of choice, of self-trust, of embracing the unknown. And that, she realized, was the greatest gift he could have given her.

Nyomi stepped back from her painting, wiping her hands on a cloth, and took in the piece in its entirety. She felt a sense of satisfaction, a quiet pride in the work she had done. It was a piece that spoke to her own journey—the transformation she had undergone, the girl she had been and the woman she had become.

As she stood there, the light catching on the canvas, she felt a familiar warmth stir within her, a gentle hum that reminded her of the magic that lived inside her. She didn't need it to come to life outside her paintings, didn't need to see her creations lift from the canvas. It was enough that the magic was there, that it was part of her. She knew now that her powers were not something to control or contain; they were simply a piece of her heart, a part of her soul.

Outside, the sky was beginning to turn the soft shades of twilight, the day fading into evening. Nyomi walked to the window, looking out over the city she had come to love, a place where she had found not only her voice as an artist but her peace as a person with gifts unlike any other.

As she stood there, watching the world soften under the colors of dusk, she thought about her journey, the years of learning, of growing, of discovering. She knew that her story was far from over—that life would bring new challenges, new lessons, new people who would add richness and color to the canvas of her existence. And for the first time, she felt ready for whatever came next, embracing it with an open heart.

With one last look at the fading light, she turned back to her studio, her mind already swirling with ideas for her next piece. She felt a sense of anticipation, the same excitement that had once made her fearful but now filled her with quiet joy. She was an artist, a creator, a woman with magic in her veins and dreams in her heart.

And she knew, as surely as she knew her own name, that she would continue to paint her story—one brushstroke, one memory, one dream at a time.

AFTERWORD

As I sit down to write this afterword, I'm struck by how much Nyomi's journey has mirrored the paths many of us walk—paths filled with self-doubt, unexpected challenges, and, ultimately, moments of growth that surprise even us. The Butterfly Touch began as a story about magic, but along the way, it became something far more personal. It became a reflection of the ways we learn to embrace who we are, even the parts of ourselves that don't quite fit into the world's mold.

In Nyomi, I wanted to explore what it means to live with a gift that doesn't always feel like a gift, a part of ourselves that we sometimes want to hide. Her powers, with all their beauty and unpredictability, represent the unique qualities each of us possesses—the things that make us different, that set us apart, and, sometimes, the things that make us feel isolated. Like Nyomi, I think we all go through periods where we wrestle with these parts of ourselves, struggling to find a balance between self-acceptance and the pressures of expectation.

Thomas was another character who took on a life of his own as the story unfolded. I hadn't originally intended for him to play such an integral role, but his quiet wisdom and sense of responsibility emerged as essential to Nyomi's growth. In many ways, Thomas represents the mentors we meet along the way, the guides who help us see our potential even when we're blinded by our fears. He reminded me, too, of the people in my life who have gently nudged me toward my own path, even when I wasn't quite ready to take the next step.

The Butterfly Touch is not just about magic; it's about friendship, loyalty, and the courage it takes to face ourselves. Through Nyomi's friendship with Callie, I wanted to celebrate the kinds of relationships that keep us grounded, the people who see us for who we truly are and love us in spite—or perhaps because—of our differences. In a world that often feels chaotic and uncertain, these connections are our anchors, reminding us of where we come from and who we want to be.

As Nyomi moves into her future, my hope is that her story resonates with each reader who has ever felt like they didn't quite fit. I hope that her journey encourages you to embrace the parts of yourself that feel "other" and to find strength in your uniqueness. Our greatest powers often lie in the things we try hardest to hide, and as Nyomi learns, these gifts have the potential to bring beauty into the world in ways we might never imagine.

Writing this book has been a journey of discovery for me, just as it has been for Nyomi. I've learned that stories have a way of teaching us about ourselves, sometimes in the most unexpected ways. I am deeply grateful to each reader who has walked this path with her and, in doing so, shared in her struggles, her triumphs, and her quiet moments of peace.

Thank you for reading, and for allowing The Butterfly Touch to become a part of your journey, too. May we all find the courage to embrace our own magic, to celebrate our unique paths, and to create a life that feels true to who we are.

With gratitude,

Hector L. Bones